I dedicate this book to my wonderful friends and family who have supported me. I also dedicate this book to my good friend Brittany who helped me build this book into my personal masterpiece. Thank you sincerely.

Table of contents

Chapter 1	pg 7
Chapter 2	pg 12
Chapter 3	pg 16
Chapter 4	pg 20
Chapter 5	pg 25
Chapter 6	pg 29
Chapter 7	pg 36
Chapter 8	pg 41
Chapter 9	pg 50
Chapter 10	pg 56
Chapter 11	pg 60
Chapter 12	pg 75
Chapter 13	pg 86
Chapter 14	pg 90
Chapter 15	pg 95
Chapter 16	pg 109
Chapter 17	pg 118
Chapter 18	pg 127
Chapter 19	pg 132
Chapter 20	pg 146
Chapter 21	pg 155
Chapter 22	pg 162
Chapter 23	pg 170
Chapter 24	pg 174
Chapter 25	pg 183

Chapter 26	pg 196
Chapter 27	pg 211
Chapter 28	pg 227
Chapter 29	pg 238
Chapter 30	pg 248
Chapter 31	pg 261
Chapter 32	pg 275
Chapter 33	pg 284

Sacred Sword

In the ever-complicated maze of life, our imagination is our map to our happiness.

Copyright © 2016 by Dylan Armstrong
All rights reserved. No part of this publication may be reproduced, distributed, or transmitted in any form or by any means, including photocopying, recording, or other electronic or mechanical methods, without the prior written permission of the publisher, except in the case of brief quotations embodied in critical reviews and certain other noncommercial uses permitted by copyright law.
First published in 2016.
Author's email: dylanarmstrong43@yahoo.com

Chapter 1

Devlin's eyes opened lazily to the bright, golden light of the morning sun flooding through his open window. He yawned long and loud, his mouth wide open as he wiped the sleep from his eyes. As Devlin sat up, he felt the soft give of his low-lying, feather-stuffed mattress that he slept on almost every night. It was far from luxurious, but it suited him well enough. The beds of his brothers were in adjacent sections of the room. Derek's bed, of course, was neatly made and organized to match. In contrast was Roark's side, looking like the aftermath of a tornado, his clothes strewn across the floor and bed sheets a tangled mess. It was a miracle that Devlin's and Derek's sides were unscathed. Devlin laughed slightly at the sight. Mother always nagged Roark about his messy part of the room, calling it a disgrace to the family. Devlin related well in that regard, as he was no different at Roark's age.

Cecelia had her own room since she was the only daughter. It was well kept and organized, even putting Derek's work to shame as not a single thing was out of place. His brothers think it was just to keep mom off her back, but Devlin figured she was more a daddy's little girl than momma's perfect daughter, even though she didn't care for favoritism.

As he, at last, garnered the motivation to out of bed and got dressed, Devlin could hear the eager footsteps of his brothers outside, heading towards the small stone home in which he lived. They most likely smelled the fresh breakfast on the range. The smell was quickly growing prevalent in the air.

Devlin picked out a red, faded shirt and a pair of tan cotton pants. Knowing it was mid-late spring, he wouldn't need anything too warm. Devlin took a quick glance in the mirror. His hair was a tangled mess, pieces sticking up in multiple places. Devlin's tired expression showed clearly through his drooping eyelids, barely showing his deep, green eyes, the eyes of his father. Devlin's chin was entirely his mother's in shape, however.

Devlin quickly fixed his hair with a spare brush and wondered how late he had slept in, seeing as how the sun was already well above the horizon. He recalled, not too fondly, countless times his father had grabbed and shook him awake at the crack of dawn, yelling at him to start his morning chores. Had today of all days not been his eighteenth birthday, his father would undoubtedly be giving him an earful even now. He walked out of the bedroom and down to the kitchen.

As he walked into the kitchen, he noticed the steaming-hot piece of ham and scrambled egg on a plate and instinctively reached for it, only to have his hand smacked with his mother's spoon. "Oww!" Devlin yelped as he quickly retracted his hand to the protection of his body.

"I don't care if today is your birthday, Devlin. You will wait until everyone is here before you begin stuffing yourself," Devlin's mother said sternly as she started preparing the rest of the plates. The sting in his hand receded to a dull ache. His mother was fierce with a spoon and, growing up, he had quickly learned to fear his mother with it. Devlin looked up to see both Derek and Roark run through the doorway, grinning as they saw the food, but wisely chose not to pick it up as Devlin had.

"Well well, look who's finally risen from the dead. Roark and I were just about to bet chores on how long you'd stay asleep, Devlin," Derek said, laughing with mirth and joined the table next to Mother and Devlin.

"I seem to recall that I'm the one usually waking you up in the morning, Derek," Devlin retorted, playfully slugging him in the arm. Devlin couldn't help but notice he was laughing too. Devlin loved his brothers just like any brother would. They sometimes fought, teased, and played little pranks on each other, but all of them were inseparable.

"I coulda gotten out of dishes for a week if you would have stayed asleep a couple more hours," Roark said with mock disappointment in his voice as he sat down too. Roark was always the playful one of the three brothers. His parents were never as strict with him as they were with Devin and Derek. He had vibrant, blue eyes. A unique trait in the family, as everyone had at least a bit of green to them where Roark had none. He also had light brown hair, the lightest of the family as well, as everyone else favored darker shades. However, he had his father's strength and his mother's will. It was never pleasant when Roark and mother got into an argument. "You were out like a light on that bed, Devlin. It looked like you hadn't slept in days."

"Enough, boys. Is your father coming in soon?" Mother asked expectantly while crossing her arms. She looked aged from the stress of living on a farm, but she still had a good deal of youth to her. She stood slightly shorter than the three brothers, who were similar in height with Derek standing the tallest of the three, and had a slim but slightly toned build due to her years helping father tend the fields. Her skin was the color of the wheat they grew, slightly tan, but still light.

The three brothers shone a tad darker shade due to countless days under the harsh, beating sun. Roark was the shortest and the youngest, two years younger than Devlin. Grime clung to his skin and his old green tunic and boots. He also hated fighting people, which seemed odd to Devlin, but he respected it. Roark would still help him train, and he was a very gifted fighter, but Devlin could tell that if it came to blows, Roark wouldn't have the heart to hurt anyone.

Derek was the eldest by a year, barely taller than Devlin, and was the most muscular of the three. He was the spitting image of Father, just like how Cece was for Mother. He had striking green eyes that glow like emeralds when he laughs. His dark brown hair was a trait all the brothers had, but Derek's was smooth as silk and flowed down just above his eyes. He had the build of a warrior and was proud of it, though he would never seek the life of a soldier; no matter how luxurious it was in the higher ranks of the king's men because he knew his family came first. "I think he was just checking on the seeds. He should be in soon," Roark answered. "When will Cecelia be getting back?"

Devlin had almost forgotten about Cece. Cecelia is Devlin's younger sister, eleven months older than Roark. Cecelia had dirty blonde hair that flowed down to her shoulders. She had blueish-green eyes like her mother and a slight, delicate smile that was impossible to ignore. Cecelia's smile could disarm any tension, even when Devlin and Derek had been on the verge of all-out war.

Cecelia also had her fair share of chores to do. She went into town to buy supplies and catch up on gossip. Devlin, Roark, or father would sometimes accompany her, but she usually took care of the trip fairly well alone. "She should be back soon. I sent her to town early this morning. As soon as she gets back, we will eat our breakfast and head off to the carnival."

Devlin had been dreaming about the carnival for many nights prior. It was filled with fun things to do, such as archery targets for competitions, and rings for the massive fighters that fought until submission. The fighters have always been a favorite among the villagers and home to many wagers on who wins. There were also many travelers from all around Crestialis that have set up shop there and sold their many wares. Devlin himself had bought a new pair of boots there once.

"Is everyone ready?" Father asked, entering the door behind Cecelia. Her usual working blouse replaced the close-fitting skirt made for long walks, which she wore with her traveling shoes. Father stood a head taller than her and wore his usual working cotton shirt and jeans. Age showed clearly on his wind-burned skin and graying hair. "I met up with Cece on the road back."

"Yes, Anthony, that's everyone," Mother answered quickly, smiling as she looked upon Cecelia.

"Can we eat then?" Roark groaned, putting a hand on his stomach gingerly. "I'm wasting away over here." Mother quickly shot Roark a dark look that even made Devlin flinch, however, conceded with an exasperated sigh. "Oh, very well."

The ham was moist and melted in Devlin's mouth. It didn't take long for him to completely devour the slab of meat. He ate his scrambled eggs and drank his fresh milk in similar quickness.

"That hit the spot!" Devlin said, licking his lips.

"Yeah, I bet mom cooks food better than the king's own chefs." Roark sprawled in his seat.

"I can't believe you two even taste the food… Was chewing ever taught to you, boys?" Cecelia said, concealing a laugh. Father washed his dish with the bucket of water they kept for dishes and a wet rag as everyone else had when they finished.

"Well, we better be setting off," Father said curtly, walking back towards the table. "We'll want to get there quickly before too many people crowd the place."

Chapter 2

    The six of them set off for the carnival due northeast from their home. The dirt path that cut through the forest was big enough for a full-sized wagon to travel it, leaving plenty of room for the family to walk. The sky was clear and Devlin could hear birds chirping in the trees. He even saw squirrels running amongst the tree branches and the occasional deer jaunting through the trees. The walk was quiet as everyone enjoyed the peace of silence and the grace of nature.

    Devlin wondered if there would be any notable fighters this year. Over the whole week that the carnival takes place, there have been many bouts with warriors wishing to test themselves in combat. Most fighters were no-names, average guys that just want to make a name for themselves. However, the occasional famed soldier usually comes to compete. The most famous of them all is the Knight Luke. He was proclaimed the king's champion for his amazing feats in combat. Devlin had seen him fight once and dreamed of maybe one day meeting him in person, but it was unlikely since the knight has many duties and spends a good deal of time at the castle by the king's side. He also had a dream to be the best fighter in the country. He wanted to be strong so people would look up to him. So Luke was a prominent milestone if Devlin ever wanted that dream to be a reality.

    Devlin was quickly pulled from his thoughts when Cecelia grabbed his hand with hers in a firm but loving grip. "Is something wrong, Devlin? You seem distracted..." There was both concern and curiosity in her expression, and Devlin knew once Cecelia got curious about something, she would be determined to find the answer.

Seeing no harm in telling her his thoughts, he said, "I'm just wondering about the matches this year. I'm curious to see who will be fighting."

A look of understanding crossed her face as she looked at him. "You're thinking about Luke aren't you?" Cecelia questioned joyfully, then looked at the sky to watch the clouds.

"Huh? How did you know?" Devlin asked, looking at Cecelia with a perplexed expression.

"I still remember the look on your face when you saw Luke fight at the last festival. You were completely awestruck by him, and I can understand why. He is famous for his bravery and skill for a reason after all. He is unmatched by any one warrior in the entire kingdom. That, and you wouldn't stop talking about him for weeks afterward," Cecelia answered reminiscently, looking back at him again.

"You know me too well, Cece; you read my thoughts as if they are written on my forehead," Devlin conceded with a smile and slightly lowered his head. Devlin felt somewhat embarrassed that what he was so easy to read, and resolved internally to fix that.

"I bet Luke will be there today, just you wait. Maybe this time around you can meet him in person?" Cecelia said optimistically with that same sweet smile that never failed to lift Devlin's spirits.

"I hope so. What I wouldn't give just to meet Luke." Devlin smiled back. "Thanks for talking to me, Cece." Cece's kindness was only matched by her generosity. She would always lend a helping hand to any that would need it. She had helped him get through many grueling days of work just by supporting him like she has.

She had known hard work too, during the rare times mom got sick or had to go on a long errand to the capital; she took over the chores and did her best to keep everything in order. Mom was more than proud one time when she came home, and the house looked cleaner than when she left. Roark, Derek, and Devlin also help her by carrying some of the supplies or lifting a particularly heavy object. Devlin wanted to be a good big brother to her.

"Of course, Devlin. It's a woman's labor to know what troubles a man." She giggled slightly at the jest and smiled at him. "We should be arriving before long now; I guess we will see for ourselves if Luke makes an appearance."

"You're right," Devlin acknowledged with enthusiasm and new determination.

"If you two are done chatting, pick up the pace or we'll leave you behind," Father called out, the rest of the family several meters ahead.

"Sorry, Father!" Devlin and Cecelia called back as they began running back up to join their family.

The carnival was full of people walking the paths and in the shops scattered all around. Devlin saw Derek's eyes light up like a spark to dry wood as he saw a new sword with a gilded leather hilt with a four-foot blade. Devlin doubted even the entire King's army could have stopped him from getting to that sword.

"That boy is a sucker for a pretty sword," Father muttered, exasperated, then followed him over to the shop. Devlin saw many different stands selling all kinds of trinkets, from amulets to simple tools, to fresh fruit, and other native grown foods. He even saw the stand where he bought his boots before. As he looked, however, he wasn't overly impressed with what he saw.

"You see anything good, Devlin?" Roark asked, looking at different stands.

"No, not really," Devlin answered indifferently as he glanced at a few old charms. "I think I'm going to head to the arena. If you guys find something, let me know."

"I'll go with you then," Cecelia said. Devlin could tell she had grown bored with looking at the many wares of the shops. "Looking at this junk is about as exciting as watching the grass grow."

"Very well," Mom said dismissing them. "Just make sure to wait at the archery stands when you're done. We'll meet up there." Devlin and Cecelia quickly headed off in the direction of the fighting arena.

Chapter 3

King Renard MacArthur sat dignified on his throne as he listened to the Squire ramble, attempting, and failing, to hide the complete boredom he was feeling. He had grown weary of all these petty requests and audiences. How he wished he could be free of the pressures and responsibilities of being king, but he suffered it, as he wanted to be a good king to his people and hear them out. "As you know, sire, the yields from the farms are going well; your coffers are much larger now after collecting taxes and the intake of ore from the mining regions. Everything seems to be faring well for now," the squire said, reading the paper.

King MacArthur found his eyes wandering the room, almost toning out the Squire as he blathered on about trivial events and attempted to make them sound significant. He took in the gilded masterpiece given to the royal family by a famous artisan as recompense for a crime he committed, the red carpeting that adorned the audience hall flooring, and the trophy case full of trophies won by his knights in competitions.

The King was relieved to hear things were going smoothly, however. The recent bandit attacks on his caravans had taken many if his sleeping hours. He had sent a contingent of soldiers to settle the matter, but the ruffians know every nook and cranny of the roads and surrounding areas, some of which could be easily overlooked by a careless soldier. He prayed this was proof that the soldiers had taken care of the issue, but he wasn't holding his breath. He felt better that at least bandits were all he had to worry about, as the other kingdoms have been rather quiet as of late. MacArthur supposed it did help that his kingdom was one of the more powerful, their only rival being Grandis.

His thoughts then went to Luke. His Knight-Champion had gone to some festival near his hometown. The king had seen him off with his blessing but wished he could have led the group of soldiers looking for the bandits to set his mind more at ease. "Thank you, Squire. You may take your leave, but tell the collectors to lower the taxes on the people by thirty percent. With such prosperity, the people deserve the respite."

"Of course, Your Majesty. It shall be done with all possible haste." As the Squire left the audience chamber, Renard turned to his adviser, Grimik. "Are there any more who wish an audience?" King MacArthur was shocked to see the doors open suddenly, with one of the guards from outside rushing inside.

"Your Majesty! Your daughter, Princess Sophia, wishes to see you. She claims it's very urgent," The guard told him dutifully.

"See her in then." The King stroked his brown, well-kept beard as he always did when he thought about something, but let the thoughts pass quick enough. Sophia entered as the large, oak doors opened wide. Sophia was tall but stood half a head shorter than the king himself. She had long, flowing blonde hair kept in many intricate curls that went well with her silk dress, fitted to her slight features, and complimented by her simple, yet elegant, heels. She was the perfect image of her deceased mother, a fact that King MacArthur took pride in, as with her daughter, the King felt like a part of his departed wife was still with him. Her face was attempted to feign composure, but he could see the worry in her features clearly. "Father, may I have a moment?" Sophia asked curtly but stood tense.

"Very well, daughter. What is it that troubles you so?" The king felt a pit of worry in his stomach. He hoped it wasn't too worrisome an issue, but the looks of Sophia told otherwise.

"It's Michael, Father. His caravan was attacked by bandits, and he was wounded in the fight." Sophia barely managed to hold back tears as she shared the grim news.

"Blast those barbarians!" The king yelled in his fit of sudden rage. It wasn't bad enough that they stole from his supplies, but now they harmed his flesh and blood. Michael was his second born son, passed his twentieth year, a fierce and capable fighter, almost as capable as his first born son, Anders, who was but a mere two years older. He turned to the guard. "Call the soldiers and renew the search for the lawless scum at once! I want every stone overturned until they are found and dispatched!"

"Yes, Your Majesty!" The guard saluted then quickly ran out of the room.

"Michael lays in the healing wing of the castle, and he requested to see you in person. He said he had a message for you." Sophia said, waiting for the guard to leave to make sure she didn't interrupt.

"Lead me to him, Sophia."

* * *

King MacArthur and Princess Sophia raced down the labyrinthine halls of the castle, down the maze of stairways, and through countless doors until, finally, they came to the healing wing of the castle. King MacArthur opened the door to the specified chamber, and his eyes went wide with shock. His beloved son, Michael, lay motionless on the bed, his clothes a bloody mess, and his skin a sickly, pale color.

The nursemaid was treating him with a salve over an open wound. Michael groaned in incredible pain but made no move to stop her. It grieved his father greatly to see his son in such a state. The nursemaid looked up at the King as she finished applying the salve and re-bandaged the wound.

"He is stable my lord, but his wounds are severe. He will live, but he will need two weeks of bed rest, possibly more to recuperate." The nurse then looked down then. "I have done all I can for him."

The king looked on crestfallen. He loved his son greatly and knowing he was beaten so brutally hit his heart like a hammer blow. "Oh, my son... My brave, brave son." Sophia was in utter shock. Not crying, not even moving, she just stood there staring at him like a possessed doll, before she fell to her hands and knees and started crying, rivers of tears flowing down her face.

"What's with all the tears you two? I'm not dead, am I?" Michael's voice was weak, and his left eye was swollen shut, but he managed a small grin and looked at them with his good eye. "I probably look like a real mess huh, Father? Not the prettiest sight, I know, but I need to show you something. Nurse, can you reach into my travel bag and get the piece of paper for me?" The nurse did as she was told and gave him the folded piece of paper. "I found this map on one of the bandits I killed; I thought you might find it useful."

The king regained his composure, took the map, and opened it. The map was marked and labeled with different ambush spots and their main hideout inside a hidden cave. A renewed rage and vengeance burst through him as he traced the location of the cave to a nearby mountain. He went outside the room to the nearest guard. "Retrieve Prince Anders at once! I swear on my honor that those scum will pay!"

"Of course, Your Majesty," the guard saluted.

Chapter 4

Devlin and Cecelia finally made it to the arena. It was a circular ring surrounded by wooden, stair-like seats for the spectators, and a single open passage to enter the ring. Devlin looked to the ring for the fighters and went up close to the edge for a better view. So far, two no-name fighters were fighting in hand-to-hand combat, and they seemed to be evenly matched. Each was dodging the others blows or blocking them as they came. "The fighters sure are tough. I wouldn't want to go against either one of them." Cecelia muttered.

"Agreed," Devlin nodded slowly, even though he couldn't care less about these fighters. "Now if only I could find Luke..."

"I think I see him..." Cecelia said as she examined the other side of the arena seats. "Over there! He's amongst the crowd." Cecelia pointed to a part of the crowd on the other edge of the arena, and Devlin saw a tall man sporting full-plate armor with the intimidating crest of the Crestialis Kingdom, a griffin with its wings unfurled, painted on his chest and the shield strapped to his arm. He saw the long, intricate sword strapped to his belt that had seen many battles, along with a dagger next to it. He took another good look at his face, that unforgettable face of a man that has seen death. It was a look of determination set in his eyes and an unyielding sense of purpose in his stance.

"That's him alright," Devlin said resolutely.

The fight in the ring reached its conclusion when one of the fighters tripped on an out-poking rock. The opponent saw the opportunity, quickly grappled his opponent, and twisted his arms until the stumbled fighter submitted and accepted defeat. The fighters got up and shook hands on a good match, although the loser did look disappointed, unlike the winner who walked off with pride in his step. As they left, they walked right past Devlin and Cecelia, but Devlin was too focused on Luke to notice. Luke leaped into the ring and stood at the center.

"What man or woman is brave enough to face my steel? I fight with swords and honor. Ready your blade and face me!" Luke spoke out. Everyone around the ring looked about, seeing if anyone was brave or foolish enough to fight him, but they didn't have to look long.

"I will face you!" Devlin yelled over the edge. This was Devlin's chance, his chance to meet Luke in combat. He had dreamt of this fight, and he was ready for it. The entire crowd was gaping at him; Luke, still in the ring, was the only exception. His expression was one of expectation and a bit of amusement.

"Devlin, have you taken leave of your senses?!" Cecelia whispered panicked in his ear.

"Don't worry, Cece, my senses are still here," Devlin joked with a confident smile as he walked past the opening to the ring.

"You're a brave lad, very well, meet me at this stage so we may make our ancestors proud," Luke commended as Devlin entered the arena. He grabbed a sword from the rack at the entrance to the ring that looked about his size and tested its weight in his palm. He had learned a few skills with the sword from an old veteran soldier and practiced with his brothers a lot in the past, but this was the king's champion he was up against. Devlin resolved to give everything he had against Luke, anything less would be an insult to himself and The Knight Champion. "Tell me, boy, what is your name?" Luke asked as he removed his plate armor and shield, revealing his chainmail and leather breeches. He then drew his sword.

"My name is Devlin Slade," Devlin announced to him, readying his sword.

"A good name, I shall remember it well. Now let us give these people a show."

Luke readied his sword. Devlin could feel his intense gaze, reading and sizing up his opponent. Devlin did the same and began the match with swinging his sword from the left, then redirected the cut at the last second with a spin and slashed from the right. Luke read the diversion expertly, blocking the real attack and performed a downward slash. Devlin sidestepped, greeting Luke with a downward strike of his own. This would have bested a lesser opponent, but Luke's practiced speed parried the slash mid-strike.

"Not bad. You are obviously more skilled than your age lets on. Show me what else you can do." Luke smiled confidently.

Luke pushed Devlin back, forcing Devlin to stumble backward. With the sheer force of will alone, Devlin regained his footing and charged for Luke. Devlin swung in a flurry of blows from all directions, sidestepping, pivoting and faking blows. None touched Luke as he blocked every blow effortlessly. Devlin stood dumbfounded at his skill. He was fast, inhumanly so, and overwhelmingly strong. He took everything Devlin threw at him and had barely broken a sweat. Devlin needed to do better than old fashion tricks. Luke was no fool with a sword; he would see right through them. Devlin needed to find a way to surprise him, but how?

Devlin sidestepped another slash and leaped backward and noticed the out-poking rock behind him. Luke charged him and swung his sword, falling right into Devlin's trap. Devlin stepped back, revealing the outcropping rock that had been the end of the last fighter. Luke saw the rock too late and fell off balance during his charge. As the opportunity revealed itself, Devlin slashed at him. However, Luke's body compensated for the loss of balance and Luke was left only with a scratch on his cheek.

"Clever boy, using the environment to your advantage. You may prove to be a worthy foe yet." Luke let loose a flurry of blows towards Devlin, who struggled to block each stroke. When Luke seemed to tire from the relentless blows, Devlin pushed Luke back. Devlin was breathing hard, his body exhausted from the onslaught, but he couldn't lose, he staked his pride on this match.

"I hope you're ready, Luke, because I don't plan on losing!" Devlin said, though, despite how worried he was of losing, despite the fact that he could even die in this arena, he couldn't help but smile. It was a smile full of pride, and a bit of excitement.

"Those are big words, but can you back them up?" Luke asked with the very same look on his face.

Devlin put the last bits of energy he had into his final assault, garnered all the resolve he had to win, and honed it so that the resolve he had dreamed for all these years aided his steps. He charged Luke again as fast as his legs were able, and at the last second pivoted in an attempt to get behind Luke. Luke caught on to the tactic and swung his sword towards Devlin from the side. Devlin ducked the swing, and the momentum from his pivot quickly put him behind Luke. Seeing his chance, Devlin tried to swing at Luke from behind. What happened next, however, was a blur to Devlin.

Luke spun so fast that the sheer force of his sword hitting Devlin's knocked Devlin's sword out of his hand. The sword was sent spinning through the air; each second felt like an eternity. When the sword finally hit the ground, so did Devlin. Too tired to fight any longer, his legs gave out. Devlin fell onto his back and was surprised to find Luke's sword at his throat. A bit of fear coursed through him as he looked at the sharp blade, realizing that had this been a true fight, he would be dead now. However, in spite of himself, Devlin smiled sadly. *I suppose that's what I should expect trying to fight the best knight in the kingdom.*

"I submit to you, Luke. You have bested me," Devlin conceded ruefully. Disappointment flooded through Devlin's mind like water filling an empty glass. *So I truly am not strong enough... He defeated me as easily as a novice...* Devlin thought, berating himself. *I have to get stronger. I have to get a lot stronger, or I'll never be able to beat him.*

Luke nodded with a grin and returned his sword to his scabbard, helping Devlin to his feet. Devlin felt a bit weak, but he managed to stand at least with Luke. They clasped arms as a show of good sportsmanship, and the crowd cheered for them, long and loud. So loud it seemed as if it could be heard for miles. "It was truly wonderful to duel you, Luke. I learned much from facing you." Devlin hated losing, but he wasn't about to be a sore loser in front of all these people.

"You have a true heart and a brave soul. It was an honor to fight you, Devlin. I hope we can face off again when your skills have improved even more. Until that day, take this amulet." Luke took off the amulet hidden under his chain mail. It had the shape of a griffin, just like the crest of the royal family. "Wear it with pride, for it shows proof of your bravery against me this day. May we meet again soon my friend." They clasped hands one last time; the crowd again roared its approval.

Devlin stumbled a little to the edge of the arena, Cecelia helping him as he stepped over the boundary. The crowd parted for Devlin and his sister, his arm wrapped around her shoulder for support, as a show of respect to Devlin. Devlin felt sorry for making Cece worry, but he felt like a changed man as he left the arena and that the change was only just beginning.

Chapter 5

The King's forces, led by Prince Anders, had arrived at the bandits' hideout. The entire force hid on top of a wall of stone overlooking the refuge itself. He wanted vengeance for his brother just as much as Father did. He loved his brother Michael dearly, and seeing him beaten and bloodied had stirred up a rage inside him like none other. So here he was, laying in wait to spring the trap that would defeat the bandits once and for all.

The army planned to split in half and ambush the bandits on two sides as soon as they returned to their hideout. It was a simple plan, but Anders liked it that way. Simple plans were easy to remember and execute. "They have returned, milord," a soldier next to him whispered, gesturing to a large gathering of rugged men.

"Wait until they're comfortable, then we strike. They will be most vulnerable when resting rather than if they are already walking, but exercise caution. Even surprised, these bandits are capable fighters." Anders held their position for a bit longer until the bandits were setting up camp. Anders wanted the bandits thinking they had won the day, and now they could relax. They would be slow at best to react to a surprise attack on their hideout which they thought was hidden from the king.

"CHARGE!!" Anders yelled, getting out from behind his hiding spot, the many hundreds of soldiers close behind. The bandits were numbered in the hundreds as well, so it was a mostly even in numbers, but Anders and his soldiers had surprise on their side, as well as experience. Anders ran up to a group of five bandits drinking booze. He interrupted their drink with one quick slash with his greatsword - a heavy blade as long as a man.

The heavy sword cut through their necks like butter, and their heads rolled with the look of drunken pleasure forever implanted on their faces. He even stabbed the man next to the dead bodies, the blade leaving a gaping hole in his chest as Anders pulled it out before the men finally realized they were being attacked.

The two bandits that were left pulled out daggers, but the booze they had drunk made them clumsy and disoriented. Anders easily avoided the blade of a bandit trying to attack him, cutting the bandit in half as he passed. Anders wheeled around, quickly stabbing the last one in the heart and he sank to his knees, dead. Breathing hard, Anders looked over towards the other soldiers.

His fellow soldiers were having similar success with the other bandits, killing well over fifty of them in a single stroke, but there were still many left even though the soldiers held the advantage. The bandits began to regroup and grabbed their weapons, everything from maces and long swords, to broad axes. The soldiers met them with drawn swords and shields, maces, and spears. The fight was bloody, soldiers and bandits alike stabbing or hacking each other apart.

Anders joined his fellow soldiers in the fray, blocking strike after strike with the flat of his blade, each impact sending a jolt of pain right through him. He slashed in a sweeping arc, slashing through multiple bandits at a time, killing them instantly, and parried a slash from the right. He saw a soldier being ganged up on and rushed to his aid, much to the relief of the soldier. He angrily slashed one of the bandits in the back, ripping through his leather armor, and stabbed another running to swing at him, lifted the sword with the man's body still stabbed on it, and swung the sword hard and fast in a semicircle arc perpendicular to the ground. The bandit was flung off the sword like a cannonball from a cannon and flew several feet above the ground. The soldier was able to trip one haphazardly and stab him in the heart. The soldier grinned at Anders showing his gratitude.

Together with his soldiers, Anders traded blow after blow with the bandits. His armor received countless dents and scratches. Anders himself received many bruises from his armor absorbing blows. He dodged a hammer swing, which instead smashed into the body of a soldier behind him. Anders kicked the bandit in the gut, before stabbing him in the heart, feeling sorrow for his fallen comrade. Anders turned toward the other groups of bandits and ran straight into them.

    He slashed and slashed, not even bothering to block anymore in his fit of rage. He hacked men's bodies clean in half with a sweeping side slash and killed man after man until dead bodies lay in bloody heaps around him. After he had dispatched the last bandit in front of him, he looked around and saw a lone group of twenty bandits surrounded by his fellow soldiers, each too frightened to move. Anders walked over to join them and stabbed his blade into the earth to act as a temporary sheath. He felt a weight on his heart as he observed the battlefield. Many of his fellow soldiers lay dead or dying, but it was worth it to help rid the country of these criminals.

    "Lower your weapons and surrender now, or die where you stand," Anders ordered sternly.

    "Surren'er? Bah! You'll probly kill us when our backs turn, or worse, leave us to rot in you lo'sy dungeons. I'd rather die on meh feet with a sword in meh hand!"

    "Aye!" some of the bandits murmured in agreement.

    "You are obviously far better armed and organized than other groups of bandits. Your ambushes, though crude at times, also show devastating leadership. Tell us who you are working with. Cooperate, and we will let you go free. This I swear on my life." This gave the bandits a pause. The promise of freedom seemed to, at least slightly, put them at ease.

    "What's y'ur name, pretty boy?" A bandit spat out.

    "Prince Anders MacArthur, heir to the throne of Crestialis." The bandits grew wide-eyed at that and hesitantly dropped their swords.

    "Fine, we'll go, y'ur highness. We'll cooperate." The head bandit said derisively.

"Good. Then we will escort you to the castle." Anders turned to his second in command and took out his greatsword from the earth to latch it onto his back. "Tie them up securely, and escort them out."

"We're unwort'y of y'ur kindness milord," The head bandit said, bowing his head in mock politeness. The soldiers tied the bandits and took them out of the cave, toward the main road, but, little did Anders know, one bandit was hiding a dagger. While Anders had his back turned, and the tired guards weren't paying attention, he quietly cut his bindings and ran up to Anders, thrusting the dagger into his back below the greatsword.

"Foolish princey, you shoulda just killed us," The bandit sneered. Anders grunted in shock as he turned and looked at the bandit in horror as Anders fell to the ground.

Chapter 6

    Devlin analyzed every moment he spent dueling Luke. The amulet he wore around his neck served as a reminder that he still had much room to improve. He held the charm in his hand and just stared at it as every slash, every maneuver replayed a hundred times in his head. Cecelia noticed Devlin's internal dispute and figured praise was the best way to cheer him up. "You were amazing in that duel, Devlin! I can't believe you held your own against one of the best swordsmen in the kingdom," Cecelia praised, and made the biggest smile she could manage. "I knew you trained a lot growing up and that you and Derek would spar, but I never realized how good were!"

    "I may have held my own, but I still have so much to improve. I fought him putting my all into defeating him, but I lost. If my best was no match, I still have much to learn..." Devlin said thoughtfully. *I suppose it's not all bad, though. I did learn a few things from our duel. For one, I need to get faster, or at least faster reactions.*

    "You shouldn't put yourself down, Devlin. Luke is the best for a reason. No one has beaten him since he claimed the title of Knight Champion. That doesn't mean you're inadequate," Cecelia assured him. Cecelia hated seeing Devlin depressed because he is his worst critic, he is always putting too much on his shoulders.

    "I told you about my dream, right? About how I want to be the best warrior in the country?" Devlin asked finally looking at Cece intently.

    "Yes, I remember you going on about it every five minutes years ago," Cecelia recalled teasingly but then smiled sweetly in affirmation. "You always said you wanted people to respect you and look up to you."

"Yes that's right, but you missed part of it. I don't just want people's respect; I also want to protect you and my family. I don't ever want you to get hurt. So if someone as strong as Luke, or even Luke himself tries to hurt you, I want to be able to stop them." Devlin loved his family more than his life, and he would give anything to protect them. It was his driving motivation to get stronger.

There he goes again... Putting too much weight on his shoulders... Cecelia mentally sighed in exasperation. Cecelia looked on in front of them and noticed the archery lanes with the rest of their family gathered behind Roark.

"There's everyone over there; I see them next to Roark shooting his bow," Cecelia told him as they walked over. "Hello, Father. How was shopping with Derek?"

"You mean besides him just staring at the sword and drooling like some hypnotized toddler?" Father asked poking fun at Derek. "I was worried hell would freeze over before he finally bought it."

Devlin looked at Derek to see if he was even paying attention, and sure enough, he just held the sheathed sword in his hands as if the sword itself was made of solid gold. Devlin just laughed inwardly and looked over to Roark shooting at the targets. He had struck one bulls-eye, and a few more arrows were scattered on the target.

"Not bad, Roark. Keep practicing and maybe you'll get more than just one bulls-eye," Devlin jeered as his brother lowered his bow.

"Keep talking, brother, and the next eye my arrow hits will be yours," Roark retorted with a sneer.

"Haha, I'm shaking in my boots." Devlin laughed and playfully punched his brother in the arm.

"I'm honestly surprised you're practicing with a bow, Roark, knowing how much you hate fighting," Derek said finally managing to look away from the sword. "Fifty yards isn't an easy shot either." Devlin knew for a fact that he wouldn't even make it on the target.

"I want to be ready in case I ever need to help you guys. You never know what the future will bring, but if it falls to me one day to protect my family, I want to be ready for it," Roark explained. *I will protect my family with my life if I have to, even if that means fighting.*

Devlin heard the words from his mouth and realized just how much alike he was to his brothers. They all shared that motivation to protect their family. *I have to get stronger, so they don't have to.*

"When do you think we should head back, Father?" Cecelia asked indifferently.

"Not sure, but most likely soon. It's Devlin's birthday, though, so he should decide." Father looked to Devlin.

"Oh yeah." Derek's face lit up in realization. "How does it feel to finally be a man, Devlin? There's so much you can do now that you're eighteen," Derek said matter-of-factly.

"Like what? Get married? Join the army? I don't care about stuff like that," Devlin rolled his eyes. "I have my whole life to worry of such trivialities." Devlin happened to look up after speaking and noticed a small tower of smoke building itself into the sky. Cecelia noticed it also, and bewilderment morphed into concern in her features.

"Is that smoke over there?" Cecelia asked interjectionally.

"It's probably just a bonfire. They have a lot of those during the festival, remember?" Derek said with a nonchalant tone. "Don't worry so much; that's mother's job." Mother gave Derek a cold look at that comment but didn't dwell on the matter.

"Maybe we should see more of the festival. We've hardly seen much," Mother suggested.

"Agreed," Devlin said. The family walked down the road but as they continued; Devlin noticed more and more smoke joining the original cloud. A pit of worry formed in his stomach and he hoped nothing was amiss, but he knew how dry the weather has been lately and worried it was a fire getting out of control. No one else seemed to point out the extra smoke, but he could feel the tension in the air. "Maybe we should go home after all?" Devlin finally said, unable to stop looking upon the gradually growing black stream.

"Aye," The rest of the family said at once.

"I don't like this, Devlin. I feel like something's very wrong," Cecelia whispered to him uneasily.

"I know, Cece. We just have to go, and hope it's some crazy accident." Devlin tried to sound confident, but he was actually trying to convince himself. As the smoke grew larger and closer, Devlin noticed he was walking even faster than he meant to, but his family was doing the same.

"I wonder what the h-hell is going o-on back there." Roark tried to hide the fear in his voice but failed miserably.

"Something tells me we don't want to find out," Devlin muttered to himself. He dared to look back one more time and, to his horror, finally saw what caused the smoke. Men wearing crudely made armor of leather and chainmail were carrying torches, burning every tent in sight. As a result, the dry grass also caught on fire, making a wall of flames behind the mercenaries.

"Oh, my..." Mother covered her mouth with her hand. Devlin saw people running frantically away from the bandits that were at least a few hundred feet away and closing fast. He saw guards attempting to fight against them, but they were easily overrun and dispatched by the mercenaries' cruel blades. Some fired arrows, felling soldiers no more than twenty feet away from Devlin and his family. Then, to Devlin's great horror, a few stray arrows flew towards them.

"Move!" Devlin yelled, shoving his mother out of the way of an arrow. He felt a sharp pain as the arrow grazed his shoulder. "Argh!" Devlin felt agony as he tried covering up the wound with his hand.

"Devlin, are you okay?" Mother asked concerned.

"It's fine, just a scratch." Devlin bit his lip, trying to ignore the pain which seemed to scream at him relentlessly. Before anyone could react, a second arrow flew towards them; this one found its mark in Mother's chest. Devlin felt his entire world collapse as he realized the shot was fatal. Time slowed to a standstill as Devlin's mother slowly fell towards the ground. The fall slowed every second as if time itself wished to torture Devlin with this horrifying image.

"Mom, no!" Devlin could do nothing but watch as her life trickled away, bit by bit as she fell to her knees and hit the ground with a thud. She had a devastated look on her face as she struggled to keep his gaze. Devlin gingerly rolled her onto her back.

"Children, go... please... save yourselves..." She gasped out, her words interrupted by her coughing up blood. Her voice was so soft and strained Devlin could barely hear her. Tears streamed down his mother's face, tears of regret that she could no longer protect her own children. "My only regret... is not being able... to protect you now... My beautiful children... Please... listen to your mother... and go..." Mother said, straining out her final words, the bell ringing on her last moment, as the final drop of life she had left her. Tears streamed down Devlin's face as he looked at her dead on the ground. Every memory he had of her poured through him at once, like a river of grief.

"Mother, no, please no. You can't die... You can't!" Devlin sobbed, slamming his fists on the ground beside her helplessly.

"Devlin, I know it's hard, but she's right. We have to go. Mother wouldn't want us to die with her here," Derek spoke quietly. His face was twisted with sorrow; Devlin looked at his father, who looked cold as ice.

"You all get out of here. I'll hold them off as best I can. If I can kill at least one of these scum, I will die happy. Now go!" Father ordered.

"But, Father! You'll be killed! It's suicide to go against them!" Roark pleaded, but one look from his father told him he knew that already.

"Listen, all of you. Your mother's dying wish was for you to live, and I'll be damned before I see one of you die. I'm gonna do my job as a father and protect my kids. I've already failed your mother, please don't let me fail you too," Father pleaded. A single tear ran down his face as he turned toward the rapidly approaching horde of bandits.

"Let's go, Devlin," Cecelia spoke quietly. She was sobbing heavily, but she tried to look strong. Devlin was torn up inside. His mother lay dead on the ground, and his father faced certain death. He felt like his whole world had fallen apart in just a few, short moments. Devlin slowly got to his feet. Tears streamed down his face, and he let them. He couldn't stop his sadness, and he didn't want to. He felt something else too... Rage. Powerful rage and hatred that was building up within him and drowned the sadness. He didn't care what happened to him anymore; he just wanted revenge. He guessed this is how his father felt, and he didn't blame him.

"Thank you, Father... I love you," Devlin said while getting up.

"I love you too son. Now get out of here," his Father said, looking back at them with sad eyes. Devlin could see a soft smile on his Father's face as he turned and ran toward the attacking mercenaries, picking up a sword that lay in the dirt. Devlin picked up a sword from a fallen soldier and, sheathing it, he tied it to his belt and ran, along with his two brothers who were each armed, Roark with the bow he used before and Derek with the sword he bought. His sister was following close behind. They ran as fast as they could across the clearing, but as they ran, the mercenaries were closing around them like a vice. Some managed to catch up to them, and Devlin had step back and repel the mercenaries with the swing of his sword. Roark helped him by shooting a couple of arrows, slowing down the mercenaries even more.

As Devlin ran faster, trying to outpace the mercenaries close behind and also to catch up with the siblings, in the back of his mind, Devlin wondered if his father was dead, or alive and still fighting. He also thought of Luke and wondered what fate befell him. They were almost to the forest as the mercenaries closed in. Derek was swinging his sword as well as Devlin, with Roark firing arrow after arrow with surprising accuracy. Devlin guessed the threat of death must have improved his aim. Cecelia, being unarmed, stayed close to Devlin. Once they finally made it into the forest, two dozen men dropped from the trees.

Roark killed a few with his arrows, but he was quickly running out. Realizing this, he grabbed a broad ax from a fallen mercenary. Devlin, Derek, and Roark wasted no time fighting against the brutes. Both Devlin and Derek stabbed and slashed while Roark smashed armor and heads with the flat of his ax. Cecelia tried to stay out of the way, but with so many mercenaries around, Devlin was struggling to keep them off of her. Devlin then saw that the rest of the mercenaries, coming to reinforce their comrades, and he realized this would only get worse.

"Derek, Roark, try and break a hole into the weakest gap you can find. This losing battle will cost us our lives if we stay," Devlin ordered while holding off the mercenaries. Derek responded by slashing at a side with the least amount of men and Roark quickly joined him. "Cece, stay close, this will get bloody."

Devlin ran toward the gap that his brothers had made with Cecelia close behind, but two mercenaries managed to sneak up behind Roark and Derek and hit them on their heads with the pommels of their swords, knocking them out. The mercenaries then did the same with Cecelia, and Devlin could tell within seconds he would be next, but the strangest thing happened. It was so strange that he thought he'd lost his mind. Some form had emerged from the tree and grabbed him, dragging him into the tree, as if magically merging with it. The rest was a mix of blurred vision, and his thoughts were all but consumed in black, save for the need to save his family.

Chapter 7

Luke galloped smoothly down the dirt pathway. He had left shortly after his match with Devlin and met his guard outside the arena. He had wished to stay longer with his fellow villagers, but he had to deal with matters of the king. He had heard that bandits had mortally wounded Prince Michael. The news left a pit in his stomach that he could not shake. He had a sinking feeling something was going on in the kingdom, behind the eyes of the people that lived there. The rising number of attacks by surprisingly well-organized bandits did nothing to ease his worries.

He unconsciously spurred his horse and raced down the path, his fellow soldiers close behind. He could feel their uneasiness too. It was like a dense fog that hung in the air and clung to them.

As the day wore on and the riding continued, Luke's thoughts strayed to his battle with Devlin. He was still just grasping the way of the sword, but Luke could sense something about him, something about him was different. The very air about him seemed alive and full of energy. Luke wondered, then, what the fates had in store for Devlin. A boy so different, it was unlikely he would grow up to be just another farm boy like he almost had.

If not for the King, he would be little more than a shepherd who favored a sword to this day, completely ignorant of the outside world. He had seen much, been to many different places. He didn't regret leaving the farm. He had done so much a regular farm boy could never dream of. Maybe fate had something in store for him, some destiny of which he was unaware. Regardless, Luke chose to follow where his heart leads him.

When the capital was in sight, he spurred his horse even faster. The walls of the capital were fifty meters tall, much taller than the small buildings that it encompassed. The walls were made of cut stone, and the walls had three entrances: one to the south, one to the east, and one to the west. Each gate was heavily guarded, and the gate itself had a wooden door reinforced with steel. As he drew near to the gate, he slowed to a stop in front of the guards. Recognizing Luke, they opened it for him.

The capital looked almost exactly as he left it; the stone paved roads and brick houses shone bright white in the afternoon sunlight. The capital was comprised of many merchant shops and homes for the residents. The residents themselves were organized by class, the less fortunate on the edge of the city next to the walls, typically the homes of the rookie recruits were here. As Luke got closer to the palace, he saw the homes get much bigger in size and much more decorated. These were the homes of the nobles, politicians, and higher ranking men in the king's army. The richest of the rich lived in the castle itself, the exception being the staff.

The road was relatively free of traffic, making it easy for Luke to traverse the complex maze of turns and alleys. He made it to the castle gates with his contingent halting in front of a pair of guardsmen. He got off of his horse, as did his comrades. Stable boys immediately ran over and led away the horses. "I wish to enter the castle," Luke spoke in an even tone.

"Of course, sir. Go right ahead." The guards opened the gates and Luke walked forward. As Luke entered the inner courtyard, he was reminded of the sheer brilliance of the castle. The courtyard itself was full of open areas of grass and trees with a beautifully decorated fountain in the very center. The grass and trees were well maintained by the dedicated staff, and the courtyard had the beauty to show for it. Luke himself had spent many days simply relaxing here in his days as a cadet. It was also the site of many of the comical attempts of the Master-Servant to teach Luke etiquette before entering the castle, a nearly impossible task knowing himself as a young boy.

As Luke opened the front door to the castle, he went over the mental map he had made over his many years here, and went straight to the King's chamber, through the twisting hallways and stairs. Luke wasted no time making it to the top floor where the audience chamber was located. He nodded respectfully to the guards who saluted him in return before opening the door to the chamber. Luke noticed the King sitting on his throne, deep in thought. So much so, he didn't even notice that Luke had come in. As Luke stood before him and kneeled with his head bowed, King MacArthur managed to free himself from his troubled thoughts.

"Luke, thank the Maker you are back. I feel as if my entire kingdom has been thrown off its hinges," King MacArthur said dismayed, rubbing his tired eyes with his hands. "I hope you at least enjoyed the festival?"

"I did, my King. I met some old friends and fought a worthy foe in the arena," Luke told him, looking up as he did so. "I came back early when I heard the news. Tell me Michael's condition?"

"My brave son, Michael… he is thankfully recovering… though his condition is still poor. I thank the Maker he spared him. If I had lost both sons so soon… I dare not even think of it." King MacArthur's head drooped in his grief, overwhelmed by so many tragedies to his family.

Luke's blood went cold at the words. "Both sons, milord?"

"Ah, yes, you haven't heard yet have you?" King MacArthur's head rose to look at Luke, but Luke barely recognized him. His eyes, once so proud and full of determination, were hollow and lifeless, as if he were looking into the eyes of a skeleton. "I sent my son Anders to a bandit hideout in the mountain side. When he returned… maker... the looks on my men's faces said it all. My poor son lays dying in the hospital bed. How much time he has left…? I dare not even think of it."

"My deepest condolences, Your Majesty. If there is anything I can do to help…" Luke offered.

"You have my thanks, Luke. The best thing we can do is try to stop these bandits. They get more organized, and more dangerous, with each attack. I even received word that they had attacked the festival you attended, and I feared the worst." King MacArther's voice was low and rasping as if he was an old man on the brink of death.

When Luke absorbed the gravity of the king's words, he was speechless. His best friends growing up were at that festival. He also felt great sadness, seeing his kind in this terrible state. "My people are in danger... Luke, I am afraid you are the only person left I can turn to," King MacArthur said solemnly. "Is there anything you'd recommend?"

Luke tried assessing the situation. "I believe the first step would be to gather information."

"The force I sent to attack the bandits did bring back a few live prisoners. We have been interrogating them since they arrived, but they have refused to speak, unfortunately," the King ventured, gesturing for Luke to rise.

Luke's heart jumped at the words. He wanted to interrogate the men himself and find each and every one of the scum that had attacked his family and friends, for service to the king and his own personal revenge. He was furious with the invisible threat, but also with himself for not stopping it.

"I will do all I can to combat this threat, my King. My sword is yours to command," Luke said as he rose to his feet. The King nodded affirmatively, regaining some of the life in his features.

"Yes, we will most certainly need your leadership, Luke. You may be able to start with the hideout Anders attacked. I am sure there will be some clues there," King MacArthur reasoned. "I will send out as many soldiers as I can spare to find who is attacking us. I am sorry that I cannot spare any more men for you than your current guard," the King said regrettably. "I will have my men continue the interrogations while you investigate, Luke."

Luke was amazed at the King's new development. The hope of saving his kingdom resurrected the corpse of the King to his former life.

"Understood, my liege," Luke said, bowing, and left the room.

Chapter 8

Devlin awoke amongst a bed of leaves in what looked to be a small hut. His head was throbbing, but he felt relatively well besides. He raised himself upright and noticed a strange man working on a table a few feet away. He was rather tall, of slim build, middle aged, and had distinctly pointed ears.

"Ah, so the young one finally awakens. For a moment, we thought you had died in the morphing."

"Where am I? How long have I been out? Why does my head hurt so much? I don't remember getting hit," Devlin blurted out as the torrent of questions in his mind found his voice.

"It's a side-effect of the salve we used. It should wear off soon. You are in one of the many hidden elven villages in this forest. You were found fighting off those barbarians, and some of our more adventurous youths took pity on you. Had they not, you'd likely have been killed or captured like those other humans. You fell unconscious for half a day due to the morphing," the healer explained simply.

"My family," Devlin gasped in horror. "They ambushed them. They're in danger. I have to help them!" Devlin tried getting up but his body, too weak to stand, collapsed back onto the bed.

"What you need, boy, is rest. Humans that experience a morphing for the first time tend to wear out quickly and need rest for at least a few days afterward. And you were in battle no less! You won't do your family any favors going off after them in your state," the elf stated cooly.

"Then what should I do?" Devlin asked desperately, frustrated at his inability even to stand. *I need to help them. They could die if I don't, but I can't even move, and I'll need at least a small army to save them now.*

"You need to rest up for now. The King has surely begun an investigation of what happened, and they will most likely find your family," the elf explained.

"They could be long dead by the time they are found. I have to do something!" Devlin pleaded.

"You certainly are a stubborn child," the elf conceded. "Very well, boy. Once you can walk properly, without straining yourself, you may be escorted out of the forest. Until then, sleep."

I hate it, but he's right. I can't do anything as I am now... Devlin thought, defeated. *I have to get stronger... I will get stronger. I will save my family no matter what it takes.* Devlin slowly laid his head back down and went to sleep as best he could. His dreams were filled with memories of his family, how only this morning he was happily eating breakfast with them. Now, they were gone, and he could do nothing.

"What a great birthday present for me, huh?" Devlin said in spite of himself as a tear ran down his cheek and he forced himself to sleep.

* * *

When Devlin opened his eyes again, he noticed the bright morning sunlight flowing in from the open window next to the door. He heard the birds chirping and saw the sun low in the east. He looked around the hut, taking it in for the first time. He noticed the room was filled with herbs of all kinds, most likely for medicinal purposes. As Devlin wiped the sleep from his eyes, a young elven girl, likely the same age as Devlin entered the hut. "Are you feeling well, sir?" the elven girl asked shyly, slowly walking over to him. She wore a fitted tunic and a skirt that went down to her knees, and worn leather boots. She had the same wild eyes and pointy ears as the healer.

Devlin wasn't expecting a visitor. He wondered who she was, but restrained himself from prying. "No, not really," Devlin said as he unconsciously rubbed his temple. *How can I ever feel okay after having my family stolen away? How could I ever forgive myself for not protecting them like I promised I would?* She smiled slightly at him.

"I understand. I remember my first experience with the salve. You get used to the effect, though," Elena told him quietly.

"That's good, but hopefully, I won't have to use it again soon," Devlin said as he continued to rub his forehead. *Derek, Roark, Cecelia, Mother, and Father. I've lost all of them. They could already be dead, and I don't even know it. They could be suffering or being tortured at this very moment, and I am completely powerless...* Devlin clenched his fists so hard the knuckles turned white.

"My name is Elena by the way; I'm the one that saved you before," Elena said, trying to open up to Devlin. "I'm sorry about your family." Hearing her say "family" was another blow. Another reminder of his inadequacy.

"It's my fault for not being able to save them, but thank you for saving me. I owe you my life, and I take that seriously," Devlin said sincerely, finally looking up to meet her eyes again.

"Of course, only one with a cold heart would turn a blind eye to someone in need. If it pleases you, sir, may I ask your name?" Elena offered, sitting down next to him, and trying to hide her nerves.

What purpose does my name serve now that I may be the only one that still holds it? "Devlin Slade, but I go by Devlin. It is a pleasure to meet you, Elena," Devlin said kindly.

"Would you like a tour of the village? I find a nice walk to be a great way to ease aches and pains," Elena suggested.

"Sure, I'd love to be out of this hut. Even for a little bit." *Maybe it will distract me from the hole in my chest...* Elena helped Devlin to his feet and supported him as he walked by wrapping his arm around her. "If you get tired, just tell me, and we can rest.

I know you'll still be a bit weak from the morphing, so no need to push yourself."

"Thank you, I think I should be fine," Devlin said awkwardly as he stumbled out of the cottage with her. He felt something rattle under his shirt and reached into it to see what it was, revealing the griffin-shaped amulet Luke had given Devlin as a show of respect. That fight seemed so long ago now, and Devlin had completely forgotten about it. Devlin stuffed it back under his shirt and continued.

As they walked, Elena showed Devlin the center of town where a good deal of the elves went to work on things for the village. The village itself was made up of a couple of dozen wooden huts much like the one Devlin was just in. There were also little shops scattered all around the village, most of them just selling natural fruits and vegetables. The elves looked kindly to each other; the only exception was when they saw Devlin. Many giving him an apprehensive look, or one of shock. Here he was, a human, in a village full of elves. Devlin had heard stories that the elves and humans had rather nasty histories and felt a little self-conscious.

"The elves seem so friendly to each other," Devlin observed awkwardly as he stood with Elena. *And so not friendly to me.*

"That's because we are a small village. Everyone knows everyone here. Just give it a little time, they'll warm up to you," Elena said sympathetically. Elena waved to a few of the passing elves who warily returned the gesture. "I have to admit, though, Devlin, I'm curious about you. I noticed that you are fairly skilled with a sword; where did you learn how to fight?"

Seeing no harm in telling her, Devlin explained his story. "I first learned the art of the sword from a kind, old soldier named Henric. He lived in the village I lived in, and I used to visit him now and then, because of the wonderful stories he'd tell me of his time in the King's army. He told me of the grueling battles he fought in and the fun times he had with his comrades."

"Before long, I was eager to learn how to use a sword myself, and he taught me on one condition: 'never use the sword recklessly.' When I told my brothers about it, they wanted to learn too, and we all took lessons together under Henric's supervision. At first, it was just a pastime for us, something to do when we got bored, but as we grew up, it became more than that. When we grew up, we became aware of how dangerous the world can truly be, and we started training harder and harder to protect our family."

"What was it that made you aware of the dangers of the world?" Elena asked thoughtfully.

"I believe I was ten years old at the time," Devlin recalled distantly. "An escaped criminal made his way onto our farm one day. If it weren't for Father, he would've killed all of us I'm sure. I always knew my father was good with a sword, but he would never teach us anything. He killed the man effortlessly and reported it to the Army. I still remember the look in father's eyes as he killed the man. They were cold and ruthless as if it were natural for him to kill someone. I'm glad he stopped the criminal, but those eyes, those merciless eyes, I would never forget them for the rest of my life."

"Do you know anything else about your father?" Elena asked concerned.

"No, he never told us anything about his past or Mother's. I don't know why they were always so secretive about it, but they wouldn't even tell us about how they met," Devlin confessed sadly.

"That is very strange…" Elena agreed solemnly.

* * *

A few days passed as Devlin slowly recovered his strength. Elena would guide him around the village, meeting all sorts of different elves. Devlin started to feel a hesitant but growing friendship with Elena as each day passed. She kept

Devlin company, and Devlin told her more about his life growing up, and about his family as a way of distracting himself from the worry as he healed. The healer elf said it took so long because Devlin would sneak out in the night and attempted to train. He barely made it back to the hut the first time he tried. One week after Devlin's arrival, Elena entered the hut with the same cheerful smile she always had.

    "Devlin, I have somewhere for you to visit today if you're feeling up to it," Elena offered. Devlin slowly got out of bed, still rousing his body from its slumber.

    "I'm ready when you are," Devlin told her, yawning loudly shortly after.

    Elena led Devlin to the front of a decorated hut, more ornate than the others. "The Elder lives in this dwelling. He said he was interested in meeting you." Elena's words were soft but kind and welcoming. Devlin felt nervous, however. He hoped he would not somehow offend the elder after all the elves have done for him. Elena opened one of the double doors and helped Devlin inside.

    The hut was full of traditional elven works and items. Devlin had to look over each several times just to comprehend every last detail. As he looked around, he noticed an aged elf with a small white beard and staff in his hand. "Ah, Elena, it's so good to see you again. This is our unusual guest, I presume?" the Elder asked, looking suspiciously at Devlin.

    "Yes, Elder, our very eager guest, Devlin, woke up this morning. I have spent the week helping him recover," Elena said uncomfortably.

    "How are you feeling then, Devlin? I trust you have been accommodated well enough?" The elder stepped closer but still was a few feet away.

    "I have actually. I can't thank you all enough for everything you have done for me. I owe you my freedom as well as my life." Devlin bowed respectfully to the Elder, hoping to build a bridge over the histories between the two races.

"There's no need for such gratitude, Devlin. Elena did want her heart felt was right. She is the one deserving of your thanks, not I. However, I also heard of the unfortunate capture of your family. I offer my deepest condolences to you, but I am curious. What will you do now?" the Elder asked rubbing his beard.

Family. Family. Family. Why does that word make me feel so hollow inside? "I want to save them, even if I have to go to the pits of hell and back to do it." Devlin felt his fists clench with fresh determination as he said it. Since he was recovered now, he owed it to them to do anything he could to save them. The Elder nodded, satisfied with his answer, which lifted the worry from Elena's shoulders.

"Understandable, though it will not be easy. I want to help any way I can; perhaps you could talk with our weapons master for guidance. I feel it might just save your life," the Elder suggested.

"Thank you, Elder. Any help you offer would be appreciated." Devlin bowed.

"I wish you good fortune with your endeavors Devlin. I will have our outfitters fit you with their best armor and sword. I feel great disturbances from the trees beginning to form. Lux has also been very reactive lately. It may be a hunch, but you may be walking right into a very terrible darkness." The Elder's features took on a worried expression. Devlin gave a skeptical look, but the look vanished before the elder looked at him again.

"If it pleases you, Elder, I would like to accompany Devlin in his journey. I worry what the future will bring since Lux has begun to shine again," Elena said stepping forward.

"Are you sure about this, Elena? Devlin's path is to be full of hardship with death being more than just a possibility," The Elder spoke sadly.

"I'm aware, Elder, but I still want to go. I want to protect this land from any danger that approaches. If Devlin's path leads to it, I want to do anything I can to put a stop to it. Also, I doubt Devlin would last five seconds without me," Elena winked at Devlin as she said this, with Devlin rolling his eyes with a smirk in response.

"Always the confident one," The Elder laughed then looked seriously at Devlin. "It's up to you, Devlin, it's your journey. Do you wish to have her along? I can vouch for her masterful swordsmanship and stealth abilities. She will not be a hindrance; I assure you." The elder looked a little saddened, yet also proud that Elena had volunteered.

I suppose a second hand couldn't hurt. She seems trustworthy at least. "It would be an honor, sir. I'm sure she would be a great help to me." Devlin smiled big with confidence. "If you aren't scared that is, Elena."

"I don't get scared, can you say the same, Devlin?" Elena challenged snidely.

"The one that says no fear always holds it closest," Devlin grinned.

"I would be careful if I were you, Devlin, Elena is a mischievous girl. Watch your back if you know what's good for you!" The Elder chuckled at his jest. "You may leave whenever you feel prepared. Elena, I ask that you wait a moment please." Devlin nodded to him and bowed slightly. "Thank you, Elder, I am undeserving of such kindness." *Assuming I am not about to be kicked out or worse.* Devlin backed out of the hut and closed the door behind him, giving the two of them privacy.

"What do you think of this boy, Elena? You are the one who has been with him all this week," the Elder asked her curtly.

"I believe he is trustworthy, Elder. I don't sense any malicious intent from him, just a deep sadness that looms over him like a cloud. The sadness dulls his spirit, makes him seem distant and spiteful. I will do my best to ease his sadness over the loss of his family," Elena answered sincerely.

"This may be the chance we have been waiting for. That boy could help us with our relations with the humans, and close the gap between our races," the Elder reasoned. "I ask that you be careful, Elena, and continue to keep an eye on the boy."

"Consider it done," Elena said dutifully. Elena bowed slightly and walked out the door where Devlin waited. Elena felt pure relief from getting the Elder's approval of Devlin, who she had truly grown to know as a friend.

"So I guess this makes us partners, huh?" Devlin asked cautiously as she closed the door gingerly behind her.

"I believe so. Just try not to slow me down ok, hotshot? You should maybe get some training in tomorrow. Trust me; you'll need it where you're going," Elena said amused. "Until then, want to check out the other shops?"

"Of course. Lead the way." Devlin conceded. *Although I'd much rather be training…*

Elena started leading Devlin away from the Elder's hut and toward the sparse merchant area.

The shopping dragged on the rest of the day, but Devlin only bought some fresh fruit, and a slim, silver ring said to bless the wearer with good fortune. It was engraved in a language Devlin didn't know, but Elena said the writing was ancient elven scripture. Elena took him back to the recuperation hut, and Devlin tucked himself in after waving goodbye to Elena. "Thank you, Elena, I had a lot of fun with you today. I hope we become great partners." Devlin wanted to get along with Elena, so he wanted to be kind to her. *If she's as good with the sword as the elder claims, maybe she can help me train.*

"Sweet dreams, Devlin. May the forest smile upon you." Elena genuinely smiled at him and faded out of view as Devlin quickly went to sleep.

Chapter 9

Derek woke up in a cell enclosed by stone bricks and locked with steel bars. His head throbbed from the sedatives the thugs had given him on the journey here, but he disregarded the pain and looked out from his cell. His vision blurred, yet another side effect, but he managed to make out the structure of the building as a long hallway with prison cells on both sides. As Derek's vision amended itself, he saw that each cell held one person, all male from what Derek could see, and some he knew as his fellow villagers and neighbors. He looked around again and saw Roark still passed out on the floor in his cell. He felt sadness for him, but at least he was still alive. He couldn't see Cecelia anywhere, though. He hoped she was just in a different cell further down or free from the clutches of this prison altogether. He couldn't find Devlin either and prayed he was safe.

Roark started to stir then, finally waking from unconsciousness. "What? Where am I?" Roark looked shaken but otherwise unharmed.

"Roark, over here." Derek kept his voice low. He didn't want to draw too much attention to himself.

"Derek? What are we doing here? The last thing I remember is getting ambushed by those thugs. How did we end up in a prison?" Roark asked still a little unsteady.

"They gave us sedatives while they dragged us here, remember? Also, if they were regular thugs, they wouldn't have bothered to capture all these people. It would've been easier just to cut our throats in the field. They must have been working for someone who wanted to capture people. We might even end up as slaves." Saying the words himself sent shivers down his spine.

The last thing he wanted was to be stuck as a slave. He was used to laboring, sure, but he remembered stories of what other countries do to slaves. Most died young or worked *until* they died. Each day at the end of a whip, forced to work until they dropped on the ground.

"I'm scared, brother. How could this happen?" Roark sounded more afraid with every passing moment.

"We'll get out of here, Roark. I promise." Derek just hoped he could keep that promise. "Can you see Cecelia or Devlin from your cell?" Roark moved to the front of his cell and looked left and right, all around.

"I don't see them." Roark sulked, and Derek feared for their welfare.

"Then I pray they are free and away from here because I'd rather not think of the alternative." Derek heard a screech and then many footsteps. Several guards in full suits of armor came down the hallway and stopped in the middle of the passage. A single man stood out from the guards. His armor was far more elaborate than the others, a clear sign of his rank, Derek guessed. He stepped forward; as he did Derek noticed the keys on his belt.

"Hello, prisoners. I do hope you're enjoying your stay here. I am your warden, and, as I'm sure you can guess, my word is law. Those who see fit to disregard what I say will be punished accordingly." Derek could see him smirk as he said *punished*. "Am I understood?" The silence was all that followed. "Splendid. You will get water and two meals a day; any complaints will be completely ignored. Should you become a nuisance, the guards will be the ones to decide your fate. That is all you need to know."

The warden walked out the door, but the guards stayed put inside the hall. Derek noticed an older man who could barely walk on his own, head toward the front of his cell.

"Please, sir, I'm dreadfully cold down to my aching bones. Might you spare a blanket or two?" The old man pleaded.

"Shut up and deal with it. No one gets special treatment," the guard ordered.

"Please, sir, just one blanket?" the old man begged again. The annoyed guard opened the door to his cell with his keys and punched the man right in the face. The old man went sprawling to the back of the cell and slammed against the wall with a grunt. Before he collapsed, the guard punched the old man, again and again, raining blows on his bony stomach and face. The beating went on for what seemed like hours, but when the guard finally stopped, the old man just fell to the floor, completely limp. He didn't look to be breathing. The guard stamped on the old man's head. The old man didn't even move. He just laid there, dead.

"Whoops, looks like I hit him a little too hard. Oh well, I doubt he's cold now." The guard laughed to himself and picked up the man. "Hey boys, I just made some more room!" With that, he tossed the body into a slot in the wall that led to who knows where.

Derek just stood there, shocked at what he just saw. An uncontrollable rage shot through him like fire in his veins. "That man couldn't even defend himself, you coward!" Derek screamed. The guard looked over at Derek with a sneer.

"Derek, calm down, or they'll beat you too!" Roark panicked but kept his voice low.

"What did you say, boy?" The guard demanded.

"I said you are a weak-minded, sniveling coward. You aren't strong enough to handle someone your own size so you take it out on old men that can barely walk?!" Derek screamed, cursing everything about the guard to his face.

"Derek!" Roark pleaded. *Damn it you prideful fool; you're going to get yourself killed!*

"Oh I'm a coward, am I? I merely helped the old man stop feeling cold. If he could still talk, he'd be thanking me." The guards laughed loudly at that. Each laugh was an abomination to Derek's nerves.

"You're nothing but scum! Every breath you take is an insult to our race," Derek yelled, enraged.

"I think we have ourselves a little rebel here." A guard responded. "Time to teach you a lesson, boy." The guard opened the door to the cell followed by two others. Two of the guards tried to grab him, but Derek was quicker and dodged their advances. The other guard, though, was right on top of him and backhanded Derek with his gauntlet. Derek was sent reeling with the force of the blow. The other prisoners watched in horror as the other two guards each grabbed Derek's arms and held him. Derek recovered himself, though, and stamped down hard on a guard's foot, causing him to howl in agony and let go. The other guard loosened his grip momentarily in shock. Derek ripped his arm free and punched the guard as hard as he could right under his chin. The jaw-shattering blow launched the guard across the cell to the stone wall, knocking him out on the spot.

However, the first guard grabbed Derek and brought him down to the cold, hard ground. "I'm going to enjoy hearing you scream, boy." The guard looked at his companion who had just recovered from Derek stomping on his foot. "You, tie his feet together!" The guard took a bit of rope and wrapped it securely around Derek's ankles. Derek struggled all he could, but the guard had him completely subdued. Roark watched in horror as the guard on Derek tied Derek's hands together, and carried him out of the prison hall and through a door at the end of the hall.

The guards took him to a wide circular room and set him down on a platform with shackles attached to the ceiling. The guard untied the rope and put Derek's wrists in the shackles. The guard opened a spot on the platform near the center, revealing a second pair of chains, and did the same process with his ankles as his wrists, and took off Derek's shirt. The second guard pulled a lever and Derek was raised off the ground by his shackles until he was held tight, his arms being pulled up, his legs being pulled down, three feet off the ground.

"What is the meaning of this?" Derek shouted, outraged.

"You're about to get the worst whipping of your life, boy. You should feel honored. The warden himself will be the one dealing out punishment, and he had this setup specially made so that no prisoner could get away!" Derek saw the tall man in his fancy armor walk in through the door.

"I can't go one lousy hour without someone causing trouble in my jail. You'll pay for interrupting my nap you pathetic rat." The warden angrily stepped onto a raised platform and removed the viper-like whip from his belt. It had a bolt on the end of the whip that looked both jagged and sharp, and Derek realized that he was about to find out how effective it was first hand.

"I'm not afraid of you and your little string." Derek steeled himself; he did not fear a whip, as his father had whipped him plenty of times in his youth for misbehaving. *How ironic,* Derek thought to himself. *I'm about to be whipped again for "misbehaving."*

"This 'little string' is going to rip you to shreds." The warden pulled his whip back behind his head, and the length of the whip was clearly visible. It looked at least the length of a grown man and slim as a snake. The warden brought his arm back down, and the whip went sailing right into Derek's back. The metal bolt sank into Derek's skin and tissue like a knife to his back. The pain was excruciating as Derek's back screamed outrage at the tear. Then, as quickly as it came, the warden pulled back on the whip, ripping even more of Derek's back. The pain was unbearable to the point where Derek had to bite his tongue to keep from screaming out in pain.

"You're a tough, little squirt, if you're not screaming from that. Oh well, we'll loosen that tongue of yours." The other guards just laughed at that, enjoying the spectacle they were seeing.

These men are pure filth. If I had a sword, they would be running scared like little dogs. They think us prisoners are below them, so they think they can do whatever they please and not get in trouble for it. Derek wished more and more he could fight back, to teach the cowards that mercilessly killed an old man a lesson.

He wanted to free his family and everyone else wrongfully imprisoned here. But first, he needed to survive this ordeal. His family would have no use for a dead man.

The whip came down again, and Derek's mind exploded from the pain. The pain was doubled from the bolt hitting already ripped flesh and then multiplied even more when the whip was pulled back out. The process repeated, again and again, the pain exploding throughout his body so belligerently that Derek couldn't even form a coherent thought. He just hung there, taking whip after whip, using every ounce of will he had to fight through the pain until it was so unbearable that Derek couldn't take it anymore. Derek's body, overwhelmed by pain, shut down leaving him unconsciousness.

When Derek finally woke up again, the pain was the first thing that greeted him. Derek groaned, knowing that even though he couldn't see his back, he knew it must be ripped and raw. He was laying on his stomach and noticed the bandages wrapped around his torso. The cell floor felt cold even through the bandages and as he looked around, he noticed his shirt laying right next to him. *At least I'm still alive*, Derek thought to himself and passed out again.

Chapter 10

    Luke rode his steed down the beaten trail to the hideout Prince Anders had ambushed. Luke hoped that perhaps he could find something amongst the debris and a hint as to who these well-trained bandits were working for. His guard, of course, followed closely behind him, and they rode at a steady pace. They made it to the crevice in the rock that led into the cave, and Luke dismounted his horse, as did the guards. They stepped, with caution, into the crevice, each of them with one hand wrapped around the hilts of their swords.

    Luke looked around the cave. The opening was several feet high but only a few feet wide, forcing Luke and his guard to enter single file. The opening to the cave kept its cramped shape for several meters before widening out into the main cavern. The stretch before them held no visible enemies, so he continued down the path. At the other side, the scene of the battlefield was laid out right in front of them. Bodies lay in piles and littered the cave. There were rats and insects swarming over dead bodies, eating the flesh off them. Luke felt himself gag at the sight, even more so from the smell but pressed onward. He surveyed some of the tents and found nothing but stolen goods; gold, valuables, and the like, as well as some rotten food.

    The guards started searching the bodies, somehow managing to hold in their stomachs, but found nothing. Luke looked at the armory; it was further back in the cave. He examined each weapon closely, looking for any engravings on it, any marks, but they looked like weapons they had stolen off of guards or people traveling. Then he noticed a small nook in the wall; he rubbed his fingers on it and felt a slight give. When he pushed on it, a section of the wall broke away, revealing a small room.

"Men, come to the armory! I believe I've found something!" Moments later, the guards gathered in, and everyone started searching the room. Luke opened a piece of parchment on a table and looked over it. It was the inventory of all the weapons, with prices to the side, all neatly ordered, meaning the Bandits did indeed receive their weapons from someone. However, the parchment didn't specify any nation or country.

"Sir, I've found something of interest. There are several other swords of the same style in a couple of barrels too," the guard said as held a strange dagger in his palm. Luke took the dagger and examined it carefully. The blade was intricately made and curved like a wave.

"I've seen this style of smiting before; it's Seamander's style. The wave-like formation of the blade is their specialty." Luke rubbed his chin as he examined further. "The hilt is gilded, and it looks like it's rarely seen use. The grip isn't worn at all. There's an inscription at the pommel of the hilt. However, I don't recognize the writing. We should head back to the castle. Take anything of interest with you but don't encumber yourself."

"Yes, sir!"

*   *   *

As Luke and his guards ran through the town to the castle, Luke ran through his mind what his plan was. He was going to have the High Scholar look into the inscription on the dagger, as well as a few documents found in the room. However, they didn't find much else of interest. In the castle, Luke went to the bottom of the stairwell and opened the doors. They opened to a large library, with shelves and large stacks of books. Each book held its own story, everything from past conquests in the lands before the Great Wars to every history imaginable. There were even biographies of the kings before King MacArthur, and books of his deeds from taking the throne to now.

Several of the people that read over these books were considered scholars and the oldest and most accomplished scholar was given the title of High Scholar. This ancient, wizened man is said to have read every book in the library many times over. Luke saw him in the center, where he usually was, reading a book with intricate penmanship on the pages. "Nathaniel, I loath to disturb you, but I am in need your help with an investigation. I found a strange dagger, with an inscription on the end in a language I have never seen before. Can you look it over?"

"Ah, the instruments of war. They go everywhere, even in the room meant solely for the peace and tranquility of learning." Nathaniel gave an exasperated sigh. "Very well Luke, I will inspect it for you. Hand it over." Luke gave Nathaniel the dagger, and he immediately started to examine. He checked the blade closely on each side, then, seeing nothing, examined the hilt and the inscription.

"This is indeed curious... The inscription is of an old tribe called the Azukas. I've barely seen it in any of our many books, in fact, but I can help you." Nathaniel paused, gathering his thoughts. "The inscription itself means power, a tribute to one of their gods to aid in battle. Likely, the man who owned this blade was from Seamander and took it to the tribe to be blessed."

"So our best hope is finding this tribe?" Luke mused.

"Exactly, but they will not be easy to find. They are in a very dangerous part of the continent Luke. The tribes there will also hinder you at any chance they get." Nathaniel eyed Luke expectantly, but there was a bit of concern in his voice.

"My fellow soldiers and I are no strangers to risking our lives. We will be fine, sir. On what part of the continent are they from?" Luke was eager to hear where his journey lies.

"They inhabit the northern country of Reshina. You will have to head there and search for the main capital, Reshim," Nathaniel pointed at a large map as he said this, and pointed out other cities, as well as the capital. Then he slid his finger a bit to the left of it. "They live just west of the capitol. But make no mistake; they will not greet you warmly. Keep your sword close at all times, lest you be stabbed in the back on the road."

"Thank you for your help, Nathaniel." Luke bowed. Nathaniel nodded his approval, and Luke quickly left the library.

Chapter 11

Elena Spellweaver was a pure-blooded elf. She had shoulder-length, brown hair, typically braided or in a bun in preparation for combat. She had deep green eyes and a smooth face. She had a scar on her cheek, a battle wound, and traditional tattoos on her face. The tattoos flowed like waves as they curved and angled on her cheeks and forehead. Fae received these tattoos when they reach the age of adulthood, and it was a symbol of pride for Elena. She stood fairly tall, about as tall as a normal man, and kept fit from all of her training.

She had been raised to be a warrior by the Elder's command. The Elder had said that he had sensed great potential in Elena, and he hadn't been wrong. Elena's magic had surfaced at the age of five years, magic surfacing that early was almost unheard of. She learned to master her power perfectly by the age of ten, using it in many different forms, such as elemental spells.

She was also taught sword combat as well as hand-to-hand combat, and she preferred the latter. She even mixed her magic with her combat abilities such as enhancing her muscles with magic to superhuman strength, setting her hands aflame which left burns on contact as well as the blow. She spent her pre-teenage years and some of her teenage years in the forest patrols. The forest patrols taught her the value of stealth and precision. She had to see the intruder without being seen herself as well as subdue the threat should it come to it. She learned to make her strikes count, and it also taught her patience.

Elena was determined, dedicated, and willful even if she came off as overwhelming to others. She had fears, of course, she didn't want to let anyone down, and she did everything she could to make others proud of her. She also feared being an outcast, so she made a conscious effort to be a kind person, and a person others looked up to.

Elena had seen Devlin and his family fighting the other humans when she had taken over a patrol for a sick friend. She didn't know how to respond to it at first, seeing as the men weren't likely to threaten the Elven village, but she felt pity for the four people around her own age being assaulted by those brutes. Elena hesitated at first, not wanting to get involved in human affairs. Elves and humans had bitter histories and many feuds, but her heart went out to the people when she saw them being overwhelmed. She couldn't just stand by and do nothing.

Elena had to act quickly, and the idea that came to mind was the morphing, even if it was risky. She could only take one person with her, though, which happened to be the cornered Devlin. Performing the morphing had been easy enough, and it went smoothly as she took the boy to the village. The morphing had drained her, however, and she had to rely on two other elves that saw her attempting to drag the unconscious Devlin. At first, the elves were alarmed that Devlin was a human, but they must have decided that he wasn't likely to pose a threat. *He was surprisingly heavy,* she recalled. After she had taken the boy to the recuperation hut she felt a sort of obligation to the boy. She checked on him regularly hoping to see him awake. Another part of her was apprehensive of the boy as she had never come into close contact with a human before, and she was worried that he would end up a threat after all. Elena also didn't know if she should trust a human, or how having him here would affect the villagers. Elena could only wait and see when he awoke.

Elena's first meeting with Devlin was a huge weight off of her shoulders. He looked tired and lost, which made sense, but she also sensed great sadness in him, and Elena could guess why. She felt somewhat responsible for his sadness, so she wanted to be kind to him, if anything, to at least distract him from his pain. She did hesitate to open up to Devlin, but she did want to give him a chance. She was surprised at him as a person, however. He was so genuine, so kind and forthcoming, yet determined and strong, even in his lowest moments. Elena could see through his mask, however, him using his determination to hide the grief he felt. She understood how he felt, as she had done the same when her parents died. Elena wanted to do what she could to help, and she genuinely bonded with Devlin over the days they spent together. Elena started to stop seeing Devlin as a dangerous human, and more of a close friend.

When she decided to join Devlin in his quest, she saw it as a chance to repay her debt to Devlin and ease the Elder's worries. For now, Elena planned to help Devlin train, any way she possibly could.

* * *

Devlin started each day by touring the village as he did before with Elena. He had grown to like the humble Elven village, as well as Elena, who supported him unconditionally. Elena's prediction about the villagers was correct also. After some time the elves grew used to Devlin's presence around the village. Upon seeing that he wasn't a threat to them they opened up to him as Elena had. Through all the differences between elf and human, Devlin found a lot of similarities as well. As close as he felt to Elena, however, Devlin realized that he barely knew anything about her. Devlin asked Elena about her past, curious to know of her life. Elena left out her history with magic but told him about her training to become a warrior as well as her time in the patrols. She told him she had a gift for marksmanship, hand-to-hand combat, and the blade.

Elena even showed Devlin what she knew, and he noticed she had a certain grace in the way she moved. Her movements seemed smooth and fluid, much unlike Devlin who relied more on strength rather than speed. Devlin made notes of her moves and resolved to add more smooth movements to his style. *If I want to fight better, I have to be faster, not just stronger. I can learn a lot from watching her.*

Elena was dangerous even without a blade. She told him about all the different ways she had learned to disarm an opponent, as well as incapacitate them. She also had surprising strength, which she demonstrated by punching a tree and snapping it in two like a twig. Elena had explained that there was a certain knack for it that she would tell Devlin about later.

Devlin started training himself in the open grounds. He did a quick warm up, moving the blade this way and that, making sure it felt right. Then, he would practice his stance and multiple strikes with his sword. Once he was sure he was warmed up, he tried incorporating some of the movements of Elena's style into his own. It was difficult, because he was considerably slower than she was, and Devlin had to find different ways to compensate for the strange style.

Devlin practiced the strikes and combinations repeatedly, getting drenched in sweat. *This is a lot harder than I thought… At this rate I'll never be as good as her,* Devlin thought to himself. Devlin used his frustration to fuel his training. He found better ways to use Elena's style and it got much easier to move. Devlin could feel himself adapting, getting smoother and less sloppy. However, the duress of the training became too much, and Devlin decided to rest in the trees which had plentiful fruits to spare. Devlin grabbed some sturdy branches and climbed up the tree with ease. He pulled out his dagger to quickly stab into the tree for a handhold. When Devlin finally got to the top of the tree, he grabbed an apple from one of the branches.

"You've been working hard," Elena's voice called out to him, surprising Devlin so much that he almost fell out of the tree. "I saw you practicing all morning; you're getting better." Devlin looked around, trying to follow her voice. He saw her standing curiously on a branch close to where Devlin sat.

"Don't surprise me like that. I'm going to fall on my head one of these days because of you, I swear it." Elena simply started laughing at that.

"It's good to know I'm still quiet enough to surprise you, Devlin. It's good practice for the field, facing real humans, and you're much warier than most to begin with." Devlin merely rolled his eyes as Elena attempted to stifle her laugh.

That was one thing about Elena Devlin wasn't so fond of. The Elder had been all too right when he said she was mischievous at times, and she liked playing little pranks on Devlin. He could never understand how she moved so quietly. *I may as well get used to it, and, to be honest, she doesn't mean any harm,* Devlin conceded mentally. *I'll just have to get her back for it later.*

"I'm going to sneak up on you one of these days, and maybe I'll give you a heart attack like the ones you give me," Devlin told her almost jokingly. Almost.

"We shall see," Elena said, relaxing on the branch. "I'll be sure to watch my back from now on." They both started laughing out loud; an odd sound for a field of battle. Devlin jumped down from the tree and ran out to practice again. Elena dropped down and ran after him. "How about a sparring match, Devlin? A moving target is always better than a still one," Elena said to him, smiling dangerously.

"Alright, but don't be sad when you lose," Devlin retorted confidently. Elena walked over to the weapons stand and grabbed a practice sword. Devlin walked over to her, with the sword he had been using, observing the other swords and testing their weights. When he was satisfied, he took his stance facing Elena. Each looked the other dead in the eye and stood there waiting for the other to make the first move.

"Something tells me I'm going to enjoy beating you senseless," Elena challenged, somewhat amused.

"That's assuming you can even touch me," Devlin shot back with a snide grin.

Both started forward, each with their blade at the ready. They swung their swords toward the other and the dull steel blades collided with a resounding clang. Devlin wasn't able to overpower her, so he pushed the blade up, separating them and quickly swung his sword from the right. Elena saw it coming though and parried the strike, forcing Devlin back. Devlin swung around again, but he faked at the last second and brought his sword up for a downward strike. Elena dodged the strike and thrust her sword toward Devlin but he leaped sideways; just managing to dodge the dull point. In mid-air, Devlin swung his sword around, but Elena ducked out of the way effortlessly. Devlin rolled to his feet to recover from the leap, parried a blow from Elena, and jumped back.

They went at it again and again, neither of them able to hit the other. Their swords danced through the air in a myriad of different ways as each tried to outmaneuver the other. However, as the battle progressed, both of them kept in perfect rhythm with the other in a graceful dance of steel; the swords sang a ringing ballad as they continually collided with each other. This continued even when they were both out of breath; the fatigue catching up to them.

The ringing ballad of honor reached a decrescendo to the final note, one last clang of their swords, and each fell to their knees from pure exhaustion. "I guess... we can consider this... a draw," Devlin gasped between breaths.

"Fair enough... good match... Devlin," Elena wheezed, drinking some water from her waterskin. Devlin got to his feet and offered her a hand up. "Well, aren't you a gentleman; thank you," she said, grinning, and took his hand. As they put away their swords, Devlin looked at the sky. It was a bright shade of orange with the sun sinking low over the trees.

"It's getting dark already? How long were we fighting?" Devlin asked, bewildered.

"I think we started a bit after noon. Time really does fly when you are having fun."

"Indeed it does. You two went at it for quite awhile; that was a match only two youngsters could manage." Both Devlin and Elena were surprised at the unexpected voice. It came from a tall elf, at least a head taller than Devlin, with large, muscular arms that carried scars of battle.

"Master Irou, it is good to see you again," Elena said getting up. "Devlin, this is the sword master that the elder spoke of. He is the best warrior in our village and taught me how to fight."

"You flatter me with your praise, young one, but I still have a long way to go before I truly may call myself a master. From what I remember, you taught me more than I taught you. Your method of swordplay is original, fresh, and much more sophisticated than others. You have a grace about you when you fight that can't be replicated easily."

"You seem to have your own style also, Devlin, and that match spoke volumes of it. Every stroke between you two was superb, truly proficient. You both should be proud." Irou praised them with a kind smile.

"I have been training to get stronger, faster, anything to help me save my family." Devlin felt proud of himself that he was at least a bit successful in that regard. "Elena was a tough opponent. So much so that I'm glad we are on the same side."

"Being your friend doesn't mean I'm going to let you slack off, though. We can't have matches like that if you get lazy. I truly enjoyed that fight; I felt like I learned some new things from it." Elena patted Devlin on the back with a determined look on her face.

"You better not slack either then, or next time I'm going to win." Devlin returned the look, then turned to the Sword master. "Is there anything you can teach me in the way of the sword, sir?" Devin was curious if there was something he was missing.

"I will correct you where I see any significant error, however, warriors improve the best on their own. I can show you a few techniques you may build off of, and incorporate into your own style. I want you to have your own style. Any page can simply copy another's. The ones that develop their own are truly above the rest," Irou insisted dutifully.

"Very well, sir. Shall we meet tomorrow?" Devlin inquired.

"I think I'll come too; it's been too long since I've been to one of the master's sessions," Elena smiled enthusiastically.

"Very well, we will have a joint session between the two of you. If it's anything like today's match, it should be very interesting. One thing though Devlin, we will have to teach you how to defend against magic. If Elena had used any of hers, she would have beaten you like it was child's play."

"You know magic?" Devlin asked incredulously. "I guess that explains how you can break trees in half with a single punch…" He had never known anyone that could cast spells; it seemed so foreign to him. Now he thought back to the match, *what if she had used magic?*

"Yes, I do. Magic is uncommon at best among the elves, but a rarity among humans. It uses energy in yourself, as well as energy in the world around you. You must have a strong soul to handle the toll it takes on you; most don't have that. If your parents had magical abilities, though, you are much more likely to have it, but it's still only a possibility."

"Why did you keep it a secret, though?" Devlin asked incredulously.

"People have always treated me differently because I was the 'gifted one' growing up. I didn't want that to happen with you too…" Elena admitted. "I'm sorry…"

"I understand, that's no big deal. It doesn't change who you are at all," Devlin replied kindly.

"Thank you, Devlin, honestly," Elena smiled genuinely.

"So... how exactly do you know if you're gifted?" Devlin wondered if he himself were possibly gifted. He had no idea whether or not he had magic, and he doubted his mother or father were magical, but he still wanted to try.

"You would either have to have another mage check for you, or the magic could appear on its own at some point. However, another mage can unlock magical energy you have a bit early if it's there. I can do it for you, but don't get your hopes up." She seemed to think about that a second with her eyes wandering, then she looked back at Devlin.

"Very well, thank you, Elena. How is it done?" Devlin was filled with anticipation and a bit of dread. He hoped he was gifted, but if he was, how would it affect him? Would it change him completely or would it simply be another method of fighting?

"The process is done by the mage placing their two first fingers on the recipient's forehead. It takes a couple minutes. For better or for worse, though, unless you learn to suppress your power you will shine like a beacon to every mage close by," the Sword master advised. "Even non-gifted can sense it if you aren't careful."

"As you say, Master. I will begin if you are ready, Devlin." She looked right into his eyes; her expression showed deep concentration, as well as a bit of concern.

"I am." Devlin stood erect. He was determined, shaking off all inhibitions. Elena raised her hand, her two fingers pointing out, and, to Devlin's amazement, the tips of her fingers started to glow with a faint light shining from them. His awe probably showed on his face because Elena smiled. She brought her index and middle fingers forward towards Devlin and rested them on his forehead. They felt warm to the touch. The glow from Elena's fingertips started shining brighter and began enveloping Devlin's head, then his chest, all the way down to his feet. This continued until he was shining as bright as the sun in the evening sky. The light faded ever so slowly until it was completely gone.

They all stood there in shock, especially Devlin. "So, does that mean I'm gifted?" Devlin asked with a lump in his throat.

"I've never seen someone shine that brightly, not in all my years." Sword master Irou was slack-jawed.

"I could feel it... Your strength Devlin; it was massive. Now I'm the one that is glad we are on the same side." Elena said this very seriously with a mixture of awe shown on her face, then she grinned and broke out laughing. "Your strength could even rival Sher'ni himself, the elf that wielded Lux and fought the greatest evil of the past if you work hard enough."

"Lux? Sher'ni? Oh yeah, the elder mentioned Lux when I met him. What is Lux? Who's Sher'ni?" Devlin asked contemplatively.

"There's an old legend or story, as most would call it, of a lone elf with incredible magical abilities fighting an entire army of men trying to destroy everything that opposed their cruelty. Sher'ni was given a sword crafted by the best dwarven smiths and imbued with power by the elves' spell casters. It's said to be indestructible; full of different spells like healing, molding magic in various ways, like making a short term bridge, or wreaking absolute havoc to those who oppose it.

"It's also said that it chooses its owner and will not budge for anyone else. It will take one with pure qualities and a strong heart to handle its immense strength. So it was left somewhere deep in the forest by Sher'ni himself after the great battle. They say he took on ten million men, alone. Not one of those ten million survived the onslaught," Irou recalled.

"That's unbelievable. Ten million men all by himself?" Devlin was just trying to imagine one million men. *The amount of one million alone was exuberant, but ten?*

"That's what they say. But ten million probably isn't the real number because people exaggerate stories, so we will never truly know. Since there is time left in the day, I should probably show you the ropes of magic. It's better to start right away. Are we still having our session tomorrow, Sword master?" Elena asked. Devlin's mind was running in circles. He couldn't even think straight trying to imagine how Elena would teach him magic. Just this morning, all he thought he was going to do was practice with his sword.

"Yes, I will see you first thing in the morning. I'll leave you two to your practice just don't overdo it. If his power streams all at once, we may need a new forest to call home." The master showed a bit of mirth and a touch of seriousness on his face at the same time. Elena watched him go and then looked straight at Devlin; she had an excited smile on her face. She grabbed his wrist and started dragging him to a section of the woods.

"Where are we going?" Devlin managed to keep up with her brisk pace, but he struggled to not trip over all the roots that made up most of the forest floor.

"To the Sage's Clearing. It's specially charmed for mages to train." They ran deeper and deeper until the trees suddenly turned a light shade of blue. It was the strangest thing he'd ever seen. Large brown barked trees with sky blue leaves surrounded a clearing that was at least a square mile. Stranger still was the grass which was the same color as the leaves on the trees. The air hummed with energy pressing down on Devlin like a blanket. "This is where I'll be training you. Don't worry about burning the place down; the trees and grass are charmed to absorb spells that touch them." Elena went out to the middle of the clearing with Devlin in tow. When she stopped, she let go of his arm and smiled at him.

"This place is so strange. The air feels so different here, and the blue shade of the trees feels so otherworldly," Devlin described in awe.

"You get used to it after a bit, don't worry. There is magic in the very air around us. It's perfect for casting spells. So, ready to get started?" She looked at him expectantly.

"As ready as I'll ever be." Devlin shrugged.

"Good. So first, clear your mind of any distracting thoughts. This gets easier as you practice." Devlin did as she said and cleared his mind. He concentrated and he left his mind blank. Luckily for Devlin, he was used to that already thanks to him training with a sword, where a misplaced thought could mean life or death in battle. "Once you do that, you will need to think of the type of spell you want to cast. Some people use incantations to help with this but if you can think hard enough, that is unnecessary. But be careful, because different spells take different amounts of energy. If you use too much at once you could exhaust or even kill yourself. So it's important to know your limits. To start, how about making a small flame?" Elena explained.

Devlin closed his eyes, crossed his legs, and thought of campfires he'd seen on the farm growing up. He'd shared many with his family on fall nights. He thought of the flame itself and all its heat.

"You've almost got it, Devlin, just concentrate. Feel the fire; be its fuel; fire needs fuel to burn. Look inside yourself for that fuel." Elena watched as he sat, his face full of concentration. He sat almost completely motionless for seconds that turned into minutes that turned into hours, to the point where it was well past sunset. Devlin concentrated and concentrated, desperately trying to grasp his magic, but grew more and more frustrated. The sun had sunk under the trees long ago, and the sky had grown dark as the shroud of night enveloped the sky.

"Maybe we should call it a day," Elena suggested as she yawned and her eyes grew heavy.

"I'll get it, just give me a little more time," Devlin told her, taking a deep breath to calm his nerves.

Devlin focused inwardly and looked at every bit of himself. He felt calm, in his own world. As he tried looked deeper, he finally felt something different. It was still him, but it felt different. He eagerly reached for this part inside himself; it flowed all through his body and he felt it. That was his magical strength. He focused this strength to a point in front of him and thought of fires again.

"You're doing it, Devlin! It's working!" Elena was excited as she saw a small flame burst into life in midair in front of Devlin and grew larger very gradually. Devlin felt his magic flow from him to this point and he opened his eyes. Before him was the flame; it was the size of a normal campfire now. He could hear it crackling and felt its warmth. The large flame lit up the area around them as the sky grew darker and darker. It was indeed fire. Devlin focused on it. He poured more of his strength into his magic and it doubled, then tripled in size.

"Great. Now try to dissipate it. Just cut off the fuel you're using." Devlin did as she said and stopped his magic from flowing. The fire grew smaller and smaller very quickly and then disappeared completely along with the remaining light the flame provided leaving them in the now dark blue forest. It wasn't completely black, however, as the strange grass gave off its own eerie, blue light.

"I did it! I can't believe it, but I finally did it!" Devlin's voice was shaking, so thrilled that he did magic for the first time. He looked himself with a new respect. He couldn't believe it. Devlin stood up but felt a bit lightheaded.

"You did it, Devlin. Just be careful. The first time takes a lot out of you, even for those with large reserves like you." Elena could see Devlin was a bit wobbly, so she had him wrap his arm around her shoulders and she supported him as he walked. The faded light of the charmed grass grew stronger as the night progressed, so much so that it even light up the forest enough to be navigable. However, once they walked out of the clearing, through the many blue trees, Elena was forced to create her own orb of light to see through the thick darkness. The light was bright enough to light the way a short distance but dim enough to not attract unwanted attention. When they got to her hut, she sat him down in a chair to rest and chopped up some food for them both. "How do you feel?"

"Very tired... I feel like I just lifted a boulder." Devlin's voice was shaky but he did seem better.

Elena nodded and put his plate down in front of him. "I felt the same way my first time, trust me. I almost collapsed." Elena made her own plate of chopped vegetables and fruits and sat next to Devlin. "It's also late too, which doesn't help much..."

"I wonder... can you use magic to lift food into your mouth for you?" The idea was so absurd, Elena couldn't help but break out laughing.

"You are a funny one, Devlin, but I haven't actually tried that. I would never even think of it." Devlin adjusted himself in his chair.

"It couldn't hurt to try," Devlin said, smiling at her, and then concentrated. He looked for his power like before and focused it on a slice of fruit. Then he lifted it with his magic and guided the fruit to his open mouth. Devlin ate it as if it was natural.

Elena broke out laughing again. "You are certainly full of surprises, Devlin." Elena tried it herself and she did it effortlessly.

"Show off," Devlin said as the toll from the spell, and all his training, took effect. The growing exhaustion made Devlin slump in his chair, his eyes struggling to stay open. "Ugh, don't think I'll be doing that again." Devlin ate his food by hand while Elena just lifted food into her mouth with magic.

"I could get used to this. I should've thought of it sooner!" Elena laughed again, while Devlin just rolled his eyes, suppressing a laugh as he ate his food.

"Thank you for the dinner, Elena. Cut up fruits and vegetables reminds me of back home. Mother would always serve at least one meal of it a day." Devlin patted his belly at the memory and looked to her. "You have a very nice home by the way."

"Thank you. I built it with the help of a couple friends of mine. It took some work but it was nothing an elf couldn't handle," Elena recalled. "You should get some rest, Devlin. Using so much magic will drain you, especially on your first trail. But you should be proud, many have a hard time just creating a small flame their first time, you made one the size of a tree. You've done more in one day than most would in months." Devlin could see the awe in her eyes but it was equally accompanied by compassion. That look she gave him made it feel like he really did something to be proud of.

"I'd love to get some rest, but you might have to help me up. That little stunt with the fruit sapped the last of my strength." Elena merely rolled her eyes and smiled as she got up from her seat. She pulled Devlin up from his chair and gave him her shoulder again. She walked him to a soft bed in a room across from hers and laid him down.

"Sweet dreams, Devlin. We have a lot of training tomorrow." Devlin didn't even hear her, because as soon as he was on the bed, he was fast asleep.

Chapter 12

When Derek woke up again, his body felt like it had been thrashed. He struggled to so much as move as pain shot up and down his body like needles stabbing into his body. Simply getting up for him was excruciating as his aching limbs roared in protest. He looked over at the other cells and spotted Roark.

"Derek, you're awake! Thank the gods... You were laying there for hours not moving a muscle; I feared you'd breathed your last." Roark looked a bit worse for wear but was otherwise completely fine especially compared to Derek. He looked around before turning back to Roark.

"Quite frankly I'm surprised I didn't. That warden was brutal... Has anything happened while I was out?" Derek questioned urgently.

"Nothing unusual, just the guards patrolling the hallways. I don't like this Derek. I feel like at any second they're just going to come in here and ship us all off into slavery." Roark was shaking. He had the look of a stricken dog. Derek wanted desperately to calm his brother.

"Just relax, we'll get through this." Derek hoped that what he said is true, but he wasn't so sure himself anymore.

"Derek, there's something I've noticed about all the prisoners here. They're all men and boys, no women at all." When Derek thought about it, it was true. There were only men in these cells.

"Then they must have the women stored elsewhere. That would explain why we can't find Cecelia; we have to find her." Derek just wished there was something he could do to escape.

Just then, Derek saw a large group of guards leave their posts and ran down the hall to the exit, leaving the room completely unguarded. "What the hell?" Derek just looked at the door that was just thrown open and closed just as quickly. He couldn't fathom it. *Why would all the guards just suddenly leave? Did someone escape, or was there some sort of intruder?*

Derek's question was promptly answered when the metal door was blown off of its hinges, showing a lone figure in a dark cloak. *Is he a mage? What else but magic could blow through a door so effortlessly? What is his purpose here?* Derek heard a faint click and all the cell doors swung open.

"If you all want to live come with me now! We do not have time to waste!" The mage's voice rang out throughout the room. He did not have to speak twice. The prisoners ran swiftly out of their cells in a massive flurry of movement, following the mage out the door. Derek leaned on the wall and bars for support, but the pain up and down his body was overwhelming. Just taking a few steps felt like a hundred knives stabbing him up and down his back. He saw Roark running over to him.

"Come on, Derek, I'm not leaving without you. Put your arm on my shoulders, I'll support you." Derek did so, and he felt some relief from the explosive pain, but it was still unrelenting. Derek hobbled along with Roark following the crowd. They moved considerably slower but the huge mass of people made it so it barely made a difference anyway. As Derek and Roark got to the door another prisoner came up to them. He was dressed in worn rags like all the other prisoners. He was older but not middle aged, most likely in his upper twenties. He was most likely a worker with how toned and tall he was.

"You're the boy that stood up to those guards... That back of yours is in really bad shape... Let me help, it's the least I can do for such a brave lad." Roark and Derek both nodded thanks and the man had Derek grab onto the man's back and shoulders. They all ran with the crowd, down hallways, and saw many guards laid unconscious on the ground. Some looked especially ravaged; Derek guessed at least more than half of them were dead.

They came to a pair of huge doors; the mage was standing in front of them. Derek could hear him muttering some strange words, and then the doors opened wide. Outside those doors was an army of at least a hundred guards all armed with different weapons: some held swords, some maces, and some had huge battle axes.

The mage raised his hand toward the guards. Derek heard him muttering a spell again and seconds later, a huge fire engulfed all around them. The huge conflagration left the guards as charred husks. An entire army of guards wiped out in seconds... Derek couldn't believe his eyes. The mage himself looked very tired but hadn't a scratch on him. He dropped to one knee, clearly exhausted. After taking a moment to catch his breath he turned toward the prisoners.

"Follow me!" The mage shouted then started running off in one direction. Everyone followed him. The prison was surrounded by an open plain, a large, nondescript grassland.

"I don't like this. We don't even know who this mage is. He could be someone even worse than that warden," Derek said as they moved. *What are his intentions? Just where is he taking us? Where are we in this world?* Derek wished to be home, back on the farm taking care of the livestock and fields. How had his life changed so much in so little time?

"Don't worry so much, brother. If he was willing to risk his life like this just to free us he can't be that bad." Roark sounded confident when he said that, but Derek just wasn't so sure. He wanted answers. *Why did this man save us? Is he alone, or affiliated with some group? Why had they been taken in the first place?*

"I agree with you, lad. I don't like the looks of this stranger. Mages, especially human mages, are very rare. He must be working with someone. The question is whether or not that person has goodwill towards us, or if he's just using us for his own personal gain. One thing I'm sure of, though: going with him is better than rotting in that accursed prison." Roark nodded at that and looked at Derek, concern plainly written on his face.

"How are you feeling, brother?" Roark asked Derek tentatively.

"My back is killing me, but all things aside, I've never been better," Derek answered somewhat sarcastically, cringing as another wave of pain shot up his back.

"So, you two are brothers then? I thought as much since you look alike." The man looked plainly at Roark. He was a hard man. He looked like he'd seen his fair share of work with his wind-burned face and slightly tan colored skin.

"Yes, we are. If you don't mind me asking, sir, just who are you?" Derek could see the look of curiosity on Roark's face as he said that.

"I'm just a carpenter from a small village in Crestialis. My name is Vantos." Derek nodded in understanding.

"We're from a village close to Crestialis's capital. My name is Derek, and this is my youngest brother Roark." Derek said gesturing to Roark.

"'Youngest'? Then you have others?" The man looked back at Derek and he nodded.

"We have another brother named Devlin, but we haven't seen him. We aren't sure if he's among this group or not. But wherever he is, I just hope he's ok."

"We also have a sister named Cecelia. We haven't seen her either. Even in this massive horde of people, I have yet to see a single woman. Are they located at another prison perhaps?" Roark looked on with concern. Derek shared that sentiment. He couldn't think of what he would do if she were hurt or killed. Derek wouldn't be able to forgive himself.

"I see. I haven't heard anythin' about the women, I'm sorry to say. I hope you boys find your family. I'm a loner myself. I guess that's coming in handy now. Don't have anyone to worry about." Derek noticed Vantos' head dip ever so slightly after he said that. *What is it like, to be alone in the world, to not know the value of having someone else there for you?* Derek didn't want to imagine. He didn't know what he'd do if he lost any of his siblings.

He still felt the blow from the death of his parents. He missed them dearly. His father was strict at times but he had a gentle side to him. Derek remembered when father held Roark in his arms, he looked so happy then. Mother too, she would always laugh and tell us funny stories from her younger years, and taught them to read and write. She always said, "You never know when you may need to just sit down and read something."

"I suppose so." Derek still lowered his head in thought. At that moment everyone stopped.

"We're here." The mage's voice echoed. Derek heard the mage speak another spell. The ground in front of him began to shift, and Derek felt the ground shaking through Vantos. A hole in the ground opened up and revealed a passage leading deep underground. The mage walked down into it and the former prisoners hesitantly followed. They walked the tunnel and as soon as the last person entered the hole closed up, leaving the tunnel pitch black. The mage made a ball of light that lit up the area in front of him but that wasn't much help for Derek, Roark, and Vantos who were close to the back; the light fading as the distance increased. Everyone went slowly going on what little light they had. After what seemed like a day they came to a wide cavern. Derek's eyes went wide with shock at the site: it was a huge cavern housing a camp at least four times the size of Derek's own village.

The mage led them to the center of the camp where a stand was set up with a woman standing on it. She wore combat armor of strong, silver steel, a sword and dagger on her belt, and a set of eyes even sharper than the weapons she wore. The sight of her sent a chill down his spine. She looked to be as tall as Roark perhaps slightly shorter with jet-black hair and eyes black as coal. She bore a scar that ran from her left ear down her cheek. It was thin but still big enough to be intimidating. Derek looked at Roark and his eyes were wide with fear. He even noticed some of the people a bit on edge. As the mage came close to her he stopped and made a slight bow of respect. Everyone else just stood there in awe of her, none daring to move and draw attention to themselves.

"You three," She pointed directly at Derek and Vantos. "Come here, now." Derek felt fear all over him now. *What could this woman want from us?* Vantos reluctantly stepped forward. The crowd parted for him. Derek could see the worried look on Roark's face, debating whether he should step forward as well. He did. As Vantos and Roark made it to the woman on the stand, she gazed fully at Derek, her hard eyes observing him.

"I'm assuming you are wounded since he is carrying you, and you seem to be the only one." Her eyes darted from Vantos back to Derek. Derek nodded, trying not to look scared, though he was sure he wasn't succeeding. "What are your wounds?" Derek's face grew hard at the memory, completely forgetting his fear before.

"I was whipped while in the prison, for beating up a couple guards." The nameless woman just started laughing. It was much unexpected coming from the battle-hardened warrior.

"We have ourselves an upstart then? I bet the look on the warden's face was priceless when he found out a mere boy in rags could beat up a 'couple' of his experienced, armored guards." The woman laughed even harder imagining it. The crowd just stood there in shock as they watched. Some even laughed with her albeit nervously. The woman regained her composure and looked at Derek with a small smile on her face. "I like you, boy. What's your name?"

"Isn't it only proper that you introduce yourself first?" Derek was determined not to look weak in front of her. His pride wouldn't allow it.

"Very well. My name is Valcara; I am the leader of this camp," she said loud enough so all could hear. "Your turn."

"I am Derek Slade, eldest of the Slade family," Derek returned with pride. She looked at the mage; her stern look returned. "Athon, see to it that Derek is healed properly. We need all the able hands we can muster." The mage nodded, looked at Vantos, giving him a waving gesture to follow, and walked off. Vantos, carrying Derek, walked off with Roark following close behind. They came to a large tent the size of a hut and entered. Inside was a woman of a slight frame with a white gown. She looked rather young still but older than Derek. She had short blonde hair that seemed to almost shine.

"Hello, Athon. I'm guessing I have a patient?" she asked as she looked over Derek on Vantos' back. She had a very smooth and soothing voice as if she was born to be a healer. Derek just nodded not sure what to say to her. "Well let's see the problem then." Derek got off Vantos with the help of Roark and sat next to the woman after removing his shirt and examined the jagged skin and ripped tissue that had only just started to heal.

"Oh goodness, someone really did a number on you. I've seen worse, though, so consider yourself lucky." The woman bent over onto her knees and laid her hands almost right on Derek's back. Her hands started to glow with a soothing white light and it shined on Derek's back. He felt an itchy sensation as he felt his skin and tissue mend, the pain slowly going away. His body felt warm like how he felt on a perfect day outside when everything was peaceful. The sensation grew smaller and smaller until he felt nothing at all.

"There we go all better," she said, patting his back as she got up. "Now, if no one else needs to be healed I suggest you go see Valcara. She will likely have something she will need for you to do." Derek got up, amazed at how much better he felt.

"Thank you for healing my wounds. I feel much better." She merely smiled at him and gestured towards the entrance.

"A patient saying 'thank you' and here I thought fighting had made people lose their manners. How sweet. It's no trouble, just make sure I won't have to see you too much," the healer said, winking at him. Derek bowed slightly out of respect and put on his shirt.

"Athon, can you lead us to Valcara?" The mage looked at him like a dog would to a distasteful meal, as if escorting him would be such an insult to him, but he rolled his eyes and started walking.

"Fine then, follow me. She's likely back in her tent by now." The mage seemed to walk faster now that Derek was healed, which was fine with Derek. He wanted some answers, and who better to ask than the boss herself? Derek was happy to finally be able to walk without the pain in his back again. He felt like he could run for miles without stopping.

After a walk through the side of the camp, they came to a larger tent; larger than all the others around it. The entrance had guards in front of it, two of them, armed with swords on their belts and shields on their arms.

"State your business," the guard said but looked like he recognized Athon.

"These people here need a role; therefore, I seek council with Valcara." The guard looked over at Derek, Roark, and Vantos for a minute.

"Very well, you may pass." The guard looked ahead for anyone else. Athon walked through, Derek started to walk forward, but then the guards blocked the entrance. "Sorry, but only those with a 'true' position here may enter the tent. You three will just have to wait," Athon said mockingly.

"So we have to be members to gain entry? Great." Derek was annoyed by this but he could see their reasoning. For all they knew, Derek could be an assassin. Just then, Valcara came through the entrance followed by Athon.

"So, you're all healed up? Good. Now I want to see what you can do." She smiled at Derek devilishly and gestured to Athon. "Athon, give him your sword and seal the edges. I'd hate to have to heal him twice in one day."

"I'm not exactly a beginner with a blade. You'd best watch out," Derek retorted, somewhat nervous. Athon took his sword from his sheath and put his hand over it. The blade glowed for a second but then the glow vanished. Athon tossed the sword high in the air. As it dropped, Derek effortlessly shot his hand up toward the sword and grabbed the hilt. Derek tested the weight of the blade as Athon sealed Valcara's blade.

"Well, show off, are you ready? Since the blades are sealed, the blades will not cut you, but you will feel it when it hits." Valcara took up her stance, sword pointed straight at Derek's head.

"Ready when you are," Derek said, then, when she nodded, he charged her. He swung hard from the right, which Valcara easily dodged under. She then stabbed her blade onto Derek's chest launching him back with a grunt. *Man, she's fast. If this were real, I'd already be dead.* Derek combed his mind for a strategy but Valcara was already upon him. Giving him no time to plan as he had to devote every thought to blocking her strikes.

Derek parried each blow, but it was hard to keep up with this speedy devil. Each strike was a blur each move calculated and Derek was immediately feeling overwhelmed. He caught a break when she slipped up on a stroke giving Derek just enough time to not only parry the strike but also force her back a few steps.

Then it was Derek's turn as he used the momentum and swung at Valcara. He made every blow count because he knew if he let up even a little, Valcara would outmaneuver him and he would be at her mercy. After a quick blow from the left, he bent down and swept her legs with his right foot, but Valcara saw this coming and jumped over his kick. Derek compensated with a quick upward strike, which Valcara again parried. Having no support from the ground, though, she was pushed back several feet before landing. As she landed, she dug her hand in the ground to help her stop, but she still slid back.

She used the leverage from her hand to rocket herself forward in a running dash toward Derek. She faked a slash and sent a roundhouse kick straight to Derek's head. Luckily Derek managed to duck in time, but he felt the whoosh of air her leg made as it just missed him. She came around with another sword slash which Derek barely managed to parry in time.

As the two were locked in the clash they looked each other right in the eyes. Derek saw a spark in them. It was obvious to him then that she was enjoying this duel and then Derek smiled. He forced his blade forward, pushing her back and began slashing relentlessly; left, right, thrust, right, he just kept on slashing. He was forcing her back, step after step, until they clashed again. Derek was getting exhausted very quickly but in contrast Valcara looked as if she'd barely broke a sweat. *What is this girl? I'm about to pass out and she's barely lost her breath. Such ridiculous endurance, no wonder she's so fast.*

"Alright, that's enough," Valcara said as she relaxed her sword. "You're not bad kid, not bad at all. I haven't had to actually try in a match for awhile now. Most of the people I fight are clumsy dogs but you actually held your own. Impressive."

"I don't know how I managed to keep up with you at first; I've never seen anyone move so fast. You'd probably give the best knight in my kingdom a run for his money." Derek's breath returned to him and he smiled at her. She smiled back and then sheathed her sword. "Don't you have to unseal your sword?"

"The spell wears off once the sword is sheathed. Don't worry." Athon walked over to Derek and took the sword. He had a look of respect in his eyes now.

"Not bad, kid, it's been awhile since I've seen Valcara struggle a bit. She used to be a top class knight. Most would feel proud just lasting five seconds," Athon said matter-of-factly.

"Wow, Derek, I couldn't believe my eyes. I've never seen a fight like that, even among two knights! You two went at it like devils!" Roark came running up to him.

"I agree with Roark. In all my years, I've never seen a fight that fierce," Vantos said as he stood beside Roark.

"He has potential, I'll admit. Don't go getting cocky though or next time I won't be so gentle," Valcara said with a serious look. "We'll train you, you'll get much better and you can be one of my top warriors."

"It would be nice to get better, but what's in it for me?" Derek wondered just what her purpose was. What had they gotten themselves into?

"You will have a place among our ranks, and safety from the nation above looking to enslave you all. I suggest you accept. All that's above is miles of grassland and surely a few armies looking for their escaped prisoners." Valcara uncrossed her arms, walked toward Derek, and reached out her arm.

"Point taken," Derek clasped her hand and shook it. "Where do we start?"

Chapter 13

Cecelia opened her eyes slowly as her mind struggled through the haze of her involuntary sleep. She was laid on a cold stone floor with steel bars enclosing a box-shaped cell. Cecelia looked around trying to orient herself, and the memories of the carnival came flooding back to her. All of the pain, sorrow, and anguish flooded through her all at once until tears began flooding out as well. Cecelia felt helpless not knowing what happened to her dear brothers as she was the first one knocked out. She was all alone now in this dank, gray cell, and her brothers were nowhere in sight. In fact, as Cecelia looked more and more, she didn't see a single man. In every cell she looked in, she only saw women and girls ranging from only a few years younger than Cecelia herself to women twice as old as her departed mother.

"I don't understand... Why am I here? Where are my brothers...? Why did this happen?" Cecelia questioned to herself, as she sobbed.

"Are you okay?" a girl in the cell across from hers asked. She had a very sympathetic look on her face, but Cecelia didn't care. She just wanted to see her family again.

"Of course not. I'm trapped in this awful cell and my family is nowhere to be found..." Cecelia said spitefully as she continued sobbing.

"Then are you unhurt at least?" the girl asked, still sympathetic. Cecelia didn't have any injuries besides for a small ache in the back of her head, so she nodded slightly.

"Why do you care?" Cecelia asked bitterly still in shock.

"Because I'm in the exact same position you are... I have an older brother and two parents. Both of my parents were killed right in front of me, and they kidnapped my brother before they finally took me in too. I hope he's alright..." the girl said sadly. Cecelia looked at her, wiping away her tears. *She's right, she's in the same position I am, she just woke up sooner...*

"I'm terribly sorry about that..." Cecelia told the woman, offering her condolences. Cecelia looked at the woman and took in her features. She looked only a year or two older than Cecelia about Derek's age. She had fine blonde hair and slight features. She wore rags for clothing, much like Cecelia at the moment. The woman's tunic was torn and ripped in several places. She had dirt all over her face and exposed skin, but Cecelia could still see her pale skin and blue eyes. She didn't look like she was from Crestialis, as her people typically had brownish hair and green eyes.

"What is your name?" The woman asked. "I go by Anna."

"My name is Cecelia," she told her, and Anna smiled sweetly.

"Such a lovely name," Anna said sweetly. "My best advice for you here is to keep quiet around the guards; they are merciless filth through and through. We are nothing to them just a bunch of slaves to sell off at some point. I've even seen them rape other girls in their cells..." Anna looked like she was about to cry from indignation. "I still remember their cries, the helplessness I felt. That's partially why they do it, to crush our hopes, to make us feel like we can do nothing but sit in our cells and take it." Anna's indignation turned to rage as she thought of it. "The worst part is the warden doesn't even bat an eye to it. He just acts like it doesn't happen."

"I'm really sorry, Anna. I can't even imagine what it must be like to have to watch that..." Cecelia said empathetically. "But I'm sure we can get through this. We just have to wait for the right opportunity."

"For both our sakes, I hope you're right, Cecelia," Anna said hopelessly. Cecelia felt bad for Anna; she looked so miserable. Cecelia wondered more and more what had happened to her brothers. She prayed they were still alive and well. She felt terrible for Devlin. The day meant to celebrate his birthday went so horribly wrong, and now she didn't even know if he was still alive.

*   *   *

Cecelia had been sleeping on the uncomfortable and filthy cell mattress trying to get some proper sleep. When she woke up, she heard a commotion outside her cell. She looked to see, and she saw a woman being beaten to death by several guards. Cecelia was in utter shock at the sight and wondered what could have sparked such a beating.

"Cecelia, look away. If you think it's ugly now you haven't seen anything yet," Anna advised. Cecelia looked to her to see bitter hatred in her eyes looking at the guards.

"What happened? Why are they all beating her like that?" Cecelia asked her in shock.

"She tried to escape. She managed to grab the keys off of one of the guards and ran. When they caught her the beating started. The warden said she would be an example to anyone who tries to escape," Anna explained.

"Are they going to kill her?" Cecelia asked hesitantly realizing the true horror of this place.

"They'll beat her within an inch of her life then leave her in her cell. The warden doesn't like killing the young girls because they're worth the most," Anna explained. "She won't be moving for awhile, though." Once the beating was done, the guards threw the girl back in her cell. She was bloody and discolored everywhere on her body. Her face was swelling so much it didn't even look human anymore. The sight of it sent a wave of fear through Cecelia. She hated violence and seeing that girl get beaten so badly only reinforced that. She didn't want to give up, though. She would come up with a plan to escape this prison, and hopefully soon. The guards walked around threateningly as if just waiting for a reason to beat up another girl. Cecelia put on a brave face and looked away from the guards. She had to wait for the right opportunity. Until then, Cecelia resolved to stay alive.

Chapter 14

Anders woke up in the bed of the empty medical wing chamber. He tried getting up, but he felt a sharp pain in his back. The pain was so excruciating he nearly passed out again. As he lay in his bed in agony the door to his chamber opened slightly. A young girl entered the room and looked at him, concern immediately showing on her face.

"Prince Anders, thank goodness you're still alive!" She ran over to him, her concern deepening.

She looks a bit older than Sophia but not by much. Perhaps seventeen years at least? "Who are you? What happened to me? The last thing I remember is walking out of the bandit's hideout..." Anders felt weak like he was dying and death just wouldn't come. He was barely clinging to the bit of life he had.

"My name is Amanda, I'm a healer. I'm here to help heal your wounds, so can you try and lay on your stomach?" Anders tried to process this. *Mages are a rarity among humans, mages that studied healing even more so. Could she really help? Well, I suppose letting her try couldn't hurt.*

Anders tried to flip himself onto his stomach. It was agonizing, but he managed. When he was finally on his stomach, Amanda placed her hands over his back, and her hands took on a strange glow. The glow grew brighter and started to envelop Anders' back as she located the wound and closed it with her magic. The wound tingled slightly as the flesh slowly closed, and he felt the insides of his back shift as she probed the inside of him with her magic. With intense concentration, she started healing all of his muscles and tissue that were ripped apart by the stab. Tissue and muscle mended together as if of its own accord, every fiber and tendon reattaching themselves. The sensation was painful at first; as it progressed it developed into an annoying itch then nothing at all.

"There. I'm done." Amanda let out a sigh of relief and watched Anders rise from the bed.

"To think... Moments ago, I was on the brink of death. Amazing." Anders stood up and realized he was wearing a medical robe.

"I hate to rush you after you just recuperated but we must go! I need your help, Prince Anders, but we can't talk here. There's too many people around. We must leave here quickly." The girl had a pleading look on her face, and Anders felt indebted to her. *The least I can do is help her; it shouldn't be too much trouble.*

"Please, change into these and come with me, but try not to let the whole castle know we're leaving." Amanda handed him a leather bag with a rider's tunic and breeches. She left the room and Anders quickly changed. The clothes Anders put on seemed to fit him well enough, if not a bit tight, and he walked over to his sword with its sheath and tied the sheath over his shoulder. Walking felt strange after just recently being mortally wounded, but he welcomed the sensation and strode onward. He walked over to the large wooden doors to leave; Amanda was already opening them. The corridor was empty but for the one guard. Amanda stayed out of sight of the guard and looked relieved to see Anders out. Anders nodded to her.

"Wait here, I need to leave a message for Father." Anders stepped up to a guard. As the guard looked at him, he nearly lost his composure in his shock.

"My p-prince! How are you up and about? Not moments ago I saw you near death in bed!" The guard looked baffled, searching for an explanation to the prince's sudden and miraculous recovery.

"I am well, soldier, but please keep this quiet for now. I need you to pass along a message to my father. Tell him I am alive and well. However, I have urgent business to attend to, so I must leave with all possible haste. Please wait to notify them until the morning, for my recovery would certainly cause an uproar. Do you understand?" Anders looked at the guard seriously, conveying the gravity of his orders, and the guard seemed to understand him and gave a short nod.

"Very well, sir, but please be careful. I may speak on the king's behalf at that." The guard saluted him and remained at his post. Anders quickly went to Amanda's side and led her out of the castle, the castle that he knew from top to bottom like the back of his own hand.

As they walked out of the castle through a back entrance, Anders grabbed two horses for himself and Amanda at the stable next to the castle wall, doing his best to remain unnoticed. As they rode out of town and went a considerable distance away, Anders and Amanda stopped. Anders looked around quickly and dismounted from his horse.

"We should be relatively alone here. So tell me, what is it that's so urgent that we must leave the castle like this?" Anders looked over to her as she dismounted. She wore a tunic much like the one Anders wore. However, her's seemed to fit perfectly. When he looked to her belt he noticed a sheathed dagger, which seemed fitting considering her small frame.

Anders, looking over her in detail for the first time, noticed she had dark-brown hair tied back into a ponytail and slight features much like Sophia's. Her face was a bit wind-scarred from obvious travel, and a bit of grime showed on her pale, white skin. She had brown eyes, both intense and delicate; she looked determined to accomplish whatever it was she needed to do. Those eyes looked straight at him, the resolve showing clearly on her face.

"I come from a far off village; we had a mage, called Nassaru, that sees prophecies. One of these prophecies depicts a great darkness befalling the world. This darkness will destroy everything in its path, and already it is growing in strength.

Nassaru told us the only way to defeat this darkness is to raise the sacred sword, Lux, the very same sword that fell the army of darkness from so long ago. He also said the one to wield it currently resides in the forest of elves, but he will not be there much longer. We must find this boy, Anders, or else we will be swallowed by darkness." Amanda had a pleading look on her face.

Anders had heard of the almost frightening accuracy of prophecies spoken by mages. Anders was shocked at this one; it raised a hundred questions in his mind. *What is the darkness? When will they strike and in what form? Who is this boy she speaks of?* The sword, however, made sense. Lux was known far and wide in Crestialis as the sword of legend. *If a person could wield it, he could most certainly defeat any foe that stands in his way.*

"This certainly is a problem. But why do you need my help?" Anders asked suspiciously.

"I need your help because the elves are much more trusting of the royal family. If I went alone I'd be lucky not to get shot on sight much less allowed to wander the elven villages," Amanda explained. "And I figured that if I healed you, you would return the favor."

"Good point… Did the mage give a description of the boy?" *It'll be easier to find the boy than it will be to fight whatever darkness she speaks of.*

"Only that he is a very gifted mage. I will try and locate him through my magic, but I make no guarantees for how effective that will be. He has likely learned how to conceal his magic energy by now, or will have by the time we may get close. For now, we should head to the forest. Once we reach an elven village we can ask around. Humans in the villages of elves aren't exactly common, so surely he shouldn't be too difficult to find," Amanda said supportively.

Anders thought this over in his mind for a moment. *We have no idea how long the boy will stay in the forest or even what he looks like. The only real option is to head to the forest, but can we get there in time? If not, he will be off to god knows where. Also, will the elves even speak to us? It was possible since it was he that was going, but elves are still rather guarded around humans.*

"Since it seems like our best bet is the forest, we should head there quickly. The sooner we get there, the better our chances." Anders looked at Amanda who was looking to him as her horse ate the grass of the fields. "Come on Amanda, they should be full by now; we've been sitting here for awhile; let's get moving."

"Yes, we should," Amanda walked over to her horse and pet its neck. Then spoke low to herself so that Anders couldn't hear. "You won't have to worry about a thing, teacher," Anders couldn't see it, but a single tear ran down Amanda's cheek, because though she didn't say it to Anders, she thought of home. However, that village had burned to the ground and she, the only survivor, had to run to fulfill the last prophecy. She mounted the horse and waited for Anders to join her. As the setting sun burned the sky with orange, the two set off down the beaten path.

Chapter 15

Devlin woke up to a bright, sunny morning. His days were mostly filled with arduous training. Between swordplay and his lessons in magic Devlin went to bed exhausted every night. So much so, that after several nights he slept a whole day and didn't even notice. Devlin, of course, always slept in Elena's guest bed, and usually spent breakfast eating the fruits and vegetables grown by the elves. Elena was happy to spend the time with Devlin and after the couple weeks since he'd arrived they had grown inseparable.

The Elder was readying for their departure, gathering the resources they needed. Soon they would finally be able to set out to find Devlin's family. Until then, Devlin was determined to be as prepared as he could. His magical abilities were skyrocketing; where it once took all he had to create a single flame, now he could make multiple flames the size of an elven house and barely break a sweat. He experimented with other types of magic and found that his endurance was rapidly improving. He could even mostly hide his magic power now too, thanks to the help of Elena, but he was still working on it.

His duels with Elena continued each day under Sword master Irou's supervision, and each battle always seemed relatively equal. The duels usually ended in both Elena and Devlin being too exhausted to continue, even when they used magic. Sometimes other elves would come watch the two duel and were awestruck as the young duo continuously fought. Their latest match was the most intense, however, as it had gone on for many hours without a break. When they did finally stop their swords were ruined. Even with the magical spell placed on the swords to protect the blade they had dents and marks all over them. "I guess all that fighting was just too much for the spell to handle. I'll have to see what went wrong so we can keep sparring next time," Elena had said.

"Hey, Devlin, are you getting lost in your thoughts again?" Elena asked him as he sat at the table.

"Oh, yeah. I'm sorry, Elena, I was just thinking about the past few days," Devlin said thoughtfully as he looked at her to see that she had a solemn and slightly hopeful look on her face.

"This could likely be your last day here so that doesn't surprise me," Elena said to him looking towards the door. "At any moment, the Elder may be sending a messenger to get us then we will be able to leave."

"Derek, Roark, and Cecelia... I really hope they're safe," Devlin said morosely. "Please, Maker, let them be safe."

"Until then, how about we practice magic again? You have all the elemental magics mastered for the most part. So how about we focus on more advanced magic?" Elena said as she stood close to the door.

"Sounds good to me. I want to try making myself levitate, or maybe see things over long distances!" Devlin got up eagerly, not unlike a small child waiting for a desert, and started fast-walking towards the door.

"You are an interesting man, Devlin," Elena laughed out loud and playfully pushed him. "Fine then, we shall head out." Elena opened the door and noticed a paper on the door. "What's this?" Elena asked with a furrowed brow as she read the parchment.

"Is this the message you were talking about before? The Elder's message?" Devlin asked. He tried reading the message but it was inscribed in a language Devlin did not know.

"It's a message, granted, but not from the Elder... It's an omen, a warning. It's a report that Lux is glowing, and that only happens when danger draws near..." Elena paused for a second, trying to collect herself through her fear. "Whenever Lux glows...

everyone in the village is to know, hence the message on the door." Elena paused again, looking toward the forest as if expecting to see a monster suddenly jump from the thick, oak trees. She looked down again at the parchment and eyed it sadly. She opened her mouth to speak, but her words quivered and Devlin had to strain his ears to hear. "Do you remember before when we talked about the legend of Sher'ni? The sacred sword that Sher'ni used? It's said that the sword always glowed brightly every time Sher'ni used it in the battle, but when the threat was gone, the sword's glow vanished as well. Since then, the sword has glowed multiple times, and each time it does a disaster of some sort occurred. That is why they make these reports: to warn us of the possible danger." Elena went quiet again after the last word. She didn't make a motion, so Devlin figured she had said all she wanted to say.

Devlin could see the great fear in her eyes. A stark contrast to her typical goofy smile. It was a look Devlin had never seen on Elena before. *Is it true then? Whenever the sword glows a disaster will occur?* Devlin didn't want to think so, but the fear on Elena's face was quite real. Devlin wondered if the danger that was approaching had anything to do with the bandits that burned down the festival and kidnaped his siblings. It was certainly possible. Either way, Devlin had to help Elena.

"Listen, Elena, everything is going to be alright. Whatever danger comes along, we can fight it. We're partners right?" Elena slowly looked to Devlin, looked into his eyes for a very long moment. She looked away and gave a hesitant smile; it wasn't the same old smile she always had, but it was a welcome sight for Devlin.

"Yeah. That's right, partner," Elena hugged him firmly, then looked into his eyes again. She saw the unyielding determination in them and some of her own confidence flowed back into her. "Thanks, Devlin."

"So, do you still want to train? I'll understand if you've changed your mind," Devlin said, standing next to her intently.

"Yes. We should," Elena said softly, slowly leading Devlin into the woods. "Just don't overwork yourself again, alright?"

"I'll try," Devlin answered back with a kindhearted grin, running towards the forest after Elena.

Devlin ran easily through the trees dodging the roots and low-hanging branches. The forest looked as it always had; deep green from all the leaves and mysterious as the path twisted and turned to accommodate the numerous oaks. The trees ranged from young sprouts barely as tall as Devlin to full-grown trees reaching up to a hundred feet. Devlin saw many different animals each time he visited ranging from deer and squirrels to large hogs fishing in the streams. Elena managed to catch up to Devlin also dodging the large roots of trees and sometimes even climbing on limbs. They reached the odd colored clearing and everything felt heavier around them, like the air itself took on weight.

"Let's get started. Our first spell will be the farseeing spell. This spell allows you to see any place or person you want so long as you have an image of it in your mind. This spell can be used many different ways, but it's mostly used to scope out the land you see. It's also used for defending cities because you can spot oncoming enemies. For this spell, you will need a reflective surface, such as a pool of water or a mirror. This is why some mages carry a mirror with them at all times," Elena explained to Devlin as he sat in the grass.

"Alright," Devlin said. Looking over the area, he saw a small pond across the clearing, then got up and walked over to it. "Will this do?"

"Yes, exactly." Elena walked over next to him. "Now that you have your reflective surface you need to take the image of the place or person and focus your magic at the same time. Doing both of these at once is a lot harder than just one or the other which is why it's a more advanced spell. Once you've done that, push your magic to the surface of the water."

"Thank you, Miss Textbook, that was very informative." Devlin laughed at the joke while Elena gave him a devilish look.

Out of nowhere, a wave of water splashed over Devlin. Now it was Elena that was laughing as Devlin was knocked over, drenched in water.

"I guess the water doesn't like you very much, Devlin," Elena said in between her bouts of laughter.

"One of these days I'm going to get you back for that," Devlin said as he focused his magic and collected every drop of water from his soaked clothes. Devlin focused it into a ball-ish form about the size of his head and threw it back into the pool, leaving him as dry as he was before.

"Not bad. You're getting better at this," Elena winked at him. Devlin stuck his tongue out at her and sat next to the water.

Devlin focused his mind on an image of his brothers first. He had to know if they were safe. He kept the image of them in his mind then pulled his magic again. The mental struggle of doing both of these put a lot of strain on Devlin as he focused his magic on the water. The water rippled slightly but no image appeared. Devlin tried focusing on the image again and felt his magic flow through his body. This time, both Derek and Roark appeared on the water's surface. They seemed to be training each other with their swords, which surprised Devlin. When he looked at their surroundings, they seemed to be in some sort of underground village. *At least they are safe.* Next, he thought of Cecelia. The image of his brothers fighting each other vanished, and he was shown a dank prison cell made from stone and iron bars. Cecelia was sitting in a corner of the cell. She looked distraught, but unharmed, which was a relief to Devlin.

"Were those your siblings?" Elena guessed as she observed.

"Yes, and it appears that they are alive. Thank the maker," Devlin said as he felt a bit of his worry lift from his shoulders. Finally, he thought of his home on the farm. It felt strange now. Thinking back, it felt like a lifetime ago. He focused it on the water again, but instead of the image of his home, an image of a burnt up wasteland appeared.

"Interesting choice. What is it?" Elena asked him curiously.

"My home..." Devlin said horrified. The shock was evident on his face as he got up and started running for the trees. Elena, with utter shock and horror at the revelation, followed him.

"Devlin, wait! What do you mean?" Elena shouted after him. "That couldn't have been your home. Are you sure you used the right image?" Elena and Devlin were running through the woods, with Devlin running at his full speed and showing no signs of slowing. It was hard for Elena to keep up. "Devlin!"

"I did it exactly the same way all three times, so there was no mistake on my part. I have to see for myself," Devlin shouted back. *It didn't make any sense. Why would my home be in ruins? Did the bandits burn it too after kidnapping everyone?* He had to know if it was true, to see it with his own eyes.

"We would need to perform a morphing to get there from here, Devlin!" Elena shouted. Hearing this, Devlin slowed down to a stop. He remembered the morphing. That was the same method Elena used to save him from the bandits that kidnapped his family. The method that supposedly let you meld into the trees. Elena stopped and stood beside him, catching her breath.

"How do we do that?" Devlin asked a look of determined seriousness on his face as he looked to Elena. She gave him with a troubled look, an uncertain one, which then formed into resolution.

"Morphing is dangerous for humans, Devlin. We elves can come and go from a morphing as we please because we are communed with nature. Humans, however, are a different story. So, I will ask you this: are you sure you want to go through with this?" Elena looked at him but she could already tell what he was about to say. It was clearly written in his eyes.

"Let's do it," Devlin said to her his determination not wavering in the slightest.

"I thought so." Elena looked determined as well and grabbed his hand. "Don't let go of me whatever you do." Devlin nodded and gripped her hand as well. She ran toward a tree, but instead of just slamming into the bark like one would expect she melded with it.

Devlin, despite himself, was still shocked that this happened and after her hand merged into the tree, his began to as well. In seconds, his whole body merged into the tree and his whole world spun. It was just like the last time, but slightly different. This time, he was not spinning into blackness, he felt like a part of the very trees themselves. He couldn't believe the sensation. It almost felt natural. The spinning got faster and faster, so much so that Devlin felt like a human tornado. But then it started to slow; at first only slightly, then drastically, until it was almost as if he was still. At the moment when the world was still he was pushed forward as if launched, and he was catapulted from the tree, still holding Elena's hand.

Devlin let go and flew in the air across the clearing, and rolled as he hit the ground. The rolling spared Devlin the injury from the fall, but he couldn't stop himself and slammed right into a tree.

"Oww," Devlin groaned as he got up feeling a sharp pain in his back from where he hit the tree. "Are you alright, Elena?" Devlin asked as he saw her laid out on the grass. He slowly started getting up.

"I'm fine, I'm just tired. I've done so many morphings and I still never get used to the sensation. Are you ok? The morphing didn't hurt you at all?" Elena asked him while getting up, looking at him with concern.

"That tree did more damage than the morphing did. Ouch," Devlin said, tentatively rubbing his back. Devlin looked around the area to see where they were but didn't see anything familiar. "Where are we?" Devlin asked her still looking around.

"The exact same spot where I saved you from the bandits. I don't know where you used to live so I thought this was the best place," Elena said to him. The reasoning made sense, and Devlin could find his way back. As he looked again, he noticed scratches on some of the trees and broken branches where the bandits had ambushed them. If this was the same spot then the path to his village wasn't far. Devlin studied the ground and saw the sword Derek had bought in the carnival hidden behind a tree. Seeing it brought back the still fresh memories in his mind. Devlin tied the sword to his belt as it was still in good condition.

"We have to find the path to my village. It should be close by somewhere to the west," Devlin said to her and started walking in the westerly direction.

"Very well," Elena responded indifferently and followed. After a few minutes of walking through the woods, they came to the beaten, dirt road. The same dirt road that Devlin had walked on with his family so many days ago.

"This way," Devlin directed down the path. "My village is down a few miles and my home is just beyond it."

"Then let's not waste any time," Elena said and started down the path. "What was your village like, Devlin? Your home, I mean." Devlin lowered his head morosely at the thought of it all as he walked down the path with Elena.

"My village was a typical one, humble and full of simple farmers, doing what they've always done: trading crops, trading for supplies, and other things. Everyone had a place, each person a role to fill. The women would cook and clean while the men went out to the fields. Sometimes the young children would even shop for the parents, just like my sister did."

Devlin felt a tear drop down his cheek as he thought of Cecelia. "My mother was a devoted wife, never above any task as long as it helped us. She even helped us in the fields whenever one of us was too sick to pick up the slack. Cecelia was like a young version of her; she did everything she could to help out around the home. She cared so much, and she worked herself tirelessly to help make the rest of our lives easier."

Elena could feel the pain in Devlin's voice like a knife straight to her heart. She wanted to comfort him, to support her friend who obviously still hadn't completely gotten over the shock of losing his loved ones. Devlin continued after a pause.

"My brothers, Derek and Roark, were my best friends. We did everything together from field work to training. We would always joke around about the simplest things and dad would tell us to get back to work. Dad was always the proud one, the worker, the proud father. He was what kept the farm alive. He worked the fields more than my brothers and I could ever imagine. He supported us, he taught us right from wrong, he did everything he could to protect us, even giving his life. I hope that one day I may grow up to be half the man he was. He gave us everything a man could give and never thought twice about it."

Devlin felt tears streaming down his face now. He sobbed, thinking of his dead parents, his siblings in danger, and his inability to do anything. He didn't want to cry, but the tears wouldn't stop. They just kept coming, as if a wall broke down and the blocked emotions just came flooding out all at once.

"I just want my family back... I would do anything just to see them all standing here again... I know they are still alive but for how long? They could end up dead before I can get to them," Devlin fell to his knees, sobbing uncontrollably.

"We'll get them back, Devlin. I swear we will. So please, get up and stand strong. Your family is waiting for you to save them." Elena rested a reassuring hand on Devlin's back. Devlin sat there, absorbing her words. After a moment, his mind finally broke through his grief and he saw the truth in her words. He managed to wipe the tears from his eyes and slowly stood up.

"You're right, thank you. We will save them... Together, we can do anything." Devlin started walking down the path again, the village not far off. Assuming it was even there, that is.

When Devlin saw his village down the road, his worst fear was realized. Each hut was burned to ash; nothing remained of them but the stone walls that simply looked like shells of the homes they once were. Devlin's eyes went wide with shock as he surveyed every single part of the village; it was completely desolate. Devlin ran down the path that led to his home, Elena in tow.

She looked at the burnt huts with a tear running down her face at the atrocity. Every man, woman, and child needlessly abducted from their once peaceful lives in the blink of an eye. Countless families torn apart, just as Devlin's was, as the barbarians mercilessly slaughtered or captured every soul in the village. It was a tragedy; one that could never be undone even if the families returned. What happened here would haunt them just as it haunted Devlin.

Then Devlin saw it. It was the exact same image as before; nothing remained of his home. It was completely destroyed, nothing but cinders all around. "So it's true... They destroyed it..." Devlin uttered. At the sight of his burnt home, his sadness ebbed off; he had felt enough grief to last him a lifetime and he was sick of it. Devlin lost his sadness as if a glass filled with his grief had toppled upon looking at his village. Now that the container was empty, rage started seeping in. Rage, fierce and raw, burned inside Devlin with an intensity that made him sweat.

The insult the bandits had thrown at him by burning his home and taking his family away like common dogs; killing his mother in cold blood right in front of him; hurting his sister that he so desperately wanted to protect; hurting his brothers that were closer to him than anything in this godforsaken world. The unprovoked destruction of his home. The capturing and killing of his friends. One offense after another piled up in Devlin's mind. Each insult added kindling to the flame that grew and grew each passing moment to the point where Devlin was shaking. He wanted them to pay and he would make sure they did. What Devlin didn't realize was that his rage wasn't just raw emotion. The emotion Devlin felt slipped, and he unconsciously drew into himself. Raw power enveloped Devlin, causing the ground itself to shake. The shaking was hardly noticeable at first but gradually grew more and more violent.

"What's going on?! Is this an earthquake?!" Elena yelped as she fell to her knees. She looked to Devlin, sensing his magic going out of control. *If he lets out all his magic at once, the devastation could be enormous. I have to calm him down before...*

Elena dared not finish the thought as she desperately tried to stand but quickly realized that the intensity of the earthquake made it impossible. Elena was forced to crawl to Devlin. Quickly grabbing onto him, she wrapped her arms around him and focused her own magic. She allowed her magic to flow into Devlin, in an attempt to snuff his magic out at the source. It was like going against the tides of a rapid, but slowly, she managed to needle her way to the core of Devlin's magic. She surrounded it with her magic and pushed against the core. The effects were immediate; Devlin's magic cut off, the ground eased back to stillness. Looking into Devlin's eyes, however, Elena realized that she had only calmed his magic, not Devlin himself. She saw the rage in his eyes like those of a wild animal. Elena placed her hand gently on Devlin's cheek. He looked at her blankly, as if seeing her but not recognizing who she was. Frustrated, Elena brought her hand back from his cheek, and swung it around to his face again. The resounding slap seemed audible for miles as she felt the numbing of her hand. Elena, unsure if the slap had done the job, looked over Devlin again. His eyes regained their previous life, but also a tinge of pain as he unconsciously brought his hand to his assaulted cheek.

"OW! What did you do that for?!" Devlin cried out in shock.

"Sometimes a woman's touch is all a man needs," Elena responded satisfied.

"Maker, that hurt. Did you have to hit me so hard?" Devlin asked rhetorically, as he gently rubbed his cheek.

"That's what you get for losing control," Elena reasoned. "Now that you're a mage, you can't just go losing your cool like that. Magic can be triggered by emotion if it's powerful enough, and you almost unleashed enough to destroy this farm five times over."

"I'm sorry," Devlin conceded.

"There is great wisdom in her words, Devlin, you'd do well to heed them." Devlin turned to the voice, something about it so very familiar. Seeing him, Devlin understood why; before him stood the Elder from the village he had taken refuge in. The Elder's expression was one of sorrow, the air around him taking a solemn tone. "However, it truly is a tragedy that this happened."

"Elder? How did you know we were here?" Devlin asked him incredulously. Devlin looked at Elena who didn't look surprised at all; in fact, she smiled.

"Because the Elder can trace any morphings that take place within his village. He must have followed us here. Our Elder is a sly one; I learned that the hard way many years ago." As Elena spoke, the Elder merely nodded. "So let me take a wild guess; it's time, isn't it?"

"It is indeed. That is why I followed you here. That and I wanted to see the damage done with my own eyes. You morphing here just gave me the excuse I needed. Seeing this destruction, it only further proves what I've feared these past moons. We must hurry, young ones." After he spoke those final words, the Elder slowly moved to the nearest tree. Before Devlin could say another word, the Elder melded gradually into the tree as if part of the tree himself. Skin absorbed to the bark in a twisted fusion as he left the two in silence, finally disappearing. Devlin and Elena looked at each other. Simultaneously, they nodded, locking arms, and ran straight into the nearest tree. It was an oak, its trunk just large enough for the both of them. Following the Elder's lead, they melded into the wood. Their bodies were consumed by the tree as the morphing took hold.

When the spinning stopped and they flew out of the tree; they flipped in the air from the force. This time, Devlin managed to land on his feet. They were next to the Elder's home and the Elder himself stood in front of them.

"Follow me," The Elder said simply and started walking toward the entrance to the large hut and entered. Elena and Devlin swiftly followed him in.

Inside the hut sat the elder and two packs, next to the packs, were two sets of armor. "These packs here hold all the essentials you will need, tools for hunting, building fires, etc., and these armor pieces are the lightest and strongest pieces ever made in our village. They are even spelled to protect you against deadly spells, and will help deflect blows from whatever you may come across. Do not depend on these armor pieces, however, they are not perfect, and too many blows at once will still cripple them. The spells use the energy of the wearer to activate, but as long as you both keep your wits about you, you should be fine. These pieces will even protect against thieves, for I have bonded a spell that lets the suits recognize your energies. I also took the liberty of duplicating this spell to your supplies. I wish you good fortune on your journey and a safe, successful return," The Elder nodded to them and gave them a slight bow. "Oh, and one more thing, the suits are spelled to equip and unequip at a thought, just think your intent and they will do so." After that, he left Elena and Devlin in the hut. The thought of a thought being all he needed to equip this armor astounded him.

   Just then, one of the suits started shaking and flew toward Elena. All the pieces of the armor, from the breastplate to the armored leggings, strapped themselves onto her. After the armor finished, she picked up the boots that came with it and changed into them.

   "I'm glad they excluded the helm, they always make fighting awkward," Elena looked to Devlin, still armorless. "Well go ahead, Devlin, it won't bite." Devlin steeled himself and focused his mind. He thought "equip" toward the armor and held himself ready. Just as Elena's armor did, his started shaking and flew toward him. Devlin could feel every strap wrap around him, and in mere seconds he was wearing the magical suit of armor same as Elena. He grabbed the boots and changed just as Elena had done and picked up the pack.

   "It's amazing, I can barely feel it. The pack isn't heavy either," Devlin said amazed, jumping up and down to emphasize his point. "We'd better get going, Elena." Elena smiled sadly at the words. Leaving felt bitter-sweet to her, she was glad to help Devlin, but she would miss her home dearly.

"Yes, we should," Elena said agreeing walked with Devlin both walked out the door, out of the village, and down the forest path. "So where do we head to first?"

"We head to the capital. We can gather some information there and figure out where to go next," Devlin said calmly, and they both walked, down the start of their perilous journey.

Chapter 16

Luke and his faithful guard on horseback rode down the long dirt path. It had been a quiet journey. They had occasionally stopped in towns for provisions but little else, wanting to waste no time finding the tribesmen. Luke had yet to see any suspicious characters and voiced a silent prayer that they wouldn't happen upon any for the rest of the journey. Luke planned to head into Reshim and gather information on the Azukas. He and his men kept their eyes open for traps, so far not finding any on the road. Neither did they see other travelers on the roads of Reshina which bothered Luke. The lack of danger, even the lack of ambient noise, did little to ease his nerves. Luke gave a signal and they all stopped on the road. Luke turned his horse and faced them.

"We should be arriving at Reshim, soon. You all remember the plan? Each of you are to branch off alone and gather what information you can about the Azukas. Anything you can gather: typical greetings, their customs, anything that will aid us in contacting with them," Luke said and looked at each of them. They each had the face of a warrior, hardened by battle, eyes that had seen death, and hands that caused death as well as prevented it. They met his eyes and each looked determined.

"Right!" His men spoke at once.

"Then as soon as we enter the city, split up, but be careful to not draw attention to yourself," Luke said giving the signal to move. Moments later the city came into few, at first just a spec on the horizon, but then got bigger and bigger as they continued down the path. As they got within a league of the city Luke diverged from the path and under some low bearing trees.

"Marcus, you watch over the horses, we will need to enter the city on foot, lest we go parading through the streets on horseback drawing every eye to us," Luke ordered and the men dismounted, Marcus giving a salute.

"The horses will be safe for you, sir," Marcus pledged. Marcus was a younger soldier of the bunch, but his skill in battle was undeniable. He had brownish-blonde hair and emerald green eyes, creating an interesting sight with his tanned skin. Luke trusted him to be able to handle this easily. Some of them grabbed small packs as well.

They wore light armor, the heavier armor in the horse's packs. Luke hoped that less armor would make them less noticeable, and restricted everyone to a single hidden dagger, including himself. Luke hoped that he wouldn't have to use the dagger, but Luke didn't want to take chances without one. He and his five men got on the path again and walked toward the city. He trusted each of these men with his life.

Connel, an archer and swordsman, could shoot an arrow into an enemy's heart even at 200 yards. Jasmine, the lone woman of the group, relied on her dexterity, and was arguably the fastest of them, being able to slit a man's throat in a split second. Jacob, the eldest next to Luke himself, was his right-hand man. They had fought together for many years, even being his squire at one point before he graduated to a full knight. There was no man he trusted more, they were like brothers, always have been.

Finally, there was Noah, the second youngest. He was reckless, at times even foolhardy, but the most honorable soldier you'd ever lay eyes on. Luke saw a lot of himself in him, so much so that it almost scared him. Luke remembered when he was his age, he was the exact same way as him, and he caused many headaches on the battlefield. Luke remembered the look on King MacArthur's face one time he charged into battle too soon, the memory almost made him lose his composure from laughter.

As they passed through the city gates cut finely from stone, each of the six headed off in different directions, blending in with the many people walking in the city. Luke took in the surroundings of the city. The city walls were tall and made of the same stone throughout. The paths of the city consisted of dirt paths like the road Luke had been traveling on to get here. The main path was surrounded by shabby, stone buildings Luke guessed were either homes or businesses.

Luke saw many stands, selling provisions, supplies, tools, and other items. Luke even spied a stand selling books that peaked his interest and looked over the stock of books. Some were useful for other purposes, such as a guide to survival in the wilds, others were old stories or fanciful tales, nothing related to what Luke needed, though, so he left the stand to walk amongst the people again. After walking for a bit in the crowded city streets, full of beggars, thieves, and the like, Luke spotted a pub, one of the best places to gather information in Luke's experience, and made his way to it, dodging around people moving to and fro.

As he opened the wooden door to the pub he sat at a round, wooden table accompanied by three short stools. The place was half full of patrons drinking bottles of cheap beer and whiskey some already stupidly drunk. A tall woman came up to him, dressed rather obscenely, and crossed her arms. An extremely bored look shown plain on her face before she looked him over then her eyes showed a spark of interest, obviously noticing his chainmail. "What is a soldier like you doing here? Come to drink away after a victory perhaps, or just looking for something to numb the woes?" She asked him, her speech was slow, almost hypnotically so. Luke merely looked her in the eye and rose from his seat so that they stood close together. Luke kept his voice low and brought his head close to her ear to make sure he wasn't overheard.

"I'm looking for information on the Azuka tribe due west of here. I need to know how to communicate to them. Any information you can give me will be rewarded handsomely," After Luke finished speaking he backed up slightly and waited for her response. The woman smiled at him, very interested in the reward.

"If the reward is as handsome as you, I'll gladly help. We have one girl that works here that is a member of their tribe. If you pay the both of us, I guarantee she'd be happy to help, the service will not be cheap, though, you sure you want to go through with it?" The woman spoke, her lips so close to Luke's ear he could feel her breath on his skin. Luke grabbed two sacks of gold coins from his pack he had brought for a time like this and handed one to her.

"How does that suit you?" Luke almost whispering to her. He wanted to be done with this already. He felt uncomfortable in this place like there were a million eyes on him even though he knew no one was looking his way.

"Very nicely, thank you," She whispered in his ear and kissed him on the cheek. Luke bristled at the touch inside like a spider had just bit his cheek, but he made no sign of it. "Sharla, come here!" The woman yelled towards the back of the pub, her face gone from amused to serious. Luke tensed up at the sudden raising of her voice, but no one seemed to notice, so he eased himself a little. A woman opened a door in the back of the pub. Her skin looked different than most others here, but only slightly. She looked to be a few years younger than Luke and wore a set of ear pieces that looked indigenous in origin. She looked rather annoyed and walked quickly, but surprisingly quiet to them.

"What?" She spat the word out like it tasted poorly in her mouth looking only at the woman.

"We have a customer in need of you, Sharla. Don't be rude, say hi." The woman gestured to Luke and Sharla looked at him for the first time, then her eyes fell to the sack in his hand and she smiled.

"And what do I owe this pleasure, milord," She said the word "milord" so sarcastically that Luke almost fidgeted with anger.

"I hear that you are a member of the Azuka tribe, I wish to do business with them, so I am requesting your help. I will, of course, compensate you," Luke said trying to keep his composure and handed her the second sack of gold coins.

"I see," Sharla smiled at him. "I can indeed help you, but on one condition: we travel alone. The tribesmen get restless around too many strangers. Do we have a deal?"

"That will be just fine, thank you," Luke looked at her up and down, he did not trust this woman, but he knew that he had no choice in the matter so he withheld his suspicions.

"Good, then meet me at the western gate in an hour so I may finish up here." She said to him and after Luke nodded she left to the back of the bar again while the woman just smiled at him, winked, and went to another table. Luke left the bar and headed towards the southern gate where he first started. Just outside the gate stood the other five of his group, all looking at him as he walked through the crowd.

"I have found us a guide to the Azukas, but I must go alone. You all go back to the spot Marcus waits and follow us, but stay well enough away so that you aren't noticed. If I need you I will give a signal, understood?" Luke looked on sternly.

"Yes, sir!" They responded in unison and walked off to the spot in which Marcus waited. Luke then turned around and headed down the winding roads of Reshim. Luke made it to the center. It was a massive, open court, full of people coming and going, with many more extravagant shops here than just the measly stalls on the gate streets. The dirt path was replaced with a loose stone street in the large, circular plaza. The air felt different in this part of town. It felt cleaner, more civilized, but Luke had doubts that it was little better than it's surrounding areas. Luke walked down the westerly road, which looked much the same as the dirt path on the south side, and made it to the gate. By the time he got there it had been almost an hour walking through the massive city. He did not have to wait long before Sharla came along.

"Thank goodness you're already here, waiting for you would've been such a bore," she said in a mocking tone.

The sooner we will be finished with this the better, Luke thought to himself.

"Do try to smile once in awhile, soldier-boy, you look so grim and serious." Luke sighed and followed her as she walked ahead. Sharla wore a different, more casual, attire for the road, as opposed to her high heels, she wore low boots, to her skimpy dress, she now wore a simple skirt and shirt. Luke welcomed the change from her look before, as he would've been embarrassed to be seen with a woman dressed like a prostitute for whatever the reason.

"Now that I think about it, I never did catch your name," Sharla spoke with a seriousness that almost surprised Luke.

"My name is Luke," He said simply, not bothering to state his title as she would likely just mock that anyway.

"Seems like a good name for you, short and to the point, your parents must've been seers, right, or just really smart?" The mocking tone was back in her voice again, and Luke could feel himself boiling from indignation.

"It's just the name I was given, so it's the name I live by," Luke stated simply again.

"So if they named you fool or failure, you'd live by those names too? Very interesting," Sharla merely looked at him, a smirk on her face as she mocked him. Luke did his best to keep his composure, but the rage of those insults burned in his gut. If he did not need her help, he wouldn't stand for it a moment longer, but he managed to calm himself.

"May we be on our way? We lose more daylight with each passing moment," Luke said trying to get this trip over with.

"Yes, I suppose," Sharla dragged out the words as if talking was too much of a chore. Sharla lead the way down the westerly path, and Luke followed close behind her. Not long did they travel before Luke already saw the encampment far off in the distance.

"So what business do you have with the Azukas, Luke? They are a rather boring tribe, always clinging to tradition and the old ways. If I didn't have my job I would die of boredom in that dunghole," Sharla looked back at him curiosity lit up her face.

"I come on business of my king, which is none of your concern," Luke replied indifferently. The sun was high in the sky; the heat was bearing down like a heavy blanket. Luke had been trained in all sorts of environments such as this one; he knew all about the dangers of dehydration, and heat exhaustion, and he was also used to it. Nevertheless, Luke felt drops of sweat on his forehead as he walked.

"If you say so," Sharla said with a dismissive wave of her hand. When they reached the entrance to the village, Sharla stopped, and no sooner than she did two men came up to them. Luke guessed they were the guards; They went on talking to Sharla in a tongue Luke couldn't understand. After they finished the men nodded approvingly and let them pass.

Luke was curious as to what had been said but dismissed the thought when they were inside. The village was full of large tents made of canvas, as well as other villagers going about their business. Luke could feel a thousand eyes on him as he walked beside Sharla, causing Luke to unconsciously grab the hilt of his dagger. Tribesmen of all ages and sorts looked upon Luke with disgust, but they made no move to stop him. Sharla stopped at a tent much larger than the others; this one had guards outside it too. Sharla went up to one of them and talked to them in their tongue. The guard walked to the entrance of the tent speaking loudly into it. After a moment another voice answered. The voice inside sounded old, and tired, Luke guessed it was an elder's voice. After the "elder" finished speaking, the guard moved away from the tent and simply took his position before, but now paid no attention to him and Sharla.

"Let's go, we've been invited inside," Sharla said to him. Luke fell in behind her as she walked inside the large tent. The inside was a simple, traditional feel, with a couple of old relics adorning sets on stands that looked able to be compressed into a more portable position, it seemed these people were nomadic by nature. The elder sat in the middle of the tent on the ground, in some sort of meditative position, however, his eyes were completely faded, meaning he must have been meditating or sleeping before Luke and Sharla's arrival.

The elder spoke, but as before it was in the tongue Luke could not understand. Sharla next to Luke spoke as a translator. "It's not too often we get outsiders here in our village. What is your purpose here?" The elder's eyes narrowed at him as Sharla finished translating.

"I come on a mission of my king, investigating the mysteriously well-armed bandits in our country. I found an item in their base, a dagger, bearing an inscription in your tribe's writing. I wish to know if you have any helpful information on this dagger that will aid my case," Luke said then Sharla translated, interest lighting up her face and Luke knew why. The Elder looked slightly unsettled and thoughtful of this and spoke once more.

"Then show me this dagger you speak of. We do not bless weapons very often, so I'm sure I will recognize it," Sharla translated for the elder, and the elder looked at him seriously. Luke took out the sheathed dagger from his pack and handed it to him and his expert eyes fell over the dagger. He unsheathed the blade and examined it taking in every last detail, then he did something that surprised Luke. He tapped the end of the hilt with his finger and the end came off, revealing a tiny piece of paper. He re-sheathed the dagger and set it down, reading the piece of paper. "I definitely remember this dagger; an outsider, like you came here with it, wishing for a blessing. He was a rather brutish man, tall and lean, but rough in his features. He also had the smell of salt to him. He also told me this: 'I own a massive stock of weapons in my shop; if you ever find yourself in Seamander, come find me at my store: the Iron Knave.' My best guess is there you will find the answers you seek." Sharla stated for the elder then said her own words.

"You're just as interesting as I thought you'd be soldier boy; if you're ever in town again be sure to stop by the bar. We will make you feel welcome." Sharla winked as she said "welcome", which sent a shiver up Luke's spine.

"Err, thank you, I'll be sure to keep that in mind," Luke said uncomfortably then bowed to them. "I will take my leave then, thank you for your time." Luke stammered out of the tent and noticed a lot of eyes on him again. This time, a crowd was forming on the edges of the street.

It seems I've overstayed my welcome, Luke thought inwardly. Luke started walking faster down the main street and wanted to leave as soon as possible to deliver the findings. As he walked toward the edge of the village, he noticed the glint of a blade behind him, as a lone man came running for him, a dagger in hand. The man was fast but small and crude; Luke easily dodged out of the way, got behind the man, brought his arm back, and grabbed the dagger. Luke threw the dagger to the ground so it was half buried in the dirt and tied the man's hands behind his back with rope from his belt.

The man cursed in the same language the elder spoke and bore the resemblance to the other tribesmen. Luke guessed this man didn't like strangers in his village, and he must have figured that since he was alone he was vulnerable. Luke pushed the man roughly off and then noticed everyone looking at him. Some looked at him with derision and disgust, others wore blank faces, and surprisingly, a few wore sympathetic looks. This did nothing but further his motivation to leave this place, wanting to be gone before another would-be assassin makes an attempt. Luke exited the gates of the village and down the path leading to Reshim, then to the Capitol of his home.

Chapter 17

    Prince Anders and Amanda were well on their way to the Elven Forest as the sun was still high in the sky. The sky was perfect: free of clouds, and warm with a light cool breeze across the lightly wooded area. Soon they would be shrouded in trees and shadows of the forest, so they took in the beautiful weather while it lasted. They pushed their horses hard the past two days, and the forest itself was within a day's ride from here. Amanda was riding close to the side of him, but not too close as she let Anders lead. *For once all those geography lessons are coming in handy,* Anders thought to himself. If we follow this path, it'll lead us right into the heart of the forest where Lux was located. Anders wondered if the boy was still there, it was unlikely, but if he left it would be very difficult to find him. He could only hope he was and that he'd be easy to recognize.

    They were entering the forest now not missing a step. The path was small, barely big enough for the two horses to use, but they continued on unrelenting. Thousands of trees all around them took up his view. All Anders could do was follow the path and hope it led to Lux. Each meter they traveled inward, the forest got thicker and thicker, so much so that it seemed like there was a literal wall of trees on either side. The path grew narrow as well, forcing Amanda to ride behind Anders. Fortunately, however, it was short-lived.

    After another 200 meters, the forest opened up to a wide clearing in the middle of which was an oddly shaped stone that acted as a stone sheath with the sword sticking out of it. The sword looked beautiful, a perfect masterpiece of a blade. It was double-edged, white-as-snow blade with supposedly a sharp point where the edges met. An ornate leather hilt gilded with gold, long enough to hold with two hands but still would be considered a hand-and-a-half length. He couldn't tell how long the blade actually was thanks to it being buried with only a foot's length of the blade actually visible.

"It's such a beautiful sword, does it really kill anyone it deems unworthy?" Amanda asked in awe.

"No it doesn't, that was just a myth the Elves spread around to discourage people from trying to claim it and disrupting the forest. If it deems you unworthy it simply will not budge," Anders stated calmly, almost repeating the exact answer his father gave him when he asked that question years ago. The curious nature of the sword never failed to pick at Anders, what if he were the one that was worthy? Is what is father said untrue as well, that it's just a regular sword in a stone?

The curiosity pegged at Anders and he dismounted, as did Amanda, then stepped up to the sword. The sword just stood there in the curiously shaped rock, almost invitingly. Anders took hold of the hilt and grasped it with both hands. He took a deep breath and cleared his mind to make sure he pulled with all his might. He pulled and pulled but the sword did not budge. Anders let go of the sword, disappointed with himself and turned around away from it back to where Amanda stood, the horses behind her.

"I guess I'm not worthy after all. It would have been nice to have a sword like that," Anders spoke in a murmur. Amanda put a reassuring hand on his back.

"Don't let it bother you, you don't need a fancy sword to fight, you won battles on your own didn't you?" Amanda spoke softly trying to counsel him.

"You know of me in battle?" Anders was honestly surprised but also garnered a bit of pride from it.

"Yes, I hear about your valiant efforts to quash the bandits terrorizing villages, even taking on that whole bandit horde. You are an inspiration," Amanda said smiling at him and Anders could feel himself blush at the praise.

"I just do what I can for my people, I want to be a good king like my father." Anders noticed a glow then from behind. "What the... the sword?" Anders said as he turned around. The sword was giving off a faint glow as if someone had lit a fire inside it. The glow was pure white, and glowing like a wave.

"So the prophecy was right... darkness is coming. I remember my teacher explaining to me Lux's warning. When danger approaches, Lux shines brightly as a beacon to breach it. We have to hurry, Prince Anders," Amanda said in shock of the sword and ran for her horse. They both mounted the horses and rode to where Anders knew the closest village would be. Anders knew there were around five notable Elven settlements in this forest, so it was very likely that the first one could be the right one. Anders hoped beyond hope that it was because he knew the boy wouldn't stay long. "Say, Anders, there's been something that's been bugging me for a while now. How do we know the boy won't simply stay in the village? What makes you so certain he will leave soon?" Amanda spoke curiously.

"I know how elves and humans are. A human wouldn't just stay in an elven village, he would have to have a reason for being there. Elves aren't really fond of humans... We have a bitter history," Anders stated.

"Have you ever met an elf?" Amanda asked him. "I know I haven't."

"Just an ambassador or two, rarely do elves ever venture from the forest besides for merchants. It's like their holy land," Anders said remembering the first time he met an elf. He was an elder of a village; a wizened man and very honorable, but you could easily tell he felt out of place. A few more trees flew past and they arrived in a clearing. It was small and empty except for two elves with notched bows and full quivers. They had arrows pointed directly at Amanda and Anders. They stopped the horses in fear at the sight of the weapons and eyed the hooded figures nervously.

"What is your purpose for trespassing in our woods, sir?" The elf to the left side of Anders said flatly.

"We are looking for a certain boy, a human boy. Have you seen one in the village ahead?" Anders spoke plainly regaining his composure.

"We are border patrol, we don't go into the village much," The same elf spoke.

"We need to find the boy quickly, can you take us to the village?" Anders spoke. The elf thought about this for a second.

"Please, sir, we must see him," Amanda pleaded to the elf, obviously nervous that they might be told to move on.

"Before I even consider letting outsiders rummage about in my village, I must at least ask you your names first," The elf spoke, challenging them.

"I am Prince Anders MacArthur," Anders took out his royal pendant, an item only a royal would have. The elf's eyes went wide with shock upon seeing it, the companion held no response.

"My name is Amanda Lythroot, aide to his highness," Amanda spoke to them in a dignified voice.

"We apologize for the suspicion, Your Highness," The other elf spoke this time. He sounded much more mature than the other elf, his speech was curt and with an underlying threat in his voice. "You may pass, but cause trouble and we will personally escort you out." They bowed slightly as a show of respect then wordlessly vanished into the trees.

"If we keep going along this path here we should be there in an hour at most." Anders surmised, and pointed to a path just beyond the clearing. Without a word, Anders and Amanda rode down the clearing and down the path. Anders looked to Amanda with conviction, she returned with a look of unease.

"Is everything okay?" Anders spoke to her. Amanda looked to him again after staring down the path as if transfixed by it.

"I just hope that we make it in time," Amanda said. "If not, then we could never find him." Anders rode close to her, trying to reassure her.

"Don't worry, if we don't make it, we can ask around. One of the elves would have seen him go," Anders said supportively.

"We had best hurry then, we won't make gains by wasting time," Amanda surged forward along the road, speeding ahead of Anders. He had to admire her tenacity.

Anders sped up to keep up with her and before long they reached another clearing, but this one was much larger and had nut shaped huts all around. They slowed their horses to a trot and looked around. "I don't see anyone," Amanda spoke aloud, looking left and right. "Not even a single elf."

"They must be gathered somewhere else, or hiding in their houses. Maybe, today is some elven holiday or something?" Anders said looking around himself. Then Anders spotted a young elf boy hiding behind a pile of logs. The boy was huddled up to the logs as if there was a terrible monster just beyond the trees. Anders didn't want to scare the boy further by just going up to him, but he also needed answers. Before Anders made up his mind though Amanda ran over to the frightened, elf boy. *Amanda, you fool if you just run up to him you'll scare him even worse!* Anders was screaming in his mind as she was now just a few feet from the boy. Amanda slowed when she got close and stopped next to him. Anders had no choice but to stay put and buried his face in his palm out of exasperation.

"Are you okay?" She asked simply but concern was etched on her face. As if the boy just woke up from a nightmare, the boy looked up. His eyes were green like the trees but were filled with fear. The fear did not seem to be directed at Amanda however, as the boy simply responded with a nod.

"I saw you hiding ever here so I was a little worried. Do you know where everyone is?" Amanda bent over a little so she was close to his height as the elf boy sat up.

"Everyone was worried when the sword started shining, so everyone is hiding in their houses. I wanted to hide too, but everyone locked their doors, so I can't get in," said the elf. "I'm really scared." Amanda pitied the poor elf boy, but her goal came to mind then.

"Do you know where the elder of this village is?" Amanda asked him sweetly. The elf nodded and pointed off in some direction.

"His hut is in the middle of the village; it's the biggest one so you can't miss it." The elf boy looked around again.

"Thank you. Stay safe, little one," Amanda smiled at him as she thanked him, and gave him a light hug. The elf sat there in shock as Amanda got up and ran back to her horse. "Well? Let's head to the village center." Anders just looked at her dumbfounded before regaining his composure.

Amanda and Anders rode off, Anders looking ahead with a pit of worry in his stomach. *Just what have I gotten myself into here?* The Elder's hut wasn't difficult to find as the boy had described, and there were some elves wandering around this part of the village, most likely the ones that work to provide for themselves and can't afford to do otherwise. Anders stopped close to the tent, as did Amanda, drawing glances from elves nearby but they moved on shortly enough.

An attendant in front of the tent looked to Anders and Amanda, who walked towards the elf. "We wish to speak with the elder of this village. May we go in?" Anders spoke formally and politely to the elf. The attendant studied him for a moment. He eyed him suspiciously but hesitantly moved aside.

"Please watch where you step inside, the elder's belongings are all valuable antiques and damaging them will not earn you his favor. Also, leave your weapons out here, please," the attendant spoke flatly. Amanda and Anders exchanged bewildered looks but disarmed before continuing on inside. The elder elf was perusing the many relics he had adorning his hut and barely even looked at Anders and Amanda when they approached him. When he finished looking at a text he looked up at Anders.

"May I help you?" the Elder spoke, the disinterest clearly showing in his voice.

"My name is Prince Anders MacArthur and this is my associate Amanda. We are here looking for a human boy, we need to find him and figured you'd know if a human was inhabiting your village." Anders said matter-of-factly. The Elder looked at him suspiciously.

"Just what purpose do you have in mind for this boy?" The Elder asked him, then proceeded to wave his hand in the air, most likely to cast some sort of spell. "And don't bother lying, I shall know if you do."

"My village that I come from had a powerful prophecy mage who foretold a dark prophecy involving that boy. Please sir, if we don't find him all is lost!" Amanda pleaded to the aged elf. The elder narrowed his eyes and examined her carefully, then nodded satisfied.

"Very well, but first tell me this prophecy you speak of, child," The elder said calmly.

"The prophecy mage foretold of a time not long from now, that a darkness would rise up and conquer us all. He said that our only hope is a boy just reaching the age of man, would fight this darkness with the sword of piercing light, Lux. He said we would find this boy under the care of the elves, growing his strength for a decisive journey. That is why we are here." Amanda told him recounting the dying moments of the mage, bringing a tear to her eye.

"That is very troubling indeed. I'm afraid the boy you search for has already left this forest, however. He left for your capital just a few hours prior to your arrival." The Elder said downcast.

"I see, that is very disappointing. Can you possibly give his a description of the boy?" Anders asked hopefully. "Maybe once we know what he looks like, we will find him more easily."

"Yes, of course. The boy you speak of, Devlin, is a head taller than this young girl here, and slim but toned. He has dark brown hair and green eyes and he looks older than his age lets on. He is also traveling with Elena, an elven girl. They shouldn't be too far ahead but I would move quickly if I were you."

"Thank you, sir, we will leave at once." Anders bowed slightly to show his gratitude.

"You have no need to thank me, just please, hurry." The elder spoke urgently.

*   *   *

Anders and Amanda rode onto the path toward the capital. "Do you think we'll catch them?" Amanda asked.

"The elder said they were traveling on foot. They have no reason to stray from the path as it leads straight to the capital, but once the forest ends, the path splits in many different directions. If they get onto one of those paths before we find them it will be significantly harder to find them. So we have to find them before then." Anders spoke while scowling.

"So there are multiple ways to get to the capital?" Amanda concluded.

"Yes, the king designed it that way to help disperse traffic. Each path leads to the four different entrances to the city, which is why we can't simply wait for them there." Anders whipped the horse's reins and urged it faster, Amanda did the same, trying to keep up.

"You're sure you can't just have your father post lookouts for him and the girl?" Amanda asked thoughtfully.

"No, that would take too much time, and Father's forces are spread thin as it is," Anders answered dismissively.

"That just means we have to hurry and hope they haven't traveled too far yet," Amanda said, staying optimistic.

"The forest path doesn't last for too much longer, though. I hope we make it in time." Anders pushed his horse even harder and the forest trees rushed by them. They had the wind at their backs, making it a bit easier as if the force of nature itself was guiding them. *Please let us make it in time.* The same thought echoing strongly in both their minds.

Chapter 18

Devlin and Elena walked down the forest path leading to the capital. "We're finally almost out of the forest, we're making great time so far," Devlin observed. "The path splits and all of them lead to the capital, right?"

"Yeah, that's right. Of course, some take longer than others, so I made sure to pick the one that is the shortest beforehand. We will worry about that when we get there, though, because we still have a bit of time before we arrive," Elena said expertly.

Devlin then heard a sound from behind them as they neared the edge of the forest, the open field finally in view. It sounded like a steady rumbling, and as they walked it got progressively louder. Devlin had heard this sound plenty of times before; the identity of it was just out of his mind. Devlin looked back and saw it: two horses, each with a rider. They were approaching quickly and almost seemed like they weren't going to slow down. Devlin pulled Elena to the side off of the path and Devlin finally got a good look. Two elves rushed by, obviously merchants. They gave a passing wave of their hands as they rushed by.

"Well someone is in a hurry," Devlin said slightly irritated. "That must be the third group of merchants we've seen so far."

"Merchants use this pathway a lot getting to and from the village, I'm surprised we haven't seen more of them running around." Elena sighed, the elven pair fading from view ahead of them.

"I kind of wish the elder gave us a pair of horses. This trip would go so much faster." Devlin complained as he walked, thinking of his tired body from walking all day.

"Oh relax, it'll keep us in shape for the journey. It's also a lot more peaceful not having to listen to the horse's gallop as we go." Elena smiled. Devlin rolled his eyes and smiled a little. *At least we have each other.* Devlin looked over to Elena still grinning a little. *Elena definitely keeps things interesting.*

As they finally made it out of the forest, the split in the path came into view. The path branched off into many different directions; Devlin counted seven in all. They came to the break and looked at each path, each as unremarkable as the next. "So which one are we taking?" Devlin asked looking over to Elena.

"The path on my map showed the fourth path from the left being the most direct route," Elena said pointing to the corresponding path. Just then, Devlin heard another rumbling, similar to the sound of the merchants from before.

"Not again..." Devlin groaned.

* * *

Anders and Amanda rode fiercely the forest becoming thinner and thinner as they rushed by. Each bound made Anders feel less and less optimistic. "Where are they?!" Anders accidently saying his thoughts aloud. *Are we really too late? Have they already made it out of the forest?* Anders' teeth clenched in frustration and he gripped the reins even tighter. *Please let us make it!* The forest then finally opened up and revealed an open field.

"Anders, look!" Amanda pointed to two lone travelers on the road far in front of them. Just beyond them, the path split seven ways.

"Unbelievable, that's them it has to be. A young man and elven girl, just like the elder said," Anders realized, relief lifting the worry off his shoulders. Anders even felt himself smiling as he got closer and closer. The traveling pair obviously noticed them, looking back toward Anders and Amanda. As they approached, the boy and girl noticing they were slowing down stayed where they were. The boy, Devlin, looked at them with a mixture of curiosity and confusion. Elena, to her credit, remained expressionless. Finally, Anders and Amanda stopped a few yards in front of them and dismounted.

"You are Devlin and Elena, correct?" Anders asked, but looking at him close up he knew that they were, the descriptions were a perfect match.

"Yes we are, and who are you two?" Devlin asked, his voice full of suspicion.

"I am Prince Anders, and this is my associate Amanda, who has been looking for you," Anders spoke calmly and kindly, hoping to ease their suspicions.

"We need your help, Devlin, the entire world does. The darkness is growing in strength and I was entrusted with a prophecy of you. When the darkness reveals itself completely, all will be lost unless a boy saved by elves, faces it." Amanda said pleading to him. Devlin's eyes went wide with shock at her words.

"You know of the darkness?" Devlin said surprised, then his eyes gave a determined look. "Very well then, what do you want us to do about it?"

"The prophecy states that you will take the ancient sword Lux in hand and do battle with the darkness, to save us all from destruction."

"A prophecy? You mean those fanciful visions of the future?" Devlin scoffed.

"Please, Devlin, you have to believe me," Amanda said undeterred. Devlin looked to Anders. "I find it hard to believe the prince himself would be traveling with just a girl," Devlin's eyes intensified. "Show me proof of your claim and I shall believe you." Anders didn't expect them to believe what they said right off the bat, but proving his royal heritage was an easy request to answer.

So Anders took out his royal pendant. Devlin looked at it and recognized it immediately.

"I trust this is sufficient?" Anders said, returning the pendant under his shirt. Devlin sighed but relaxed. Elena also seemed to loosen her guard a little.

"Fine, so you are who you say you are," Devlin said. "Then I'll help you on one condition... I save my siblings first before I help you."

"Understood," Anders said agreeing, "Then we will help you save your family immediately." Devlin nodded in respect.

"We'll probably need it, in all honesty, all we know is that they were kidnapped by bandits rampaging at the carnival near my village." Devlin's eyes lowered in sadness at the words.

"So you're also victims of the bandit uprisings as of late?" Amanda said walking closer to Devlin. Anders could tell that she knew all too well the pain of losing those you love most. "It would be an honor to help you save them, Devlin, I can't fight very well, but my healing spells saved the life of the man you see beside me."

"I can sense her magical energy. She speaks the truth, Devlin; she'd be an invaluable asset." Elena speaking for the first time, surprising Anders a little. Devlin merely nodded and looked to Anders again.

"I assume from the giant sword and fancy armor you wear that you are a gifted warrior?" Devlin questioned.

"I was trained by the king's finest knights and tacticians, and that has allowed me to claim the title of general of the King's army. I fight for honor and glory for my people, as you will soon enough." Anders spoke recounting his past.

"It's funny," Devlin said thoughtfully. "I certainly never thought of fighting in a major battle before. A mere farm boy such as me, destined to save the world?" Devlin paused. "It's a daunting task, to say the least, but I will do all I can. I assume you will too, Elena?"

Devlin looked toward Elena and she smiled enthusiastically. "Of course, you couldn't keep me away if you tried."

"Thank you, thank you both so much." Amanda bowed low to them.

"I think the best course of action will be to meet with father to see if he has found out anything regarding the bandits," Anders said as he started remounting his horse. "Amanda, you climb on this horse with me. You two can share that horse." Anders gestured towards the unmanned horse and Amanda climbed on behind Anders, wrapping her arms around his back looking back toward Devlin expectantly.

"Darn, I was really enjoying the peace and quiet..." Elena muttered somewhat bitterly. Devlin needed no encouragement and climbed onto the unoccupied horse, Elena got on behind him mirroring Amanda.

"Let us be off then, and hope for the best," Devlin spoke to them.

Chapter 19

"What do you mean we found them?" Derek asked Valcara confused as she studied her map.

"I mean we found the place where they are holding the women and children the armies have captured. You said you had a sister right? She's most likely there then along with plenty of other potential hands for the rebellion. Luckily they aren't too far from us so it won't be long before we see what we get."

"I'm finally going to see my sister again, after all this time," Derek said almost not believing it. Derek had been through a lot after joining Valcara's ranks. Derek wore strong steel armor like Valcara and rose to the top of her ranks through his skill in combat and claiming a commanding rank. Vantos, being great with his hands, joined the construction crew, and he has helped build many of the barracks and homes in the rebel base. Roark became Derek's right-hand man helping him train for upcoming battles. Roark was improving remarkably fast as well, beating many of the average fighters in sword-to-sword combat and even some of those more experienced.

As if called by his thoughts, Roark entered the tent with them, looking somewhat fatigued from all the tasks he was required to do. Derek gave him a sympathetic look and Roark returned a tired smile.

"How goes everything?" Roark asked disinterestedly.

"We might've finally found Cecelia, Roark," Derek smiled confidently. "We'll be that much closer to being all together again."

"You're serious?" Roark's head snapped to Derek faster than he could swing a sword. Derek nodded with a bit of hope growing in his features. "Please tell me we are leaving now," Roark asked with a rush of enthusiasm.

"Yes, you are. In fact, you two are leading the charge. I'm going to need you two to help break into that stronghold. They have it heavily guarded thanks to our recent raid on the other prison. You ready to get your hands dirty, boys?" Valcara said smirking at them.

"As ready as we'll ever be," Derek said with a confident grin.

"Good, then I'm placing one hundred men under your command, and Athon will be joining you as well," Valcara told Derek. "Just try not to get yourself killed alright?"

* * *

Cecelia was growing frantic waiting in her cell, watching the guards on their patrols. She had been formulating a plan to try and escape this place. Cecelia thought about starting a riot, but that would require for her to steal one of the keys off of the guards and let enough prisoners free to outnumber the guards. The problem was the key was locked securely around a metal ring around the guard's belt. However, their belts were made of leather, meaning they could be cut with something sharp.

Cecelia did have a blade hidden in her boot, but it wasn't used to cut leather, just ropes, so she didn't know how effective it would be, but she had to try. Luckily, the opportunity of a lifetime revealed itself to her. A guard took a nap next to her cell, and the keys on his belt were within arms reach. Cecelia made sure that no other guards could see her, then took out her hidden knife.

She slowly sawed the belt with her knife, slowly but surely cutting through it. Cecelia moved very slowly and gently, as to not wake the guard. Cecelia looked over to Anna, who had an incredulous look on her face when she realized what Cecelia was doing. Cecelia mouthed the words "Be ready" to her, and Anna nodded understandingly. Cecelia managed to finally cut through the leather belt with her knife, and she slowly took off the key ring. She even grabbed the short sword on his belt.

Cecelia had no skill with a blade like her brothers did, but that didn't mean she couldn't at least use it now. Cecelia took the sword, then she noticed the guard start to awaken. *I have to move fast!* Cecelia screamed in her mind. She thought of all the ways to inflict a fatal injury to the guard and which would be the quickest, the armor made it hard to decide, however. She looked over the armor and noticed small ridges in it to allow the armor to breathe. She stuck the sword through one of these closest to the heart. It took every ounce of will and hatred she had to stab the guard right through the heart.

There's no turning back now. Cecelia opened the cell door and dragged the guard inside it. As she looked at the body she felt like she was going to vomit. She had never killed anyone or anything before, and having to do it now disgusted her, but she steeled her resolve and exited the cell. Luckily, the hall of cells had many decent places to hide, which Cecelia would take advantage of, but for some reason, all of the guards suddenly started running for the exit as if the building were about to collapse.

Here's my chance! Cecelia ran to Anna's cell and unlocked it.

"Are you any good with a sword?" Cecelia asked quickly.

"My dad taught me the basics in case I ever needed to defend myself, so I suppose so," Anna responded. Cecelia gave the sword to Anna, not wanting to hold the accursed thing any longer, and ran to the other cells to free the other women. The crowd of women grew as Cecelia systematically freed every single woman in each cell.

* * *

As Derek arrived before the stronghold, he studied every aspect of it. They hid in the grasses that made up the prairie and

Derek tried forming a plan of attack, Roark and Athon crouched just behind him. The stronghold consisted of three entrances, the front entrance and two side entrances, each heavily guarded with around a dozen soldiers at each door. If the inside was anything like the prison he was in, the prisoners will be in the back of the fortress. The grasses were the most important part, however. The grass kept Derek's army hidden from view, and Derek noticed that the front had significantly less than the sides, making the side entrance the most favorable.

"Roark, I think I've thought of the best route. Do you see that tuft of grass over there?" Derek said directing him.

"Yeah, I see it. I'm guessing you want to move to there then?" Roark asked looking at him.

"Yes, and Athon, do you think once we get over there, you can incapacitate those guards for a couple minutes? Just long enough for us to rush over and attack? I want to make sure nothing goes wrong." Derek asked looking to the stern mage. Athon merely nodded understanding, and the army walked into position. As soon as everyone was set, Athon cast his spell on the guards a hundred yards away from them, and Derek immediately saw the guards all clutching their heads in agony.

"Now!" Derek commanded silently to everyone behind him, and two dozen of Derek's army followed him to take down the guards. Derek quickly closed the gap and began slashing down the incapacitated soldiers, taking down the first three effortlessly. The other soldiers quickly grabbed onto each of the guards and slit their throats quietly. Derek, seeing that the threat was eliminated, opened the door just enough to peek through. As he figured, the inside was full of guards, completely unaware of what just happened outside. As Derek had instructed before the soldiers came up a dozen at a time to keep from being noticed. Derek estimated the inside room to have another dozen guards, this time, they would have to rely on their steel, as Derek wanted to conserve Athon's strength for when they really needed it.

Derek waited for the last of the soldiers to arrive behind him and opened the door wide, shocking all the guards inside. Derek and his force swarmed the guards like fire ants and chopped them down with little resistance. They barely made a sound, thanks to their quick, surprise attack. Derek looked around at the room he was in and noticed it was completely nondescript, nothing but brick walls and the two large wooden doors, as if the room's only purpose was to act as a buffer between the wall and the inside of the fortress.

"Let's keep moving," Derek instructed as he walked to the other set of doors across from the first. Derek peeked into the second door and saw a long, empty hallway. Derek opened the door completely and as some of his soldiers filtered in, a guard opened a door close to them and reeled back in shock as he noticed the army in the hallway. His reaction stirred many of the guards inside the now open room much larger than the hall, and Derek found that he was quickly outnumbered two to one.

"So much for the sneaky route," Derek sighed exasperated. "Athon!" As Derek said the word he unleashed a very powerful lightning spell, quickly wiping out a third of the guards. "Charge!" Derek yelled as he rushed forward to meet the first guard, clashing swords with him. The warriors were not far behind and they all rushed to meet the mass of guards behind the door. Derek easily overwhelmed the guard he was clashed with, with strength alone he pushed back the guard, eyes wide with fear as Derek half-chopped off his head.

Derek jumped over the dead guard and joined his force in the wide, circular room. As Derek studied the battle, the guards, even though they previously outnumbered Derek's force, were little match for the trained army. Derek noticed the number of guards drop dramatically with minimal casualties, but that didn't stop half a dozen men to charge straight for Derek. Derek charged the men head on and stabbed the first one in the heart, two guards from the left swung down at him with their swords, so Derek rose his shield to block them, also dodging another from the right. Derek slashed at the guards to his right and managed to slash one guard down his front, making him crumple to the floor and tripping two guards in the process. Roark came to Derek's aide and killed the fallen guards with quick stabs to the back. Derek nodded thanks and kicked one guard in the chest, making him fall backward, and stabbed another guard through his neck. Roark chopped off the head of the guard Derek kicked and chopped off the sword hand of the last guard, making it an easy kill for Derek. The rest of his soldiers finished killing off the last of the guards, who put up a sloppy counter at best.

Derek took stock of his men and noticed only half a dozen men were killed, none injured beyond a few cuts and bruises. Derek smiled confidently at that; this would be an easy victory at this rate. *But then again, I doubt these men expected a full army to attack,* Derek thought to himself. Athon walked up behind Derek, recovering from his previous spells and Roark was uninjured besides for one small cut on his cheek.

"Impressive work, Derek. These men were amateurs but you handled yourself well." Athon smirked at him.

"They weren't much but at least now it should be smooth going from here on," Derek smirked back. Derek looked around the room again and noticed several doors, meaning this was likely the center of the fortress. "Let's find the prisoners quickly, spread out and search."

Derek looked at each door with respect to the one he had entered from. The door to the prison cells were likely in the door across from where he entered. Derek walked over to a door across the room and opened it, but it was just a stockroom. It wasn't what Derek was looking for, but made note of it anyway as supplies for the rebellion. Some soldiers seemed to have the same idea and started putting the supplies into bags. Derek checked a door adjacent from the door he just opened and discovered a strangely shaped hallway that seemed to go around the storeroom. Derek walked along the hall a few steps and found that it led to the back of the structure.

"This way," Derek ordered to the soldiers and they followed him along, Roark and Athon close behind him. The hallway wrapped along the wall of the storeroom like a semicircle and it opened to a long hall, prison cells on each side. To Derek's surprise, however, the cells were empty, and he saw a huge crowd of women with Cecelia and some girl leading them.

"What the hell?" Derek asked confused.

"Looks like these women don't need to be freed after all," Roark laughed, and relief overflowed in him as he spotted Cecelia as well. When Cecelia noticed them, she just looked at them shocked.

"Derek, Roark? Is that you?" Cecelia asked in disbelief.

"You know them?" Anna asked her.

"Those are my brothers," Cecelia answered, fresh tears streaming down her grime-covered face. Cecelia walked to her brothers, wanting to make sure it wasn't a dream and she embraced them both firmly.

"I was so worried about you two," Cecelia sobbed, her head buried in Derek's shoulder.

"We missed you too, Cece," Derek and Roark both said simultaneously.

"It's a pleasure to meet you two, thank you for coming for us," Anna seemingly trying to smile but unable to. A man in the crowd behind Derek suddenly came forward, looking shocked and relieved.

"Anna, is that you? By the maker thank goodness you're still alive!" the man exclaimed happily. When Anna looked at the man her eyes were wide as plates, then she started crying as she embraced him. She sobbed uncontrollably into his chest, and Derek felt happy for her, seeing as how he was in the exact same situation. The Slade siblings broke their embrace and Derek laid a reassuring hand on Cecelia's shoulder.

"You did an amazing job, Cece, Mother would be proud," Derek told her, prompting more tears from Cecelia along with a genuine smile.

"I'm just glad to see you two alive and well. That is all that matters to me," Cecelia told him.

"We have to find the warden, we need to get information out of him." Derek started running down the hall opposite from where they entered and found a door right next to the opening to the prison block. As Roark opened the door for Derek he saw the Warden in the corner of the room alone, cowering in fear as he looked at Derek. Derek walked over to the warden with contempt.

"You don't know how lucky you are that I've been told to take you alive. I would enjoy killing you the most." Derek said to the cowering man as he glared at him. Derek grabbed his shirt and forced him up, pushing him to a group of soldiers who subdued him.

"What do you plan to do with me?" The Warden asked almost crying.

"The leader wants you for interrogation, and we can also use you as a shield in case your friends try anything funny," Derek explained to him coldly. "Let's get out of here."

* * *

As Derek made his way back down to the underground base, escorting all the former prisoners Cecelia walked up beside him.

"Derek, I have to ask. Just how did you end up a leader of such a large army?" Cecelia spoke concerned.

"I was saved by this group of rebels, rose in their ranks, and I came to save you." Derek smiled at her, Cecelia smiled back albeit a soft one.

"Thank you then, for saving me. They treated us terribly in that prison, starving us and beating us without provocation." Cecelia shed a tear and brushed it away. Derek's face darkened as she said that. His hatred toward the warden growing even further.

"Everything's okay now, Cece, you saved all the prisoners and we captured the warden." Derek tried smiling again but was unable to thanks to the dark thoughts that kept poking into his head.

"Where's Devlin?" Cecelia asked worriedly. "Is he not with you?"

"Devlin is nowhere to be found. We assumed he escaped somehow and is probably still back in our hometown. I have no doubt that he'll try and look for us." Derek didn't want to say that he could also be dead, he didn't want to imagine that happening to his best friend and brother.

"I hope you're right, Derek, I hope for nothing more so. I can't imagine losing any of you. You're the only family I have especially now that mother and father are dead." Cecelia felt a tear roll down her face at that realization. "I still can't believe they're really gone." Cecelia's cries turning to sobs and Derek hugged her tight. Cecelia's tears flowing out of her eyes as she held onto Derek.

"I know how you feel, I miss them too," Derek said downcast. *I can imagine how hard all this has been on her. After spending all that time in that cell after just losing not only our parents but our home too.* Seeing the moment they were having the other soldiers wisely stood away from the mourning siblings. As Roark and Anna noticed what was going on, however, they rushed over, concern etched on their faces. Roark waited for Cecelia to calm down a little before speaking and Anna went to help comfort Cecelia.

"Do you think that Devlin might be in another prison?" Roark asked softly.

"It's possible, but we'd need to find out from the Warden we captured. I suppose we'll know the truth once we interrogate him." Derek surmised. Roark looked worried as he studied Cecelia, who was completely withdrawn into herself and clearly not paying attention. Roark and Derek escorted the prisoners to the taskmasters to get their respective jobs, Cecelia awkwardly following behind them.

"So what are these 'rebels' planning exactly?" Anna asked Derek, who turned to face her.

"All I know is that they are trying to free as many prisoners as possible to build up their army. What they intend to do with that army is beyond me," Derek answered sincerely.

"It's kind of strange that Valcara is being so secretive to her own right-hand commander," Roark concluded suspiciously, looking to Derek who turned his head to face him, then scratched his chin as he thought about it.

"I can understand why she'd be suspicious of me. We did just get here a couple weeks ago. She probably doesn't completely trust me yet and is keeping me close by." Derek concluded, nodding to himself as he thought it over again.

"I hope she isn't planning anything devious. I'm grateful to be out of that prison, but I don't want to stand by a cause that will put innocents in harm's way." Cecelia said frowning distastefully.

"Those are very nice morals you have, miss, and your concern is understandable," Valcara said, revealing herself from around a corner shortly ahead of the Shade family gathering. "But you have nothing to fear as our cause is just. We wish to overthrow a tyrant, nothing more, nothing less. That same tyrant is the one who is responsible for bringing you to those prisons, although he did have a little help I'm sure." Valcara stared directly at Derek, awaiting their response to this sudden development.

"So, where exactly are we then?" Anna asked her. The same question had crossed Derek's mind many times since he got here but never had the right opportunity to ask.

"You are close to the edge of Seamander, the plain filled land famous for its ports," Valcara responded, seemingly expecting the question. "Seamander is the definition of corruption and filth, no thanks to that barbaric pirate they call a king. That 'king', also known as Henry 'Scurvy Jaw' Russel, is the person we are trying to get rid of."

"What will you do with us once the king is overthrown?" Roark asked her, his eyes determined.

"I would like to try and claim the throne for myself," Valcara stated optimistically. "Once that is settled, I would like to find out who the king is conspiring with for all the help he's getting, and get rid of them. Afterward, I'd like to send all the prisoners back to their homes or at least offer them a new one here." This seemed to put Cecelia, Anna, and Roark a bit more at ease and Derek felt like a weight was just lifted off his shoulders. Finally, they knew for sure what was intended for them. Derek felt like he was one step closer to going home with his family and starting their life over again. Although, he felt a sinking feeling that it wouldn't turn out that way.

"What did you mean when you said that Scurvy Jaw is getting help?" Derek asked her, the thought burning in his head when she mentioned it. Valcara looked at Derek purposefully.

"The king is likely receiving outside help with his little invasion force. His armies are well-known pirates, but terrible on land, yet they have entire prisons full of talented swordsman. So, someone must be getting their hands dirty with Seamander." Valcara answered frankly. "One thing that I want to know is, where is it that you hail from, Derek?"

"We lived in the kingdom of Crestialis on a small farm outside of a small village. We were at a carnival when we were kidnapped by mercenaries," Derek said to her. "If that king is really behind that then this is personal for us. Those scum killed our parents in cold blood, and I will avenge them." Derek held new conviction in his heart. He wanted to make that murderer pay. Valcara smirked at him.

"I like that attitude. If it comes down to it, maybe I'll let you execute him." Valcara laughed out loud and Derek just smiled.

Roark looked at Derek with a new respect. He was in awe of him. After all they have been through, he still finds something to fight for. Roark wanted revenge too, the memory of seeing mother with an arrow through her chest was too much to go unanswered. He wanted revenge for Cecelia too, He hated seeing her like this: sad and confused. He hated that she, of all people, had to go through this suffering in the first place. Most of all, though, he just wanted his old life back; he would trade plowing the fields for this any day because Roark didn't like to fight and kill. He was a gentler man than Derek and Devlin, being the youngest of the three. He would do anything to protect his family, but it still put grief in his heart that he had to fight these people.

"I have one more question, Valcara. How exactly did you end up here?" Roark asked her. Valcara seemed caught off guard by the question, not expecting it to come from Roark, but she quickly regained her composure.

"This country wasn't always ruled by that tyrant. We had a king, much like yours, a kind, devoted king. That all changed though when those pirates attacked us out of nowhere. It was a slaughter, and the king volunteered his life in exchange for the lives of his subjects, Scurvy Jaw agreed to it and spared the rest of the city. He saved many lives that day, and Scurvy took over as king. I was a member of the king's guard, so I fled the city and gathered this rebellion with Athon, who worked under the king as well. The original force was just a ragtag group of people against the tyrant, but we have grown in strength, thanks to the bravery of all the men and women here." Valcara spoke with hatred that was palpable. "I swore I would kill him for what he did to my king, my father. So, is there anything else you wish to ask?" Valcara looked at them, amused by their expressions. Derek, Roark, and Cecelia all silent in shock of the story Valcara had told them. Derek finally got up the nerve to respond.

"So you mean to tell us that you are a princess?!" Derek asked his voice cracking as he struggled to regain his composure. Valcara simply laughed.

"The expression I get whenever I tell someone that is always so amusing." Valcara continuously laughing as she spoke. "You all look like fools." Valcara laughed even harder which made

Derek feel a bit embarrassed. The Slade siblings finally gathered themselves, but Derek still couldn't believe it. He had fought sword-to-sword with a princess. He simply didn't know how to feel about that.

"Have you seen the warden yet?" Derek asked, trying to change the subject.

"Not yet and I look forward to meeting him. I've already got a couple of interrogators ready to make him feel 'welcome'." Valcara made an evil smile as she said "welcome", and the smile made Derek shudder a little inwardly, he almost felt bad for the warden now. Almost.

"Shall we go to him then?" Derek asked her suggestively.

"Yes, I'd hate to let him get lonely," Valcara said smirking again.

"I don't know whether to be scared of that woman or admire her. She's so unpredictable it keeps you on edge." Roark whispered to Derek as Valcara was out of earshot.

"I know what you mean. I still can't get used to her sometimes, but she is a great leader." Derek whispered back and started following Valcara to the tent where the warden was being held, but then looked back at him remembering Cecelia. "Roark, can you make sure Cecelia gets settled? I'll join you in a bit."

"If you say so." Roark shrugged then grabbed Cecelia's arm gently. "Let's go, Cece." Cecelia merely nodded slightly and gave Derek a worried expression before rushing off to the residency tents, Anna and her brother followed.

As Derek entered the tent, Valcara, of course, already in it, he noticed the warden. His hands were bound behind his back a piece of rope attached to a spike in the ground, and his feet tied to the stool he sat on.

"Interesting setup you have here," Derek said raising an eyebrow at Valcara.

"I designed it myself, and no one has ever escaped it. I'm quite proud of my work," Valcara said with a satisfied smile. "Did you want to test it out for yourself, Derek? I'd hate for you to feel left out."

"I don't doubt your work, I've just never seen someone tied down like that before..." Derek mumbled. "So, where are these special interrogators you mentioned?"

"We are the special interrogators." Valcara smiled evilly at him.

"I was afraid you'd say that." Derek brought his palm to his forehead in exasperation.

"Don't worry, it'll be fun." Valcara now looked at the prisoner, and he stiffened like a board, terror shown clearly in his eyes. "Don't look so scared little guy, as long as you tell us what we want to know, this will be quick and painless."

"I-I-I'm n-n-not telling y-you anything," the prisoner stuttered.

"I was hoping you'd say that," Valcara said, her face suddenly cold.

Chapter 20

As Luke rode down the beaten path, his thoughts faded out with the hoofbeats of his horse. He looked upon the horizon, and as before, he saw nothing but open fields with the straight path that guided him and his guardsmen. Then, the memory of his encounter with the Azukas flooded his thoughts and reminded him of the weight of his journey.

"Do you know how much longer we have?" Marcus called out, seeming fatigued from the long journey.

"We are less than a day's ride from the capital if we keep this pace," Jacob answered him. "Sir, do you know what we should do once we reach the capital?"

"We will have to inform the King on what we discovered and head to Seamander to search for that blacksmith. The faster we get this sorted out, the faster we may bring peace back to Crestialis."

"Understood," Jacob spoke looking forward again.

*　　*　　*

As Luke and his guard made their way to the gates, the door opened hastily for
them as they drew close. The border guards saluted him as he passed, a gesture which Luke returned. They rode quickly to the castle, not skipping a beat, and dismounted their horses near the castle doors. Luke was greeted by the guards at the main doorway to the castle and they opened the door for him. Luke went straight to the audience chamber where the king usually was most of the day. The guard outside noticed him and stood erect.

"State your business, Sir," The guard said mechanically from protocol.

"I am here to report to the king on my findings for a mission I attended," Luke responded automatically. The guard nodded understanding.

"The King isn't busy at this moment, please head inside," The guard said as he opened the large wooden door. "Your Majesty, the Knight-Champion Luke wishes to speak with you!" The guard announced. The king looked startled to see him again but the shock quickly faded to relief.

"Thank you, Mathus," The king said dismissing him. "Luke, thank the maker you are back. Please, share what you have found."

"The arms we found were made by a certain smith in Seamander. We plan to investigate there and see what we can find. Hopefully, we find the source of all of Seamander's soldiers," Luke said optimistically.

"Agreed, we must end their destruction of my kingdom while we still can," The King said with a furrowed brow of concentration. "I give you the authority Luke, you have my blessing to go. I hear there is also a rebellion taking hold there, perhaps you may seek them as allies if you can, but it is not necessary to do so."

"Your majesty, I have urgent news!" The guard yelled out as he opened the large oak doors.

"What is it?" The king asked eager to hear and somewhat apprehensive about what it might be.

"Prince Anders has returned to the capital! He is riding toward the gates as we speak!" The guard spoke loudly. "He is accompanied by three others and one looks to be an elf."

"What strange and wondrous news, I could only imagine what could have transpired. Guide them to the castle with all due haste!" The King told the guard who then saluted and ran to fulfill his order.

*   *   *

As the group made their way down the trail to the capital, which grew ever closer over the horizon, Devlin wondered what would transpire. Anders had said that he would report to the king and see if any more information was gathered, but what information would they find? What was in store for them? Devlin looked up at the capital's walls, the entire structure a hive of activity as they approached. Devlin expected to be stopped at the gate, but surprisingly, as they approached, the guards made no move to stop them. In fact, it looked like they wanted them to go through. Luckily, there was no traffic on the route so it did not take long to get into the city streets as they made their way to the castle.

*   *   *

Anders drove his horse onward through the streets and came to the castle gates. A guard ran up to Anders stopped on his horse. "Sir, His Majesty awaits you and your company in the audience chamber, please make all due haste."

"Thank you." Anders nodded approval and quickly dismounted his horse, as did the others. The intricate wooden doors carved by the best of artisans were guarded by a pair of guards. They recognized him immediately and opened the door for him. Inside stood Luke, who looked to Anders with interest. Soon after, his gaze fell on Devlin and his eyes went wide with shock. Then there was King MacArthur, his father, who looked at Anders intently. Devlin also noticed Luke but he wasn't too surprised to see him here.

"Anders, my son, it's good to see you safe and alive again. I had worried much of your fate these many weeks you had gone, thankfully it has brought you safely back. Please, tell me, what drove you to leave so suddenly, when no one even thought you still had the ability to live?" King MacArthur asked, his face grave.

"I was healed by Amanda," Anders gestured towards Amanda and the King's gaze followed, taking in the girl. "She has superb healing magic and she had me up and able very quickly. She is also the reason I left, however, as she has a prophecy of the times to come; it's rather unsettling, so I set off with her to try and stop it."

"What exactly is this prophecy?" King MacArthur clearly focused on Anders.

"A wave of darkness will wash over this and all other lands unless a certain boy found by the elves takes the sacred blade in hand to fight it," Amanda answered the King.

"That is most troubling indeed. I assume the lad next to you is the prophesied child?" The King asked as he looked over Devlin. Devlin simply looked down, his head bowed before the king, but occasionally dared to meet his eyes and they held a strength and intensity the King liked.

"I know the boy for his name, Devlin. He and I fought at the recent festival; he has a lot of skill with the blade, Your Majesty." Luke spoke aloud looking hard at Devlin. "Do you still have the amulet I gave you, Devlin?" To answer his question, Devlin revealed the amulet from under his shirt, and Luke nodded approval.

"To fight you on equal terms?! That speaks volumes for itself!" The king laughed, somewhat lifting the mood of the room. "Devlin is your name then? Be proud lad, most that face off with Luke do not usually live to tell the tale!"

"He was certainly too much for me in the end, but I've grown stronger now," Devlin said to himself somewhat embarrassed, scratching the back of his head.

"Then who is the companion beside you, young Devlin?" The King finally looked toward Elena and she held his gaze.

"My name is Elena, I am Devlin's partner and friend on his journey to save his family, Your Majesty." Elena bowed slightly as a show of respect.

"It's not often I get the pleasure of meeting an elf. Even less so I find a human and elf are friends. I thank the maker there is still hope that our races can coexist. I wish you the best of luck on your journey," King MacArthur said in his proud voice and looked back to Anders. "What do you plan to do henceforth, Anders?"

"Devlin and I agreed that he would fight the 'darkness' after he finds his family. We were hoping you had found a lead on the bandits that have been attacking us as of late." Anders responded back.

"What impeccable timing you have! In truth, Luke here has just told me of such a lead," King MacArthur said joyfully.

"We believe that the country of Seamander as a tie with the bandits. I was planning to investigate there further. If you wish you may come with me and aid me in my investigation," Luke offered. "Truth be told I'm curious to see how Devlin has grown since our last meeting."

"That's settled then, I assume all five of you are going?" King MacArthur assumed.

"Yes, I believe so, Father," Anders said with a chuckle.

"You couldn't stop me if you tried," Devlin said with a confident grin. Just then there came a loud bang as Devlin saw a young girl in a pretty dress about his age run through the large oak doors drawing the eyes of everyone in the room. "Sophia, what is the matter? You look like you've seen a ghost," Anders said running up to her as she caught her breath.

"It's the bandits, there's an army of them and they are heading toward the city gates!" Sophia exclaimed in between breaths.

"They've grown bold if they are trying to ransack this great city. I will gather the army immediately!" King MacArthur said as he got up hurriedly.

"That won't be necessary, Your Highness; let me take care of them. It'll be good practice for what I'm going to do to the scum that stole my family." Devlin had a wild look in his eyes that exuded power, and a thirst for vengeance.

"Devlin, you can't be serious. There have to be hundreds of them out there. They'll kill you!" Anders said with disbelief.

Sophia looked at Devlin, seeing him for the first time, it took her breath away. *Who is that boy?*

"If I can't kill a few hundred bandits then maybe I deserve to die," Devlin responded coldly. "Give me five minutes, Your Majesty. I'll have them running back to whatever hole they crawled out of by then." Devlin ran out of the room passed the large oaken doors. Elena just giggled watching him go.

"Don't worry, Prince Anders, Devlin will be fine. If he screws up I'll help him out, but I doubt he'll need it." Elena ran out after Devlin, leaving the room quiet.

* * *

As Devlin exited the city gates, the large mass of bandits was little more than a half-mile away and a small group of guards was gathering in front of the city. "Guards, step back if you don't want to get hurt, I can't guarantee I can control myself completely if you get in the way," Devlin said as he walked forward toward the approaching army. At first, the guards looked at him with disbelief but after seeing Devlin's magic flare to life around him they decided to step back.

Devlin drew his sword with his right hand as he went, the sword ringing as it slid out of the sheath. When Devlin's sword was fully drawn, the army was almost upon him. Devlin raised the point of his sword toward the bandits and as soon as he did a massive ring of flame spouted right out of the end of it. The flames consumed many of the approaching bandits and when Devlin finished the spell, half of the entire army was reduced to ash and rubble. "Hard to believe he used to have trouble just drawing the energy forth, now he can decimate half an army in a breath. Amazing," Elena said observing the aftermath of Devlin's work next to the guards.

"How is that even possible?" One guard asked incredulously.

"Who is he?!" exclaimed another. Devlin lowered his sword to his side and charged at the remaining bandits, who were completely disoriented and confused. Devlin slashed one bandit after another with ease, slitting their throats, cutting them in half or stabbing them in the heart. Devlin worked like a machine, wiping out the army before it could even regroup. A bandit tried swinging at Devlin as he stabbed another. Seeing that Devlin couldn't bring his sword around to block him, he raised his left palm toward the bandit and out came a bolt of lightning, electrocuting him and every bandit behind him. Another tried to swing at Devlin from the rear, but the armor simply bounced off the attack like the sword was a toothpick. Devlin also used his shield multiple times, blocking blow after blow. Devlin moved gracefully and purposefully as he felled foe after foe, tearing through any resistance they put up. When Devlin had wiped out over three-quarters of the bandits, they dropped their weapons out of fear and ran for their lives. Satisfied with his complete victory over them, yet also partially from exhaustion, he let them escape.

"Not bad, Devlin, but I'm pretty sure that was ten minutes," Elena teased.

"Ah shut up," Devlin said leaning on his sword that he lodged in the ground. "I'm just a bit rusty after being on the road, that's all." When Devlin's breathing slowed, he retracted his sword from the ground and cleaned it with a wet rag in his pack, wiping off the blood from the sword and cleaning the rag through water he magically collected from the ground. "This armor works like a charm but it really takes it out of you. I didn't realize how much of my magic energy it uses protecting me."

"Good reason to be more careful when you fight then," Elena advised. "You honestly surprised me, Devlin, I didn't think you could summon a flame that large. No wonder you're so tired."

"Should we get back to the castle? We need to get Luke and the rest of our group if we want to leave," Devin said as he finished cleaning his sword and sheathing it.

"They will show themselves soon enough. Especially Luke, you know he did say he wanted to see you in action," Elena told him as King MacArthur, Sophia, Anders, Luke and Amanda walked out to meet them. "Ah, here they are now." Every face Devlin saw was a mix of disbelief and awe, especially Luke's.

"Never before have I seen such a display of power and magic. Devlin, you are truly something special," King MacArthur said still shocked.

"You've grown very strong, Devlin, you should feel proud," Luke told him, patting him on the back. To hear such words of praise from the man he had always looked up to, Devlin couldn't be happier.

"I had a good teacher and partner. If it weren't for Elena, I wouldn't be even half as strong," Devlin said embarrassed.

"Shall we head out then, Luke? Time is of the essence here," Anders said to Luke with urgency.

"We wish you a safe and successful journey, Devlin," Sophia told him with a wary smile.

"Your graces flatter me, Princess, I pray we may be more properly introduced the when I return with my troublesome siblings," Devlin said laughing a little at the thought of Derek's expression meeting the princess. Devlin turned to Elena. "We should go get the horses. We'll need three if Luke is coming along."

"Very true," Elena responded and she walked over to King MacArthur. "Your Majesty, we will need three horses for the journey, may you arrange this quickly?"

"Of course, of course," The King affirmed. "They shall be packed and ready immediately." The King walked over to a few attendants to relay the request.

"Then we shall leave as soon as they are ready," Devlin said in anticipation.

Chapter 21

"That didn't take long. You had him talking in five minutes," Derek said to Valcara, somewhat surprised after they sat in the council room.

"It certainly helped that he had about as much backbone as a jellyfish. However, he gave us a lot of insight into the capital's defenses, but he said he has never seen anyone fitting your brother's description," Valcara said to Derek sympathetically.

"Do you think he was still hiding it?" Derek asked a bit disappointed.

"No, he told the truth. You can't lie when you have a truth serum crammed down your throat, compliments of Athon himself," Valcara explained sympathetically. "I'm sorry, Derek, alive or not, your brother is not here. Your best hope is that he escaped those bandits somehow."

"Then all I can do is pray that's the case. If he's dead, I'll never be able to look Cecelia in the eye anymore," Derek said regrettably. "So, what's our next move?"

"We must strike at the capital. Our numbers are bolstering and the greatest they'll ever be at this point," Valcara explained further. "We must hit that tyrant where it hurts before we lose strength. Are you ready for this Derek? It won't be easy and death is more than a possibility for all of us. If we fail, there is no retreat."

"My family is part of this rebellion now. I can't afford to not take part. Also, once you are queen, you can help me look for my missing brother," Derek said resolutely. "It's the duty of the eldest to take care of the young. I will protect my siblings with my life."

"I wouldn't expect anything less coming from you." Valcara smiled, then her face turned serious. "The capital is half a day from here. When we approach, it will be at nightfall, when the city is at it's weakest. If everything goes according to plan, the pirate king will be dead by daybreak."

"What is the plan exactly?" Derek said curiously.

"We'll head to one of the side gates, while our main force attacks the front gate. The diversion created at the front gate will draw all the soldiers to that gate, making it a simple matter to sneak inside. While they are distracted, you, Roark, I can sneak up to the castle and assassinate the king." Valcara told him, gesturing to different points on the map.

"If we are the assassination crew, who will lead the army?" Derek asked.

"I'm leaving that up to Athon. It should be a simple matter for him. Also, your sister will remain, along with the women and children we saved, here, so you won't have to worry about her. I will tell them that if the battle doesn't go well to evacuate immediately. I will send a message to them within the day if we win. If they don't get it, they'll know we did not succeed."

"When do we attack?" Derek asked with finality.

"We attack a week from today. That will give me enough time to prep the troops and tie up any loose ends." Valcara answered quickly. "Also don't forget to tell Roark the plan."

*　　*　　*

The night sky was cloudy and dark, the clouds only allowing enough moonlight to see a few dozen meters ahead. Taking the lead, Valcara rode her horse up slowly behind the hills in front of the gate. Looking through his scope, Derek observed the guards atop the gate.

"Once Athon unleashes the signal, we go forward," Valcara reminded Devlin and Roark.

"It was a great idea getting us these uniforms. Even if the guards see us, they won't think anything of it," Roark said awestruck.

"You can thank our scouts for that. Their spying helped us figure out what their uniforms look like. It's just too bad we didn't have the resources to do it for the entire army," Valcara said disappointedly. Devlin nearly jumped out of his armor as he saw the sky light up with a greenish light, and a loud crash closely following.

"There's the signal," Valcara observed. Derek looked through the scope again and saw every guard on the gate running off toward the light.

"The guards are leaving too. Just like we planned." Derek said relieved.

"Then let's go, quickly," Valcara ordered. They all dismounted their horses and ran toward the gate. With barely any guards still there and the few that remained in total chaos, they managed to get all the way to the gate without being noticed. The gate itself consisted of two large wooden doors reinforced with steel.

"We have to move, they'll probably be closing the gate soon with the commotion at the front gate," Valcara ordered. As they carefully made their way around the gate doors and out into the inner courtyard, Derek could hear the gigantic doors begin to close, as if on cue with Valcara's fears.

"I'm sure glad we didn't wait around," Derek said not wanting to think about what would happen if they hadn't slipped through in time.

"We should be fine now but don't draw unnecessary attention to yourselves," Valcara warned. The silent trio made their way to the castle, managing to blend in with the other guards who didn't even give the three of them a second glance with their identical uniforms. Derek just hoped his and Roark's darker skin didn't give them away because these guards were much paler by comparison. Luckily, with the uniform covering most of the body, and the limited lighting of night, Derek and Roark were easily concealed. Derek couldn't make out much of the city, but most of what he saw consisted of paved pathways and brick buildings more inland, with the docks and ships all on the sea. Derek made a silent reminder to himself to see this place in the sunlight when this was finished.

Valcara, being native to this city, made an excellent guide. She even used a few secret passageways in the city to avoid detection. When they finally made it to the castle through a secret escape hatch, it was practically empty. Derek only saw a couple guards running through the halls, most likely to relay that the city was under attack. Derek was more than a little surprised when a guard addressed him suddenly.

"You three, ya know the city is under attack right?" The guard asked quickly. "Spread word to the others that haven't woken up yet, will ya?"

"Of course, sir!" Valcara answered. The guard ran off in another direction, and Roark and Derek just laughed to themselves silently, before Valcara gave them a look of death to shut them up. "This way morons."

The three of them went higher and higher into the castle, managing to avoid most of the guards. Derek even noticed some soldiers dressed in much better armor, but could smell a stench on them that made Derek want to vomit. "I'm going to go out on a limb here and say the king made his crew higher-ups in the army?" Derek asked quietly to Valcara.

"Correct, but no matter how high their rank they are still pirates," Valcara answered.

"Smell like them too…" Roark said holding his nose. "Odor like that, no wonder they're outlaws. That stench is criminal." Valcara just rolled her eyes, trying to conceal a small grin and pressed forward. The entrance to the audience chamber was a disturbing one. It had a massive jolly roger painted on the doors with two guards in front of it. Valcara took out a small ball shaped object and threw it at the guards. The ball exploded, letting loose some gas, and within a few seconds, the guards fell unconscious.

"So why not kill the guards? Wouldn't that be easier?" Roark asked confused.

"I don't want to kill them. Those guards are men I worked with growing up. It's just the higher ups that are pirates." Valcara said like it was obvious. The three of them quietly made their way to the door. Valcara put her ear to the door in an attempt to listen for anyone on the other side. Inside, she heard Scurvy's voice barking orders to some men, she assumed more guards. "He's in there, I know that voice all too well," Valcara said darkly.

"Don't move!" A shout rang out that sent a shiver down Derek's spine. When he turned to find the source he saw a large group of guards surrounding them. The guards quickly grabbed all three of them before any of them could react and opened the door to the audience chamber. What scared Derek the most was that the look on Scurvy's face wasn't one of shock. He was smiling, a triumphant grin showing some missing teeth, and the one's he did have looked rotted. The sight of it made Derek gag.

"Well looky 'ere! Look who 'cided to join our lil pardy!" Scurvy Jaws cackled.

"How did you know we were coming?" Roark shouted angrily.

"Ya walked inta a trap kiddo," Scurvy said joyfully. "Ya fell for it hook, line, an' sinker too. Best part is, ya have yur lil frien' Vally 'ere to thank for it!" Derek felt his world turn upside down at the words, and Scurvy just laughed and laughed. His words came out jumbled and almost unintelligible from his missing teeth, but every sound from his mouth was like a blow to Derek's ears. He looked like a rat dressed in a tuxedo and smelled like one too. He was about Derek's height, but chubby, and he had a crude face that was scarred and twisted.

"You're lying! Valcara would never do something like that!" Derek shouted, hoping he really was lying, but from the look on

Valcara's face, he knew Scurvy was telling the truth, at least for once.

"I'm sorry Derek, Roark, but he's right. We made a deal shortly after Scurvy became king. The deal was, that if I gathered a group of rebels into a trap for him, he would spare my little brother," Valcara cried, as she said it. "He said he would do terrible things to my brother if I didn't do as he said." Derek tried absorbing her words. The devastating part for him was, he completely understood. Derek would have done the same thing in her shoes. Derek didn't want to imagine Devlin or Roark dying by torture or worse by this heartless criminal.

"What a great job she did too," Scurvy Jaws cackled. "'Er 'ntire force is mine now. She singlehand'ly gathered ev'ry piece a scum in me country an' I barely had to lift a finger."

"I gave you what you want now let my brother go," Valcara reminded him angerly.

"'Bout that lil detail, my deary, one o' me boys took a dislikin' to the brat and wanted 'im executed. I'm 'fraid me hands 'rrrre tied." Scurvy laughed hard at Valcara and her face twisted with rage. "Guards! Get these upstarts out of me sight! Lock 'em up and see to it 'at they don' get out!"

"You promised!" Valcara screamed in outrage as the guards started pulling the three of them out of the room.

"'Ere's a lil word of advice, me deary, ne'er trust a pirate," Scurvy laughed evilly as Valcara, Derek, and Roark were dragged out of the throne room.

*   *   *

The guards threw all three of them into their own cell, Derek on one end Roark on the other. When the guards left Derek went to the edge of his cell behind the bars. "You two okay?" Derek said quietly trying not to draw the guards back.

"I'm a little bruised, but I'll live," Roark responded.

"I'm sorry, Derek, Roark, I was a fool to trust him," Valcara cried her head tucked into her knees. "I don't expect you to forgive me."

"You're right, you were a fool," Derek told her. "But that's what family does to people. We're all fools for our family, it's just how people are." Through all of Valcara's sadness, she smiled at that in spite of herself. "If anyone could understand what you did it would be me, because I know I would probably do much more foolish things to save my family. However, getting down on yourself won't do anything."

"How can you be so strong?" Valcara asked him. "How can you still be willing to fight?"

"When you have something to protect, you fight like hell to protect it. Those were words my father lived by and instilled in me. I will fight until my last breath to protect my family," Derek told her honestly. "What you really should be asking, Valcara, is what are you willing to risk your life to protect?"

"My brother, and everyone in the rebellion," Valcara spoke silently to herself as the realization dawned on her. Valcara couldn't help but feel impressed at Derek's resolve. *Even in this hopeless situation, he still doesn't give up. Well, if he won't give up, what a pathetic leader that would make me to be outdone by my soldiers. What kind of leader would I be if I let all these people die for my selfishness?* She wanted to save her brother more than anything, but she also had a responsibility to the rebellion.

"You're right, Derek. I don't have time to get down on myself. Let us find a way out of here," Valcara resolved. "And thank you. As unworthy a commander I may be now, I ask that you lend me your steel, and I promise you, I won't fall again."

Derek just smiled proudly at the words. "I wouldn't have it any other way."

Chapter 22

As Devlin's group got on their horses, with Devlin and Elena on one horse, Anders and Amanda sharing one, and Luke on the third horse, the portion of King MacArthur's men that had gathered all saluted them at once. A true sign of respect to the group as it began its maiden voyage. Luke wished he could've brought his guard along with him, but they had to restrict their numbers if they wanted to move fast. He also wondered about the combat effectiveness of their group; he had a decent grasp of Devlin's and Anders' skill, but Elena and Amanda were still unknown, save for Amanda's miraculous healing abilities and the dagger she wielded.

If Elena was anywhere close to Devlin's magical abilities, this group would be the equal of a small army. Luke still wondered, though, if healing was the only skill Amanda had. If not, she could be just as versatile as Elena. Luke knew he could rely on Anders' leadership, should they need to split up for some reason, and he was mostly on par with Luke himself in terms of skill with a sword. Luke took stock of their group as they traveled down the beaten path, and imagined different combinations for them in possible combat situations.

They rode in a triangular formation, with Luke in the front since he was currently the fastest. They made good progress in their travels, riding most of the day and camping at night. Devlin left the hunting up to Elena, as she grew up a silent hunter in the woods, hunting for food was literally child's play to her. Devlin was curious about his companions, especially Amanda. She was a sore thumb to him. It bothered him to no end why she would take up this quest, being about the same age as his little sister.

One night, when Devlin had finished his list of things to do, he sat next to Amanda by the fire.

"So Amanda... we're traveling together and I don't know a thing about you. Care to enlighten me?" Devlin asked awkwardly.

"I was thinking the same thing actually. It would be a pleasure to hear about you, Devlin." Amanda smiled sweetly at him. Her smile reminded him even more of his sister.

"You said you were a healer. Do you have any other skills?" Devlin questioned, flicking a fire into life above his fingertip to emphasize his point.

"I'm not very good at elemental magic like you, but I can remove curses and diseases from the body as long as I know the composition of them. My teacher made me study every disease she could get her hands on, and it came in handy whenever I felt sick," Amanda said, recalling past memories.

"I envy you then. I remember catching the flu as a kid, and remember no worse feeling," Devlin recalled and cringed at the thought of it. "I guess having mother take care of me wasn't all bad, though. And it gave me a break from doing chores."

"Having a mother to care for you... I bet there's no better feeling." Amanda's face filled with sorrow at the thought. "I never had a mother actually. My parents died when I was very young. My teacher was the one that raised me."

"I'm so sorry, Amanda. I can't even imagine what that must be like," Devlin said compassionately. "I really do miss her, though. My mom died a few weeks ago when the bandits attacked. If growing up without one feels anything like how being without one now feels, I can understand how you feel."

"At least we have each other now, all of us together like this. Anders is like a big brother to me now, so kind and strong, then there's you, who understands me better than anyone does." Amanda laughed sweetly as she looked at him.

She's so innocent, Devlin thought to himself.

"You remind me so much of my little sister. She was always such a kindhearted, innocent girl before she was kidnapped. I really hope she's alright." Devlin looked at the stars and wondered if was she looking at these same stars now.

"We'll find her, Devlin. I promise." Amanda laid a reassuring hand on his shoulder and smiled that same sweet smile his sister would give him, and, for the first time in a long time, he truly felt at peace.

"Thanks." Devlin smiled back. "So, tell me more about your teacher?"

"She was a very kind woman. She was proud and always wanted to have a say, especially if I was involved. Her silver hair draped over her shoulders like a tapestry, and her eyes were blue like sapphires. She had a smile that could ease any troubles you had and made you feel safe. She was the mother I never had, and I loved her for it. She taught me everything I know, from my literacy, to my healing powers when she discovered I had magic. She loved reading books and discovering things. She even read a few books to me as a child." Amanda smiled admiringly, but the smile was hiding the grief she felt. Amanda still felt the pain of losing her village, and remembering her teacher made her want to curl up and cry. Devlin could tell she cared a lot about her teacher. "So Devlin, who taught you magic?" Amanda asked trying to change the subject.

"Elena did," Devlin answered quickly. "She taught me the ropes and I grew from there. I tried experimenting with different spells and elements. Water is my favorite, but I always end up using other spells offensively."

"Did you learn swordsmanship from her too?" Amanda asked.

"No, I was first taught by an old soldier. He saw that I liked his sword one day and taught me how to use it. I developed on my own from there, but me and my brother Derek did practice together sometimes, although Elena did give me a couple pointers," Devlin said, remembering all the grueling days he practiced in the elven forest. Devlin felt a hand grab his shoulder which made him nearly jump ten feet.

"You two aren't getting too comfy are ya?" Elena teased.

"Elena also takes any chance she gets to scare the living hell out of me," Devlin grumbled, glaring at her.

"I can't help it when you make it so easy," Elena laughed. "Sorry, Amanda, I'll have to steal Devlin for a minute, but I promise he can talk later." Elena winked at her, and Amanda simply laughed.

"It's no trouble, Elena. Take your time," Amanda said smiling. "I should probably check our supplies anyway."

Elena bowed slightly and pulled Devlin toward the forest. "So what is it you need?" Devlin asked, confused.

"I'm so glad you asked," Elena said, handing him a dull sword. "We're gonna spar. It's been too long since I've served your butt to you on a silver platter."

"You're so on!" Devlin laughed, taking a ready position.

*   *   *

Luke was amazed watching Elena and Devlin spar. He had noticed Elena pulling Devlin into the forest, and curiosity got the better of him. Devlin had a new grace to his style he had not seen in their previous bout. Luke noticed that same grace in Elena's steps, only more pronounced than in Devlin's. Luke heard Anders walk up behind him and he looked upon the match next to Luke.

"I heard swords clashing. I am curious to see Devlin's skill for myself," Anders said, looking on. "It kind of reminds me of when you and I used to spar. 'Those two fight like demons' people would say, remember?"

"Brings back memories, doesn't it? We were about the same age too," Anders recalled. "We were always neck and neck, every match... I miss those times."

"Maybe we should spar then," Anders suggested, grinning at Luke. "Like old times."

"Very well, but I hope you don't regret those words," Luke grinned back, drawing his sword.

"Get ready, old friend," Anders told him as he drew a long sword from his belt just for times like this. "It's been awhile since I've held a smaller sword, I hope I'm not too rusty."

* * *

Amanda simply watched the sparring matches, one between Luke and Anders, and another with Devlin versus Elena. They were both exciting. Even though Anders wasn't quite as good as Luke, it was far from one-sided, as Anders was surprisingly fast. Elena and Devlin were like twins in terms of skill, they matched blow for blow, but Amanda wondered if Elena was holding back. She noticed from time to time Elena had a chance to get a quick strike and didn't take it. Amanda doubted Devlin noticed, though.

Elena was very good with her strikes and made each one purposeful, Devlin's were still a bit sloppy at times, full of unnecessary movement. *Just how good is Elena? Is she so that much faster than Devlin that she'd have to hold back? She must but very familiar with Devlin's skill, because she matches him perfectly.*

Anders and Luke were a different story, however, neither one held back most likely because their pride wouldn't allow it. The difference between them being clear as day, Amanda guessed Luke must get in more practice as a knight than Anders who had his duties as a prince to deal with.

Amanda herself relied on her dagger for close combat, or simply used her spells to incapacitate the enemy.

When the sparring matches ended, Elena and Devlin looked like they were about to pass out from exhaustion. *Do they always train so hard?* Anders and Luke looked winded but they were fine compared to the other two. Amanda jumped tree branch to tree branch and dropped down next to Elena and Devlin, both of whom were sprawled on the forest floor. They only had minor bruises from what Amanda could tell, so she healed them quickly enough.

"What?" Devlin asked, raising his head. "Oh, hey, Amanda, didn't see you come over."

"How do you two fight so hard? You look so exhausted," Amanda sighed.

"We've always fought like this. We like pushing ourselves. Can't get better by taking it easy." Elena laughed as she sat up. "Thanks for healing us, Amanda. I was worried I'd feel those bruises tomorrow. Devlin's actually starting to keep up with me."

"Next time, I'll be faster than you," Devlin said smugly. Amanda just giggled and playfully punched Devlin's arm above the elbow.

"Ow!" Devlin yelped, rubbing his arm.

"Whoops! Missed one!" Amanda laughed, healing that last bruise. Elena laughed so hard she nearly fell back down as she stood up.

"You did that on purpose, didn't you?" Devlin questioned, finally getting up.

"Of course not, I'm not thaaat mean," Amanda said facetiously, then giggled. "I promise."

"We should probably get dinner set up before it gets too late," Elena advised. "I finished hunting a little bit ago, so the meat will need to be thawed."

"You froze the meat? How?" Devlin asked, confused.

"Yes, I couldn't let it go bad, so I covered the meat with water and froze the water," Elena explained. "It's an easy trick, Devlin, I'm surprised you haven't figured it out yet."

"It's not that I can't do it, I just wouldn't think to do something like that. I would just let it cook over the fire."

"And that is why you are not the cook. We'd starve to death in your hands," Elena teased.

"I'm a very good cook, actually. I've just never had to hunt for my meat before," Devlin said truthfully. Devlin's mom was an amazing chef, and she had taught Devlin how to cook also. It never hurt to have more than one chef in the family.

As the five of them neared the campfire, all save Elena sat calmly by the fire. When Elena started walking off to a different part of the camp to get the meat, Amanda got up and followed.

"Where are you going, Amanda?" Devlin asked noticing her getting up.

"I just want to ask Elena something," Amanda said truthfully, the curiosity getting the better of her. When the two of them were out of earshot, Amanda walked up to Elena.

"Hey, Amanda. What is it?" Elena asked.

"I wanted to ask you why you're holding back when you sparred with Devlin. I noticed it earlier and it's bugging me," Amanda stated. "I don't wish to pry, so if you don't want to answer it's fine." Elena was a little shocked when Amanda said this, and her face turned serious.

"I hold back with Devlin, because if he thinks we're equals, he'll train harder. Men have pride that makes them hate losing, so if he thinks we're evenly matched, he'll train harder to try and beat me. Every time we spar I notice his growth, he is worlds apart from the kid I found trapped in the forest." Elena reasoned, looking away for a second as she recalled Devlin and the three others fighting off those men.

"Is that how you two met? I did wonder why Devlin was in an Elven village of all places" Amanda said thoughtfully, involuntarily bringing her hand to her chin, the universal sign of one in thought. "Just how much better are you?"

"It's hard to say, Devlin's moves are still unrefined and sloppy at times, but I noticed it happening a lot less this time around. He's also getting better at blocking different strikes even though he still needs to get faster to block them effectively. I'm still twice as fast as he is, but he makes up for it with just stamina," Elena elaborated, looking Amanda in the eye. "At this point, my speed is the only real advantage I still have over him.

"I'm sure your speed helps a lot sneaking around? I wondered about that since you seemed to sneak up on Devlin so easily earlier," Amanda asked, and giggled a little remembering the look on Devlin's face when Elena snuck up on him. Elena laughed too and smiled reminiscently.

"The fool makes it so easy sometimes," Elena said jokingly. "But yes, I used to be a part of the village border patrol. You probably encountered some of them on your way to my village."

"I remember them, two elves with bows, I didn't even see them until they revealed themselves," Amanda recalled the tense encounter.

"The patrols thrive on stealth, so they hammered it into me for the whole time I was there. To their credit, it stuck, and now sneaking is just a habit for me. I was never very good with a bow, though, so I relied on my swordsmanship." Elena explained, reminded of the grueling training she went through as a child to get into the patrols.

"What was the training like?" Amanda asked as if reading Elena's mind.

"To make us faster they fastened these rings around our ankles and weighed them down with magic. Walking around with twenty to thirty extra pounds on your legs was pure hell, but it worked wonders, and after a few times you get used to them." Elena said involuntarily rubbing her ankles.

"Thank you for talking to me, Elena, I'll let you get to the food," Amanda curtsied and returned to the fire.

"Only a week to get to Seamander and this ends the first day," Elena said to herself. "I can't shake this feeling of dread I have, that when we get there the darkness will rise."

Chapter 23

As Michael woke up, gasping for breath, in a cold sweat, he realized it was just another nightmare. Michael had bad dreams a lot lately, most of them not even distinguishable anymore as he wakes up. Michael had finally recovered from the bandit ambush and had recently started training his body again. In three short weeks Michael felt completely out of shape, so much so that he nearly vomited from his old training regimen when he first attempted it.

Michael preferred using a staff or spear as his weapon, only relying on his sword as a backup. Michael's staff was made of fine steel, which he preferred because wood would shatter with one good swing of a sword, and other metals were just too heavy to be effective. Michael remembered the first time he wielded a staff, he had bruises all over his body from the times the staff smacked him. It took awhile to get used to it.

Whenever Michael or Anders trained Sophia would come and watch, Michael wasn't sure why, but he guessed it was because she worried about them. Sophia was definitely not a fighter, in fact, she hated fighting. That's why it was hard on her, having two older brothers that play leading roles in the King's army.

When Michael received word six days ago that Anders had left with a small group to Seamander to put an end to the bandit problem, he wanted desperately to go with him. He wanted to get out of the city he had been cooped up in for so long now that it made him twitch. Sadly, Father wouldn't allow it after he had just recovered. So, he was in the open courtyard, where he practiced his staff movements fluidly. He remembered the words of his teacher all too well. "If you wield the staff, you must be fluid like water. When you use the flow and momentum of the enemy to your advantage, the staff makes you invincible."

"Prince Michael!" a messenger boy yelled. As Michael turned to the boy and fastened his staff to his clamp, the boy ran quickly over to him. "I am terribly sorry to interrupt your training, but King MacArthur requested you immediately to the council chamber. It's very urgent."

"Thank you, squire, I shall head there now. You are dismissed," Michael ordered in accordance with standard protocol. As the boy ran off, Michael sighed and collected his thoughts before heading off toward the council chamber. It wasn't a long ways away, but it gave Michael enough time to wonder what the importance of his summoning was. As Michael opened the door to the chamber, he saw his father, King MacArthur, as well as Grimik and some Guard Captains.

"I believe you summoned me, Father?" Michael said giving a small bow of respect and walked over to the table.

"Yes, and now that you are here, I can explain why." King MacArthur gave a short pause and gestured to the map. "Our scouts have reported that an extremely large contingent of soldiers is heading toward the capital. The army is hostile and it will be here in a matter of hours." The news shocked Michael and he wondered who would possibly be attacking.

"Do we know how large the army is?" Michael questioned viewing the map.

"Our scouts estimate their numbers in the hundreds of thousands," The King said gravely. "It greatly outnumbers us at the current moment, as I had most of the army out searching for clues on the bandit uprisings."

"So we are doomed," Michael said bluntly. "They would slaughter us if we try to resist them."

"I know that. That is why I have contacted the elves. We will evacuate all of the citizens to the forest. The Elders have agreed to hide us until we can come up with a countermeasure. I have sent messages to the surrounding villages as well to evacuate."

"You're sure retreat is the only option? I mean no disrespect, My King, but I do not wish to see my home destroyed if we can prevent it," a Guard Captain said outraged.

"Yes, I am afraid retreat is the only option. Even if we secured the capital, we don't have nearly enough men to fend them off. I don't wish to see men die without cause," King MacArthur said solemnly. "We must live to fight another day when we have our entire force we can fight them on even terms." Michael could tell this wasn't an easy decision for father. He loved this city, he had no desire to see his people's homes and businesses destroyed, but he also didn't want to see people die needlessly.
It was better this way, homes can be replaced, lives can't, Michael thought to himself. The Guard Captain grudgingly accepted this and slammed his fist down on the table in frustration.

"Michael, since Anders is gone, you are in charge of the military. I know you can handle this," King MacArthur said faithfully. "Please help guide my people to safety."

"I will do all I can father," Michael bowed. King MacArthur smiled, the first time Michael had seen it in a long time, and Michael's determination flared brightly.

"Then this meeting is concluded. You are all dismissed," King MacArthur ordered.

*   *   *

Michael finally managed to gather all of the townspeople and evacuate them smoothly. Michael had to be delicate with his words, because if he lost his composure, everyone would panic. Michael ordered the soldiers to guide the civilians into wagons to transport faster, the soldiers riding on horseback alongside them.

Thankfully there were no problems and everyone was out of the city within a couple hours.

"I believe that is everyone, Father," Michael told him as he rode next to his horse.

"Good, then let's hope the army doesn't find out where we went. We should be long gone before they get here, but it's too close for my liking," King MacArthur said looking back at the city again.

"I made sure there were no traces of our departure. I just wish I knew who was attacking us," Michael said frustrated.

"Most likely the ones orchestrating those bandit uprisings. They figured they would hit us at our weakest, and it almost worked," King MacArthur said begrudgingly. "Blast it, if only I had kept more soldiers in the city, we wouldn't have to run. If we had Devlin's group here as well, we would be unstoppable."

"You mean the boy that wiped out a small army by himself?" Michael asked, remembering the report.

"Granted bandits aren't quite as combat effective as soldiers are, he destroyed half the army with a single spell. At least a hundred men burnt to a crisp. I have never seen anything like it in all my years." King MacArthur said in awe of the memory. "It almost worries me what he will do if he improves even more, such power wielded irresponsibly could very well do much more harm than good."

"I hope he can control his power then, for all our sakes," Michael said as he spurred his horse.

Chapter 24

    Raven led the massive army of soldiers on horseback, heading toward the Crestialis capital. She looked forward to crushing the King's forces after all her planning to weaken them. King MacArthur, the name she hated more than anything in this world. The same name of the man that had ruined her life and caused the murders of her family in cold blood. She would never forgive the MacArthur family for that suffering. She would not rest until MacArthur's head rested on a pike and his subjects bowed to her every whim.

    All of her careful planning was finally falling into place. Raven was the reigning Queen of Grandis, and she made sure everyone there knew it. She was in her mid-twenties and very beautiful. She had used her beauty many times to steal her way to the throne. That was when she stopped being weak and learned the true weaknesses of men. She had done many things in her life she wasn't proud of, many things that disgusted her to this day, but power takes sacrifice and that she knew all too well.

    She had long, jet-black hair and brown eyes that turn black when she angers. She had near flawless skin that was smooth and tanned from head to toe. She had a slim but fit frame and she stood only a bit shorter than the average man. She carried around a very intricately carved staff that she used to enhance her magic, made by the greatest of craftsmen. The very tip had a raven carved from a rare wizard gem.

    She was a harsh but fair queen, and while she did enjoy putting men in their place, she did feel sympathy for the few she didn't find detestable. Though she ruled with fear, the people loved her, because she wasn't afraid to do what needed to be done, and she got it done quickly. Today, though, she led a charge for revenge. The former King of Grandis, a cousin of King MacArthur's, was a cruel and heartless king, one she had held great hatred towards. Because of him, Raven's life was a living torment. Because of him, she had lost all those close to her. Because of him, she wanted to rid the world of him and all of his family, including the MacArthurs.

As Raven lead her hundreds of thousands of soldiers behind her to the capital, she saw it quickly coming into view. Raven smiled. Soon she would be rid of the scum.

As she got closer to the city gates, Raven noticed something off. There were no guards in sight. She guessed they might just be hiding and waiting for her to get close before attacking. Raven sent a powerful ball of energy toward the gate, which completely blew the huge steel doors off their hinges. As she rode through the gates, followed by her many soldiers, she was enraged to see the city completely empty.

"Where the hell are they?!" she screamed in frustration. "Drake! You said you made sure that every scout was killed!" Raven turned to her second-in-command.

"I did, My Queen. I hunted down every single one. They must have sent the message on before I got to them..." Drake said fearfully.

"They knew we were coming and ran before we got here. Not even a single villager to interrogate! You had better hope you find out where they went before I make you take their place!" Raven said, seething. Drake immediately deployed the troops, who systematically flooded the capital. Raven felt robbed like a common thief had just made a fool of her, and she couldn't stand it. She couldn't even enjoy watching the tainted city get ransacked by her soldiers. The soldiers made sure to steer clear of Raven, knowing all too well how she gets when she's mad. She would have to leave the city. She knew that if the king fled, he would be gathering his forces to strike back at her. Fighting his army at full force was not a risk she wanted to take.

"Soldiers! To me!" Raven ordered and her captains quickly went to her side. "Since the Great King Macoward managed to get away, we will head back to Grandis, but before that, destroy everything! Just the sight of this place now angers me beyond reason!" The soldiers quickly did as she asked, tearing apart houses and shops. Raven even shot a few energy blasts herself, using some of the houses as target practice. After she had vented some of her anger, she turned toward the castle. The castle was the thing she wanted to destroy the most. It was the symbol of King MacArthur's reign, and it was an insult to her. Raven walked over to the castle gates, easily blowing them aside as she had done to the first gate.

"Say goodbye to your beloved castle, Macoward. I hope you enjoy this little memento." Raven gathered every single ounce of magical energy she had and focused it on the ground beneath the castle. The ground started shaking, like the earth itself was trembling with Raven's power. Cracks in the earth opened all around the castle, and then cracks started appearing on the castle walls. Stone bricks ripped apart like paper as the castle started collapsing from the force of the earthquake Raven conjured. Raven didn't stop it until the castle had completely collapsed, and was no more than a pile of debris. The sight of the destroyed castle lifted Raven's spirits a little bit, but she wouldn't be satisfied until she had King MacArthur kissing her boots. "That arrogant fool... has evaded me... long enough," Raven said gasping, trying to recover her strength. As she turned around, she saw Drake and some of her captains, immediately tensing when she looked at them.

"Today's your lucky day, Drake, because now I'm too tired to kill you," Raven said, starting to regain her breath. "Fail me again, and I'll make killing you my first priority."

"I promise you I will not fail againnnnnnn!" Drake screamed as a crack as wide as Raven was tall formed right underneath him and swallowed him whole. The crack then slammed together with a loud crash, and Raven could smell the blood of Drake's crushed body.

"I know you won't fail me again, but I'm afraid I had some strength left after all." Raven observed the guards as she walked toward her horse. The captains quickly backed away from her like frightened children. Then Raven stopped and looked to one of her captains.

"Gorren, you are my new General. Make sure you don't make the same mistake Drake did, or I promise you I will do to you far worse than his quick death," Raven threatened coldly. She had to make sure failure would not be tolerated in her ranks. Fear, she felt, was the best way to control men. Kindness was a sign of weakness to her. Kindness gets people taken advantage of, and that was one thing she couldn't take anymore.

"Of course, Your Majesty!" Gorren responded dutifully.

"Good. Then let us head back to Grandis. I grow tired of this place, and I think MacArthur will greatly appreciate my little present." Raven yawned from boredom and mounted her black steed. She needed more power, enough power so that next time, he wouldn't escape, and Raven could have her revenge. For now, she would have to settle with destroying his home. She remembered a legend about a sword, a twin of Lux that had been made by a group of dwarves and elves that wanted it's power for their own. Maybe she would start there.

*   *   *

Raven, age eight, lived in a poor, hardened village in Grandis. She grew up a normal child, orphaned at age four, and having to beg for most of her meals on the side of the dirt road covered in filth. "Get away from me, demon!" they would scream at her, slapping her, or calling her other cruel, horrible names. Her village was influenced heavily by a false, cultist religion. They view mages as devil worshipers and demons in human bodies. In fact, that's how her parents were killed; people discovered her parents were both mages and burned them at the stake. That's why people looked at her like she was one too, but couldn't kill her unless she showed actual signs. She could still remember their screaming in her dreams. Their endless, horrid screams would ring on and on forever in her head. "Help me! Please God, it burns!" "Don't make me leave my children behind!" She woke up every morning crying and moist with cold sweat.

The thing she hated most was she couldn't even remember her parents' faces, just that they were kind and loving, more than any kid could ask for. "You're so beautiful, Raven, and you have your mother's eyes," her father would say. They didn't deserve the death they suffered, they were just unfortunate enough to have the rare power most humans weren't blessed with. Raven hated magic for it. She hated the cult for killing her parents, she hated that the only reason they were killed was because they had powers, and she hated all the people that had cheered as her parents were burned alive.

Raven herself didn't show any signs of magic. That was the sole reason she was still alive. Raven had nightmares day after day of her parent's deaths, and feared even more that one day, her own magic powers might surface and she would be killed just as painfully. All the family she had left was her one little brother, Crow, who was two years younger than Raven was. Crow was probably the only reason she ever got food, because he had such an adorable voice, that people just couldn't help but love him. "Sister, why are you crying?" he would ask her sometimes, even when Raven hadn't even realized she was crying.

Raven loved Crow for a lot more than that, though. He was the only friendly face she knew, the only person that didn't look at her like a demon waiting to reveal itself. Crow was the only person she trusted, and she would protect him with her life if she needed to. She would spend most of her time with him, playing with him, talking with him, and teaching him grown up things he had to know to survive. "Stay out of people's way, and be as polite as much as you can," she would tell him.

Two years later, her worst nightmare became reality. She discovered her magic powers and her brother's had surfaced within the same week. The discovery terrified her, partly because she knew that if she was discovered, she would die, but also for her little brother, who was just an innocent kid who didn't know any better. She tried hiding it the best she could, but one slip up was all it would take. Every day was filled with fear for her and Crow. She wanted to run away, but she knew she would die in the wilderness. She was too young and frail to defend herself from the wild beasts of the forests and she didn't know the first thing about survival there. All she had was that run down village, and a tinderbox just waiting to be lit.

Growing up was hard for Raven, but she at least managed to keep her powers in check. Crow was another story. He loved his powers and had almost gotten caught using them a couple times. She tried telling him it was dangerous, that he shouldn't use his powers around people, but he just didn't realize how much people feared magic. When Raven was eleven years old, her entire world was finally broken to pieces.

Crow was playing with water down by the creek, using the water to clean himself, and a priest saw him with water floating all around Crow. Before Raven even knew what had happened, the monks of the cult snatched her brother from her. "Noooo!!! Let him go! He's just a kid, he hasn't done anything wrong!" Raven cried helplessly, pounding her fists on the monks. They just spat on her and kicked her away. Raven tried getting up, tried to save him. She had to save him, but she was too late. The monks took Crow to the High Priest, who held a ritual dagger in his hand.

"Consider yourself lucky, demon, that you are too young by law to burn at the stake. We will just burn your body instead," the High Priest spat as he took the dagger, ready to kill Crow. He stopped to perform a short prayer first. Raven ran over to Crow, trying to break him free, suddenly wishing she knew magic that could release him, but she was punched hard in the face by a monk, and another two monks restrained her as the High Priest finished his prayer.

"Quit hurting my sister! Stop, please stop!" The High Priest grabbed the screaming Crow's shoulder and plunged the dagger into his heart. Crow's screaming ceased and his body just fell, like a puppet that had just had it's strings cut. The look of agony was still very present on his face even as he died. Raven watched in horror as her only brother, the only person in the whole god-forsaken world she loved, hit the ground with a thud. That thud was the final cord of Raven's sanity and she snapped along with it.

Raven screamed, a horrible, ear-piercing scream as all of her magical energy that she hid burst through her at once. Raw magical energy reacted with her rage and she completely lost control herself. The two monks holding her were catapulted through the air and died upon impact with the ground. The energy sparked like lightning, a physical manifestation of her current storm of emotions. Her hatred for the high priest had shown purely in Raven's eyes, and with a simple wave of her hand, she hit him with a wave of pure magic. She blew a row of cheap, wooden houses to pieces along with him. Raven's rage was palpable in the very air, amplified by her energy, creating a whirlwind of destruction all around her. Whole houses and buildings were ripped from their foundations and thrown into the air. When she finally ran out of energy and fell unconscious from the strain on her body, she had reduced the entire village to dust and debris, having killed every person there.

When Raven woke up a whole day later, she was shocked at the complete destruction of the village she grew up in. *Did I really do all this?* She cried, horrified at what she had done. The only thing around her left intact was her brother's body. His limp body had since relaxed, but his eyes were still wide open. Raven sobbed above him for what seemed like hours, unable to stop, unable to get a hold of herself. She was the only one alive in a destroyed village. She hated the High Priest, she hadn't regretted killing him, but she didn't want to kill everyone else. She hated her magic. Why had she been cursed with it in the first place? Magic had caused nothing but misery for her her entire life, and now the only person she loved was dead.

"So you are the one that did this," an old woman spoke, walking up to Raven.

"Go away," Raven cried, not even able to muster up any strength to move. "Those people were right, I am a demon."

"You are hardly a demon, child," the old woman laughed. "These people got what was coming to them, one way or another, and now they are dead. Their irrational fear starting the very flame they hoped to contain."

"That doesn't mean I wanted to kill them. I never wanted any of this," Raven pleaded.

"Of course you didn't. But sometimes things out of our control twist our lives completely around, and time doesn't wait for you to rebuild yourself. It just keeps flowing like a river and doesn't stop," the old woman explained. Raven looked back at her, taking her in for the first time. She was ancient looking, wrinkles all over her face from age, and her hair was white as snow. Though she was old, the woman had a strength about her, like the very air hummed with her energy.

"You can sense it, can't you?" the woman asked her. "I can tell by the look on your face. I suppose I'm not hiding it very well, but I'm still impressed you can sense the magic of other people at such an early age."

"So you're just like me then, you're a mage," Raven said sullenly, then smiled in spite of herself.

"I can teach you how to control your magic, my dear, and make you more powerful than you ever thought possible," the old woman offered.

"Why would you help me?" Raven asked her with disbelief. "You don't know anything about me, besides the fact that I'm a murderer."

"I suppose it's because you remind me of myself at your age. Also, I'd hate to see so much potential go to waste. I feel like fate has something in store for you, and I have little better to do at my age." The old woman laughed. "What is your name, little one?"

"Raven, and yours?" Raven asked.

"Call me Cassandra," she told Raven.

Raven trained under Cassandra, learning to control her magic and shape it into manipulative forms. Her magic was very powerful and her strength only grew as each year passed. At age sixteen, she had learned everything Cassandra had to teach her. Raven had learned to accept her power, and she relished in it. She felt such power coursing through her, and it was an exhilarating feeling for her. She was hardened after the destruction of her village. She didn't care about others anymore. She wanted to change things in the country, to take control and right the injustices done to her, starting with the king. Then started Raven's long rise to power.

Chapter 25

As Devlin watched the road pass by him, he yearned to see his brothers and sister again. Riding on his horse with Elena wrapping her arms securely around him they rode full speed toward the capital of Seamander. Anders riding with Amanda, and Luke riding his own horse were close behind him. They were still half a day's ride from the Capital, meaning it would be dark by the time they got there. Luke had suggested camping another night, but the city wasn't that far off and Devlin wanted to sleep in a real bed again. Luke didn't argue his point, so Devlin knew he wanted to just as much as Devlin did.

Still having a long way to go, Elena and Devlin viewed the scenery. The plains, already golden from the long grass surrounding them, reflected off a golden, amber-ish glow from the sun as it finished setting on the day. Devlin couldn't take his eyes off the beautiful sight as the red, yellow, and orange of the diminishing light intermingled into a cascade of flame-like brilliance over the void of the vast prairie. *This is what it's like to travel. Taking in the sights like this and seeing new places. I hope I can travel more, once things settle down,* Devlin thought awestruck to himself. Elena watched the scenery as well, never seeing anything like it having lived in a forest most of her life. The sun's rays dimmed and dimmed, until it was completely set, exchanging the warm blanket of sunlight, with the chilling breeze and dark shroud of night, like a blanket covering the sky in slow motion. Devlin passed the time keeping a lookout for anything in front of them. Sadly, the plains weren't much fun to look at, as every patch of grass in front of them looked the same as the patch behind them.

Devlin could feel himself fidgeting, getting impatient. He wanted to get there and start looking for clues, he felt like he was so close to finally finding his family.

"Devlin, aren't you getting tired at all? Maybe I should lead for a while." Elena asked concerned.

"I'm fine, we're almost there anyway," Devlin insisted, denying his onsetting fatigue.

"Alright, but if you start falling asleep, I'm taking over tough guy," Elena warned him in that usual half-serious half-joking manner of hers. Devlin appreciated Elena looking out for him, she really was a caring person when she wasn't busy teasing or playing pranks on him. Devlin didn't mind it much, though. In fact, he liked it. She helped lighten the mood for him whenever he was feeling down on himself. *I hope I'll still see her when all this is over.* Devlin looked ahead again, and to his relief, he saw the port capital of Seamander, not too much farther ahead. His relief, however, was quickly replaced with shock, as he saw a massive, off-colored explosion at the gate closest to them, no more than a hundred meters ahead. As Devlin looked closer to the fallen gate, Devlin saw a huge group of people storm through it.

"What the heck is going on?" Devlin asked incredulously, seeing the ragtag army led by a single mage.

"Those could only be the rebels of this country. They must have planned an attack on the capital. What timing, that we should see the attack in progress like this," Luke told him.

"Should we join them?" Anders asked Luke, the same question burning in Devlin's mind.

"Let's see what happens first before we go storming in," Luke said hesitantly. Devlin wondered if his siblings were in that army. If they were, they were most definitely in danger. Devlin felt conflicted, should he risk his life, saving the ones he loved who may not even be there, or stay behind and keep out of it?

"Let's go," Devlin said making his decision.

"Devlin, wait, I know how you must feel but your siblings most likely aren't even in that army," Elena objected.

"She's right, Devlin, we have to wait and scope out the situation first," Anders told him.

"And what if they are in that army? What if they are about to die and need my help? I wouldn't be able to live with myself if any of them died, especially when I could have stopped it," Devlin said angrily. Luke, despite himself, smiled at Devlin's resolve. Luke expected no less from him, and that was the thing he respected most about him.

"Well, Luke?" Anders asked again.

"Let's go," Luke ordered and rode his horse to the fallen gate.

"You won't have to tell me twice." Devlin smiled and spurred his horse to full speed with Anders and Amanda close behind.

"Devlin, before you go jumping into battle and all, look at the walls." Elena pointed. Following her hand he saw row upon row of archers on the wall, all preparing to fire when the army entered the gate.

"They're walking into a trap! Those archers will kill at least half of them in one swoop," Devlin said shocked. "Damnit! Anders, take my horse! Elena, you take one side of the gate, I'll take the other!" Devlin and Elena worked as one as they both simultaneously jumped off the horse. As Devlin came close to the ground he used magic to catapult him to the top of the wall, Elena doing the same. Time seemed to slow for Devlin as he flew through the air, hurtling toward the top of the barricades. When Devlin got close to the top of the wall he adjusted himself with his magic and used it to resist the fall, dropping Devlin onto the stone ground as if he had only jumped two feet up.

As Devlin landed on top of the wall, right next to at least three-dozen archers with notched arrows, he incapacitated them all with a bolt of lightning from his palm, the spell jumping from archer to archer in a matter of seconds. Satisfied that he'd foiled the trap, he looked over to see that Elena had a similar success, using wind magic to whip them all off the wall and down thirty meters to the hard ground below. Not wanting to waste energy getting down, Devlin quickly ran to the nearest ladder. He slid down the ladder, grabbing onto the smooth edges, and down to the fray below. As Devlin hit the ground he was surprised to see the mage who was leading the charge before with his palm towards Devlin.

"Are you friend or foe, boy?" Athon asked him threateningly. "Speak carefully, or you die where you stand."

"I just happened to be in the neighborhood and saw that you needed some help. Don't worry, you can thank me later," Devlin said facetiously. Athon simply laughed at that.

"Fair enough, then how about you head toward the castle? Our leader is leading an assassination plan for the King up there, and it never hurts to have a little backup. We can handle it from here," Athon told him then ran before Devlin could respond as if expecting him to do it.

"Very well," Devlin said as he ran to the only castle-like structure he saw.

* * *

As Luke reached the gate, he dismounted his horse and ran to the closest group of soldiers he could find. As he ran, he watched the exchange between Athon and Devlin and saw him running toward the castle. He was a bit surprised and also somewhat relieved to see Elena close behind Luke, sword drawn. Luke drew his sword as well and readied his shield as he slashed at the closest guard to him. Luke could tell the guards were very well trained, however, as the soldier blocked his slash at the last second. However, a rebel took advantage of Luke's distraction and stabbed the soldier in the heart.

Elena seemed to have trouble as well, the guards blocked her slashes, even though she was too quick for them to touch her. Frustrated, Elena infused her sword with electricity, and each slash afterward was crippling even though the soldiers blocked her. *Clever girl,* Luke thought as he outmaneuvered a soldier with a fake slash, and stabbed him in the stomach. Anders seemed to have less trouble, his greatsword sweeping through a few soldiers at a time. Amanda stayed close to him, watching his back with a drawn dagger. She was surprisingly quick with it, striking like a snake at whatever soldier came near her. After about half of the men were either killed or injured, the rest simply lost what little will they had to fight and dropped their swords.

These men are victims, Luke reminded himself. He doubted they really wanted to fight them in the first place, only complying out of fear for their lives. Luke had heard the story of how a pirate had taken over this country; this was a nation taken hostage. Luke watched Athon as he approached a single soldier.

"You win, please spare us, I don't wish to fight my own kin anymore." The soldier said pitifully.

"Agreed," Athon told him. The rebels and the soldiers, fellow countrymen both, withdrew their arms. What Luke saw next was something he wasn't expecting. Several men formally on opposing sides reached out and embraced each other. Most of them were brothers, father and son, or just old friends separated by duty. Luke couldn't imagine having to kill his own brother, and he didn't want to. *A war among brothers was the worst kind of war, no matter the result, both sides lose.* As Luke headed over to the group of soldiers he noticed a dirty, rat-faced man screaming at the soldiers.

"What do you cowards think you're doing?! Kill the rebels, or die!" The man ordered. He looked out of place in his fine clothes, like a dressed up vermin. Luke drew a throwing dagger from his belt and hurled it at the pirate. The dagger flew, spinning end over end, and lodged into the pirate's throat. His threats quickly replaced with muffled gags, as he collapsed to the ground. The soldiers looked at Luke, shocked at what he had just done, then cheered, like oppressed slaves that had just been freed.

* * *

Devlin ran through the empty pathways to the castle. Luckily, the path to the castle was pretty straight forward, so Devlin had no issues navigating to it. Devlin was curious as to what the king was like to a cause a civil war such as this. He also wondered what the "leader" was like. Devlin wished the mage had at least given him a description of them. There were a couple guards at the closed castle gate who, upon seeing Devlin, immediately ran to engage him.

The guard on the right slashed downward at Devlin, which he easily dodged with a sidestep. Devlin brought his blade down for the guard's exposed neck, but the second guard covered for him with his shield. The second guard then tried stabbing at Devlin, which he deflected with his sword. The first guard got up and tried another downward slash at Devlin, forcing him to step backward.

Devlin was getting frustrated from this, he could just use magic to take care of them, but that would cost him more energy he did not want to use. Devlin got a lucky break when the first guard charged him, leaving himself open. Devlin waited until the guard swung at him to dodge behind him, and decapitated him from behind. What Devlin wasn't expecting, however, was that the second guard charged him. The guard was on top of him before Devlin had time to react. Having no choice, Devlin placed his palm toward the guard, and magic shot outward with a blast of pure force. The guard was sent hurtling toward a stone building and crashed into a wall.

Devlin knew the sound of the fight would draw attention to him, so he quickly ran to the castle gate. Using the same spell he had used to get to the archers, Devlin rocketed over the gate itself and landed on the other side. *I can't waste any more energy. I'm already getting tired from all the spells I used.* Devlin ran up to the giant wooden doors, and quickly entered the castle.

*　　*　　*

"So, Valcara, how exactly do we plan to get out of here?" Derek asked her.

"Easy, those fools only striped us of our weapons, but I always keep a pick or two in my boot in case I get caged. My father used to throw me into a cell like this as a punishment sometimes, picking this lock will be child's play." Valcara explained searching the inside of her boot. Valcara took out the pick and gently twisted the pick inside the lock mechanism of the cell. After a minute of this, the cell opened with a satisfying clank. Valcara opened Derek's and Roark's cells with the same method, and they grabbed their weapons off the ground in the corner of the room.

"I'm impressed, Valcara, I never pegged you as a lockpick," Roark said gratefully as he attached his sword to his belt.

"How else do you think I survived as a king's daughter?" Valcara scoffed and ran toward the end of the row of cells. "I needed to kill time somehow, and it wasn't going to be timeout in a prison cell."

"I kind of feel bad for your dad." Derek laughed following close behind her. "You must've been a handful."

"You better believe it!" Valcara laughed at one memory in particular when she had made father so mad his face turned red.

Valcara, Derek, and Roark stood against the wall, waiting for Valcara's signal. Valcara made a chopping motion with her hand and kicked open the door. There was a single guard outside the door, caught completely off guard by Valcara's sudden entrance. Valcara took advantage of the guard's slow reaction and hit him with a really hard punch to the gut, knocking the wind out of him. Then she hit him in the back the head with the pommel of her sword.

"What do we do now?" Roark asked. "Are we still going to assassinate the king?"

"The rotten toothed pirate has a lot to answer for. You better believe we are killing him," Valcara said coldly. "I swear on my life itself if he so much as touches my brother, I'll cut off all his fingers and feed them to him."

With Valcara taking the lead, the trio ran quickly down the hall to once again meet Scurvy Jaw.

* * *

Sneaking around in the castle, Devlin made his way to the top floor of the castle. The way Devlin figured it, a big, important room like an audience chamber would be at the top of the castle. He decided to follow that ideology and work his way down. He was tempted to interrogate a guard, but Devlin didn't want to risk losing more energy than he already had. Once he made it to the top floor, Devlin noticed it was nearly empty. In fact, the only guards he saw were the two guarding a pair of doors, he guessed were to the audience chamber.

The guards looked bored and exhausted, meaning Devlin could easily take them out if he wanted to, but challenging them directly would probably just alert more guards, so Devlin came up with a little plan. Devlin focused his energy on a door handle across the room from Devlin. With his magic he pulled the door open, causing the guards to get curious. Both of them went to check the door and walked into the room. Once they were in, Devlin used his magic to push the door shut and lock it. *Perfect, and I barely broke a sweat doing it.* Now that the hallway was clear, Devlin strolled up to the door the two guards were in front of. Devlin was about to open the door a crack to try and see inside when a woman clad in the uniform of the guards tackled him. *Where the heck did she come from? I thought I just took care of the last of the guards!* Devlin was panicking and the woman drawing a sword to his throat didn't help at all.

"Who are you supposed to be? You're certainly not a guard, yet you're skulking around the corridor like a common thief," The woman questioned suspiciously. "I saw you use magic on those guards. So if you so much as twitch, and I'll cut your throat clean in two." Coming up behind her were two other men in the guard's uniform and for some reason, they looked really familiar.

"Devlin? Is that you?" The guard said in disbelief, which confused Devlin beyond reason. *How does he know my name? And why does he sound so familiar?*

"Oh maker, it's him, Derek! I'd recognize that stupid expression anywhere!" The other guard said. *Wait, Derek? No, it can't be.* The woman looked back at them just as confused as Devlin was.

"Wait, so this is your lost brother?" The woman asked. The two guards raised their visors, and when Devlin saw their faces, he could feel himself tearing up. It was his two brothers that he been looking for all this time, and here they were, standing right in front of him. Devlin felt overwhelmed, he didn't know how to react. He wasn't exactly expecting to see them with a sword at his throat, especially in guard uniforms. The woman got off Devlin, and Derek pulled him to his feet, embracing him, with Roark not far behind. Devlin wished he could pause time and just enjoy seeing his family once again. Devlin hadn't even realized until that moment just how much he missed them, and how much they had missed Devlin.

"I feared I'd never see you two again... thank the Maker you survived," Devlin said, not able to hold back his tears anymore.

"I was scared to death... thinking those mercenaries had killed you, instead of kidnapping you like they did to us," Derek told Devlin, crying just as much as Devlin was. "We had no idea what happened."

"We even found Cece in a prison just like we were, but you were nowhere to be found," Roark sobbed. "I missed you so much, brother..."

"Boys, I hate to interrupt your touching reunion, but we kind of have a job to do," Valcara said awkwardly.

"She's right, we still have to assassinate that tyrant," Derek said still trying to regain his composure.

"So I guess that means you are the 'leader' leading this assassination?" Devlin asked Valcara, wiping the tears from his eyes.

"You heard of me?" Valcara asked him.

"Yeah, a mage leading the rebels told me you'd be here. I wasn't expecting you to be dressed up as guards, though," Devlin explained.

"Athon's alive and well then?" Valcara said surprised.

"He is, although he was about to fall into a trap, my friends and I foiled it," Devlin told her.

"Thank the maker," Valcara said looking more relieved than Devlin imagined she would, but he didn't question it.

"Let's settle this, Valcara," Roark resolved.

"Right," Valcara said, collecting herself. "Let's go." Roark and Derek needed no encouragement, opening the two doors wide. This time, Scurvy sitting on his throne, most likely waiting for news of the battle. Scurvy's eyes widened with shock as he saw the four of them enter the room.

"How'd ya get out o' yer cell?" Scurvy inquired angrily. "I see ya brough' another rat wit' ya too."

"This is the guy you guys want to kill?" Devlin asked recoiling. "I'm surprised his own stench hasn't done the job for you."

"Shut it, ya sheep-brained piece a filth!" Scurvy screamed.

"Oh, I'm going to enjoy this..." Devlin said turning cold.

"Release my brother you scurvy-ridden cur!" Valcara insulted back. Roark failed to suppress a giggle, enraging Scurvy Jaw even more.

"That's it! When me boys arrre done wit' ya, I'll feed you to the sea!" Scurvy shouted, and as if on cue, a dozen pirates entered the room. Each one holding either a wave-like sword or a two-headed ax. The pirates were big, but Devlin could tell by their stance alone that they weren't very organized, or well-trained. Their stench seemed more dangerous to Devlin than their swords did. Each of the four burst into action against the pirates. Devlin slid under one pirate between his legs, pulling his ankles with him. When the pirate fell face-first to the ground, Devlin tackled the second one to the ground and stabbed him through the heart.

Valcara easily blocked slashes from two of the pirates and sidestepped when they charged her. As one pirate ran towards her she slashed at his legs, cutting off his feet. The sound of his screams annoyed Valcara, so she stabbed him in the neck, cutting his windpipe. The other pirate, enraged at seeing his friend killed, swung wildly at Valcara. As she blocked each blow, the third pirate tried striking her from behind. The pirate stabbed at her, missed, and accidentally stabbed the other pirate in the stomach. Valcara grinned venomously and slashed the last pirate in half.

Derek and Roark attacked as a team, taking on the remaining six. Luckily for them, the remaining pirates weren't as big as the others, and they took out two of them with no more than a couple of well-placed stabs. The biggest of the group bore down on Devlin with his huge ax. Devlin barely held him off, his strength overwhelming. The pirate Devlin had tripped before decided to charge him while Devlin was preoccupied. Valcara saw this and tackled the charging pirate.

Devlin, unable to bear the weight of the pirate anymore, deflected the ax to the side, and slashed at the pirate's leg, leaving a deep cut. The pirate reflexively grabbed his leg, giving Devlin an opening to slash at his neck, slitting the pirate's throat and he fell to the floor dead.

Scurvy, seeing that the battle wasn't going to his favor, started to flee. Devlin wanted to stop him, but he was completely exhausted after fighting with the huge pirate, and his two brothers were still finishing off the last of their group of pirates. Devlin looked to Valcara, who had already snapped the neck of the pirate who tried to tackle him before, and she was running toward the pirate king. Devlin held no objection to that, he was so tired he could barely move.

"I won't let you get away!" Valcara screamed ruthlessly. She grabbed a throwing dagger from her belt, aimed, and threw it straight at Scurvy Jaw. The knife sank deep into Scurvy's back, and Scurvy collapsed from the pain. Scurvy groaned every curse imaginable before Valcara kicked him in the ribs and pulled his head up by grabbing his greasy hair.

"Tell me where my brother is!" Valcara screamed.

"Why should I tell ya?" Scurvy spat out blood.

"I swear, if you don't, I'll knock out all of the teeth you have left and shove them down your throat," Valcara said coldly. The look on her face terrified Devlin, and he was suddenly really glad he was not on her bad side. Derek and Roark had finally finished off the last pirate and ran over to Valcara. He almost felt bad for the pirate, almost. Some of the rebels Devlin had seen in the battle before ran through the doors. They were accompanied by a young boy with the same eyes and skin as Valcara.

"Milady! We rescued the prince from the lower dungeons unharmed," A rebel announced to her.

"Sister!" The boy cried smiled wide at her. "It's really you!" All the coldness, the bitterness, and hate melted from her face when she laid eyes on her little brother. He looked somewhat aged from when she had last seen him, but he still looked mostly the same. Valcara left Scurvy to Derek and Roark and ran to embrace him. The smile on her face when she hugged him, was enough to make Devlin tear up all over again, the memory of how it felt to see his brothers again for the first time, still fresh in his mind. Valcara felt tears of sweet joy run down her face as he held her little brother close, but she didn't care. Valcara felt like a piece of her that she had lost, had been restored to her. Then and there, nothing could upset her, she felt complete for the first time in ages.

"Celebrate… while ya can… ya scallywags… but I be the one… havin' the las' laugh…" Scurvy grunted out, having a hard time breathing. "Ya think… yer camp was safe… from me? Ha… haha… I sen' out some a me men… from across the plains… to wipe yer camp… off the face a the earth. All yer women… all yer children, they'll be dead soon enough…" After Scurvy finished forcing out those worlds, Derek realized, with great horror, that meant Cece too.

"Arrrghhhh!" Derek screamed as he stabbed Scurvy through the heart in his rage. "Well?! Didn't you hear him? Back to the camp! Now!" Valcara ordered as she let go of her brother and ran towards the door.

Chapter 26

As Michael walked into the hut of the Elder, He saw both the Elder and Father both with very worried looks on their faces.

"Lux has started shining again, more frequently, and much more brightly. This does not bode well, Your Majesty. If your capital has truly been attacked, then this is something we cannot ignore," the Elder explained.

"Agreed. My scouts report that the troops that have attacked my capital are leaving and that they fly the flag of Grandis." King MacArthur stated uncomfortably. "It troubles me because that is the Kingdom of my cousin Gabriel. We were never close by any means, but he would never attack his own family."

"Perhaps there is a new leader in charge?" Michael suggested.

"That's certainly possible. But if that's the case, what happened to my cousin?" King MacArthur questioned thoughtfully. "I haven't heard anything from Grandis in years."

"Our main focus should be to get Devlin back here as soon as possible. The young girl, Amanda, told me Devlin was prophesied to wield Lux, making Devlin our best hope for dealing with this crisis," the Elder recalled. "I wish I had known that before he left. I could have let him take the sword and save us a lot of trouble. Do you know where he was headed last, Your Majesty?"

"He was headed for the capital of Seamander to look for clues about his missing siblings," King MacArthur answered.

"Then I shall send a messenger bird to him. It should reach there in a day or two," The Elder concluded.

"How do you know it will find him?" Michael asked confused.

"When we send a messenger bird, we can implant a homing spell on them to find the person we need the message to go to. We just need to know his general location. To make absolutely sure, I will be following its movements with a seeing spell to adjust the path of the bird if need be," the Elder explained. "What will you do, Your Majesty?" the Elder asked urgently.

"Once all of my forces have gathered, we will head back to the capital to rebuild and fortify the city. I want to make sure we are ready in case Grandis attacks again. The rest of the troops should be gathered within the next couple of days. In the meantime, I shall quickly write the letter to Devlin. He'll be more likely to recognize a letter with the royal seal on it." King MacArthur resolved.

* * *

As Raven's forces made their way back to Grandis, Raven began forming her next plan. She had heard rumors that the dark twin of Lux, Tenebrae, held the power of dominion, meaning that whoever wields it gains control of whatever it defeats, and grows stronger with each person under its control. She could turn armies against their own commanders with such a sword. She could quite literally conquer the world with Tenebrae, with no one to stand against her. No one could hurt her like she had been as a child. The only issue was finding the sword... She would have to find the sword quickly to destroy MacArthur's Kingdom. It was only a matter of time before she had the entire world in her hand.

* * *

As Devlin, and his group led the army of rebels back to the base, leaving Athon to help maintain the capital, Derek worried more and more that they would be too late. Scurvy's threat hung heavily on his mind, and Derek could tell his brothers felt the same way. Derek was greatly relieved to see Devlin alive and well, fearing the worst had happened to him back at the carnival. But his relief was overshadowed by the possibility of Cecelia's life slipping through his fingers.

Derek could feel himself getting more and more lethargic, having battled the entire night. Now, the sun was rising over the horizon, as his company hadn't stopped riding since he left Seamander's capital.

As Derek rode up to the formerly hidden passage into the camp, he felt the blood in his veins run cold as he saw the mechanism blocking the passage moved out of the way. Derek lead the horse down the lit passageway quickly, hoping beyond hope he wasn't too late. As the passageway opened wide into the rebel's camp, Derek's fears became reality before his eyes. Homes were burning or destroyed, soldiers were swarming the entire area, and some women already lay dead on the ground.

"Quickly! We have to save the women and children!" Derek shouted angrily. The men and Derek's friends behind him shouted their agreement and followed him as they charged the soldiers. These weren't the soldiers of Seamander like back at the capital; they donned different armor with a raven on the breastplate. Derek jumped off his horse and ran straight to the closest group of soldiers with Roark and Valcara close behind. All three of them slashed desperately to stop the soldier's destructive rampage. Devlin, Elena, and Amanda split off and fought as a trio as well against oncoming soldiers.

Anders and Luke cut a path right through a line of soldiers, putting their great skill to work on any man they came across. The men split off as well, aiding the three teams and fighting with everything they had, some for the very lives of their families they left here. Derek slashed the limbs off soldiers trying to cut down women indiscriminately. Valcara helped him by stabbing the armless men in the heart. Valcara left a path of death wherever she went, killing soldiers left and right, determined to protect her people. As the soldiers realized they were being attacked, many started surrounding Derek, striking at him from all directions. Roark, seeing his brother in trouble, quickly slashed his way to him, killing soldiers from behind, and pushing them out of the way. When Roark finally made it to Derek, Derek was being overwhelmed by the sheer numbers of the soldiers. Roark tried stabbing, hacking, and slashing with his sword, as well as beating soldiers with his shield. Roark's efforts gave Derek some time to recover, but the fighting still continued all around them.

Devlin, still trying to conserve his already scarce energy, relied mostly on hand-to-hand combat. Fighting at the capital had taken a huge toll on him, and he had to ride through the night without rest. Devlin felt safer having Amanda with him, knowing that she could heal him if he got too beat up. Elena was a big help as well. Her speed made her much faster than the attacking soldiers, and she had no trouble taking them out one after another with her precise strikes and efficient movements. Amanda mostly left the fighting to Elena and Devlin, but she didn't hesitate to use her dagger when a soldier got too close.

After finishing off a couple groups of the soldiers, Devlin finally spotted Cecelia. He felt great relief at seeing her sister alive, but as he observed those around her, Devlin saw a single man. The man Devlin saw fighting to protect her left him speechless from the shock. There, in full plated armor, was his father cutting through soldiers like butter. He fought like a demon gone mad and cut down every soldier who tried to harm the women and children around Cece. Devlin couldn't believe his eyes, thinking there must be some mistake. *How is he alive? I saw him run straight into a horde of mercenaries!* Devlin got over his disbelief, thankful that Cece was safe, and slowly made his way towards her.

As Devlin was heading toward Cece, however, he didn't notice that he was getting further and further away from Elena and Amanda. Before Devlin realized he was separated he was surrounded by soldiers. Emboldened by the fact that Devlin was alone, they all rushed him at once. Devlin, seeing that he couldn't stop them all, had to resort to his magic. Devlin gathered energy in the palm of his hand and placed it flat on the ground. He let the energy loose all at once, creating an explosive shock wave that toppled all of the approaching soldiers in one fell swoop.

The shockwave drew Cecelia's attention, and she saw Devlin as the soldiers around him collapsed. Her heart filled with joy and relief at the sight of him. She felt like all the weight she had carried was lifted off of her shoulders. She had felt a similar feeling when her father had come out of nowhere to rescue her. It was because of his protection that she was still alive. She realized with grief that the sight of conflict would have horrified her before her abduction, but now, she didn't care anymore. Cecelia didn't feel the same after she had killed that guard in front of her cell. Her thoughts went to Anna, and she wondered how she was doing. She hoped that she was safe from all this chaos.

Then, to Cecelia's horror, she saw a pair of soldiers charge Devlin from behind. One of them held a massive hammer, the other had a sword. The soldier with the hammer was only a few feet from her brother before Devlin realized he was being charged at. Devlin, too tired to react, was slammed by a sideways swing of the soldier's hammer. Devlin was launched in the air like a rocket and landed hard on the ground several feet from where he had been hit. Luckily for Devlin, the armor absorbed most of the hit, but it sapped the last of his strength as a result. Unable to move, Devlin was as good as dead for the other soldier, who smiled wide at the chance to take out the powerful mage-warrior.

The soldier brought the tip of his sword to Devlin's heart, as if marking the spot his sword would stand. Cecelia realized with great horror, as she saw him raise his sword high, the soldier was about to bring an end to the brother she loved. Cecelia searched for something, anything, she could use to save Devlin. She wouldn't let him die after finally seeing him again. Cecelia searched her brain for something to do, and to her amazement, noticed something she had never seen before, like a part of her that had stayed hidden and she didn't even realize it was there. It was energy, powerful energy, and as she tapped into it, the energy flowed throughout her body, as if looking for a way to be released. *Is this what I think it is? Have I had this power and just never realized it?*

Cecelia resolved herself and gathered all the energy she had into her hands. She released a powerful ball of raw energy that hit the soldier on top of Devlin as he brought his sword down for Devlin's heart. The impact sent the soldier hurtling into a collapsed hut and landed harder than any man could live through. Devlin was completely caught off guard, thinking for certain he was about to die. Devlin looked over to Cecelia, a mixture of awe and disbelief on his face. Cecelia felt just as shocked as Devlin did, but she felt so weak that she blacked out as the powerful magic she had used took it's overwhelming toll on her body.

*   *   *

When Devlin was hit from behind by the huge Warhammer, he was completely helpless as his armor absorbed the last of his strength. When the second soldier walked over to Devlin, he knew he was finished. *If I have to die here, please maker, just let my family be safe.*

Devlin watched as the sword of the soldier rose higher and higher, and Devlin braced for the blow he expected to come. To Devlin's great shock, the soldier was launched off of him and through the air into a collapsed hut, saving Devlin's life. *Did Elena save me?* Devlin looked toward the opposite direction of where the soldier had been sent flying and was even more shocked to see Cecelia with her left palm facing where the soldier had been. *My sister is a mage?! When did that happen?* Devlin didn't know what to think but reminded himself that there was still the soldier with the hammer to deal with.

To Devlin's horror, Cecelia's eyes closed and her body went limp. Before she fell down, though, Father caught her and just looked at her. Unlike Devlin, he wasn't surprised at Cecelia's magic powers. In fact, he had a look of great pride on his face. Father handed Cecelia to a strong looking woman.

"Take care of her for me would you?" Father said to her and the woman smiled proudly.

"Of course, sir." The woman bowed slightly.

Devlin tried getting up as the soldier with the hammer walked over to Devlin, clearly annoyed that now he had to get his hands dirty. The soldier was a huge, burly man, his muscles much more defined than the average soldier. His armor was also a bit nicer than the other soldiers. *This guy must be the commander, he's strong. Really strong. If it weren't for my armor, that hammer swing of his would've snapped me in half.* Devlin managed to sit up slightly but that was as far as he got when he felt excruciating pain in his ribs. "Argh!" Devlin screamed as the pain erupted in his ribs. *Blast it all. the blow must've broken a rib.* The commander grinned, realizing Devlin's inability to move.

"Just stay still boy, I'll make this quick," the commander said, raising his hammer.

"I don't think so, friend. That's my son you're standing over," Father said coldly. "I suggest you back away from him unless you want to lose an arm."

"I'm the one in charge of this army, old man. I don't take orders from anyone!" the commander yelled angrily at Father. "If you want to die first, it's fine by me. I was sent to kill all of you scum anyway. The order in which you all die makes no difference." The commander stepped toward Father and readied his massive hammer. The commander swung the hammer so fast, Devlin could barely follow it, but Father rolled out of the way almost effortlessly.

"I've fought men a lot bigger and a lot faster than you. I may be getting old, but I'm not so weak to die to a weakling like you," Father threatened as he brought his razor sharp sword down on the commander's arm just below the shoulder. The sword cut through the limb, completely cutting it off. The commander screamed in pain, his other arm letting go of the hammer and gripping his stub where his arm used to be. "I told you you'd lose an arm," Father grinned dangerously. "And unless you want to lose the other, get your men and scram."

*   *   *

As Derek fought the last of the soldiers surrounding him, he could feel himself getting more and more exhausted. It showed in his swordsmanship, as his slashes became sloppy and it took a lot longer to beat the enemy soldiers. Valcara and Roark were having the same problem, barely managing to hold off the innumerable amount of soldiers. Derek was both relieved and shocked when he saw all of the soldiers suddenly turn tail and run. Derek at least had the pleasure of seeing Valcara and Roark just as confused as he was. As the crowd of soldiers cleared, Derek saw his father. The man he had thought for certain was dead was helping Devlin get up off the ground.

"Roark, look over there, and tell me what you see? I want to make sure the lack of sleep isn't making me hallucinate," Derek said, pointing toward Father in disbelief.

"You're not crazy," Roark answered, his voice shaking. "I see him too." Derek and Roark mustered up the last of their strength to run over to Father and Devlin. As they ran over, Father noticed them and smiled with pride.

"You two look like you were run over by a pack of horses," Father laughed, looking just as rugged as they were. "Well, at least you're alive. That's what really matters."

"How exactly are you alive, Father? We all saw you run straight into a mob of mercenaries!" Roark said astonishedly.

"I'm a little curious about that myself, to say the least," Devlin agreed, looking to him while trying to hide the pain in his ribs.

"Give your old man some credit, boys," Father said pridefully. "I was an experienced swordsman back in the day. I'll tell you about it when Cecelia wakes up.

"Oh, I completely forgot! Roark, Derek! Cecelia is a mage now!" Devlin said, astonished as the memory flooded back to him, but then grunted as pain exploded in his ribs again from the excitement.

"Cecelia's a mage?!" Roark exclaimed. Derek laid a reassuring hand on Devlin's shoulder.

"We can worry about that later. We have to get you patched up Devlin, you look even worse than the rest of us," Derek said sympathetically.

"I'd reckon he would, after that hit he took from that Warhammer," Father reasoned. "Quite frankly I'm surprised that blow didn't snap a few more ribs."

"I need to get to Amanda; she has healing magic. She could fix this in no time," Devlin said roughly through the pain. "What about Valcara? What happened to her? I could have sworn she was with you two." Derek had completely forgotten about Valcara in all the excitement of seeing his father again. Derek surveyed the area and saw her with a group of rebels.

"She's doing her job, don't worry," Derek answered coolly.

"Where is this 'Amanda' girl?" Roark asked Devlin, concerned. "I can go get her while you rest." Devlin felt glad to have his family back together again. To have Roark around to worry about him again, it was like the pain that had been gnawing at him for so long was finally lifted from him. Compared to that, a couple broken ribs was nothing.

Devlin looked around himself to try and spot Amanda, who, to his surprise, was already running towards him with Elena in tow. "She's coming here now, you don't have to worry, little brother," Devlin said, leaning on Father for support.

"Says the kid who can barely stand." Father laughed as he mumbled those words. When Amanda finally reached Devlin, she gingerly put her hand on Devlin's side.

"Thank goodness you're okay. When I saw you collapse, I feared the worst," Amanda said, probing Devlin's body with her magic for injuries, immediately finding the site of the broken ribs.

"You're always getting into trouble, Devlin," Elena smirked. "Can't take my eyes off of you for one minute."

"We'll have to get this armor off so I can operate." Devlin thought how much of a pain that would be before he remembered the armor was charmed to come off and on by thought. Devlin concentrated on the armor and it harmlessly detached itself from Devlin's body, exposing his torn undershirt and discolored ribs.

"It looks like you have three broken ribs, aside from your other bruises and cuts. Bones take a bit longer to mend than most, however," Amanda said expertly, then turned to Devlin's father. "Can you set him down somewhere?" He merely nodded and took Devlin over to a campsite with a few cushions and set Devlin down on one.

"I'll go get Cece," Father told them and walked off. Amanda laid her hand softly on the spot where Devlin's ribs were broken and started working her magic to heal his bones.

"Devlin, you said that Cecelia can use magic now. I've never seen her use it at all since we found her. What happened exactly?" Derek asked Devlin.

"When I was fighting a pair of soldiers, one was about to kill me. Cece stepped in and killed him, saving my life, but she passed out right after. She most likely couldn't handle the strength that spell required and passed out from that. I remember how weak I was my first time casting a spell, so it doesn't surprise me," Devlin explained. "Funny thing is, the guy that hit me with that hammer was the commander of the army. So when Father cut off his right arm, he ran and took the whole army with him."

"That explains why all the soldiers ran away all of the sudden," Roark said finally understanding.

"Elena, what happened to Prince Anders and Luke?" Devlin asked. "I haven't seen them since the battle started."

"Last I saw of them was when they were in the midst of battle. I wouldn't worry, though, Devlin," Elena answered honestly. "Those two knuckleheads are too stubborn to die." As they all talked, Amanda made steady progress on Devlin's bones. She easily healed his minor cuts and bruises, and she had finished healing two of the three broken ribs. Bones were a lot harder to heal than other body parts due to its composition, but she had a lot of practice under her belt. When Amanda finished mending the last bone, she felt her fatigue start to take it's toll on her. She barely had much strength left before the battle, and now that it was over, she finally noticed how tired she was.

"I'm finished, Devlin, you should be fine now," Amanda said wearily.

"Thanks, Amanda, I feel a lot better now," Devlin replied gratefully. To Devlin's shock, however, Amanda fell asleep where she sat next to him, her head landing softly into Devlin's lap.

"Poor girl must be exhausted," Roark observed sympathetically. "I can't say I blame her, I'm about ready to fall asleep myself." Derek and Roark started a small campfire, as it was a bit chilly underground. Devlin would have started it himself to save some time, but he was too exhausted to move. Elena sat next to Devlin, Amanda still sound asleep with her head rested on Devlin's leg. Devlin felt a little bad that she had used the last of her strength to heal him, but she slept so peacefully. He didn't let it bother him too much. Elena stroked Amanda's long, brown hair affectionately.

"Amanda saved my life earlier in the battle. She fought hard and saved me when I was surrounded by soldiers. She even healed my wounds for me. She's a very strong girl, Devlin. I'm almost a little jealous of her," Elena admitted ruefully.

"Why would you be jealous?" Devlin asked confused, then looked down to Amanda, still sleeping soundly.

"She has more courage than anyone I know. She lost her entire village, yet devoted her life to carrying out the prophecy. She lost everyone she cared about, yet she has the courage to fight against men twice her size, and much stronger. I don't think I would be able to carry on with what she went through. She does so much and still keeps fighting," Elena explained. "I don't know how she does it."

"We all have different stories, we all come from different backgrounds. It's what makes us who we are. Amanda has had a lot of hardship in her life to make her the person she is today, but that doesn't make her better than anyone else; she just has a different perspective. I don't believe for a second that you are a weak person Elena. It took a lot of courage to come with me on this journey. Anything could happen to us, yet you chose to leave the safety of your own village to help me. In all honesty, I believe it takes a lot of courage to leave a home behind, intact or destroyed," Devlin told Elena. Elena smiled in spite of herself. Devlin knew what to say to make her feel better, and she appreciated that side of him.

Devlin looked down the path his father had gone, and saw him carrying Cecelia in his arms, still passed out from her magical rescue. He set her down gently next to the fire, and she started to stir. She woke with a start, bolting upright while she oriented herself. She looked around at her brothers, and stared at Devlin, making sure he was alright.

"Wha-what happened? Where are all the soldiers? The last thing I remember is Devlin about to be stabbed to death," Cecelia gasped hysterically.

"Everything is okay, Cece. The soldiers are gone, and Devlin is actually in better shape than the rest of us right now," Derek explained kindly. Cecelia seemed to take this in and collected herself. The noise Cecelia made waking up must have startled Amanda, because suddenly she started stirring as well. When she realized she had been sleeping on Devlin's leg, she immediately sat up, blushing so much her face was as red as a tomato. "I'm sorry, Devlin! I didn't mean to fall asleep on you..." Amanda said, embarrassed.

"It's no trouble, Amanda, you deserved a quick rest. Thank you for healing me," Devlin told her appreciatively. "I'll be sure to properly introduce my siblings to you later. Just relax for now." Amanda nodded slowly and looked to Devlin's father.

"Father, you said you had an explanation?" Roark inquired.

"Yeah, yeah," Father said dismissively. "I was getting to that. I'll start with the beginning. Back in my younger years, I was part of a mercenary group. I was one of the best swordsmen around, and people paid me handsomely to fight for them. It wasn't always a pleasant job, of course, but it kept a roof over my head and food in my stomach. On one job, a few of my group and I had to infiltrate a tower. I was hired by a noble in Crestialis whose daughter was a mage, to sneak into the tower and liberate his daughter being held captive there."

"So, you were gifted with swordsmanship?" Devlin asked but wasn't entirely surprised. In fact, it made sense, considering the Slade family's compatibility with sword fighting.

"Indeed, I was. I trained with the best of the best when I joined the Black Claw. Men that would even put Luke to shame in terms of skill. They helped mold me into a fighting machine; smooth and deadly," Father answered nonchalantly. "I suppose that rubbed off on you boys, considering your skill."

"Why was the woman being held captive?" Cecelia asked, eyeing father expectantly. Devlin was just curious as to how this all related to how Father survived. *Is he really that good?*

"The girl was being held for ransom by some nasty outlaws. As it turns out, that woman was your mother. In fact, we first met on that mission. She was beautiful, the finest lady I'd ever seen in my life, but that didn't matter to me at the time. She was just an objective to me back then," Father explained reminiscently.

"So if Mother was a mage, that explains why Cecelia and I are gifted too," Devlin concluded purposefully.

"Aye, she was a powerful mage; the outlaws figured they could exchange her for ransom or use her magic for their own purposes. She was a worthwhile prize either way. It wasn't fun saving her either. Being noble-born, she hated my guts. She probably would've blasted me to pieces if she weren't drugged. It made traveling with her more interesting, I suppose," Father confirmed. "She finally loosened up on the way home, and she was actually a nice girl. The only problem was, she couldn't control her magic. She was like a container filled up too much because sometimes her magic would leak out, and trust me when I tell ya, that was far from pleasant."

"How did you two fall in love then?" Roark asked eagerly. Father had always kept that story a secret, no matter how much his kids bugged him about it. Father sighed exasperatedly, and gathered his thoughts, figuring that question was coming sooner or later.

"The truth is, we never truly fell in love with each other. When we brought your mother back home, it was in her best interest to seal off her magic and go into hiding so people wouldn't try kidnapping her again. The seal wasn't guaranteed to keep her magic in check, however. She was at risk, a loose cannon ready to fire, so I took it upon myself to watch over her. We got along well enough, but we never truly loved each other. I know for a fact, though, that she loved you kids, and I know I never say it much, but I love you all too.

"Marie always had a soft spot for kids, wanted her own more than anything else in the world. Each of you were her pride and joy, the things she kept close to keep her moving on. The tragic part is, if she hadn't had her power sealed up, she might still be alive. When I charged that mob, I don't know what came over me. It felt like being back in the old days again. I fought those rotten mercenaries to win back my stolen pride, but even when I killed a whole group of them, I still felt empty," Father said somberly.

"At least now, she's at peace," Cecelia said tearfully. Devlin looked to Elena, trying to take all of this in. Cecelia looked to Devlin, studying him, and trying to see his reaction to all of this.

Devlin looked back with an exasperated shrug. Devlin wasn't really sure what to think. He felt like the explanation only raised more questions than it answered.

"How did you end up here then?" Elena asked.

"I still have my old contacts. It wasn't hard to track the path the mercenaries left. The fools tried destroying all the evidence, but it was a simple matter to collect some leads. When I found out you three were with the rebels," Father said gesturing to Roark, Derek, and Cecelia. "I kept watching over you until I felt the times was right. Sadly, the unexpected attack on this base forced my hand."

"Who knew our parents held such interesting lives," Derek joked sadly. Devlin noticed Derek was a lot more serious than he used to be. It's hard to believe how much has changed since they were at the carnival.

"Devlin! We received a message for you," Valcara shouted, running over to where Devlin's group was congregated. "It has the king's seal on it, so it is no doubt urgent." Valcara handed the letter to Devlin. When Devlin broke the seal and read the contents of the letter, his eyes went wide with shock.

Chapter 27

"I'm sorry to have to leave you so soon brothers, but that message can't be ignored. I also made a promise to Anders that I have to keep," Devlin explained the next morning. Devlin found Anders and Luke in a camp not far from where Devlin was camped and quickly told them the news. The group of Anders, Luke, Devlin, Elena, Amanda, and, Cecelia set out for the forest of the elves. "I have to learn how to control my magic, and what better teacher than the person that taught my brother?" Cecelia had told him. Devlin had no problem with it, as it would probably be safer for her to come with them anyway. Devlin gave the letter to Valcara as it held some information for her, like the fact that Grandis was the country that attacked Crestialis's capital.

"Very well, brother. Just make sure you come back in one piece, alright?" Derek said, embracing his brother.

"I should be saying that to you, Derek." Devlin smiled gratefully at his brother. "You stay out of trouble too. Roark, watch Derek's back for me, okay?"

"Count on it," Roark answered proudly, embracing Devlin tightly.

"Here, little brother, take this amulet. It'll give you something to remember me by," Devlin told him, removing the amulet from around his neck, and put it around Roark's. "It's my good luck charm, maybe it'll give you a bit of luck. Derek, I have a gift for you too. I found the sword you bought at the festival when I visited our old house. I held onto it, figured you'd want it," Devlin said as he grabbed a sheathed sword from Devlin's satchel and handed it to Derek.

"I wondered what happened to this sword, thank you, brother," Derek said gratefully as he examined the blade. Cecelia embraced Derek and Roark as well. Devlin could tell it was hard for them to leave each other after what they've been through.

"We'll be heading back to Seamander's capital to rebuild. We'll figure out what to do about Grandis afterward," Derek explained and Devlin nodded in understanding.

"I'll figure out where to go after I get that sword," Devlin told Derek. "I'll send you a letter when I figure that part out. Also, do you know what happened to father? I didn't see him anywhere."

"We found a letter with his handwriting at the camp. It said he was going back to his mercenary group. He figured we would take care of things from here, and that he would find a way to contact us if need be. He said he was proud of us… Proud of the men we've grown up to be…" Derek smiled sadly as Devlin got on his horse. "I'll miss him. As tough a man as he was, I'll miss him."

"Agreed," Devlin and Roark responded sadly.

"Don't worry, Derek, we won't let him die, even if he screws up somehow," Elena told him confidently. Derek, relieved by her words, shook her hand.

"Wait!" A voice screamed in the distance. Cecelia recognized the voice immediately. Anna didn't stop running until she was right beside Cecelia.

"Anna? What are you doing here?" Cecelia asked her as she grabbed Anna's hands.

"I heard you were leaving. I didn't want to miss saying goodbye, or thank you. You helped me get through the worst time of my life," Anna answered sadly.

"You helped me through mine as well, Anna. I can't thank you enough for what you did for me, but this isn't goodbye, I hope. Once this war is over, come look for me at the capital. Maker willing, I will be there after this unrest is passed," Cecelia said hopefully. Nothing would make Cecelia happier than to see her friend that helped her get through the worst time in her life again.

"My brother and I were planning to head back to Crestialis soon anyway. I will be sure to look for you, and I pray for your safety on your journey," Anna told her with a smile.

Cecelia finished saying her goodbyes to Anna and Devlin's group set off to the elven forest. Amanda and Elena were riding together. Anders and Luke each got their own horse, and Devlin and Cecelia rode together as well. Devlin got on the horse, Cecelia getting on behind him, and spurred his horse to a trot along the path. Luke, Anders, and Elena followed behind Devlin's horse and they quickly left the rebel base. Taking off down the beaten path, the morning sun was already high in the sky as they set off back to Crestialis.

*   *   *

Raven grew impatient sitting on her throne; she had sent out men to search for the ancestors of the dwarves that had created Tenebrae. She had heard of rumors of dwarven settlements in the mountains to the north, so she had sent most of her men there. The only problem was Dwarves lived underground, so they couldn't simply spot the settlements.

The throne room was built mostly of stone and marble. The entrance doors were made of solid wood reinforced with steel. It was simple but effective. There were many intricate paintings and tapestries along the stone brick walls. Raven didn't really care for the finery, but she needed to keep appearances.

As Raven read a book of spells on her throne, her peace was interrupted by a loud knock on the door. She tried to keep her annoyance in check until she heard what the interruption was about. A pair of soldiers pulled in a bound man behind them. The man was very short and rough looking. He was covered in dirt and wore very cheap clothing, but he seemed to match the general description of dwarves.

"We found this lone dwarf in the mountains you suggested we look at, Your Majesty. He occupied a lone hut on the mountainside so we, unfortunately, didn't find any settlements. However, this dwarf seems willing to talk," one of the guards announced.

"Very well, let's hear him talk then," Raven ordered. The guards pulled the dwarf in front of Raven's throne, practically throwing him forward. The dwarf stumbled but regained himself and looked to Raven with hard eyes. "What is your name, dwarf?"

"I go by Ironclad Rorren, Ya Majes'y," Rorren said in his rough dialect. His speech made Raven cringe inwardly, but she restrained herself. "I'm one o' the bes' blacksmiths in the realm."

"If you are one of the best, then why do you live outside of a settlement?" Raven questioned indifferently.

"Petty jealousy, milady. Me works was unmatched by any in the mountains, so a bus'ness rival had me exiled. I haven't been undaground since," Rorren explained bitterly.

"I don't particularly care about your life story, dwarf," Raven announced indifferently. I need to know about a certain sword. Are you well versed in history?"

"Of cou'se, ma'am," Rorren answered blankly.

"Interesting," Raven said gaining interest. "I don't suppose you've heard of a sword called Tenebrae?"

"E'ry dwarf wort' his steel know's about dat sword. It lies in a to'er, guarded by dragons, and none have touched it since the group dat craf'ed the sword died off," Rorren scoffed.

"Can you lead me to this tower?" Raven stood up in anticipation. "You will be richly rewarded, I promise you."

"I can, milady, I jus' hope yer ready to take the risks. It's not exactly a stroll through the mountainside," Rorren smiled greedily.

"I've been taking risks since I was a child, drawf. Do not patronize me," Raven warned, then turned to the guards. "Unbind this dwarf immediately and get him into a bath. He is now a guest here, so treat him as such."

"Yes, Your Majesty!" The guards saluted her and quickly untied the dwarf.

"Pleasure doin' bus'ness wit' ya, milady." Rorren bowed.

* * *

Derek didn't know what to feel as he watched his younger brother and sister ride away. He was immensely relieved Devlin was alive and well, but it seemed like as soon as the family had been reunited again, they were separated just as quickly. Derek looked to Roark, and he seemed to have the same mixed emotions Derek had.

"You certainly have an interesting family, Derek," Valcara said casually, walking up behind them. "Your father leaving late last night to Maker knows where, and your brother has connections with the king of Crestialis. Not to mention half of your family is gifted with magic."

"We certainly are one of a kind," Derek admitted, grinning a little. "What's the status of the camp?"

"About a third of the women and children were killed last night. Thank god it wasn't more. They destroyed quite a few houses but that doesn't matter much. Luckily, most of our supplies were spared from destruction," Valcara explained, turning serious. "I plan to get everyone moved into the city in the next week, then we can figure out if Grandis was the country conspiring with Scurvy Jaw. Hopefully, that's the case, or else we won't just have one country to deal with."

"Agreed. What should we do now then?" Roark asked her confused.

"For now, we will head to the city. I ordered the soldiers to help the women pack everything. It's time for the rebels to return home." Valcara looked back at Derek one last time before walking off. Derek headed for the stables to fetch a pair of horses for himself and Roark, Roark following close behind.

"So I guess since Scurvy's dead, Valcara will be queen now?" Roark assumed.

"I believe so. She is the heir to the throne after all," Derek reasoned, grabbing the reins of the horses.

"I wonder what will happen to us then. Will we still be leaders in her army or something else?" Roark asked concerned.

"I suppose we'll find out later," Derek said optimistically as he handed Roark his horse. "Until then, let's be off."

* * *

As Devlin's group traveled down the road, Devlin could still feel the fatigue from the night before. He could tell the rest of the group felt similarly, because when Devlin suggested they set up camp early, no one questioned it. Elena began teaching Cecelia over the course of the trip how to control her magic. Cecelia wasn't as gifted as Devlin was, making her lessons a bit more time consuming, but once she started getting the hang of it, she grew by leaps and bounds. Cecelia seemed to favor wind magic, and Amanda taught her a few healing spells after finding out she had a knack for it. Cecelia wasn't quite as good as Amanda, but she learned how to heal minor wounds and injuries. Amanda had Cecelia practice on a few animals, healing their scratches and scars.

Learning magic both fascinated and terrified Cecelia; she didn't know what to make of it, as she had only just recently discovered her powers. The more she trained, however, the stronger she got. Before long, she could cast torrents of wind effortlessly and heal even fatal wounds like Amanda, but she still lacked the skill necessary to heal overly complicated wounds. Amanda was happy to have another healer around to ease the workload, even if she didn't have the years of practice Amanda had, and Cecelia still had a long way to go before she could truly consider herself a healer.

Seeing Cecelia train inspired Devlin to train himself. He trained to focus on his energy reserves, trying to expand them and use his energy more effectively. Devlin and Cecelia even tried a few combination spells and the power of the spell shocked Devlin. He would have to keep those in mind for future battles.

Luke and Anders trained together; being evenly matched as they were, they were quite exciting to watch. Luke was still better than Devlin with a sword, but they did spar every now and then. Luke used Devlin to help defend against mages he might face, and Devlin was great for that. Luckily for Luke, his armor was charmed to negate magic to a certain point, but after it absorbed too much, the effect had to recharge and was essentially useless during that time. Devlin also learned how to avoid hostile spells thanks to Elena, getting zapped multiple times in the process.

"I swear you are a devil sometimes," Devlin would say after getting hit by a lightning spell a couple of times. Cecelia got a lot of practice in healing Devlin's burns and scratches. "If I had my armor on, none of those spells would hit me."

"Well, take it as motivation to get faster then. You can't rely on your armor too much, or you'll get yourself killed in the next battle," Elena said sternly. The group did most of their practicing when they were camped. Since the area was never exactly the same, it kept things fresh.

After a little more than a week, they finally reached the elven forest. Devlin could tell Elena was happy about it, and she seemed a lot more comfortable so close to home. However, that feeling was quickly dashed when they saw a huge pillar of light suddenly appear deeper in the forest.

"Devlin, we have to hurry!" Elena said, more worried than he'd ever seen her before. He could tell something was wrong before she told him to hurry up. The woods felt tense somehow like an uneasy presence was taking hold. As they arrived in the elven village, the same village Devlin had recuperated in, he saw the elves in a panic. *The pillar of light that had appeared before was most likely the cause,* Devlin thought as he watched the elves run into their homes for shelter. Elena immediately headed towards the Elder's hut, and when they got there, the Elder was standing outside it.

"Elder, what is happening?!" Elena asked him hysterically.

"It is the darkness my child, it is gaining strength as we speak. Never before have I seen Lux radiate with such intensity," the Elder spoke, genuine fear in his voice. "Amanda, you said you believe Devlin is the one to wield Lux; is that right?"

"It is, sir," Amanda confirmed.

"Then, Devlin, you must head to the sword quickly. Whatever is causing the sword to stir so wildly will only do us harm. I have gathered the other elders to unseal the blade once you draw it from its earthly sheath," the Elder explained urgently.

"Very well," Devlin said, spurring his horse to head to where the sword Lux was, Elena taking the lead.

"Is it true? That the intensity of Lux's shining reflects the enormity of a disaster?" Luke asked aloud.

"It is, and if it's shining that much, whatever darkness is coming must be powerful. It's like a forewarning so we may prepare ourselves," Elena explained, her voice very serious and very worried.

"Amanda and I saw it shining on our way to find Devlin. Compared to now, that was but a glimmer," Anders recalled, starting to feel afraid himself.

"What could be happening to make the sword shine like that?" Cecelia asked Devlin, awestruck by the light still visible over the trees.

"I'm not sure I want to find out," Devlin told her.

*   *   *

Raven lead a small army behind Rorren through the mountainside. Due to it being in the summer months, the mountains shown green with plants and all manner of vegetation. Raven appreciated the warm climate, but then again, she was merely wearing a tight fitting shirt that clung to her skin for free movement but let in air easily. Raven actually pitied the soldiers who wore full armor and extra equipment.

According to Rorren, they were getting close to the tower. The fact that Rorren had stated before made Raven worry, though. If there was really a pack of dragons guarding the sword, it would be no simple matter to claim it. Raven was grateful, at least, to have Rorren as a guide, as she feared it would've taken far longer to find someone to take her to the sword. Since the tower was underground, Rorren led them to a hidden tunnel in a cliffside.

"Make sure yer men stay close behind. It's easy ta get lost in these tunnels even if you know where yer goin'," Rorren advised. Raven relayed the message to Gorren and dismounted her horse since the passage was too small to ride on horseback. Raven felt herself hunch over a little in the cramped tunnels, but thankfully, as they got further down, the tunnels got larger. As the tunnel got darker, however, Raven was forced to make an impromptu torch from a fire she held in her hand.

"Will we be seeing any friends of yours down here?" Raven asked Rorren.

"I doubt it. Dwarves may build a lotta tunnels, but they hardly ever use 'em," Rorren said, looking closely at the tunnels ahead to confirm his claim. "'Specially da ones closer to da surface,"

"How exactly was this sword made?" her general, Gorren, asked suspiciously. Raven knew her guards didn't trust Rorren, and neither did she; that question had been burning in her mind as well.

"I don' know all da specifics, but it's said some dwarves mada deal wit' a demon ta make the sword as powerful as Lux," Rorren told him nonchalantly. "Though, I also heard dat sword became too powerful for them ta control, and they became slaves to it. Since the sword don't hava mind ta give orders, though, they prob'ly just waited there 'til they starved ta death." Hearing that tale sent shivers up Raven's spine, to the point where she was almost having second thoughts.

After trekking for what seemed like hours, they finally saw the tunnel gradually widen more and more. Before long, the tunnel opened up into a huge cavern with an opening in the roof like a skylight.

"We're at the dragon's lair," Rorren whispered fearfully. Raven was amazed at what she saw. A stone tower in the middle of the cavern stood at least one hundred meters tall. What she saw around the tower scared her to the bone. Thousands of skeletons littered the ground all around them. They were most likely leftovers from the dragons' meals. To Raven's good fortune the dragons were asleep around the tower. To her misfortune, however, there were at least a couple dozen of them.

"How should we proceed, Your Majesty?" Gorren asked dutifully.

"I shall go alone. I do not want to risk waking up the dragons, and I will cover a lot more ground by myself. If the dragons wake up before I get to the tower, keep them busy. Dwarf, do you know where the sword is located in the tower?" Raven ordered, trying to seem strong even though she was scared out of her wits.

"Tenebrae is said ta be at the very top'a the to'er," Rorren told her. "Try not to die milady, I can't collect me reward if yer dead." Raven rolled her eyes at that remark.

Raven steeled her resolve and walked toward the tower, making sure to avoid stepping on the bones. As she drew closer, she could hear the deep rumble of the dragons breathing. It was like hearing a man snoring, only much, much louder. Raven could feel herself trembling; she knew that, even with her magic, these dragons attacking all at once would easily tear her apart.

Raven stepped over a dragon's tail, which was particularly tricky as sometimes the tail would shift. After safely navigating around several dragons, she finally made it to the entrance to the tower. She let go of a huge sigh of relief and walked to the doors.

The doors were open and more than large enough to let one of those oversized lizards through, Sure enough, there was another dragon sleeping inside. This one, however, was twice the size of the other dragons and a lot rougher, as it had huge scars on its body. The scars looked like claw marks, battle scars from making its way to being the leader of the pack. Raven had heard leaders like these were referred to as High Dragons.

    Raven looked for the stairs to the top and saw them behind the High Dragon. "Of course it is," she muttered in annoyance under her breath. Luckily for Raven, the room was big enough that she could mostly avoid the dragon, but she completely tensed up as the dragon shifted in its sleep, fearing it was waking up. When it stopped moving, Raven realized she wasn't breathing, and took a deep breath.

    Raven carefully stepped around the dragon and silently walked up the stairs. There were three floors of the tower, not including the top, but thankfully there weren't any more dragons. The floors of the tower were filled with smithing tools and manuscripts. Raven even noticed some weird symbols in the middle of the floor. She was curious about what they meant but didn't feel like risking taking too much time to examine them.

    As she walked up the last flight of stairs, Raven could feel a weight to the air, as if it hummed with energy. When she finally reached the top floor, she saw it. The black blade, Tenebrae, just laid there on an altar-like table. The weight in the air grew heavier and heavier with each step she took. *It's so powerful. I can feel its energy in the air.* As she drew close, she noticed a dark aura around the sword; pitch-black light was radiating from it. Raven reached out to grab the sword, but the air got so heavy Raven struggled to remain standing.

    I have come this far, I am not going to quit now! Raven steeled her resolve once again and reached out for the sword once more. This time, she managed to grab the hilt of the sword, and the black light emanating from the blade shined out. The black light swallowed everything, everything around her there was nothing but black, like complete and total darkness. The feeling of it was overwhelming, like stepping into a bottomless pit. Raven could feel it; this was a test. The sword was testing her to see if she was worthy of wielding it. *I can't give in! I won't give in! I've known darkness my whole life, I will not lose to it now!* As her resolve hardened, the darkness lost its intensity.

Eventually, the darkness faded completely, and Raven was standing there, the sword she had been seeking, Tenebrae, clutched in her hand. The thrill of victory coursed through her veins. She had conquered the sword, and now she would conquer armies. She could feel the knowledge of how to use the sword enter her mind like she had known how to use it all along and had just forgotten. Raven guessed the knowledge came from a charm in the sword. In the height of her success, however, she heard a roar that shook the tower itself.

"Oh god, no. Do not tell me those blasted dragons woke up!" Raven said aloud. Surprisingly, though, Raven wasn't scared. In fact, she was excited. "The power of this sword is dominion. Time to see if that is true." Raven ran down the stairway to the bottom floor. The High Dragon that was once sleeping there was wide awake and very angry. Hearing Raven's approach, the massive beast turned toward Raven and blasted a jet of hot flame at her. Raven countered the flame with water from her palm and charged the beast.

The dragon must have woken up when I drew the sword. I guess they are linked somehow. As Raven got closer, the dragon swiped its left claw at her, barely missing as she rolled to the left. Raven used her magic to collapse the ceiling on top of the dragon. It worked, and massive chunks of stone fell onto the beast, pinning it to the ground for at least a moment. Raven hopped onto the beast's back, around where the heart would be and stabbed Tenebrae into its flesh. Instead of actually stabbing the creature, however, the blade phased through the dragon just like Raven hoped it would.

"The dragon is mine now and so is every dragon that follows it. I claim dominion!" Raven shouted, and the blade started glowing black again, this time enveloping the dragon completely. The glow faded as quickly as it came. Raven jumped off the dragon who finally managed to free itself. The High Dragon looked at Raven deeply with its eyes, eyes that felt like they cut straight through to her soul. She felt the creature's will, looking into its eyes, and she felt the sword make the dragon's will her own. As the High Dragon's will became hers, it bowed its head low to her, a demonstration of fealty to her.

As she walked outside, she saw all two dozen dragons wide awake as well, and as one, each and every one of them bowed their heads to Raven as the High Dragon had. Raven raised Tenebrae straight up in the air, and a large pillar of black light shot up into the sky from it.

* * *

Devlin's group made their way to the sacred sword Lux. Devlin could tell from the massive pillar of white light ahead that they were getting close. As they entered the clearing where Lux was located, Devlin could barely see thanks to the blinding white light. Devlin's horse was startled by the light and reared up, almost throwing Devlin and Cecelia off. Devlin dismounted the horse and, as he hit the ground, the light of Lux started to wane.

The light gradually dimmed until it was completely gone. As Devlin approached the sword, he noticed a dim aura around it, the dying remains of the white light that had just illuminated the sky moments ago. As Devlin took hold of the sword, a voice spoke in his mind. *Ye who have taken hold of me, heed my call. Expel your darkness and prove thy worth. Only then may you wield me.*

"'Darkness'? What does it mean 'darkness'?" Devlin asked to himself confused. When Devlin looked back to Elena and everyone else, they were all frozen, as if time had stopped for everything except him. Then, out of nowhere, an exact duplicate of Devlin appeared in front of him. *Is that what it meant? I have to beat the darkness in myself?* The doppelganger held a sword exactly like Devlin's. Dark Devlin swung his sword from the left, then spun and swung from the right. Devlin parried the strike and was amazed that the dark version of him even had his fighting style.

"What are you?" Devlin asked, confused and annoyed.

"I am you, just your bad side. I am your hate, your sadness, your grief, and your anger, all neatly wrapped in a single package. Lux drew me out from the depths of your heart, and it feels great to be free," Dark Devlin told him, grinning coldly. Devlin's dark half swung at him again, this time, a downward strike. Devlin dodged and slashed from the right, but Dark Devlin brought his sword back just in time to block it. They exchanged blow after blow with each other, neither one making any progress.

This is pointless. If he really is me then he knows every technique I do. Fighting him would just wear myself out. Devlin blocked a slash from the left and pushed Dark Devlin back. *I have to think of a way to beat him, but how?* Devlin tried kicking Dark Devlin's legs out from under him, but the doppelganger jumped to avoid it. *Wait. He said he was my negative emotions right? Hate, anger, grief? Maybe if I rid myself of those emotions, it'll weaken him.* Devlin tried clearing his mind of all thoughts. Unfortunately, all that accomplished was to give Devlin a headache. *Well so much for that...* Devlin blocked a series of swings from his doppelganger.

"You're gonna have to do better than this to beat me, Devlin. You're slowing down, getting weaker with every swing. Just accept that you can't beat me by yourself," Devlin's doppelganger scoffed. *Maybe he's right. This fight isn't going anywhere fast. It's going to take more than just myself to beat him.* That's when Devlin remembered. "It isn't just me. Everyone I care about is with me. My brothers, my sister, Elena, Amanda, and everyone else. You only have my negative emotion, you don't have love. You don't have the lives of so many people riding on your shoulders. All you are is darkness. That's what makes us different. That's what makes me stronger!"

With renewed motivation, Devlin charged his doppelganger and hacked at him ferociously. The doppelganger parried each strike but he was losing ground quickly. Devlin didn't stop swinging, he had to win. The doppelganger tried kicking Devlin to get him off of him, but Devlin dodged and kicked the doppelganger. He was hurled backward onto the ground and Devlin quickly brought the point of his sword to the doppelganger's neck. "How did you beat me? We are the same!" the doppelganger shouted angrily at Devlin.

"We aren't the same. My motivation is different than yours. Your drive is what can sharpen your sword or dull it. I have too much on my shoulders to lose here," Devlin said looking down at the doppelganger. Devlin withdrew his sword and the doppelganger vanished. Unaware that he was dreaming, Devlin woke up on the ground Lux in hand.

"Oh maker, what happened?" Devlin asked completely disoriented.

"Devlin, are you alright? We saw you grab the sword and you collapsed," Elena asked him concerned.

"Was it all a dream? Yeah, it had to have been," Devlin concluded. "I fought my dark half in a dream. I think the sword did it to test me."

"Indeed, it did. Perhaps I should've warned you, but Lux cannot simply be drawn; you must pass its trial in order to wield it, and it seems you were victorious," the Elder said as he morphed out of the tree. Following him were six other elves. Devlin guessed that they were the elders of other elven settlements. "Devlin, if you would be so kind as to set the sword on the ground in front of us, we may begin the unsealing." Devlin did as he asked and set Lux on the ground in front of the Elders. Looking at it carefully for the first time, Devlin admired the beautiful, snow-white blade with its gilded leather hilt.

The elders quickly gathered in a circle around the blade. They clasped hands and hummed softly. Devlin couldn't believe it when he saw Lux float in the air point toward the ground, and began to glow again. The light grew and grew as if a torch was being lit in a pitch-black room. The light grew so intense that all Devlin could see was white light. Finally, the light faded and the sword fell to the ground, embedding itself in the earth. The circle of elders parted and Devlin took hold of the hilt. He felt the strength of the sword flow through him as he lifted the sword out of the ground and held it in his hands.

Chapter 28

Derek and Roark walked quickly to the throne room, receiving a message to head there immediately. As they walked into the cleaned hall, they saw Valcara sitting awkwardly on her throne.

"Having fun as the new queen, Your Majesty?" Derek teased.

"Shut it, pretty boy, or I'll have you noosed," Valcara spat. "I cannot begin to tell you how boring being a ruler is. All the pointless formalities and squabbling over their meaningless problems. I had to settle a fight between two men over a fish... A fish!" Valcara sighed exasperatedly. Derek laughed very hard inwardly and did his best not to show it.

"So, what was it that you sent us for?" Roark asked, trying to change the subject. Derek could tell he was about to crack up too.

"Yes, yes more formalities. Derek, you are promoted to general of the forces of Seamander, Roark will be second in command," Valcara said dutifully.

"Did you ever find out who was conspiring with Scurvy Jaw?" Roark asked Valcara, impatient for some new information.

"Some of my men did some digging, but most of the evidence we found was inconclusive. Some things pointed to Grandis but there was nothing truly revealing, unfortunately." Valcara said discouragingly. As Valcara finished her sentence, one of her guards stepped into the room. "Yes, what is it?"

"Your captain wishes to speak with you on a very important matter, Your Majesty," the guard said dutifully, and Valcara just rolled her eyes.

*I've been hearing **that** all day,* Valcara groaned inwardly.

"Very well. See him in," Valcara said indifferently. Valcara's captain made his way into the throne room and bowed low before beginning.

"Forgive the interruption, milady, but I have pertinent news," the captain explained. "You remember the knaves that attacked your base camp the week before? We found their remains trying to leave the country, and we captured their commander." Valcara raised her eyebrows in disbelief but then smiled devilishly.

"Oh, I'm going to enjoy this," Valcara said in a way that sent shivers up Derek's spine. Derek almost felt pity for the commander, but then remembered that he had almost killed his brother.

* * *

"You have done well, Rorren. When we get back, I promise you will be one of the wealthiest men in the kingdom," Raven told him gratefully as she eyed the beautiful blake blade in her hand. The soldiers were scared out of their wits from the twelve-foot tall dragons behind her, too scared to even move. Gorren was the only one who didn't look like he was about to soil himself, which impressed Raven somewhat. "You soldiers head back to the castle with Rorren. I think I will fly home on my new friends," she said as the High Dragon lowered its head so Raven could pet it affectionately.

"One secon', milady. I'm a bit curious on when ya learned how to wield a sword? I thought you just relied on magic," Rorren asked her merely out of curiosity.

"I learned that when I became queen. It was the hope of one day wielding this sword that spurred my motivation, and I am certainly glad I took part in it," Raven explained before she hopped on the base of the Alpha's neck. Raven braced herself as the dragon jumped high in the air and unfurled its massive wings to fly. In no time at all, the dragon cleared the distance between the ground and the skylight at the top of the cavern. As the dragon flew up over the opening, Raven could feel the wind rushing past her as the dragon rose higher and higher. She also started to feel cold as the temperatures dropped the higher the dragon went. Raven suddenly wished she had brought her wool cloak, as her fitted clothing did nothing to fight off the cold. Raven even tried making a fire in her palm but the wind blew it out too fast for it to be of any use.

That's when the dragon breathed out short bursts of flame. The short jets warmed Raven up considerably, and she guessed dragons did that instinctively to fight off the cold temperatures. Instinct or not, Raven certainly appreciated it. She saw the dragons behind her, and they were surprisingly fast, not seeming to use much effort to keep up with her and the High Dragon.

Raven felt the adrenaline rush through her as she looked at the ground far below. Luckily, the base of the dragon's neck made a great resting place, even though she noticed that the hard scales were a bit uncomfortable. Raven was glad her pants were thick, as they protected the inside of her thighs from the rough scales, but she made sure not to move too much regardless.

"With you dragons under my command, I could conquer entire nations effortlessly," Raven said to herself.

"Yes, My Queen," the dragon spoke in her mind. At first, when Raven heard the voice, she thought she had just imagined it, but the curiosity got the better of her.

"You can talk?" Raven asked bewildered.

"Yes, My Queen," The same strong, rough voice in her head replied.

"How come I never heard you speak when we fought?" Raven asked, the question bringing back the memory of the fight.

"We dragons consider humans inferior. We eat humans; why bother talking to them?" the High Dragon explained nonchalantly. The dragon's tone angered Raven, but she accepted that it was just being honest.

"If you do not talk to humans, how do you know our language?" Raven asked again.

"We use the same language to communicate amongst ourselves, though we communicate magically instead of verbally like you humans do," the High Dragon explained.

"What is your name, dragon?" Raven asked offhandedly.

"I am called Horris, milady," Horris stated blankly. Raven was fascinated by the dragons and resolved to learn more later.

Raven directed the High Dragon to the location of her castle and landed just outside the gate of the city. When she landed on the ground, she looked to the dragon.

"Do as you wish for now. However, stay close to this city, and do not bother the humans. I will contact you when I have need of you," Raven ordered.

"As you say, My Queen," the High Dragon said understandingly and flew off with its clan. Raven could definitely learn to get used to this. One of Raven's captains ran outside to meet her, the poor fool was so frightened he was trembling. Not that Raven could blame him, but the look on his face was priceless.

"Did I s-see you j-jump off a dr-dr-dragon?" the captain stuttered.

"Indeed, you did. Thanks to my wonderful new sword, they are completely under my control. The rest of my army should be back within the day, and see to it that the dwarf gets treated nicely," Raven informed the captain.

"Yes, Your Majesty!" the captain said dutifully. "Also, my Queen, we received a report that the pirate king of Seamander has been dethroned by the rebels."

"That is of no importance to me now, I never liked that disgusting pirate in the first place. I will just do to their leader what I did to the dragons, then they will see it my way," Raven pondered indifferently. "Send a message to the new ruler for a challenge. I will fight them personally."

* * *

Devlin could feel the power flowing from the blade, enhancing his own strength greatly. He stood in awe of the sheer power of the sword.

"How do you feel, Devlin?" Amanda asked, concerned.

"I feel like I could run a mile and not get tired," Devlin said jokingly. Amanda rolled her eyes at that remark but still giggled a little.

"In your hands, you hold the light of the world, young Devlin," the Elder said cryptically. "Do not misuse it."

"No pressure," Elena added awkwardly.

"PUNY HUMAN!" A voice suddenly exploded in Devlin's mind, making him drop the sword to cover his ears in a vain attempt to silence the voice.

"YE WHO WIELD THE SACRED BLADE," the voice exploded again, making Devlin scream in agony.

"Devlin! What's wrong?!" Cecelia pleaded to him.

"A voice in my head! It's too much!" Devlin yelled in return.

"Could it be?" the Elder questioned, distant. As if to answer the Elder's question, a pure white dragon landed in the clearing. The ground itself shook as the dragon landed. The Elder looked at the dragon as if meeting an old friend for the first time in years. Everyone else just looked on in shock.

"Lower your voice guardian! You'll split the boy's head open!" the Elder shouted to the dragon.

"My apologies," The voice said at a much lower volume, but Devlin could tell he wasn't sorry. "I always forget how feeble the minds of humans are."

"Who... are... you?" Devlin asked the dragon, still recovering from the mental onslaught.

"I am the guardian of the sacred blade. The almighty Drathic. Remember that name well, human," Drathic said in his mind.

231

"Wait, so that dragon is talking to Devlin in his mind?" Anders asked, confused.

"Dragons communicate telepathically through people's minds," Elena explained, "But usually dragons don't waste time talking to humans. They just hunt them." Hearing that sent chills up Devlin's spine, and he looked at the dragon with new respect.

"Your elven friend is surprisingly well-informed," Drathic confessed snidely.

"He won't bother to talk to the rest of us, Devlin. He only talks to you because he has business with you," Elena explained further.

"What is he saying, Devlin?" Amanda asked him, frightened beyond her wits.

"The dark blade, Tenebrae, has been awakened. My brethren guarding the sword have lost their will to it," the dragon stated angrily. Devlin repeated the words aloud, and the Elder's eyes went wide as he heard that.

"Oh no, anything but that," the Elder said trembling. "That cursed sword is free?!"

"Elder, what is Tenebrae?" Elena asked him, concerned.

"That cursed sword steals the will of anything it strikes. Any wound fatal to a person causes them to lose their mind to the sword, as well as every person that directly follows that person. It was made by the dwarves who were jealous of Lux. They made a deal with a demon to give it its power. If that sword is truly free, all hope is lost." The Elder was trembling as he spoke.

"Is there a way to fight it?" Devlin asked Drathic.

"Lux is the only possible way to fight Tenebrae," Drathic stated seriously. "You must defeat the person wielding the sword, and Lux's magic will allow you to use Tenebrae to liberate all those under the sword's influence. However, should you lose, Tenebrae will swallow the light of Lux, and your soul, as well as all others, will be lost to the black blade," Devlin repeated Drathic's words to everyone else.

"Then we just can't lose," Luke concluded.

"That's easier said than done," Anders retorted. "We don't even know who holds the sword."

"The sword is in the hands of the one called Raven, the ruler of Grandis," Drathic said, answering Anders's fear.

"Raven, ruler of Grandis. Ring any bells, Prince Anders?" Devlin asked. Anders was surprised to be addressed so quickly.

"I know the country, not the name. I believed the current ruler of Grandis to be my father's cousin," Anders answered.

"That fool was killed years ago," Drathic scoffed. Devlin repeated what Drathic said in the same tone to tease Anders. Anders grew slightly indignant but quickly regained his composure.

"How do you know all this?" Devlin asked Drathic.

"I use my magic to see distant things. I believe you have used this spell to see the state of your home?" Drathic asked rhetorically. Devlin thought back to when he had used water to see his home burnt to the ground. The memory still bit at Devlin, even now.

"What is your purpose here, Drathic? Why explain all of this in the first place?" Devlin asked him.

"My purpose? I am glad you asked. I am another trial for you to overcome. As I am linked to the sword and you wield it, you wield me as well. I will make sure I am not in the hands of a coward," Drathic told him to the shock of everyone else.

"What does he have in mind for this 'trial' of his?" Amanda asked, concerned.

"I will call a friend of mine to fight you. If you survive, then I will serve you, as will the rest of my kind not under Tenebrae's spell. We have no desire to lose our will," Drathic said, then roared very loudly. Within a few minutes, a dragon half the size of Drathic landed in front of Devlin. Despite being smaller, however, he still towered over Devlin at ten feet tall. "I would fight you myself, but I suppose I have to give you a fighting chance,"

"Don't patronize me dragon. If I have to fight alongside you, I have to make sure *you* aren't a coward," Devlin challenged, glaring at Drathic. "I challenge you, Drathic." Drathic seethed, letting out a huff of blue flame.

"Very well, human. I accept, but don't blame me if you die," Drathic said, this time announcing his intentions to everyone. The pure white dragon stepped toward Devlin, preparing to strike. Everyone but Devlin backed away, Cecelia having to be pulled back by Luke and Elena, not wanting to see her beloved brother possibly lose his life to the massive dragon.

"Devlin! Please, this is madness! You can't fight that monster. You'll die!" Cecelia pleaded. Devlin looked at her with confidence that shocked her.

"I won't die, sis, don't worry. If I die, I couldn't protect you anymore. I won't let anything happen to my family, even if I have to fight the world itself," Devlin said determinedly. "I will fight you with my own strength, Drathic! If I must face you, it will be on equal terms!" As Devlin said that, he placed Lux on the ground away from himself.

"Admirable, but very foolish," Drathic said critically. The dragon blasted a jet of blue flame at Devlin. Devlin rolled out of the way, just in time, and when he looked to where the flames had struck, large icicles formed over the grass. *If that fire hits me, I'll be frozen solid!* Drathic spit forth another jet of icy flame, and Devlin jumped out of the way again. Drathic swiped at Devlin with his left-front leg. Devlin ducked below it, and jumped on top of Drathic's back, having to climb up his side to do so. In response, Drathic jumped into the air and took flight.

Devlin barely managed to hold on as he was slammed onto the back of the dragon. Drathic climbed higher and higher, then performed a barrel roll, trying to get Devlin off. Not having anything to hold onto, Devlin fell off Drathic easily, and was free falling through the air. Unfortunately for Devlin, the fast approaching ground was the least of his worries, as Drathic was quickly circling around back to Devlin. Devlin conjured a gust of wind to slow his descent and land softly on the ground, then used another gust to disrupt Drathic's flight, resulting in a head-on collision with the ground.

Drathic recovered quickly and roared in frustration. He charged Devlin, easily closing the distance between them in a few short bounds. Drathic quickly spun, slamming Devlin with his long tail. Devlin was launched in the air like a ball from a cannon, snapping a tree in half on impact. Thankfully for Devlin, his armor absorbed most of the impact, but it still knocked the breath out of him. Devlin picked himself up from the wreckage of the tree and observed Drathic.

The dragon was watching him, waiting for him to make a move. *I have to remember to watch for that tail of his. A couple more shots like that, and I'll be in major trouble.* Devlin used his magic to grab the earth under Drathic. He gripped the earth to bury Drathic's feet, holding him in place. Drathic howled in annoyance and struggled against the willed earth. Devlin took it a step further and pulled a huge clump of earth from the ground. Devlin split the clump into dozens of smaller chunks and threw it down on top of Drathic. Drathic shrieked in surprise as he was buried in a mound of dirt.

"Give up… yet?" Devlin asked the currently stunned Drathic, breathing hard from fatigue. Drathic roared again and exploded from the rubble, using his wings to bat away the earth. "I guess not…" Drathic growled furiously at Devlin but showed no signs of exhaustion.

"It will take more than that to stop me, child," Drathic raged. The dragon spat out more balls of icy flame. Devlin raised a wall of earth to block the flames, then sent a blast of energy from his feet to rocket him high over Drathic. Devlin used his magic to gather earth around him until Devlin had formed a boulder underneath him. Devlin jumped off the boulder at the last second, adding another push with his magic, for the rock to slam hard into Drathic's back. Devlin didn't wait for Drathic to recover and grabbed his tail. Using the last of his magical energy to enhance his muscles to superhuman levels, Devlin picked up Drathic, spinning him, and then threw him into a row of trees.

The sound of Drathic slamming and snapping the trees was deafening. The thundering crash echoed throughout the forest as a dozen trees collapsed at once. Devlin fell to his knees, utterly exhausted from his exertions, felt a sense of pride at being able to injure the dragon at least. To Devlin's horror, however, Drathic got up again, albeit with a struggle as the dragon started to feel the damage Devlin had done to it. Drathic was far from tired, however, just slightly rattled. The enraged dragon stalked toward the exhausted Devlin, huffing small jets of flame from his mouth in anticipation. Drathic was upon Devlin, ready to flood him with a torrent of his frozen breath. Before he could, however, the elder stepped between Drathic and Devlin.

"That is enough," the Elder declared. "I trust the boy has more than proven himself, guardian. There is no point in continuing when Devlin no longer has the strength to fight back." Drathic huffed in annoyance, seeming to debate whether to freeze the Elder as well, but instead blasted a huge pillar of flame straight upward, and then glared coldly at the Elder.

"It is not your place to interfere in a dragon's challenge, elf. You are fortunate that I am in a good mood today," Drathic huffed, then turned and walked toward the center of the clearing.

"That prideful fool would tear apart the entire forest to defend his ego. You did quite a number on his pride, Devlin. Drathic is one of the mightiest dragons alive. I am honestly surprised you were able to injure him at all. You have grown so much since you left the forest, I barely recognize you," the Elder praised, helping Devlin rise to his feet. Before Devlin could react, however, he was tackled in a bear hug by Cecelia.

"Ow! Cece, don't surprise me like that. You're worse than Elena," Devlin complained but hugged her tightly when he realized she was crying. "I told you I'd be fine, didn't I?" Cecelia just nodded and wiped the tears from her eyes. "I'm sorry for making you worry again." Devlin smiled sympathetically.

"Devlin! Are you hurt?!" Amanda asked him as she ran up to him.

"I probably have a couple bruises from when Drathic hit me with his tail..." Devlin guessed, removing his armor for Amanda. Amanda checked him over and healed a large bruise on Devlin's back.

"I'm amazed you didn't suffer worse. You were up against a huge, adult dragon. Be thankful you're still drawing breath," Amanda scolded.

"I probably wouldn't be if the Elder hadn't have stepped in... Drathic was a second away from freezing me, I'm sure," Devlin admitted. "I can't believe how strong he is. I threw everything I had at him, and he still came back for more. Maybe I should've used Lux after all."

"Drathic is the protector of our realm for a reason, Devlin. It's to be expected that he would be strong," Elena told him. "Your display was impressive, though. Not many can so much as scratch Drathic. You threw him around like a rag doll. If your endurance hadn't run out, you may have even beaten him."

"That just means that I still have room to improve," Devlin responded. He looked to Drathic, who was sitting by Lux and watching him expectantly. He walked to Drathic and picked up Lux. As he held the blade in his hand, he could feel it rejuvenating his strength.

"The wonders of this sword never cease. I feel as if I hadn't even fought just now," Devlin said in awe.

"Such is the power of the sacred sword. Now that you have proven your worth, I shall aid you in your battle, as well as every able-bodied dragon in the realm," Drathic explained.

"Our forces are already with King MacArthur in the capital. His army should be gathered by now, and it is time to go on the offensive against Grandis. We must stop Raven before she becomes too powerful," the Elder explained.

"Then it's time to prepare for war," Devlin said with finality.

Chapter 29

"Elder, may I speak with you for a moment?" Elena asked as everyone made their way back to the village.

"Of course, Elena. You needn't be so formal with me, you know that," the Elder chastised.

"Yes, I know, but I have to ask. Why have you cooperated with the humans? I thought you and the other elders were wary of them…" Elena asked him suspiciously.

"It is true, we have had grievances with humans in the past. In fact, when King MacArthur asked me for aid, I was incredulous. Part of me even wished to turn him away for fear of treachery," the Elder admitted.

"So why do you aid them then?" Elena asked insistently.

"You have Devlin to thank for that. Devlin was the first true human we have had contact with in many years. He showed me the good of the human heart as he associated with you, as he associated with all of us in the village. He made me believe that, perhaps the past was, at last, the past, and that we had nothing more to fear of the humans," the Elder explained sincerely.

The Elder's words shocked Elena, but she knew all too well what he meant. *Before I met Devlin, I had no idea beyond the recounting of others what humans were like. My kin told me the humans were to be avoided, that they would bring naught but harm to us. When I met Devlin, I realized what a human was truly like. I realized what a good person he is, and how much he cares…* Elena recounted. *I even found myself growing close to him, even risking my own life to help him, and witnessing him risk his life to protect his family. Devlin truly is a man of his word, so maybe that's why we elves were willing to trust him. Trust him so much so that we are willing to go to battle by his side.*

"He is a remarkable man, Elena. Hold onto him. Help him grow even more," the Elder instructed her. "That one man is now our only hope for peace against Tenebrae. Don't let him fail."

"I wouldn't worry about that, Elder. Devlin would never lose, not when his family is on the line. He considers us all his family almost as much as his own siblings because we all share a home here. He is the kind of man that cannot be stopped when he wants to protect his home," Elena assured him.

"I sincerely hope you're right, Elena," the Elder said looking at her purposefully.

I do too, Elder.

* * *

Valcara, Derek, and Roark were walking to the council room after interrogating the captured commander. He had told them that she was under orders of Raven, the Queen of Grandis.

"So I guess now it's official?" Roark asked Valcara. "Grandis is our target?"

"According to what that commander squealed, I believe so," Valcara confirmed.

"We'll have to start planning for the invasion then, also get in touch with the MacArthurs," Derek advised. "It would be better to have two armies instead of one."

"I'll agree to that. Let's just hope matters don't force our hand." Valcara thought about different plans to get to Grandis. She knew it was mountainous in the north, as Grandis held part of the Acopane Mountains. To the east and south, it held massive forests, thick with oak trees. She had heard they had hidden villages in the forests, to protect from invasion. Then to the west, there were the plains that connected to the plains of Seamander. They weren't next door neighbors, but they were pretty close.

"It would make the most sense to attack from the west, we could attack unobstructed by the mountains to the north and the forests to the south," Valcara said gesturing around Grandis on the map. To the southeast was Crestialis, and Derek thought about Devlin and Cecelia looking at it. Derek hoped they were doing okay.

"Your Majesty!" A messenger said opening the door to the Council room and running hastily to her.

"Thank you," Valcara said grabbing the letter. It was sealed with the seal of Grandis, which surprised Valcara. She opened the seal and began reading aloud. "Salutations, ruler of Seamander. It has come to my attention that you have dethroned my associate, the pirate, and taken the country as your own. This I congratulate you on, however, hostilities between our two countries is the last thing I need at the moment. So, in an effort to save time and lives, I propose a challenge to you. I, Queen Raven of Grandis, shall battle you one on one. You may either fight yourself or choose a champion in your place to represent you. If you accept, we shall meet on the plains of Grandor. Should you win, I shall cease all hostilities, and surrender my army to you, however, should I be victorious, you will surrender and cease hostilities between our countries. The choice is yours, I sincerely hope you make the right one. Sincerely, Raven, Queen of Grandis."

"She wants to challenge you to a duel?" Derek asked, not comprehending the sudden turn of events.

"It's too risky for my taste, she could be hiding something," Roark spoke out.

"I know it's risky, but if I win, we end this entire war without a single casualty. I am confident in my skills, I shall take part. Of course, if I lose it will be my responsibility."

"You're sure about this?" Derek asked concerned for her safety.

"Awe, are you worried about little ol' me? That's sweet of you princess, but remember the last time we fought I beat you into the ground," Valcara teased.

"That was weeks ago! I've gotten a lot better since then!" Derek responded indignantly.

"Whatever you say, princess," Valcara teased again. "Get ready for the duel. If it's a trap, I will need you on your toes."

"Of course, Your Majesty," Roark said dutifully.

* * *

Valcara waited in the open plains of Grandor like the letter requested, her army twenty meters behind her. Valcara waited patiently for over an hour, and nothing happened. When Valcara looked up, though, she saw a flock of birds in the sky. To her shock, however, that flock of birds wasn't birds. As they drew closer, Valcara got a better look and saw a couple dozen dragons all flying toward her.

Valcara was known to be a brave person, and it took a lot to scare her, but the sight of a dozen dragons sent a shiver down her spine. As the dragons came down to land, they flapped their wings hard to slow their descent, creating a gust of wind that nearly blew Valcara off her feet. When the dragons landed, a lone woman jumped off the neck of the biggest one. She wore black battle armor that looked freshly made and had a black sheath holding her sword. Little did Valcara know, that sword was Tenebrae. Valcara wore battle armor herself, it was silver on the metal outer shell and she wore a black undershirt.

"Nice pets," Valcara scoffed. "Where did you get them?"

"I found them all in a cave in the mountains, and they seem to have taken a liking to me. Dragons are creatures of power after all," Raven sneered.

"We duel until one person falls, I will be my own champion. I trust that is no issue for you?" Valcara asked her, and nearly spat at her. Valcara knew that if Raven tried anything, Derek and the rest of her army would be at her side in an instant.

"Yes, that seems appropriate," Raven said dismissively. "Get ready." Valcara did just that and got in her fighting stance. She drew her longsword and watched Raven as she drew her pure, black blade. Raven got in her fighting stance as well. Valcara could tell just by looking at her that she was no novice with a sword. Her stance was loose but rigid. Valcara saw few openings in her guard and prepared herself to strike at the ones she did see.

Raven lunged at Valcara, and Valcara blocked the strike effortlessly. Valcara noticed a black aura around the sword and felt danger from it. Valcara refused to hold back, not wanting to figure out why the sword gave her a bad feeling. Valcara did her best not to let Raven touch her, blocking every strike with purpose. Raven was a devastating foe, her strikes were precise and calculated, and they held power behind them as well. In response, Valcara swung harder as she hacked at Raven's defense.

She parried a downward strike, then swung around fast, trying to catch Raven off guard. Raven managed to block the blow to the left just in time and pushed Valcara back several steps. Valcara closed the distance immediately and swung from the right. Raven blocked again, and countered with a kick to Valcara's ribs, knocking the wind out of her lungs. Raven struck again, and Valcara barely managed to parry it. Valcara got her breath back, and her strength returned. The fight continued on, neither fighter giving any ground.

Seeing that the battle wasn't getting anywhere, Raven resorted to using her magic on Valcara. Raven had resolved to fight only with her sword, but she grew tired of this bout. Raven made the ground beneath Valcara's feet cave in, burying her feet up to her ankles. Valcara was caught off guard by the sudden turn of events and dropped her guard for a moment. That moment was all Raven needed. Raven stabbed her sword through Valcara's heart, but like with Horris, the sword just phased through her. It was a surreal feeling for Valcara, seeing the sword go through her, but she didn't understand why she didn't feel any pain, or why she was still alive.

"I claim dominion," Raven said with an evil smile.

Then she felt a dark veil cover her mind like a shroud was thrown over her. Her entire world went dark like she passed out, but she was still awake in her own body. She couldn't understand what was happening. She couldn't move, even when she instructed her limbs to function, they remained motionless. Valcara felt like a prisoner in her own body, and even though Valcara could no longer see it, the same thing was happening to her entire army, including Derek and Roark.

* * *

As Raven pulled the sword from Valcara's chest, she saw the blank look take over her eyes. "Well that takes care of that," Raven said relieved, and let out a sigh. *I did not expect to actually get a fight out of this girl. I'll be sure to train later, I cannot afford to have anyone my equal in any fashion.* Raven looked to Valcara, "I believe your army is also under my control," Raven commanded. "Step forward." In mere seconds, Valcara's army started walking forward to her. They moved almost mechanically, their bodies still freshly taken over. Raven knew they would grow more fluid as time passed. "I shall be returning to my castle, you all shall head to the war front where the rest of my troops are waiting. Understood?" Raven ordered.

"Understood, My Queen," Valcara responded robotically. Raven couldn't help but smile at the sight of a queen calling *her* queen. Raven felt a sense of satisfaction from it. Raven climbed onto Horris's neck. As Horris flew into the air, Raven looked below and watched as the new addition to her army walked the open plain. The added force would easily double her forces, and with the dragons as well, Raven had more than enough to wipe out MacArthur's army. Raven looked forward to wiping Crestialis off the face of the earth, and that accursed family would be out of her life forever. Raven also felt something else, she felt her strength surge. *That's right... I get stronger with each living thing under my will.* Raven felt even happier then, like a final nail in MacArthur's coffin.

*　　*　　*

The griffin-shaped amulet around Roark's neck began to glow. The glow enveloped his body, lifting the dark veil over his mind. *What? What happened to me?* Roark looked around and saw everyone walking around him. All of his allies walked and walked as if marching in a rhythm. Roark felt completely disoriented, the last thing he remembered was seeing Valcara stabbed, but he saw her leading the army through the plains.

Roark didn't understand, had he passed out? Had he gone mad? *If Valcara was really stabbed she would be dead right now, not leading the army.* Roark could tell they were walking in unfamiliar territory as well, as he would've recognized something if they were just heading back to Seamander. Roark looked around for Derek. He walked just behind Valcara, still wielding his regular sword and the sword Devlin had given him at his side. Roark also noticed a glow. It was the dying glow of the Griffin Amulet. *Why was this glowing? Is it magical? Is that why I'm so disoriented? Maybe I'm in a hallucination spell or something.* Roark pinched his arm very hard, the pain reassured him that everything was really happening. Roark ran up beside Derek and tried patting his shoulder.

"Derek, what's going on?" Roark asked him, trying to clear his confusion. Derek didn't respond. Roark shook his shoulder again, thinking maybe he was daydreaming. Still no response. Roark put both his hands on Derek's shoulders and shook him. Derek merely shrugged Roark's grip off and continued walking. Roark was completely caught off guard. It was as if someone had taken his brother and replaced him with a senseless doppelganger. Roark tried the same thing with Valcara with the same result.

When Roark got in front of Derek, to try and stop him, and Derek pushed Roark out of the way. Roark tried thinking this through, to come up with something to get Derek's attention, and Roark got desperate. Roark punched Derek in the face, and Derek did react, but not the way Roark was expecting. Derek drew his sword on Roark, a cold, blank look in his eyes.

That's when Roark noticed that every soldier behind him had the same look. *Are they all under a spell? Derek would never look at me that way. He always has life in his eyes, even at his worst.* Roark wondered about the amulet around his neck. *Was it that I had been under the same spell, and the amulet had freed me somehow?* Before Roark could find out, he was forced to draw his sword against Derek, as Derek swung his sword at him. This worried Roark, as Derek had always been the better fighter of the two, but Roark had a motivation, where his brother was now a lifeless puppet. Roark couldn't afford to lose, or else he would lose his dear brother.

Roark swung furiously at Derek, where Derek just mechanically blocked each blow. "Derek wake up! I'm your brother for maker's sake!" Roark shouted desperately.

"Anyone that is an enemy of Queen Raven is my enemy, family or not," Derek responded in a cold, mechanical voice. His words cut into Roark's heart. Roark knew that Derek was being controlled, but that didn't make him feel any better. Roark fought to protect his family, not harm it, otherwise, he didn't want to fight at all. *This is a fight to protect my family,* Roark realized. *If Derek was under Raven's influence then he could end up fighting Devlin. Devlin wouldn't understand until it was too late.* Roark wouldn't let that happen. Roark couldn't let that happen.

"I will protect you from yourself, brother, I will save you from yourself," Roark told him, starting another flurry of strikes. "And I will do so even at the cost of my own life!"

"I don't need saving, especially not from my enemy. I shall end you myself," Derek countered, blocking Roark's blows again.

"I looked up to you, I emulated you. You were an inspiration to me. That's way I followed you. That's why I worked as your right hand. I guess now, though, I'll have to be my own person to beat you, to save you, like you've been saving me all this time. I won't let my oldest brother down," Roark said resolved. Derek swung at Roark, but Roark ducked the swing and kicked Derek hard in the stomach. The kick stunned Derek, giving Roark enough time to put the Griffin amulet around Derek's neck. *I hope this works!* As the amulet wrapped around Derek's neck, it started to glow brightly as it had with Roark. After a couple seconds, life came back to Derek's eyes, as well as the confusion that quickly followed.

"What the hell?" Derek said confused, trying to orient himself. "Roark, what happened to me? I remember Valcara dueling then it's all a big blur." Roark was thrilled to have his older brother free of whatever spell he was under.

"I'll explain later, but for right now just act natural. You're supposed to be leading these soldiers," Roark said gesturing to the charmed soldiers. Roark ran over to Valcara and Athon and freed them the same way he had freed Derek. Valcara and Athon reacting in a similar manner to Derek, except Valcara was a bit more agitated.

"How am I not dead? I know that witch stabbed me, but I did not feel a thing from it, then all of the sudden I'm a prisoner in my own mind!" Valcara screamed. Roark covered her mouth to silence her, not wanting to risk being discovered. Derek and Athon walked up to Valcara and Roark curious themselves as to what had happened, and all four of them walked and talked in front of the army of possessed soldiers.

"Listen, I don't know the details myself, but whatever Raven did to Valcara, brainwashed everyone in her army including Valcara. I was just like you three before, but for some reason, this amulet, bless you Devlin, freed me from the spell. I'm guessing the amulet must be protective against magic, which is why it worked on you three also. The big question is, how did Raven cast the spell?" Roark explained.

"I noticed a weird aura around the sword as I fought Raven, maybe the sword is charmed in some way to cast that mind control spell over others. If that's the case, why did it only activate when she stabbed me? If she had used it when we first met, she would have won the duel without having to raise a finger," Valcara surmised.

"Maybe that's how the sword activates. It has to fatally stab a person to activate," Athon concluded. "Nothing seemed to happen when the sword merely scratched you after all." Valcara nodded confirmation.

"Roark, you saved us, and for that, I cannot thank you enough, but how will we save the rest of my men?" Valcara questioned turning to Roark.

"For now I believe we should just follow the soldiers. If Raven notices nothing amiss, maybe we can surprise her and take her sword," Roark answered.

"That sounds like a good plan to me. These soldiers are heading to the front lines anyway. We can obstruct their progress from within, and go to Devlin's side when the battle starts," Derek concluded. "I'm sure they have a massive army waiting for Raven, if she wasn't worried, she could've just wiped us out with her dragons.

"Good point..." Valcara agreed. "Very well, it's decided then. Let's follow the soldiers for now."

Chapter 30

After making sure the preparations for the elves were going smoothly, Devlin had Drathic call some dragons to give them all a ride to the capital. "I'm not some beast of burden you insufferable whelp!" Drathic screeched indignantly.

"We don't have time to ride there on horses. At least if we ride on dragons we can fly over the forest and save a lot of time," Devlin countered impatiently. Drathic roared in frustration and gave Devlin a look of death.

"Very well! But only this once. Only because the realm is in danger," Drathic fumed. Devlin and his group rode on the dragons Drathic called to get to the capital quickly. Devlin rode on the back of Drathic; his friends and sister rode on dragons Drathic had called. Devlin felt a little nervous being on Drathic's back again, given his first experience, but he ignored the feeling eventually. *At least I know if I fall off I won't be helpless...*

Devlin kept Lux in a newly made sheath, given to him by the Elder. It fit the sword perfectly, like a glove on his hand as it remained tied to his belt.

Devlin noticed the sword glowing frequently, giving him a sense of unease. When Devlin held Lux's hilt in his hand, he could actually feel the darkness it was reacting to. It felt massive and ever changing but still held the same properties as before. Unfortunately, Devlin could not sense the exact location of the darkness. He just got the vague direction of it.

Thanks to Drathic's knowledge, Devlin at least knew what he was up against: the ruling Queen of Grandis, Raven, who wielded Tenebrae, the black blade of dominion. Drathic had gathered as many as three dozen dragons to their cause, hoping to offset the powerful dragons Raven had taken over with sheer numbers. With the elves joining the cause, the size of the armies would be greater than Raven's, especially knowing that Valcara would be joining the fight as well. Devlin felt confident knowing that much, but the fact that Tenebrae could take over people's minds worried Devlin. *If I lose, I'll be no more than a mindless slave to Raven. I could unwittingly destroy everything I swore to protect.* That outcome terrified Devlin more than anything. *I can't think about what will happen if I lose. I just have to win, and everything will be back to the way it was.*

It didn't take long before the capital city came into view, but the sheer devastation he saw below amazed him. The city was completely decimated, the rebuilding making little progress. Devlin saw camps all along the inside of the walls. Devlin was worried about scaring the guards below, so Devlin told Drathic to land outside the walls, to which Drathic begrudgingly agreed. Devlin was glad he did, because as he landed, a mob of guards was surrounding them, keeping well away from the dragons. Before long, King MacArthur himself emerged from the mob of soldiers. His eyes widened as he saw Devlin and Anders with the dragons.

"What in blazes is going on? I hear a report of a possible dragon invasion and it turns out to be you all?" King MacArthur asked flabbergasted.

"Sorry, Father, but we needed to get here quickly and they offered," Anders joked.

"Well, I cannot say I am not happy to see you all. My men and I will need all the help we can get against Grandis," King MacArthur stated honestly.

"I'll do my best to take care of Raven, but her army will not pull punches. We have to watch out for that sword of hers. If she stabs you, Your Majesty, the entire battle will be lost," Devlin advised.

"What on earth do you mean?" King MacArthur questioned.

"The sword Raven wields, Tenebrae, has the power to take over the will of anyone the sword fatally wounds, as well as any person who follows them. By definition, if you are stabbed, everyone in the Kingdom would be under Raven's control. It doesn't just go for you either. If a captain falls, you could lose a huge chunk of your army," Anders explained fearfully. "That is why I recommend you stay far away from this battle, Father." As the king and prince deliberated, Michael walked up behind them.

"Do not worry, brother, I shall be fighting in his place," Michael grinned pridefully.

"Michael! You've healed!" Anders exclaimed, and quickly went to embrace his little brother.

"I am in fighting condition again and thank the Maker for it. I was so bored in that healing bed that I wanted to strangle myself. Father will be in the back of the army, protected by quite a few guards. He will not be in any danger unless we lose completely and even then, we would all be dead anyway," Michael stated bluntly.

"Thank you for the vote of confidence, my son, but Anders does raise a valid point. As a result, I shall stay behind in the capital with the civilians. I do not want to single-handedly wipe out our only hope of winning this battle. I do have one question, however: just how powerful has Lux made you, Devlin?" King MacArthur asked purposefully.

"I've not had a chance to truly test it in combat, but the sword enhances my magical reserves at least threefold," Devlin answered casually.

"Perhaps a quick match then? I'm still eager for a rematch to see how strong you have gotten, Devlin," Luke told him confidently.

"Sounds good to me. I need to blow off some steam after all that traveling we did." Devlin grinned. Everyone backed away to make room for the duo. Devlin drew Lux from his sheath; the draw had a feeling of purpose to it. The weight of this fight hung in the air. It was the first time Lux has been used in a battle for thousands of years. The feeling was surreal, as Devlin still didn't know the full capabilities of the sword. *Time to see what this sword can do.* Many onlookers viewed the fight with excitement. Most knew the old legend about Lux, and all knew Luke's skill in combat. It was a duel to end all duels before it.

As Devlin took up his stance, the memories of their last match flooded into him. The pure nostalgia of it made Devlin fidget with excitement. All of Devlin's travels, all that he learned, would be tested in this duel. Devlin resolved not to use magic in the match as he didn't want to risk hurting a bystander, and he wanted to see how much his swordsmanship had grown thus far. Luke readied his stance as well, his intricate long sword shining, showing the care Luke took with his blade. Devlin made the first move, charging Luke with his sword to his side. As Devlin got close, he swung Lux with such ferocity that surprised even Devlin. The two swords clashed in a shower of sparks, the ring of the colliding blades echoing through the air. Devlin was just getting started, however, pulling his sword back and striking at Luke from the right. The swords collided yet again, each strike only increasing in intensity.

The tension in the air was palpable as the two fought, neither one giving an inch. Devlin could tell Luke wasn't holding back either, as he could see the effort in his strikes. Devlin was so much faster thanks to his constant training, the constant fights. Each battle had honed Devlin into a warrior, the threat of death driving him to new heights. Devlin understood how Luke could be so experienced and masterful as he was a battle-hardened warrior to an even greater caliber than Devlin. His experience showed in the way he fought, as Luke didn't waste a single movement. Every step, every breath had purpose as compared to Devlin whose movements were still sloppy at best by comparison. Devlin closely observed the way Luke moved, the way he breathed, the way he attacked. Devlin started adapting his movements to match Luke's, and Devlin noticed a remarkable difference in his use of energy. Devlin noticed the same moves and combinations using less of his strength and felt like each strike was being used with purpose like Luke's were.

The pair swung back and forth, the sounds of their swords colliding ever present in the air. Noticing neither one was gaining any ground, Devlin tried even harder, his competitive drive fueling his desire to win. The tides shifted in Devlin's favor for a moment, but Luke quickly adjusted and they were back to being evenly matched. There was a difference, however. Even with Lux adding the extra fuel to Devlin's physical reserves, he was gradually getting more and more tired, whereas Luke was still going strong. *This isn't good, I'm tiring out too fast. How is he in such better shape than me? Is it just the gap in experience, or is it something else?*

Devlin kept up the pressure on Luke, fighting through his growing exhaustion. Devlin felt a bit of hope as he noticed that Luke was finally starting to feel fatigue as well. *Finally, I'm wearing him down! Maybe I still have a chance.* The duel had been going on for a couple hours. The soldiers noticed that the two were getting tired, and more people gathered, hoping to see the conclusion. *You can still win this,* said a voice in Devlin's head. The voice distracted Devlin so much that he almost threw Lux in mid swing. *What? Who is that?* Devlin asked.

I'm your partner, duh, The voice scoffed. *I am not just a pretty sword, you know.*

What do you mean I can still win? Devlin asked the voice.

I mean you can still win, answered the voice. *There are flaws in this human's technique. Don't you see them?*

No, I can't. Care to enlighten me? Devlin asked incredulously.

Sure thing. You see the way he retreats after a few swings? It's very slight, but he favors his right more when he does that, as his right hand is dominant. Try striking from the left after a few swings from the right, the voice advised. Devlin did as the voice instructed and Devlin noticed Luke reacting much slower to his strikes.

Wow, that really worked! Devlin thought in awe.

If only you would use magic. I could have told you twenty different ways to beat him already. You humans, you are so stubborn and impractical, the voice griped. Devlin followed his "partner's" advice and gained considerable ground on Luke. The voice pointed out flaws that Devlin never noticed before, and when Devlin exploited them, Luke was struggling to keep up. Devlin wore down Luke so much that the Knight Champion was gasping for breath, hands on his knees.

"I give, Devlin... You've surpassed me. I admit defeat," Luke gasped. Devlin sheathed Lux and extended his hand to Luke. He gladly accepted and shook it properly.

"Thank you for the kind words, Luke, but I haven't yet surpassed you. The sword aided me in this fight. With a blade like yours, you would have won this match, not I," Devlin admitted.

"What do you mean the sword aided you?" Luke asked him.

"The sword has intelligence somehow. It pointed out flaws in your fighting style for me. It also increased my reserves. Without it, I doubt I would've lasted," Devlin explained morosely. Devlin felt like it was a shallow victory, not quite demonstrative of his progress, and he hated that. "We shall have a true match one day. After this war is over, my friend."

"Agreed." Luke smiled at Devlin, and they clasped arms, just like they had in the arena so long ago. The crowd cheered for them, long and loud, then slowly parted as the distraction had passed.

"Devlin, you said the sword had intelligence? How is that possible?" Amanda asked him, looking at the sword.

"It's a voice in my head, like how the dragons talk to you," Devlin awkwardly explained. Amanda sighed in exasperation.

"Before today, if you would've told me that, I would've thought you were crazy," Amanda grumbled. "It's weird how much my life has changed lately. A couple months ago I never would've thought I'd so much as see a dragon, much less ride one, and now this." Devlin was curious to learn more about the sword himself.

"Amanda, I'm going to train for a bit. I'll see you all later," Devlin said walking off.

"He raises a good point, as we do have some free time. How about we do some more training Cecelia?" Elena asked her offhandedly.

"Sure thing!" Cecelia agreed happily.

As Devlin found a clear area away from the commotion and activity, he drew Lux, sat with the sword in his lap, and concentrated.

Hey, partner! You called? The voice questioned. Devlin listened to the voice, examining it for the first time. The voice was like a little girl's in pitch, but very soothing and fluid.

Do you have a name? Devlin asked bluntly.

I am the sword. If you wish to address me, just call me Lux, it responded.

How are you intelligent? Is it a charm of some sort? Devlin asked.

My intelligence was created by the same elven spell weavers that gave me my power. They thought adding a partner to the swordsman would be beneficial, Lux answered. More questions popped into his head, but Devlin didn't even have to voice them as the sword was already in his mind. *You're curious about my origins, and about Sher'ni.*

Immensely, Devlin confirmed.

It's a long story, so I will try and skip over the boring parts, but it all started when a demon got loose in the realm of man. That lone demon was causing chaos and destruction throughout the land. As it destroyed, it grew stronger, and it learned how to take over the minds of men. That demon raised armies and threatened to swallow the world in its darkness. Sher'ni, a very gifted yet hardheaded youth, was raised to be the next protector of the elven civilization. His magic was unmatched by all, and he was a master with the sword. In response to the threat of the demon, a group of dwarves created my blade, and the spell weavers blessed me with magical properties, including my intelligence, and preset spells that you may use should you need them.

When I was created, the spell weavers filled me with the knowledge of many sword masters and mages, hoping to make me a tactical aide to my wielder. When I was finished, Sher'ni wielded me against the demon and his army, and with the aid of the few free humans and elves, he banished the demon back to the spirit realm. Unfortunately, even though the demon was banished, another group of dwarves fell to his influence, and the demon put his power into a sword they created, making Tenebrae before he was banished. Lux said telling the wondrous story of its origins.

Devlin tried absorbing the knowledge Lux gave him. The sword gave him images, memories of Sher'ni's, as well as describing the events in detail. It described Sher'ni himself, a hardened elven warrior, with magical abilities that Devlin had scarcely imagined. The spells he used were different. They seemed to just flow from him effortlessly. Devlin observed the final battle with the demon. The horizon was nothing but the army taking up the landscape. Devlin watched as Sher'ni decimated wave after wave of soldiers with a simple swing of his sword, and how he fought the demon in their last confrontation. It looked terrifying, grotesque and evil. It was like the embodiment of evil itself. Devlin felt himself shiver as he watched the fight between them.

I have one more question to ask. Why did you choose me? Devlin asked Lux.

You remind me a lot of Sher'ni. You're just as stubborn as he was, and just as compassionate. You also have a strong heart, a will that doesn't break, and you have suffered great hardship. For every person that grips my hilt, I can tell very quickly whether or not they are worthy. I deemed you worthy and had you go through a trial, just to be sure, and you passed, Lux told him nonchalantly.

I suppose that's fair enough, Devlin conceded humorously. *Thank you for taking the time to explain your past to me.*

I will literally be at your side should you need anything else, Devlin, Lux responded, laughing at her own joke.

Devlin sheathed Lux and did some actual training with his magic. He wanted to improve his reserves even more. Devlin used rocks around him, ranging in size from a foot in diameter to a foot in radius. Devlin focused his energy under as many of the rocks as possible and tried lifting them all at once.

The spell was going smoothly, and Devlin had as many as ten rocks floating in the air about eye level. Devlin used his magic to lift them even higher, and when they were up twice Devlin's height, he made the rocks do acrobatics in the air. He made a few spin, a couple more flying through the air, and the remaining few fly in loops perpendicular to the ground.

When Devlin finished with that, he used his magic to break up the rocks into pieces the size of his fist and threw them in different directions. The rocks sank deep into the ground from the force of the launch. Devlin was surprised to see that he barely felt any fatigue from the display, and tried thinking up another way to train.

As Devlin stood deliberately in the field, he spotted Amanda approaching charismatically. "Amanda? What are you doing here?" Devlin asked, looking at her smiling.

"There was nothing to do back at the capital but sit around and watch a bunch of muscle-heads do construction, so after I helped Cecelia with her training, I figured I'd come watch you," Amanda explained obviously bored.

"You got bored watching a bunch of guys lift stuff? Color me surprised," Devlin laughed good-naturedly.

"So you understand my dilemma!" Amanda laughed too.

"I was just trying to come up with something else to train with," Devlin said thoughtfully.

"I have an idea! How about you try levitating me like you did to those rocks? It'd be fun to actually fly, and I don't know how to do it myself…" Amanda asked, which surprised Devlin, as he had never tried levitating someone besides himself.

"Are you sure? It could be dangerous…" Devlin warned her.

"That's what makes it interesting," Amanda giggled. "A little thrill is always fun!"

"Alright, but don't say I didn't warn you," Devlin told her laughing. He focused his magic under Amanda and reversed her gravity like he had with the rocks, causing Amanda to rise into the air. It was like lifting a rock, but Amanda didn't weigh as much. Devlin was careful raising her up, not wanting to break concentration and drop her.

"Wow! I'm so high up!" Amanda shouted so Devlin could hear. As Devlin got used to Amanda's weight distribution, holding her up was a simple task. In fact, Devlin used the same magic to lift himself up to join her. It was a bit harder lifting both, as Devlin had to focus on both himself and Amanda.

"You aren't having too much fun up here, are you?" Devlin teased as he floated up beside her.

"This is even more fun than I thought it would be. To think dragons do this sort of thing all the time," Amanda said wondering. "How are you doing, Devlin? You aren't getting tired are you?"

"This is honestly easier than throwing those rocks around, it just takes a bit more concentration lifting up an actual person," Devlin said reassuringly. "I should have enough energy to last for awhile."

"How about you try flying us back to the capital then? It's not too far from here, and it's getting late anyway," Amanda told him.

"Not a fan of walking huh?" Devlin joked, and Amanda just smirked at him. "Alright."

Devlin shifted his magic and made himself and Amanda fly off towards the capital. Devlin raised them high up so they could see the sights a bit better.

"This is one thing I love about being a mage," Devlin said thinking aloud.

"What's that over there?" Amanda said pointing off toward the northwest. When Devlin looked to where she was pointing, Devlin saw a huge army camp a few miles away. The thing that worried Devlin was, it wasn't sporting a Crestialis banner. It flew a red flag with a raven on it, and Devlin guessed it was Grandis's army camp. Curiosity got the better of Devlin, and he flew over it with Amanda to get a better look. It wasn't very active, just a few men marching around the camp. Devlin guessed it must be a scout camp, the scouts went ahead of the main army, to check the enemy's fortifications.

"This is bad. They already have troops this close to the capital?" Amanda exclaimed.

"We should warn King MacArthur if he doesn't know already. He'll want to hear this," Devlin concluded seriously. Devlin flew them both toward the capital again, this time, he flew them faster, however. Devlin could feel himself wearing down as they approached, and Devlin lowered them closer to the ground in response. Devlin started getting weaker as they flew, and he barely had any energy left as they reached the capital, which resulted in a much rougher landing, for Devlin at least. Devlin was able to set Amanda down gently, but Devlin fell to his knees as the last of his magic left him.

"Dangit... I shouldn't have flown so fast..." Devlin gasped.

"Are you okay, Devlin?" Amanda asked helping him up.

"Yeah I'm fine, just tired... Go to the king," Devlin said trying to stand up on his own. Devlin leaned on the wall of the capital, trying to regain his strength. Amanda hesitantly ran through the gate to the capital.

* * *

After several miles of walking, Valcara's former army finally made it to their destination. Valcara, Derek, Roark, and Athon acted similarly to the army of brainwashed soldiers and joined the soldiers in the crowd. Raven's soldiers must have been notified of their coming, as they had already constructed a camp for Valcara's men. *Well at least they treat their allies well, even if forced,* Valcara thought observing the camp. Valcara led Derek, Roark, Athon into a tent. As the four of them sat down, Valcara took a map from her pouch. The small map was unfortunately made for navigation, not planning, but Valcara had to compensate. Based on the miles they had traveled and the direction, Valcara pinpointed their current location on the map.

"We are around here, next to the boundary between Gradis and Crestialis. Based on the massive force of soldiers here already, we are most likely the main force of the army," Valcara told them.

"We'll have to be careful and make sure we aren't found out by the soldiers. They aren't brainwashed like our fellow soldiers, they can find us out if we aren't careful," Roark warned.

"We just have to blend in then. Valcara, you might have to act a little, seeing as how you're supposed to be the leader of this army," Derek told her.

"I know, I know," Valcara said irritated. "Wait, I hear a commotion outside." Valcara checked the outside of the tent and saw the soldiers all walking and conforming together.

"Let's go," Roark said, seeing the soldiers outside the tent. Roark didn't have to repeat himself, as everyone moved to blend in with the crowd. Valcara's army joined with Raven's army in the open field, with Raven herself sitting on Horris's neck.

Raven knew that there were four people in the army that weren't under her control, however, she couldn't tell which they are, but she didn't care. What were four soldiers to her many thousands? If they showed themselves during battle, she could kill them easily with her soldiers. She had, however, told her men to keep an eye out for any suspicious behavior. Today, Raven would lead her army to battle; to take over Crestialis, and end the MacArthur Bloodline. She would finally have her full revenge against his family, and she will stop at nothing to carry it out.

"In this battle, we will conquer Crestialis! We will conquer MacArthur and all of his pathetic subjects! Join me in battle at my side, and we shall claim glory for Grandis! For your Queen! For yourselves and your families!" Raven shouted, and in response both armies roared approval. "March!"

Chapter 31

As Devlin leaned on the wall of the castle, taking a second to recover himself. As Devlin regained his stamina he asked a guard to escort him to the king. Recognizing Devlin, the guard nodded in response and led him to the King. Devlin knew that the battle to decide the fate of the world was closing fast, and he wondered just when he would face Raven. The guard led him to King MacArthur's council tent, and walked to return to his post after giving a brief salute. "Devlin, thank the maker you are back," King MacArthur said as he looked over to him. "My scouts have reported Grandis's army is moving toward the capital. Fortunately, it will still take time for them to reach us. I estimate a week at the most. When they are close enough, we plan to meet them head on with you at the forefront. Your strength will be critical to the tide of the battle. I encourage you to take all the necessary steps to prepare for war, and I shall send a messenger to notify you in advance."

"Thank you for your consideration, Your Majesty," Devlin said gratefully. "Did Amanda inform you of the scout camps not too far from here?"

"She did indeed, it will be no issue, however, as most of our preparations are being made inside the walls. Even with scouts, they won't be able to tell what we are doing in great detail. I believe Amanda went back to see how you were doing actually, you must have just missed her," King MacArthur reasoned nonchalantly. "If you need anything in particular, Devlin, do not hesitate to ask me. I will do what I can to see it done."

"Thank you, Your Majesty, I will keep that in mind," Devlin bowed and walked out of the tent. "Time to get back to training."

* * *

A week later, Devlin led the army of men, elves, and dragons across the open grasslands. The number of men and elves combined was four hundred eighty thousand. Scouts estimated Raven's forces in the five hundred thousands, so Raven's army held the advantage in numbers thanks to the addition of Valcara's army. Devlin felt a pit of worry in his stomach that his brothers and Valcara were in that group as well, but he then realized the anti-magic properties of the amulet he gave Roark likely freed them, which Devlin confirmed earlier with a seeing spell. However, Devlin wasn't so concerned with the number of soldiers, as it didn't matter against Raven's sword. If he lost, the army lost. There would be no hope for victory should Devlin fall. *Everyone is counting on me to win, and I will not let them down!* Behind Devlin was Anders, Luke, Amanda, Cecelia, Elena, and Drathic, leader of the dragons. Michael also led part of the army as a commander of the right wing. Everyone was tense, waiting for the battle of their lives to start. The battle that would determine the fate of the entire world.

After an hour of waiting, Raven's army finally came into view. Devlin saw a woman on a dragon almost as big as Drathic leading the charge, Devlin assumed the woman was Raven. As the army drew close, Horris dropped to the ground. It was customary for the leaders of the opposing forces to converse before the battle as if a last resort for peace could be made before resulting in war. Devlin being the leading figure for the battle stepped forward, Raven did the same. When they were a mere few feet from each other, the tension in the air was thick enough to cut with a blade.

"So you are MacArthur's lapdog, boy?" Raven asked condescendingly.

"No, I am your executioner," Devlin retorted threateningly. "Retreat now, witch, and you may yet live this day. Attack, and I will see to it myself that you and that cursed sword of yours are buried six feet under."

"Big talk little man. Let's see if you can back it up!" Raven yelled, hatred clear as fresh water. Raven and Devlin drew their swords and swung. The resounding clang of the blades was the trigger to the armies advance. It was all out chaos as the two armies met, the only exception was a space in the middle where Raven and Devlin clashed. No one wanted to be caught in the middle of those two as light and dark clashed. Tenebrae and Lux were glowing as they struck one another as if the swords themselves wanted to battle as much as Raven and Devlin did. Raven was a skilled swordswoman, keeping up with Devlin blow for blow. Devlin was shocked, however, to suddenly see Valcara, Derek, Roark, and Athon jump into the unofficial no-mans land around Raven and Devlin. The four of them went to strike Raven from behind, and Raven growled in annoyance at the intrusion.

"So you are the four turncoats," Raven said venomously. Raven blasted Devlin with a shot of magical energy, sending him flying backward.

"How dare you hurt my brother!" Roark and Derek screamed. The two brothers swung at Raven like wild beasts, performing a double downward strike. Raven managed to parry their blows, however, and pulled pillars of earth to intercept them and send them flying past Devlin. Valcara ran to Raven and swung at her with seething hatred.

"You thought you could control me, huh? I will make you pay for what you did to my men!" Valcara yelled as she swung at Raven.

"Since I have your army under my control, I'm afraid I have no more use for you. But do not worry I will take good care of your men," Raven smiled wickedly and used a lightning spell to electrify Valcara. "And by the way, I was holding back the last time we fought. Since you do not seem smart enough to figure that out."

Valcara fell unconscious and Raven threw her over to Derek and Roark, Valcara's limp body knocking both of them down again. Athon, knowing his limits ran to help Valcara instead of attacking. Devlin managed to recover from the energy blast and used earth magic to restrain Raven's legs. Raven cried out in shock and tried casting a spell to remove the earth. Raven managed to free herself just in time to dodge Devlin's stab, and the two of them swung their swords, clashing once again.

Anders and Luke fought with everything they had, Anders swept through lines of soldiers with his greatsword, and Luke skillfully outmaneuvered man after man but the Grandis soldiers were very skilled. They used sheer numbers in an effort to take down the masterful duo, but the Crestialis soldiers came to their aid and struck back the oncoming wave of soldiers, saving them from being surrounded. Although the elves were powerful, they were inexperienced at war having lived peacefully in the forests, and suffered some casualties. The mages of the elves somewhat made up for this, however, as they managed to take out more soldiers than they lost. The dragons were about even, as the number of dragons on Devlin's side made up for the lack of power, as multiple dragons attacked one of Raven's.

The clash of Drathic and Horris was a bloody one, as each dragon clawed, bit, and blasted the other with their flames in the air above the armies. Drathic froze a part of Horris, and Horris spouted flame on the ice to thaw himself before continuing. Horris retaliated with a tail lash to Drathic's neck. Drathic took the blow and bit down hard on Horris's tail, prompting a roar of rage from Horris.

Whenever Devlin saw the dragons fighting, he was glad Drathic was on his side now. A problem arose when one of Raven's dragons managed to kill the dragons opposing it, and he began wiping out scores of soldiers. Devlin was about to break off his fight with Raven to help, but luckily Elena, Cecelia, and Amanda took on the dragon. Elena and Cecelia managed to keep the dragon at bay with their spells, while Amanda kept their strength up.

The fight between the two armies was bitter. Valcara's mindless soldiers fought like zombies. Even if they were wounded, they didn't care, they just kept on fighting. This distinction made itself apparent with the dragons as well, as Raven's dragons slowly gained the advantage. As the fight between the dragons began reaching its conclusion, all of Drathic's dragons were either wounded to the point of being unable to fight or dead. The trio of Amanda, Elena, and Cecelia killed the dragon they were fighting with a combined lightning spell toward the dragon, electrocuting the beast. Amanda quickly went to heal the dragons that were wounded, so they could at least survive, if not continue fighting. Drathic and Horris continued their brutal fight, but Raven still had three dragons left at her disposal.

"You are a decent fighter, Devlin, I will admit, but I can't be bothered to fight you anymore. I think I'll let my remaining dragons finish you off," Raven said coldly.

"What's wrong, Raven, too scared to fight me yourself? I'm not scared of your pet lizards. I'll skin all three of them and make myself some new boots from their hides," Devlin spat.

"If you cannot at least beat these three dragons, you aren't strong enough to defeat me, boy," Raven said condescendingly. The ground itself shook as the three twelve-foot-tall dragons dropped to the ground in front of Devlin. Devlin readied his sword to take on the dragons, and to his surprise, Roark, Derek, and Cecelia were at Devlin's side.

"You don't have to fight these overgrown lizards alone, Devlin. That's what family is for," Roark told him.

"I still owe that girl for what she did to Valcara. She'll pay for that," Derek said in a rage.

"Just make sure you don't die then," Devlin told them seriously.

"I'll take the right one," Roark volunteered.

"I'll take the left one," Derek stated.

"Cece, are you ready?" Devlin asked her.

"Whenever you are, Devlin," Cecelia reassured him.

The three brothers ran forward to the three dragons. "Remember, you have to kill them. They are under Raven's control, so they'll keep getting up even if you injure them," Devlin warned.

"Aye," Roark and Derek answered in unison. The dragons were already weakened from fighting the other dragons, so Devlin wasn't too worried about his brothers. Devlin used his magic to enhance his muscle strength, and Devlin threw a bone-shattering blow to the dragon's chest, crushing the dragon's ribs into its lungs and heart.

Derek ran up to the dragon and swung at its legs, but the sword didn't cut very deep with the dragon's tough skin. Derek made sure to keep well away from the dragon's head, and jumped onto the dragon's back. Derek tried stabbing the dragon in multiple places, but the skin prevented a fatal wound. Realizing he wasn't making progress, Derek stabbed the wings of the dragon so it couldn't fly away. The sword easily cut through the thin webbing of the wings, and the dragon screamed in outrage as Derek cut holes into its wings. The dragon reached back with its head and bit down on Derek in retaliation, and threw him off his back and onto the ground several feet away. Luckily for Derek, the armor protected him from any significant damage, but he was left with several teeth marks on his arm.

As Cecelia tended to Derek's wounds, Roark was still trying to look for a weak spot on the dragon, evading blasts of flame and the savage teeth of the dragon. When Roark watched the dragon's neck move, he noticed a different scale pattern on the nape of its neck. *Maybe that's a soft spot,* Roark thought hopeful. Roark waited for an opening and climbed onto the dragon's back just behind the neck, and stabbed his sword into the nape of the dragon's neck. The sword stabbed through like paper, and the dragon roared fiercely in pain, then quickly collapsed to the ground, dead. After Derek was quickly healed by Cecelia, Derek used the weakness Roark had discovered to kill the last dragon.

The three brothers stood victorious over the three dragons, enraging Raven to new extremes. Raven shot two blasts of energy at Derek and Roark, sending them flying several feet and knocking them both unconscious.

"How dare you!" Devlin screamed, readying Lux and swung at Raven ferociously. Raven blocked the blow, and, to Devlin's surprise, held a look of sorrow on her face.

"Protecting your family... Just how much do you care for them? That you would risk your own life?" Raven asked him contemplatively.

"My family is all that I have, but it is also all that I need. My family is everything to me, but why would you care?" Devlin asked her scornfully.

He reminds me of myself before my little brother died. "I failed my family in the past, my entire world was destroyed in one instant. When I lost him, I lost my will, my sanity. I just wanted the entire world to disappear," Raven confessed, a single tear rolled down her face as she said those words, the same words of her life that she relived every day of her life. The day she had lost her light.

"You had someone dear to you that you lost..." Devlin said thoughtfully. "And because of that you want to take over the lives of all these innocent people?!"

"No. My reasons are... that I must take vengeance on the MacArthur bloodline, for what that tyrant did to me, and I want to make sure that what I went through, does not... happen to... anyone... else," Raven answered, rage making her voice shake. "When I rule the entire world, I can use Tenebrae's power to rid the world of conflict."

"But won't that also rid every person of their free will?!" Devlin reasoned angrily.

"Yes it will," Raven answered sadly.

"Peace like that isn't peace at all. It's a mockery, a sham. If you want to rid the world of conflict, you must make peace with them, not enslave them and rob them of their own free will!" Devlin said defiantly.

"Making peace with people is a fool's errand. As long as people have will, there will be war. As long as people have the power to fight, they will fight. You cannot change that!" Raven shot back.

"I won't know until I try!" Devlin said as he pushed Raven back with her sword.

"This will be... a battle to determine our wills," Raven decided, regaining her feet. "We will decide who is right... In this battle!" Raven yelled as she charged for Devlin. Devlin braced himself as Raven swung down hard diagonally from the upper left. Devlin blocked the blow, but the force of the impact forced him to step back.

Devlin, don't forget I'm fighting with you. You're not alone in this battle. Believe in me! Lux advised, her voice resonating in his mind.

I know that thank you, Lux, Devlin responded. *Do you spot any weak points?*

It's tough when your opponent has both swordsmanship and magic... Lux said exasperatedly. *It seems that her magic is more powerful than her sword, however, so make doubly sure you watch out for her spells.*

I noticed that... Her magic is as strong as mine if not more so, Devlin confirmed.

*Luckily for you, if she pulls out something particularly nasty, I can help you counter it. I **am** gifted with great knowledge of magic, after all,* Lux bragged.

Yeah yeah, you're a regular encyclopedia, Devlin scoffed.

Raven used magic to electrify her sword, but Lux told Devlin a spell to cancel it out, by momentarily covering the sword in mud. The irritated Raven shot out bolts of electricity at Devlin. The bolts were too fast for Devlin to dodge, so he raised a wall of earth to block the bolts. Devlin then launched the wall at Raven, and she barely managed to avoid the block of earth. Raven retaliated with forming an orb of water around Devlin's head in an attempt to drown him, and Devlin had to focus his energy into dispelling the water, costing him valuable time. Raven took advantage of the delay to blast Devlin with more bolts of electricity, and they hit their mark on Devlin's body. Devlin saw the bolts hit the armor and sighed with relief when the armor absorbed the brunt of the assault.

Devlin formed a powerful gust of wind and blew Raven straight into the air, and used the wind to blow her around every different direction to disorient her, and made wind so fast that it cut into Raven like blades. Raven had scratches all over her body from the razor-like wind. Devlin formed one final gust to slam her back down to the ground, knocking the wind from Raven's lungs.

"Why do you want revenge on the MacArthurs? The king is a good man, and a fair king," Devlin reasoned, walking toward her as she got up again.

"Because one of those 'MacArthurs' was the reason why my family is dead and my country was in shambles. Since he killed my family, I shall murder his in recompense!" Raven screamed, regaining her breath.

"How did he kill them? Tell me!" Devlin demanded.

"He supported the cult that burned mages at the stake and made it legal to kill those gifted. They burned my parents at the stake and stabbed my brother in the heart. They slaughtered innocent people, simply because they feared the magic the mages held. They killed my family right in front of me, and it was out of sheer luck that I wasn't killed too. However, since I survived, I will repay him for the suffering he put me through!" Raven screamed.

"That doesn't make King MacArthur responsible! He is a good man with a family of his own. I'm sorry about what happened to your family, I know what it's like to lose those close to you. It's a hole in my heart that I could never hope to fill again, but I made new friends, and I felt that void start to fill. I moved on," Devlin confessed adamantly.

"You talk as if we are the same!" Raven scoffed. "You still have your siblings. My only brother was killed right in front of me. Until you see the terror I saw, the hopelessness I saw on his dying face, we will never be the same."

"You're right, we're not the same, but if you kill King MacArthur, how does that make you any better than the scum that killed your brother?" Devlin questioned angrily. "Is that any way to pay respects to your brother? Would he want you to kill innocents in his name?!"

"No, he would not, but this is not about just my little brother anymore... My reasons are my own, boy," Raven answered defiantly. "Enough talk, I need not explain my reasons to a man who will be my servant before long."

"Like hell I will, I'm not about to lose to someone who gives up on their family," Devlin responded outraged.

The two of them resumed their fight, chaos consumed the world around them as the two armies still collided. The sounds of swords clashing and men dying were all consuming in Devlin's ears. *So this is what war is like. It truly is a terrible thing.*

It was just like this when Sher'ni fought against that accursed demon. War consumes you, you either fight and live on or die like so many already have. That is the cruelty of war, where death can so easily take you, Lux told him in his mind.

I will end this quickly. Too many have died today, it's time to end the suffering, Devlin resolved. Both Raven and Devlin were growing tired, as they had been battling on and on, but neither one wanted to show it. They fought on without pause, but both of them were breathing hard, feeling the fatigue of the battle. Raven hacked at Devlin's neck from the right, but Devlin blocked the strike with the flat of his blade deflecting it.

Devlin's renewed resolve set his blood boiling with new strength. Devlin wanted to throw everything he had at Raven, to make sure she wouldn't get up. Raven and Devlin clashed swords, swinging at each other, each one trying to outmaneuver the other, each one trying to win. Devlin fought hard and put all his strength into every swing, forcing Raven back. Raven countered by sending rocks from the earth at Devlin, forcing him to deflect them with his magic. Thanks to the time that bought Raven, she used her magic to split the earth under Devlin, the same thing she had done to her former General, in an attempt to finally silence him. Devlin saw the move coming, however, and shielded himself as the earth came crashing together again. Devlin used his magic to mold the earth around him, making it ease him upward as if the earth were the sea instead. Devlin rose from the earth and landed down on the battlefield once again.

"Nice try," Devlin scoffed. "But I'm afraid burying me six feet under only works when I'm dead."

"Insolent brat," Raven raged as she readied her sword. "I shall amend that discrepancy soon enough!" Raven gathered the remains of her strength and formed it into a ball of pure energy into her palm. The energy was so concentrated that it was even visible. It just grew and grew, a massive sphere at the end of her hand several feet in radius. Seeing what Raven was trying to do, Devlin realized that if he didn't stop it, that sphere would take out everyone behind him as well.

"If that's how you want to play, so be it," Devlin said coldly. Devlin raised his hand and formed a ball of energy of his own. Devlin packed every bit of energy he had left into the sphere, and it grew exponentially to the same size as Raven's. The energy sphere, enhanced with Lux's power as well, appeared as a white ball of light, while Raven's was pitch black.

"They say that the form the magic of a mage takes is a reflection of their soul. My magic reflects the great darkness I hold in my heart. I wonder... will your light swallow the darkness of my soul? Or will your light be snuffed out like a candle in the wind?" Raven asked him rhetorically. Raven and Devlin pointed their arms toward the other and launched their magic. The two orbs of magic met in the middle of the battlefield. The collision was as loud as a thunderclap as the two great orbs of magic pushed against each other. As the two orbs pushed and pushed, they grew unstable and exploded. The raw force of magical energy exploded outward, launching both Raven and Devlin backward several feet from where they were standing. Devlin and Raven landed hard on their backs, the combination of exhaustion and the force of the explosion had both of them struggling to move.

"Devlin, are you alright?!" Cecelia called to him, rushing to his aid.

"I think that last shot took the last of my strength away," Devlin laughed in spite of himself. "I'll be fine, I just need to rest for a second." Cecelia tried healing his minor wounds and eased his pain somewhat, but his energy was still completely drained.

"I'm sorry I can't do more," Cecelia said morosely.

"You did more than enough, sis, thank you," Devlin thanked her genuinely.

Devlin tried getting up off his back and managed to at least sit up. Devlin looked over to Raven who was still on her hands and knees.

"Darn it, I was hoping that explosion would've finished her," Devlin complained. *Lux, do you have any magic left?*

I'm ready when you are. Lux answered.

Can you heal my sister then? Devlin asked it. In response to Devlin's plea, a strange aura surrounded Cecelia.

"What is this? My wounds are healing?" Cecelia gasped in disbelief.

"I asked the sword to heal you. This battle is far from over, so I want you in the best shape you can be," Devlin explained.

"Thank you, brother," Cecelia said with gratitude.

Devlin, I can only give you enough strength for one more spell. You better make it count! Lux explained.

Got it, Devlin understood. "Cece, do you have any strength left for another spell?"

"I believe so. Why?" Cecelia asked him.

"Want to help me finish this?" Devlin asked her.

"With pleasure," Cecelia smiled confidently.

"Hey, don't leave us out too," Derek called out behind them having recovered. "Roark and I have some strength too. Take it and finish her."

I can convert their life force into magic for you, Devlin. This may be our best chance, Lux advised.

Alright, just make sure you don't kill them, Devlin thought seriously. Devlin stood up with the help of Roark and pointed the sword toward Raven. "Grab the hilt when you're ready." As one, Cecelia, Roark, and Derek grabbed the end of the hilt. In response, the sword starting resonating the same white aura as before. That aura grew more and more dense and formed a ball of energy at the end of the shaft.

"Get ready, Raven. We're putting everything on the line for this one last spell," Devlin called out resolute.

"Do your worst, child," Raven scoffed as she created a ball of dark energy of her own.

They launched their spells and they both collided just like before, but this time was different. Devlin had his family with him this time. With his family by his side, he was invincible. The ball of darkness Raven had launched dissipated against the ball of light the Slade family had launched.

"This is it!" They all said at once, as the ball of light continued toward Raven. Raven watched in fear as the ball of light went right towards her.

"I'm sorry, brother," Raven said just before the spell hit her. The white ball of light hit Raven head on, then expanded several meters in an explosion of released energy. When the light dissipated, Raven was passed out on the ground. Of the four siblings, all but Devlin passed out as well from exhaustion. Devlin fell to his knees, unable to stand any longer.

"Devlin, are you alright?" Amanda called out rushing to help him up.

"Bring me over to Raven or give me the strength to walk. I still have to deal with that sword," Devlin ordered.

"Understood," Amanda answered, and wrapped his arm around her shoulders. Devlin, with the help of Amanda, walked over to Tenebrae. The sword was still in Raven's hand. A death grip on the sword even though she was passed out. "Devlin, aren't you going to finish her?"

"I won't kill someone who has already been defeated. I'll deal with her later. The people she's possessed are more important right now," Devlin explained. He gripped the hilt of Tenebrae. He was amazed at its power, still surging with darkness even though its wielder was unconscious.

If she had tapped into the true power of this sword, she would've killed me, Devlin realized. *It still has so much power left.*

Use that as motivation to make yourself stronger, Devlin, Lux advised. *Don't bother trying to take it from her. The sword has a defense mechanism just like I do. It'll kill you for certain.*

Understood, Devlin replied. The words to release the spell came to his mind as he gripped Tenebrae. "I claim dominion." As Devlin said those three cryptic words, a black aura resonated from the sword. Devlin felt every person taken over by the sword shift their will to his, and all at once he released the will that they had lost. All of the remaining soldiers of Valcara stopped fighting and cheered. Raven's forces, realizing that their queen was down and the Seamander soldiers now against them, surrendered their arms. The dragons that Raven had captured fled the field, besides for Horris who merely stopped fighting, and landed by Raven' collapsed body.

"Drathic," Horris said flatly. "I apologize for the damage I caused while I was under this girl's control.

"Think nothing of it," Drathic responded understandingly.

"I believe I will continue looking over this girl, however, as she still carries the sword and she is the proper wielder," Horris admitted. "I will keep in touch."

"Very well," Drathic said with a nod.

Chapter 32

When Raven woke up, still on the battlefield, her body ached all over. She focused her eyes and took in her surroundings. The boy she had fought with sat next to her. She felt anger and indignation looking upon him now.

"Why am I still alive? Why did you spare me?" Raven questioned angrily. "I have no reason left to live if I cannot even get revenge on MacArthur. If I am too weak to accomplish my own goals, I am nothing. I cannot even restore my family's honor." Despite herself, Raven started crying. She was so angry at herself for losing, she hated Devlin for stopping her, and she felt the frustration of failure burning in her gut.

"I spared you because you aren't a bad person. You may have acted on your own self-interests, but no one has ever given you a chance to do otherwise. I wanted to see if you could change," Devlin explained. "My role in this battle was to stop you from taking over Crestialis. If you promise to leave this country in peace, then I have no reason to kill you. Everyone deserves a second chance."

"I do not need your pity," Raven said defiantly as she felt her entire will fall apart. *I had thrown everything I had at this boy. I had the determination, the power, but I still lost. What was it that I lacked that this boy had?*

"How was it that you beat me? How could I lose?" Raven asked confused.

"The one big difference was... I had my family by my side. They gave me the strength to go on, the strength to win. I had their lives on the line as well as mine, and when my family is in danger, I cannot afford to lose," Devlin told her resolutely. "You fought alone and you had no one to truly fight for. You don't have the same motivation as me."

"Your family means so much to you that you would risk your own life to protect them," Raven surmised somewhat humbled, reminded of herself again before her brother died. It had been so long since then, but that feeling of protecting what she loved still resided deep in her heart. *I wish he was here. I have no idea what to do anymore.*

"The reason you lost was because you were alone. Before I found my family in Seamander, I felt alone just like you do. I made friends, though, and felt like I could accomplish anything," Devlin explained nonchalantly. "What I mean to say is, we can be friends or enemies, but I'd like to try being your friend."

"Why would you want to be friends with me?" Raven scoffed.

"Because no one deserves to be alone. No matter what they've done or how despicable they are," Devlin explained kindly. "Not even you."

"You are a fool... but I appreciate the offer," Raven said sincerely yet still spiteful.

"Is that a yes?" Devlin asked.

"The next time I see you, I promise I will try not to kill you. Will that suffice?" Raven replied, her cheeks blushing slightly.

"I suppose that'll do for now." Devlin laughed genuinely.

"You really are a fool," Raven stated with an almost imperceptible smile, but her face turned serious again. "As promised I shall give up my plans of conquest. There is no point in it anymore, seeing as my men do not even have the will to fight, and quite frankly, I am exhausted."

"Why does the will of your men matter to you? Can't you just take them over like you did to my troops?" Valcara asked walking up to her. Valcara looked a little singed but otherwise okay.

"They are my people. If I betray the men and women that trust me what kind of queen would that make me? I have a responsibility to them," Raven explained simply. "Surely you would understand that, Queen of Seamander."

"More than you would ever know. So tell me Raven, Queen of Grandis, why I shouldn't kill you right now?" Valcara asked as she drew her sword. "You have committed terrible crimes against me and my men. It's because of you that so many of my men, good men with families, are dead on the ground!"

"Kill me if you wish, it makes no difference to me," Raven said nonchalantly. In response, Valcara raised her sword angrily to stab Raven.

"Stop Valcara, if you kill her now, you'll be no better than she. Those men knew they had the possibility of dying and they went to war knowing that. If you kill her, it'll just cause more fighting, and more men will die," Devlin told her gripping her arm. Valcara looked downcast as she took in the words, knowing them to be truth but not wanting to admit it. "War is a terrible thing with death all-consuming. Let's not create more of it."

When Raven finally had the strength to move, she picked up Tenebrae and stabbed it into the earth. "Bring MacArthur and we shall discuss terms of surrender. Please fetch him quickly so that I may be done with this," Raven told Valcara and Devlin.

*   *   *

When Raven saw MacArthur and Valcara striding up in front of her, she felt renewed rage. Had she not made a promise to withdraw, she would already have his head on a pike. She restrained herself, albeit grudgingly. The king stood but a few feet from Raven, a magical amulet around his neck to protect him from her spells as well as armed guards.

"Greetings, Your Majesty. I was told you wish to discuss the terms of surrender?" King MacArthur asked, more of a statement than a question.

"Yes yes, let us be done with it," Raven replied dismissively.

"I wish no more conflict between us. As heinous as your offenses were I shall overlook them if your men aid in rebuilding the capital. I would also wish to write a treaty between the countries of Crestialis, Grandis, and Seamander, if Valcara agrees," King MacArthur explained flatly, his face completely expressionless.

"I do agree," Valcara stiffened as she stood next to King MacArthur, she also looked intently at Raven.

"I agree..." Raven said low. She hated this contemptuous man, the sooner this was done the better.

"Then I shall commit the terms to writing and send it to your kingdom in due time," King MacArthur concluded.

* * *

Derek watched Amanda as she healed his many wounds. Roark, who had already been treated, looked as if he had never gone to war besides for his dented armor.

"How are you feeling, brother?" Roark asked with concern.

"A lot better now, but I'll probably be sore tomorrow," Derek answered regrettably.

"Count yourself lucky that sore muscles are all you will suffer from, Derek. Especially since you fought a dragon," Amanda jibed.

"I'm curious, Amanda. Now that all this dirty business is cleaned up, what will you do?" Derek asked her as she healed the final cut.

"My village is gone, so I was hoping to work in the capital as a healer," Amanda said thoughtfully. "It will be a different, for certain, but I will adjust. What about you Derek?"

"I was thinking about remaining as the head of Valcara's forces. It'll be hard not seeing my family, but I have a responsibility to her now. I also know that Devlin can take care of himself. He doesn't need me watching over him anymore," Derek said proudly and also sadly.

"I figured as much. I feel the same way, Derek," Roark affirmed. "We've been through so much with Valcara, it wouldn't feel right to leave her now."

"What about Cecelia then?" Amanda asked seriously.

"It would be best if she stayed with Devlin. She wouldn't be as safe with us. Maybe she could continue to learn under you, Amanda, and continue as a healer," Roark concluded.

"The question is, what will Devlin do?" Derek asked thoughtfully.

"He's good friends with Elena, maybe he'll live in the elven forest again. He could also live in the capital," Amanda predicted.

* * *

"Devlin, are you feeling okay?" Elena asked him as he stood up.

"I'm a bit tired, but other than that..." Devlin replied.

"That's good. Just don't push yourself too hard," Elena said concerned.

"Elena, now that the war is over, what do you plan to do?" Devlin asked her, the same question in the back of her mind.

"I think I will stay in the capital. I love the forest, but it's so quiet all the time. I may return later, but for now, I think I'll stay here," Elena concluded unsurely. "What about you, Devlin?"

"I'm honestly not sure. I could just live in the capital. I thought about visiting the forest, to lay the sword to rest, but I decided against it, as there could be threats in the future. I could also live in the forest though, I'm used to the quiet life, so it is fitting," Devlin pondered.

Devlin looked around the field and saw Cecelia approaching, a troubled look on her face.

"What's wrong, Cecelia?" Devlin asked, snapping her out of her thoughtful state.

"Amanda just told me that Derek and Roark wish to return to Valcara's side in Seamander. She also told me that she'd be willing to take me on as an apprentice in the capital," Cecelia explained. "I'm not sure what to do…"

"If Amanda is willing to train you, I suggest taking it. You'd be hard pressed to find another teacher as good as her," Elena advised. "You could also make quite a living as a healer, as mage healers are rare even in the capital. I can't tell you which path you should follow, however, that is entirely your choice."

"Derek and Roark are leaving because they did what felt right to them… I suppose healing others does make me happy. I hate seeing people suffer, and I want to do anything I can to stop that," Cecelia said thoughtfully. "Devlin, what are you going to do?"

"I have a responsibility to the king since I wield Lux, so I'll be in the capital more likely than not," Devlin answered, still unsure himself. "I suppose I'll see how court life treats me and make a final call."

"I think that's a good idea, Devlin," Elena said proudly. You can even have Luke help you train."

"Speaking of which, where are Luke and Anders? I haven't seen them since before the battle started," Devlin said perplexed.

"I believe I saw them with the king," Cecelia answered him, recalling.

"Speak of the devil," Devlin said as he saw Luke walking over to them.

"Devlin, I have wonderful news, my friend," Luke told him smiling wide. "I reported the happenings of the battle to the king, and he has announced you to be knighted!"

"Me?! Knighted?!" Devlin gasped with disbelief. Being knighted was a high honor reserved for only the select few that have proven themselves worthy to the king. "I know I played a crucial part in the last battle, but I would never have imagined this…"

"You more than deserve it, Devlin. If it were not for you, we would all be under Raven's control," Cecelia praised warmly.

"He plans to hold the official ceremony after the repairs have been made to the capital. He also welcomes you to join him at the castle whenever it is built," Luke informed him. After Luke left to rejoin the king, Devlin felt an urgency to see his two brothers before they set off.

"Cecelia, do you know where Derek and Roark are?" Devlin asked quickly.

"I believe they said that they were meeting with Valcara at the capital," Cecelia answered uncertainly.

"Thank you. I want to go see them before they leave," Devlin said worriedly. It felt wrong that they were splitting up again so soon.

"I'll go with you then," Cecelia resolved. "I want to see them too."

"I guess I will go too, seeing as I was going to head to the capital anyway," Elena reasoned indifferently.

The three of them ran off toward the currently incomplete capital. As they entered the walls, the city was rife with workers and elves alike, rebuilding the decimated buildings. The workers and elven mages worked seamlessly to rebuild all the brick homes and official buildings. The mages made the work much faster by lifting all the bricks and placing them neatly in place. The workers did the more intricate work the magic didn't cover. This combination greatly accelerated the construction time, and the capital was already well on its way to being rebuilt. Devlin asked around for Valcara's location and managed to finally find her in a reconstructed home. Valcara, Derek, and Roark were all gathered in the home going over plans and getting the formalities of war sorted out.

"I'll have to take a record of all the men we lost today, and inform the families of their passing…" Valcara reminded herself. Valcara's features brightened slightly as she saw Devlin, Cecelia, and Elena walk into the home. "Hello, Devlin."

"It's good to see my two brothers are okay," Devlin said smiling broadly. The Slade siblings all embraced each other happily, even as the scars of war were still fresh.

"I owe you my entire Kingdom, Devlin," Valcara told him gratefully. "If not for you, my men would still be slaves."

"Thanks for the amulet too! It released me from Raven's control and helped my free Derek and Valcara," Roark exclaimed happily, holding up the griffin pendant.

"I'm glad it helped. I never would have imagined that the amulet would have saved you from Raven's magic," Devlin said happily. The mere thought of having to face his own brothers in battle to the death terrified him.

"Ya, I couldn't believe it myself. It was like being held prisoner in my own body," Valcara recalled sadly. "Nothing in this world was more terrifying than that sensation."

"Well, now that your men are free, are you all heading back to Seamander?" Devlin asked, already knowing the answer.

"Yes, we are," Derek confessed sadly. "We owe our lives to Valcara. We are needed in her army, as I am the commanding general and Roark is my second." Devlin looked to Roark sternly, waiting for his reaction. Roark stood proudly and nodded in the affirmative. Devlin just smiled sadly at him.

"I will miss you two more than words could ever describe," Devlin told them sincerely, struggling to hold back his tears.

"We will always carry the name Slade. The name of the proud family known the world over," Derek said confidently as he embraced Devlin one last time.

"I promise I won't let you down, Devlin," Roark swore. "Please take care of him for us, Cece."

"It would be my pleasure," Cecelia said as fresh tears cascaded down her lightly tanned cheeks. "If you two get hurt out there, I swear not even the maker himself could stop me from coming to your aid." Cecelia tried her best to wipe away her tears as she embraced Derek and Roark fiercely.

Devlin, there is something I need to do. I must do something to repay you for all you have done, Lux stated calmly.

What do you mean? Devlin asked confused.

Please instruct your two brothers and sister to place their hands on my hilt, Lux insisted. Devlin did as Lux asked and pulled out the sword from his sheath, holding it point toward the ground in front of him. Derek, Roark, and Cecelia all grabbed the hilt of Lux hesitantly. Lux started to glow dimly, that glow spread onto all of the Slade siblings' hands for but a moment, then the glow faded to nothingness.

I have placed a charm on you and your siblings. This charm now connects all of you like a magical tether, letting you know their general direction and their wellness. You will now know if one of you is injured and how severe the injury, Lux explained in Devlin's head. Devlin took a moment to comprehend what Lux was saying before repeating it back out loud.

"So now we are truly connected…" Roark stated amazed.

"Thank you, Lux. That was truly a thoughtful gift." Cecelia smiled gratefully and giggled.

"Lux just made my job easier," Cecelia smiled happily.

You guys are gonna make me blush… Lux stated bashfully. Devlin looked at Lux from tip to hilt and smiled, the blade still flawless even after the grueling fight. As Devlin sheathed Lux he looked toward Valcara purposefully.

"Take care of my brothers, alright?" Devlin asked her intently.

"You have my word as ruler of Seamander," Valcara reassured him proudly. "You will always be welcomed as an honored guest in our court, Devlin Slade."

"Good, because you better believe I'll be visiting at least every once in awhile," Devlin said, happily smiling again.

Chapter 33

Devlin looked on sadly with Elena and Cecelia as Valcara, Derek, Roark, and Athon led all of the Seamander troops back home. All of the troops packed up their supplies and gathered down the trail toward Seamander.

"It'll be a long journey for them," Devlin said looking on towards the many busy soldiers. "Most of them don't even have horses."

"That may be the case, but I believe they will be fine," Elena told him confidently. Cecelia looked on sadly, watching as the soldiers got further and further away.

"What will you do in the capital, Elena?" Devlin asked her, curiosity burning in his mind.

"I may act as an ambassador for my people. I can make sure we are keeping close ties with humans and help make peace with them. We have been blinded by fear long enough," Elena said with determination that surprised Devlin. Devlin himself wondered what he would be doing as a knight.

I'll most likely be training to make myself stronger, so I can protect my family if they need me. I also need to keep an eye on Raven. But there is one thing I know for certain... Devlin thought to himself. "I'm glad I made a friend like you, Elena. You have done so much for me... I doubt even if I thanked you every day for the rest of my life that it would be enough."

"Don't be getting all sentimental on me, Devlin. It's unlike you," Elena teased, then smiled affectionately. "But I do appreciate the kind words."

"I hope we can still train together. You are an amazing fighter," Devlin said hopefully as he half smiled.

"I hope to see you again as well. You are a wonderful teacher, Elena," Cecelia said finally looking away from the receding army. Cecelia looked downcast from the sudden goodbyes.

"Of course! Every chance I get to kick your butt up and down the training field is a chance I'd love to take Devlin. As for you Cecelia, you will have a lot of practice healing Devlin's pride later," Elena said laughing.

"Big talk, let's see you live up to it!" Devlin challenged smugly.

* * *

As the next few weeks dragged on, the construction of the capital was finally completed thanks to the efforts of the elves and civilians. King MacArthur made Elena an honored ambassador for the elves, which the elves happily agreed to. Amanda was given space in the castle to act as a master healer with Cecelia acting as an apprentice. Devlin was celebrated as a hero of Crestialis, proud warrior, and wielder of the legendary sword, Lux. To the great shock of everyone, Valcara and Derek fell in love after going through so much together with Derek being her next in command. Being so high up in ranking, Roark himself also became very popular with the women of the court, even though he humbly denies it. Valcara and her brother become very close again even after everything he had been through with Scurvy Jaw. The peace treaty, signed by King MacArthur, Valcara, and Raven, became a symbol of hope and prosperity between the three nations, but for the most part, they kept to themselves even though trade and relations were doubled between Seamander and Crestialis.

Devlin stood proudly before King MacArthur before dropping to one knee. King MacArthur nodded as he was handed the ceremonial sword for knighthood by one of the squires. MacArthur slowly unsheathed the very intricate yet purposefully dulled blade and stood over Devlin. Devlin was dressed in a fine, black silk doublet, tailored to him by the King's own servants. The King wore a ceremonial robe for the procession.

The king made sure all was quiet before proceeding and cleared his throat to speak clearly. "Devlin Slade, proud warrior and hero to Crestialis, you have aided the country in its greatest time of need and prevented our destruction. Because of these great and admirable feats that you have committed, it is my honor to dub thee a knight of Crestialis," King MacArthur announced as he brought the sword to just above Devlin's left shoulder, then his right, before slowly sheathing the blade. "May you live a long life of honor and glory for Crestialis!" King MacArthur raised his arms and the gathered crowd of onlookers burst into cheers. Among those onlookers were Amanda, Elena, Cecelia, Luke, and the members of the royal family. Devlin wished his two brothers could have been here to see it but he knew that Derek and Roark were busy rebuilding Seamander, so he understood.

When the ceremony ended and Devlin was escorted back to his chambers in the left wing of the castle, he wasted no time changing out of the fancy doublet and into a fitted tunic and trousers. No sooner did he finish changing did he hear a knock on his door. Devlin quickly opened the door to find a servant girl with a parcel in hand.

"I have messages for you, sir," the girl said bowing graciously. The sight was something Devlin was still getting used to, as, before the recent events, no one had ever bowed to him in his life unless it was his brothers mocking him.

"Thank you very much," Devlin said gratefully. The girl smiled big at him and promptly handed him the letters. Looking at the first letter, he saw his brother Derek's handwriting and immediately opened it.

Dear Devlin,

Congratulations on becoming a knight! I wish I could have been there to see it personally, but things are truly a mess here. I do have a bit of news so I'll cut right to the chase. Valcara and I are engaged to be married in a couple months. It's crazy, I know, and I'll explain the story behind it to you later in person. I have sent you this letter as an invitation to anyone you wish to bring to the wedding reception that we plan to have at the castle, and I would also like you to be my best man. It would really mean a lot to me, so I hope you'll say yes, but I will understand if you can't attend. Best regards! Love Derek.*

Devlin just stared at the letter in complete shock, trying to comprehend Derek and Valcara as a couple. The idea of it simply baffled Devlin, but he was happy for Derek for finding someone to love. Devlin had no doubt in his mind about attending the wedding. He would be there even if the sky itself was torn asunder, a thing he made sure to note in his reply letter. Shortly after finishing the reply Devlin looked at the second letter. The handwriting was unfamiliar to him, so he checked the name to find "Raven, Queen of Grandis". Pure curiosity and shock filled his expression.

Dear Devlin of Crestialis,

I have been thinking about what you said to me that day on the battlefield. I wish to take you up on your offer, so I invite you as a guest to my castle here in Grandis. No one is aloud to come with you, just you alone. Be sure that if you do decide to come to send a letter well in advance. Thank you for your time, Raven.

Devlin didn't know what to make of Raven's letter. It sounded like she was trying to branch out to him, but part of him felt like it was some sort of trap. *This could be a chance to strengthen the peace between Crestialis and Grandis. I can't just ignore it,* Devlin debated mentally. *I'll go but I'll bring Drathic just in case. He can at least keep an eye in the sky for me.*

Devlin quickly wrote the reply to Raven's letter and gave them to a messenger girl. As Devlin made his way around the castle, however, he saw a girl just a bit younger than him walking around with two armed guards. It took him a second to realize it was Sophia MacArthur, the King's daughter. Devlin had only ever seen her once, even though he knew who she was. She had beautiful blonde hair and pale, white skin dressed in a flowing formal dress. Princess Sophia looked right at Devlin and grew puzzled for a second before clarity shone on her face. Devlin bowed respectfully to her. "Good morning, Princess," Devlin said politely

"About as good as a morning can be I suppose," Sophia responded humorously. "No need to be so formal, Devlin. Quite frankly it's an honor to see you. I'm so terribly sorry we were never properly introduced."

"You're too kind," Devlin said smiling politely. "Perhaps we could become better acquainted when you have free time?"

"I am free at the moment. Father is busy taking care of the clean up for your ceremony, so I have nothing to do," Sophia told him, then looked to the guards. "You two are dismissed, I'll be more than safe with the hero of Crestialis around." The two guards merely saluted and walked off down the hall. Sophia led Devlin to a study where they had a bit of privacy. Sophia explained to Devlin about her upbringing and complained about all of the formalities of the court. Devlin in return told her about the many events leading up to the great battle with Raven and about his life before his eighteenth birthday. Sophia even told Devlin about the different things to do in the castle that she usually preoccupies herself with, things Devlin made note of for when he had some downtime in the castle.

"Thank you for the enlightening chat, Princess," Devlin said smiling kindly as he got up to leave the study.

"The pleasure is mine," Sophia responded. *He's so handsome and polite. He's also so carefree, it's hard to believe he is the same person that defended the kingdom because he seems too humble for it. He's everything I ever dreamed of in a man.*

Devlin walked down the hall to where he knew Elena usually was. He wanted to have her opinion on the letter he got from Raven, figuring maybe she had an idea for it. When Devlin entered her study, he quickly summarized the letter for her and waited for her feedback. "It does sound like a trap. We just can't be sure with Raven. She was out to kill us not a few weeks ago," Elena reasoned bemused.

"I know what you mean, I'm concerned too. That's why I wanted to possibly bring Drathic with me, in case of emergency," Devlin explained.

"How about I go with you. I will ride with Drathic while you visit and if there is a problem, you can signal us," Elena suggested.

"Okay, that does sound better, especially if I end up in a building too small for a dragon to get into," Devlin reasoned. "The only issue is how do we get in touch with Drathic?"

I can handle that, Lux told him. *He and I are linked remember?* Understanding crossed Devlin's face as he recalled the dragon saying such a thing.

"Lux can contact Drathic, so we should be ready to go in a couple weeks. She said to reply well in advance before coming. The messenger bird won't take more than a couple days to deliver the letter," Devlin informed her. *Lux, where is Drathic right now?*

He is up north encouraging the youths to breed. The recent battle took a heavy toll on the dragon population, Lux explained. *He'll be ready to move in a week or so.*

That works out just fine then, Devlin told her, then looked to Elena. "Be ready to leave in two weeks.

The story will continue in the next book *The Twin*.

Acknowledgements

This being my first ever book I was quite excited to get it underway. This book has helped me grow as a writer and has helped me build a skill for it that I hope to continue in many books to come. I started this book of my own volition, but I doubt it would have been anywhere near the quality the book is now without the aid of my close friend Brittany. She helped me by partially editing my book and through her proofreading I gained the knowledge to increase the quality of my own writing. I owe her a huge thank you in that regard, as she is one of the main contributing factors into the development of this piece of literature. Thank you to all of my readers and I hope you will be looking forward to the concluding book, *The Twin*.

Made in the USA
Lexington, KY
24 September 2016